SAVING BABE RUTH

BASED ON A TRUE STORY

TOM SWYERS

HILLCREST HOUSE PUBLISHING

Hillcrest House Publishing

949 Birchwood Lane

Schenectady, New York 12309

HillcrestHousePublishing@gmail.com

Publisher's Note: This book is a work of fiction. Names, characters, businesses, organizations, places, and incidents are product of the author's imagination or are used fictiously. Any resemblance to actual events, locales, businesses, organizations, or persons, living or dead, is coincidental.

Ordering Information: Quantity sales. Special discounts are available on quantity purchases by corporations, associations, and others. For details, contact the "Special Sales Department" at the address above.

Saving Babe Ruth/ Tom Swyers -- 1st ed. ISBN: 978-1-941440-00-1

To Cher, Randy, Mom, Dad, Arden, Ellen, and my wonderful family.
For the volunteers who serve the spirit of Babe Ruth.
For the simple goodness of baseball.
For the boys of summer.
I dedicate this novel.

I won't be happy until we have every boy in America between the ages of six and sixteen wearing a glove and swinging a bat.
—BABE RUTH

In great deeds, something abides. On great fields, something stays. Forms change and pass; bodies disappear; but spirits linger, to consecrate ground for the vision-place of souls. And reverent men and women from afar, and generations that know us not and that we know not of, heart-drawn to see where and by whom great things were suffered and done for them, shall come to this deathless field, to ponder and dream; and lo! the shadow of a mighty presence shall wrap them in its bosom, and the power of the vision pass into their souls.

—JOSHUA CHAMBERLAIN, "Dedication of the Maine Monuments," Gettysburg, October 3, 1889.

FOREWORD

My grandfather, Babe Ruth, loved children. He thought that every boy should have the opportunity to play baseball. As originally conceived in the 1950's, the Babe Ruth League was intended to provide organized baseball for 13- 15 year olds during the summer, something that did not exist at the time. Following his death, the Babe's widow and my grandmother, Claire Ruth, spent much of her life promoting Babe Ruth baseball across the country, traveling as far as Anchorage, Alaska to do so.

Sadly, events similar to those described in *Saving Babe Ruth* are transpiring not only in Upstate New York, but all across America today. Based on true events, it's a great story and a must read for teen players and their parents. The unfortunate truth is that as elite baseball teams flourish, they often do so at the expense of organizations like Babe Ruth League. Today, as a result, many boys and girls at every age level who do not play at the "elite" level, or whose families lack the considerable resources required to participate, are once again left with no options for playing baseball.

Thanks to dedicated individuals like Tom Swyers, *Saving Babe Ruth* has a happy ending. The countless volunteers who so tirelessly work to ensure the success of Babe Ruth League are the lifeblood of the organization. On behalf of the Ruth family, I wish to offer a heartfelt "thank you."

—TOM STEVENS, Babe's grandson

LAWYER DAVID THOMPSON SERIES

Saving Babe Ruth is the prequel to the Lawyer David Thompson Series and the 2015 recipient of two Benjamin Franklin Book Awards for "Best First Book, Fiction" (first place) and "Best Popular Fiction" (second place).

The Killdeer Connection, a legal thriller, is the first book in the Lawyer David Thompson Series and was selected as a 2017 winner in Amazon's international Kindle Scout writing competition.

A second legal thriller in the series is currently in development.

All books in the series can be read as standalones.

DAVID'S HILL

A rmed with a 1859 Sharps carbine, David Thompson gazed beyond the baseball field, across the asphalt and slate-shingled suburban homes of Indigo Valley, wondering how these twenty-one thousand residents would feel if they knew that baseball was dying. It was April 18, 2009, opening day, and as the town league's Babe Ruth commissioner, David had been preparing for this date since the end of last summer. It was, for him, a time of rebirth, the beginning of baseball season, and the end of the other season called winter.

But baseball wasn't the only reason David celebrated spring's arrival. The winter of 2008 had devastated his elder-law practice because most of his clients had died. Two had stroked out, another had checked out with a massive heart attack, and yet another had been laid out in a crosswalk by a teen intent on making it to Starbucks before closing time. When David had closed up his last estate before opening day, he'd half-jokingly told Annie, his wife, about his decision to pursue a new career in positive law, a specialization that he'd created through declaration. His first case would be to save the town's Babe Ruth baseball program for the benefit of their eighth-grade son and only child, Christy.

That morning, David was on the lookout for the man who had briefly visited the field for the past four days. He was determined to discover his identity. David's silvery-brown hair waved in every direction. He stroked the grizzle on his chin, wondering if he might be acting a little crazy. He felt certain Annie would think he had lost it if she knew he was at the kids' baseball field armed with a gun.

David loved his gun. The reproduction Sharps carbines turned him off; they were historically inaccurate. So David had bought an authentic one. His had been used by a Union cavalryman in defense of Gettysburg on July 1, 1863, the first day of battle. The carbine's owner had recorded the serial number in his diary, and David had cross-referenced his name against the war-casualty records.

David's infatuation with the Civil War had been sealed when he'd purchased the Sharps some twenty years earlier for his thirtieth birthday. He had been thrilled to find out that General John Buford had commanded the original owner of the gun. David already knew that his great-great-grandfather, Joseph Thompson, had fought on the Union side with the Fifth Pennsylvania Reserves at Gettysburg before being captured in a later campaign and shipped to Andersonville prison. Joseph Thompson had started a family after he'd been released at the war's end. David knew full well that if Joseph had not survived the war, he himself wouldn't be here today.

In studying the movements of Joseph Thompson's unit at Gettysburg, David had become an expert on the battle and admired Buford for his choice of ground. On the first day of the battle, Buford had ordered his men to dismount their horses and offer resistance on the outskirts of town. This decision delayed the Confederate advance and allowed the Union reinforcements to take up a superior defensive position on the high ground of Cemetery Hill and Cemetery Ridge. It was "good ground," as they say in military circles, and if Buford had not developed a strategy to defend it, there might not have been a Union victory at Gettysburg.

David checked his wristwatch. It was 6:10 a.m. For the past week, David hadn't been able to sleep past 4:30 a.m. He'd roll out of bed to work the field for an hour and then climb the hill to stew about the season ahead. But since he'd first spotted the man coming to the field each morning at the same time, he had retreated to the hill earlier.

David had left his Bardou & Son Civil War–era field glasses at home this time, as they had not given him a clear view of the man's face. He'd opted instead to bring his modern-day binoculars. With his back to the ball field, he peered straight down into the Mohawk River, more than one hundred feet below, and then across the treetops of Saratoga County on the opposite bank. He imagined this hill might be the highest point in the town of Indigo Valley. David appreciated the protection from the rear that both the high ground and the river afforded. Gazing farther north, he hoped to catch a glimpse of one of the church spires reflecting the early morning sunlight in Ballston Spa, the birthplace of General Abner Doubleday, the mythical inventor of baseball.

David's thoughts had turned to Doubleday not because of baseball but because of his role at Gettysburg. On the first day of battle, General Buford's morning success in delaying the Confederate advance had been bolstered by infantry reinforcements under the command of General John Reynolds, whose death on the battlefield had enabled General Doubleday to assume command. Doubleday's efforts had solidified the Union's position on Cemetery Hill and Cemetery Ridge. David imagined that while Doubleday probably didn't invent baseball, he sure knew how to defend it.

David considered this hill his "high ground" and found it superior to Cemetery Hill. Although Cemetery Hill was twice as high, its slope was much more gradual. David's hill shot up fifty feet above the ball field and achieved its stature within one hundred feet of its base. It also boasted a six-foot-high chain-link fence around the outfield that would mark a kill zone for any enemy assault.

Even so, David's satisfaction with his hill's defensive superiority over Cemetery Hill came up short. Cemetery Hill was a natural hill made up of underlying igneous rock. David's hill was anything but natural. The more recent generation of townspeople referred to the hill as an Indian burial mound for the indigenous Mohawk Indian tribe. Maybe that explanation would take root in history over the coming centuries. But David, a longtime resident, knew that the hill had been shaped and molded from the former town dump that had been buried, capped, and closed years earlier. Had it not been for the dumping of years' worth of refuse on the site, there would be no steepness to the hill; in fact, there would be no hill at all. David tried to convince himself that he was perched atop the town's history, an archeological site for future generations to explore. But as the hill's foul stench lingered in the air, the archaeological site once again became a landfill, a dump, an undeniable pile of crap.

David could not locate the Ballston Spa spires. His failure to locate Doubleday's birthplace reminded him that there were no reinforcements coming to his aid that day or that baseball season. He stood alone with ten live rounds of .52 caliber ammunition stored in his authentic black-leather Union cartridge box, which hung from his black-leather belt.

He picked up his son's new Derek Jeter Rawlings baseball glove and slipped it on his left hand while he began working the pocket with the fist of his right, pounding it like he was in the ready-set position during a game. Christy had always been a passionate but average player, but now, at age thirteen, puberty had bolstered his strength and speed. David was optimistic about Christy's upcoming season and was breaking the glove in for him.

David's watch read 6:20 a.m. It was about time for the man to arrive. David trampled on the grass so it did not impede his vision of the field, then slid his athletic frame face-first into position on the ground. He felt safe hidden in the high grass. David laid the glove down on his left and the carbine on his right. A shiver ran up his spine as the heat generated from the decomposing dump gently warmed his body. Through his binoculars, he scanned the parking-lot entrance for the red SUV.

Seeing no vehicles, he took in the baseball field. The dormant grass had turned to hunter green. No weeds. Not even clover. Freshly cut with a crisscross pattern, the outfield sported a morning layer of dew. The chalk baselines were perfectly straight and solid, like white icing on gingerbread. The tines of the grooming tractor had brushed the dirt of the infield in perfect, uniform strokes. The bases and pitcher's rubber and home plate had been freshly spray-painted white to match the brilliant chalk lines. There were no footprints to be found anywhere, not even within the batting boxes where David had hand raked. It was true artwork on a canvas of dirt and grass, and the field's beauty would have caused even the most diehard baseball fan, player, or coach to stop and wonder, at least for a brief moment, if that field looked too good to play on.

The popping gravel of the driveway announced the arrival of the man. The sun peaked over the hill. The SUV, a mass of red and chrome with all the subtlety of a parade float, parked facing the field along the first baseline.

The driver's door opened, and the man got out. A puff of smoke came from behind the man's head. David adjusted the focus on his binoculars. *Barkus,* he thought, *the face of baseball's death.*

Rob Barkus was the Elite Travel Baseball League promoter when he wasn't working at his dead-end midlevel management job at a regional car dealership. In his early forties, he was well over six feet tall, triple chinned with a goatee and a gut the size of a small beer keg. His flattop crew cut made his jet-black hair bristle like a scrub brush. Fat folds ran up his neck to the back of his head, as if someone had surgically implanted a pack of hot dogs.

David now understood how desperately Barkus wanted the Babe Ruth field. David was a sitting board member in charge of Indigo Valley Baseball League's Babe Ruth program, and Barkus had already started an e-mail assault directed at David personally. Barkus's teams were made up of high-school players who had enjoyed access to the Babe Ruth field for more than a decade. David wanted that usage to stop.

David had explained to his board that giving the Elite Travel Baseball League access to the Babe Ruth field was like being a bystander, or even an accomplice, to the killing of Indigo Valley's Babe Ruth program. The town league was losing players to Barkus's Elite teams at a rate that rivaled the decline in David's client base. As a result, David was dead set against giving Barkus access to the Babe Ruth field. If the Babe Ruth program folded, Christy, his friends, and other nonschool players would no longer be able to play baseball.

Board members favorable to Barkus had leaked news of David's stance. Barkus, in turn, had launched a daily e-mail campaign accusing David of bullying, acting in a disturbing manner, and trying to hurt his players and families by keeping them off the field. Barkus sent these e-mails to the parents, the high-school coaches, and all league board members. Some of the parents joined Barkus in the e-mail attacks. Members of the board were afraid of Barkus and what he might do to impact their sons' baseball careers. Many on the board had sons that played both for the school and on the Barkus teams. Nobody stepped up to defend David.

As a lawyer, David understood his legal duty of loyalty toward the survival of Indigo Valley's program, open to all teens regardless of ability. Indigo Valley's Babe Ruth program provided baseball for teens while its Cal Ripken program covered younger kids. Both programs operated under the direction of Babe Ruth League, Inc., a nationally recognized nonprofit created in the 1950s.

The Barkus teams had access to the two Indigo Valley school fields, so David thought Barkus would just move on after whining in a few e-mails. Instead, Barkus's appearance on the Babe Ruth field four days in a row strongly suggested that David had underestimated Barkus's determination. While lying on the hill, David had come to fully understand Barkus's desire to get the Babe Ruth field.

David understood that a military commander on the battlefield essentially has three choices: attack, stand pat, or withdraw. David's counterattack on the e-mail front was to more or less stand pat, though he'd told himself he was engaging in an aggressive campaign of absolute silence. David's plan was to have Barkus wear himself out and to have others question Barkus's sanity.

It wasn't in David's nature to take endless bullshit without defending himself. Being passive hadn't been in his nature, even before he'd become a lawyer. The daily e-mail thrashing had taken its toll. It required a great amount of energy to do nothing. Although David had tried to suppress the thought while lying on the hill, he couldn't help but think he should go on the offensive right then and there.

Barkus stared at the field, blowing rings of cigar smoke. He loved his cigars, and anyone could find him at the ballpark just by following his nose. He spat on the ground in the direction of the field. His three boys, his teams, and his league had played on this field for over ten years. He was infuriated with David for trying to end his reign over the best field in town. The field looked playable to him. That's all that mattered; the field's beauty blew by Barkus like a hundred-mile-per-hour fastball. He longed to have his sons, his teams, his travel league play on it right then and there. *I need this goddamn field,* he thought. *What will everyone think of me if I lose it?*

The Babe Ruth field had stadium lighting that made nighttime play possible. The ballpark had a sprinkler system that kept the field green during the hot days of summer. It had a modern concession stand that served a full range of food and beverages. It had a nice electronic scoreboard. It had a PA system that announced the games. It had rest rooms.

It had large bleachers and a fence spanning the outfield. A contractor mowed the grass every few days during the summer. The league had a grooming tractor to comb the infield dirt. All these amenities made the Babe Ruth field one of the best baseball parks in the region.

The school district owned the other two full-size baseball fields in town, and neither had any of the amenities of the Babe Ruth field. No lights. The temporary outfield fence was removed for the summer, preventing home runs from being awarded unless they were of the inside-the-park variety.

No irrigation. No restrooms, though one field had a Porta-Potty nicknamed the Red Rocket because of its color and conical shape. No concession stand. No PA system. The varsity field had a small scoreboard that was crooked and didn't work. And the chain-link backstop had long turned brown; rust fell to the ground when foul balls hit it.

When the school season was over at the end of May, the school did not maintain its fields except for an occasional mowing. The grass would get too long. Water would puddle in the infields. Weeds would begin to claim the dirt infield and baselines starting in early June. By mid-July, the weeds owned them. By August, after the baseball season had ended, the weeds seemed as high as cattails, and the fields had the swampy smell of wetlands.

Barkus walked to the passenger-side door and opened it. Out came the Great Dane that David had seen for the first time the day before. *Not again,* he thought. David had let it go the previous day; he'd stood pat and done nothing. But he didn't know if he could restrain himself this time. This was opening day; it had taken him hours to ready the field under the lights last night. He was physically exhausted, and his lack of sleep unsteadied him.

Barkus walked the dog on a tight leash toward the field entrance. The beast was the size of a man, a gray man, a gray man with the ears of a devil that galloped on all fours. Barkus opened the gate. The dog's head bumped against his belly with each step, like a Thoroughbred being placed in the starting gate. Barkus stepped onto the field and closed the gate behind him. The dog bounced up and down off the ground.

David knew what was coming. He'd seen it happen yesterday, and it was going to happen again if he let it. But what could he do? He'd brought the gun and ammunition with no real intention of doing anything, just in case. He had hoped it wouldn't happen again.

But it did happen. Barkus unhooked the leash and set the beast free. It took off in a sprint down the first baseline, obliterating the razor-sharp chalk lines and kicking up a mist of white dust. The dog raced to right field, scuffing up the crisscross pattern created by the mower's passes. It then bolted toward the infield dirt, destroying the brushstrokes between second and third, before rounding third and going home. It sniffed around home plate and left paw prints in the batter's box.

David put the binoculars down.

Reaching for his gun, David flipped up the rear sight on the barrel and set it for two hundred yards. He pulled the hammer back into the half-cocked safety position, removed a homemade paper cartridge armed with a .52 caliber bullet from his box, then dropped the trigger guard to lower the breech block and expose the chamber. He checked the pellet-primer system that fed percussion caps into position. David pushed the cartridge into the chamber.

He peered through his binoculars. Barkus stood along the first baseline. The dog was sniffing his way over to him. David laid the binoculars on the ground. He brought his Sharps up and lined up the rear and front sights to his targets, first to the dog and then to Barkus.

At that moment, David's conscience flashed to life. *What am I doing?* he thought. He heard his wife's voice. "It's only baseball," Annie would whisper as the two lay in bed when he couldn't sleep. *This isn't Gettysburg*, David reminded himself.

He put his gun down and reached for the binoculars. The dog narrowed its area of sniffing to a small circle a few feet in front of Barkus. It hit David then. The dog was searching for the perfect spot, and he was zeroing in. *Oh, my God, he is going to take a dump on my field!*

The dog assumed the squat position. David glanced at Barkus and saw a smirk. Clenching his teeth, David looked back to the dog. He was laying one of the biggest craps that David had ever seen. It swirled like a coiled snake, one layer on top of the next, a mound of crap rising high above the grass in the infield. David's eyes bulged. It continued to flow. Barkus grinned ear to ear. The dog finished his business with a shiver. Barkus patted the dog's head. It was as if he had taken the dump himself and was proud of his accomplishment.

Enough. Binoculars down, gun up.

David brought the gun to his cheek and froze. He didn't aim at anything. *The dog doesn't know any better.* He pointed the gun at Barkus, but his hands trembled, and he couldn't hold his aim. An image kept racing through his mind: *A Sharp-Shooter on Picket Duty.* It was a Winslow Homer painting. David had seen this work the previous summer in the Portland Museum of Art. Homer's painting was of a Union sharpshooter perched in a tree, aiming, finger on the trigger, at an unsuspecting Confederate soldier through the scope of a long-barreled rifle. Then David thought, *Murder.* That's the word Homer had used in a letter years later in recalling how horrified he had been by the sharpshooters, how they were as close to murderers as anyone he had seen in the army, how they had picked off unsuspecting soldiers who were disengaged from battle: having a meal, going to the bathroom, or writing letters to loved ones.

Murder, David thought again. *Am I going to kill this son of a bitch over a baseball field?*

He brought the gun down and set it on the ground. *Is Barkus really engaged in battle here?* David flicked the saddle ring around the slide bar of the carbine with his trigger finger. *Maybe I just need to walk away from this.* But he couldn't. David considered firing shots to scare them off, but he couldn't risk being caught. How would he explain his acts to Annie and Christy?

He thought about just going down to the field and telling Barkus to get lost, but any contact between David and Barkus without witnesses would be used by Barkus against him. The board would think David had lost his mind lying in the brush and spying on Barkus in the early morning. Once again, he could do nothing. He continued to spin the ring and consider his options.

Then, as a pungent reminder to all who might choose to forget its origin, David's hill belched gas through its candy-cane pipe vents. The rotten-egg odor of decades' worth of decomposing crap invaded David's nostrils. It felt as if Barkus was sticking his face right in the pile of dog shit. David's eyes welled up. A flash of anger rushed through his veins. The ground seemed to grow warmer now, the town's past fermented beneath.

In the distance, downriver, he then heard the sound of airplane engines. A gigantic C-130 transport plane—a blimp with wings and four thunderous turboprops—was on the approach to land at nearby Stratton Air Base. If history were any guide, the flight path would take the plane overhead. *Cover*, David thought, *I've got cover!* He felt like a center fielder facing a short line drive: he could now chance attacking the ball knowing he had fielder backup to his rear, in reserve.

Now might be my only chance, David thought. The plane would be able to provide noise cover for about twenty seconds, enough time to get three shots off: one before it passed, one when it was overhead, and one right after it passed. David quickly removed two more rounds from his cartridge box and set them by his side within easy reach.

He raised the gun and sighted down the shiny bluish-steel barrel and took aim. With his peripheral vision, he strained to look for a glimpse of the plane coming over the treetops. The turboprops roared louder. There was a lull in the breeze, and the dump's gaseous odor intensified. His throat was on fire, and his head pounded. He sensed the plane in the corner of his eye. He squeezed the trigger and took his shot as Barkus looked up at the plane passing. The bullet crackled out of the rifle. The gun recoiled amid a plume of smoke.

David felt good; he felt alive for the first time in months. He finally had done something, though he wasn't entirely sure of the consequences. David thought about Doubleday's memoir and imagined that's how Doubleday must have felt when he'd fired the first Union shot of the Civil War at Fort Sumter. "There is a trifling difference of opinion between us and our neighbors opposite," Doubleday had said to a fellow soldier, "and we are trying to settle it."

Dirt popped where the bullet had driven into the ground. It fell short and to the right. Barkus didn't flinch as he looked up in the opposite direction for the plane roaring above. David figured he had to adjust more for the wind. He reached for his second cartridge and quickly loaded it, took aim, and squeezed the trigger. The gun cracked like thunder.

The bullet drilled into the ground and kicked up some dirt just as the plane flew overhead. It was in line but a few feet short. Barkus continued to watch above. David reloaded for the third time and brought the gun to his cheek. He was excited by the smell of burned black powder in the air. His left arm held the barrel, and his sculpted forearm muscles aligned parallel with it. He took a deep breath, aimed, and then pulled the trigger. The bullet rocketed toward its target.

Splat, direct hit.

David picked up his binoculars to survey the damage. The dog shit had splattered all over Barkus's gray slacks. David had obliterated the pile, sending the bullet through the mess and then into the ground. Barkus seemed oblivious to the fact that his lower half was sprayed with dog crap as he followed the plane overhead.

After the plane passed, Barkus looked around and found the dog peeing in the on-deck circle. He clapped for the dog to come. The dog ran over and jumped on Barkus, with his front paws hitting his chest and working their way downward to his slacks, adding dirt to the shit splatter. Barkus pushed him away playfully, and the dog ran in a small circle, through the area of his nasty deed, and then he returned to Barkus again, placing paw prints of dirt and crap on the man's Elite Travel Baseball League jacket as he jumped on him. Barkus smiled and pushed the dog away. The dog retreated, circled in the area of the deed once more, and then added a fresh coat to Barkus.

"What a fine animal," David said out loud as he smiled ear to ear and rolled over on his back, laughing. "What a good dog," he added, trying now to contain his laughter so as not to be heard. A strong gust of wind blew the gas odor away. David drenched himself in sunlight as his laughter settled down. He put a reed of grass in his mouth and savored the moment as puffy clouds, like seamless baseballs, flew by in the light-blue sky. He wished he could celebrate his small victory with someone.

His thoughts turned to Union lieutenant Marcellus Jones, who is said by most to have fired the first shot at Gettysburg. Jones had borrowed a Sharps carbine from a soldier—the same as or a similar model to what David carried—asking the soldier for the "honor of opening this ball." Jones had fired at a Confederate officer but had missed the shot. David, in his mind, had one-upped Jones. While he had missed Barkus, he had at least sprayed his enemy with dog shit, something more than Jones had accomplished, though he had to grudgingly admit that Jones was a half mile away when he fired, not a few hundred yards.

David rolled back over to his stomach, found his binoculars, and looked for Barkus while chewing his reed. The dog was in the car with his head hanging out of the passenger window, panting away. He found Barkus now bending over a few feet away from the driver door. He was tugging at the front of his slacks with one hand while scratching a spot on them with the index finger of the other. He held the index finger to his nose and then abruptly pulled it away while his head quivered.

"There's a wake-up call for you, Barkus," David said.

At that point, David heard the popping gravel of another vehicle entering the parking area. He raised his binoculars to locate it. Another SUV, this one a mass of black and chrome, slowly crept through the lot to park next to Barkus on his driver's side. The vehicle sat there with its motor idling for a few seconds before its driver's door slowly opened. David saw a shiny black wingtip shoe touch the asphalt under the door. He then saw Barkus step back between his door and his vehicle, pulling the door toward him.

David found the feet of the other man and began to scan him from foot to head. He was dressed in a black suit with a beige trench coat and sash. David got a glimpse of a large flashy ring on his pinky finger. He had what appeared to be a blue lanyard around his neck that stood in contrast with his power-red tie.

Then it happened. *Ring.* It was long and loud, like an old-fashioned dial phone. David tossed his binoculars on the ground and rolled on his side. *Ring* again. He jammed his hand into his front pants pocket and searched for his cell phone. *Ring.* He fumbled to open the cover before it rang a fourth time. He saw Christy's number flash on the screen.

"Hello," whispered David, while rolling back onto his stomach.

"Dad? Is that you?" Christy asked.

"Yes, who did you expect?" David asked softly as he looked down the hill to locate Barkus and the man. "Why are you up so early?"

"You told me to call if I heard Mom getting up. Why are you whispering?"

"Never mind now. She's up?" David asked. He reached for his binoculars.

"I heard the TV in your room go on. She must be lying in bed now, waking up."

"Hmm, now that's a problem," David said. He couldn't locate the men, the enemy. He got off his stomach and crouched to get a better view of the field. The two vehicles stood silent, doors closed.

"Dad?"

David threw the gun sling over his head. *Maybe they're trying to flank me,* he thought. He picked up Christy's glove and tucked it under his arm. He scanned the grass around him to see if he had left any evidence that he'd been there.

"Dad, what's going on?"

"Nothing," David said as he fluffed up the grass around him so it stood straight again. "Christy, why did you turn my ringer up so loud?"

"You said you wanted me to turn it up, so that was my best guess. Your phone is ancient, Dad. You need a new one."

"Come on, Christy. I just conquered the learning curve on this one."

The sound of rustling grass sounded like static to Christy on the phone.

"Are you okay?" Christy asked. "What's with the heavy breathing?"

David wiped some perspiration from his forehead.

"You caught me in the middle of something. I'm just trying to finish up." David began moving down the opposite side of the hill that overlooked the river while crouching so as not to be seen from the baseball field below.

With his back bent, he started to circle around the field to get to his car parked a couple of hundred yards away.

"Dad? What's going on?"

"Never mind. I'm good. I'll be home in a bit. Go back to sleep. Hopefully, Mom won't see the car missing by the time I get back." If Annie found out he was at the field, David knew he would be in trouble. She already thought he spent too much time on baseball. The less she knew he worked on baseball, the better things were around the house for everyone.

"Okay," said Christy.

"I have to go now," David said, and hung up.

He got halfway down the hill so he could stand without being seen on the other side. He scanned the area around him. There was no sign of anyone. David started jogging toward his car. *Maybe I'm the hunted one now,* he thought.

He reached his 1974 pearl-white Mustang parked behind some trees and out of sight from the lot where Barkus and the man had parked. He touched the hood. He had reached third base safely in his mind. He leaned against the car for a second; he was out of breath. He brushed his jeans off and looked over his shoulder. Again, there was nobody in sight. He popped open the trunk and loaded his equipment, then looked around again before getting in the car. Still, no signs of anything moving.

Time to head for home, he thought while mounting the Mustang's driver seat. At that moment, David imagined he felt much like General Buford must have felt mounted on his white horse, "Grey Eagle," after the first day at Gettysburg: sad, exhausted, yet steadied by an underlying satisfaction of a job well done.

David approached the parking-area exit, about two hundred yards from the entrance to the main lot where Barkus and the man had entered. Both entrances connected to the same county road. He looked down to the other entrance, then in the opposite direction. No traffic, no sign of Barkus. He turned in the opposite direction of the main lot and drove off.

David checked his rearview mirror. He got a glimpse of the black-and-chrome SUV leaving the other lot and heading in his direction. His heart raced and his stomach dropped, the same feeling he got when spying a speed trap. He turned the radio off and applied some giddyap to the gas pedal.

He put a great distance between himself and the black SUV. There wasn't much traffic on the road except for the owners of a few landscaping trucks en route to care for the upscale lawns of Indigo Valley. After a number of turns, David no longer saw the black SUV in his rearview, so he figured he had lost him.

David considered the absurdity of what he had done. He prided himself on his ability to handle any situation with calmness and reason. He realized that he had risked his family's reputation and his reputation as a lawyer by acting impulsively. He was forced to consider the distinct possibility that his actions were a little more outrageous than Barkus's. But maybe, he considered, this was a matter that was best addressed by acting more absurd than the enemy. *Enemies in kids' baseball?* David thought. *How had it come to this?*

When he darted into the driveway, he felt some shame in what he had done but couldn't deny his sense of satisfaction, a sense of doing something and making it to home base safely, a sense that he knew would persist only so long as his morning maneuvers went undetected.

2

THE HOME TEAM

David got out of his car and gently pushed the door closed so as not to wake Annie. It was a little past 7:00 a.m. He looked up and could see from the driveway that the curtains to his second-story bedroom were drawn. Annie always opened the curtains when she got up so he figured she was still in bed.

He took off his sneakers before reaching the side door entrance. The treads were still caked with the infield clay mix from working the prior night. He wasn't going to risk leaving that evidence on the house floors for Annie to find. He placed the sneakers in the bushes under the water spigot, next to three other muddy pairs. His socks were wet from galloping through the grass that morning and he left wet footprints on the sidewalk. He slowly opened the door to the Cape Cod home so the hinges didn't squeak. Fifteen years ago, he had bought the house as a surprise for Annie while she was out of town on a business trip.

David tiptoed in the doorway and made his way to the living room to see if anyone might be there. The only inhabitants were a few large *Saturday Evening Post* cover illustrations painted by Mead Schaeffer depicting armed US enlisted men in various wartime poses during World War II. Schaeffer was David's great-uncle by marriage and he had worked alongside Norman Rockwell in the same town and even shared his studio for a time with him after Rockwell's studio burned to the ground. David had been given some of

Schaeffer's wartime series illustrations. Annie complained that armed men hanging around the living room did not contribute much to the country theme of the house, most notably the guy posing in a tank turret and pointing his gun barrel at the love seat. David removed his socks so he didn't damage the high-gloss maple floorboards that always seemed to remind him of baseball bat billets.

He scaled the steps to the second floor on all fours, looking to distribute his weight equally so that the stairs didn't creak. Halfway up, David could hear the television in his bedroom on low volume. He got to the top. Their door was slightly ajar. David peeked in and saw Annie buried under the covers asleep. *Good*, he thought.

This was David's second year on the baseball board of directors. His first year had been a rocky one requiring long hours of work, and Annie and Christy were growing weary of David's focus on the baseball program. So David did his baseball work in the early hours before Annie and Christy woke up for the day, or he did it after they had gone to bed.

David drifted down the hallway into his son's bedroom. He saw Christy sleeping with a Yankees quilt strewn about and his head lying on a Yankees pillowcase. He had kicked off his covers yet again to rid himself of all the blankets Annie had piled on him because she was cold. David pushed Christy's light brown hair away from his forehead before touching his skin. He felt cool so David put one blanket back over Christy's slim frame. As he pulled it up and gently tucked it in around his shoulders, David could see that Christy's arms were becoming more muscular.

All around the room was baseball memorabilia, on the walls and on top of bookcases. There were autographed baseballs and baseball cards neatly displayed in a cherry bookcase with sliding glass doors. The collection was displayed by low-level lighting that had been left on by Christy when he went to bed. He would stare at the collection while lying in bed until he drifted off to the sweet dreams of baseball seasons past. Above his bookcase was the framed sports section of an April 16, 2000, headline that screamed "3,000 Rips," celebrating the three thousandth career hit of Cal Ripken and autographed by him. A signed Ripken baseball sat on top of the bookcase. There was also signed ball from Derek Jeter and a number of his rookie cards.

But the amount of modern player memorabilia was dwarfed by the amount of vintage items in the room. His prized possession was a collection of two dozen T-205 tobacco cards from 1911. These baseball cards had a shimmering gold border surrounding bright-colored illustrations of the players of that time on the front with biographies and statistics on the back.

Christy had read a magazine article on the T-205 series a few years back and had studied all their variations: different tobacco company backs, typos, missing stats, different facial features. He had become an expert on grading them. Christy could spot a trimmed or a reproduction card in a few seconds. He would often tell vendors at card shows that their cards were underpriced or overpriced based on his evaluation. Christy had come to love the history of baseball almost as much as he loved playing the game.

David picked up his favorite card from Christy's growing T-205 collection. It was a mint card to David, though Christy said it would grade as "excellent." It was David's favorite card in the T-205 collection but it was at the bottom of the list for Christy. The difference of opinion over the card stemmed from the name of the player on it. The card was of Christy Mathewson, the earlytwentieth-century Hall of Fame pitcher for the New York Giants, and one of David's favorite players growing up. When David learned that Mathewson's father had served as a Pennsylvania volunteer in the Civil War just like David's great-great-grandfather, David wanted to name his newborn son "Christopher Thompson." Annie liked the name too. David nicknamed his son "Christy" after Mathewson and the name stuck with all of Christy's classmates through elementary school. It wasn't until the fifth grade when he was first kidded about it being a girl's name by his friends. Then things turned worse after Mrs. Cheswick, his sixth-grade music teacher, played Johnny Cash's song "A Boy Named Sue" in class as part of the school district's anti-bullying campaign. Kids kept turning their heads to look at Christy and whisper among themselves as the song played. Later on, some boys told Christy that he had the same first name as Christie Brinkley, a name they had become familiar with after seeing her, all summer long, in reruns of *National Lampoon's Vacation*. So when David gave his son a Christy Mathewson T-205 card for his birthday the following year, it could have been a mint, rare variation and Christy wouldn't have thought the better of it.

The gold borders shimmered as David moved the card around to catch the early-morning sunlight that found a crease between the curtains. A smile came to his face as it always did when he looked at the card every morning. He looked over to his son and his smile broadened.

He took a deep breath and slowly exhaled while looking at the pictures of Christy and other boys on his team this year. He had made this early-morning walk into his son's room the past few months after the e-mails from Barkus had intensified. Seeing Christy's face, the team pictures of his friends, and his room dedicated to baseball was comforting and inspirational. It reaffirmed in David's mind all that he was doing.

David put the card neatly back on the stand and went to the bathroom. He looked in the mirror and saw his messed-up hair and his stubble face and came to the realization that he could not skip the shower and shave routine as he had done often of late. Heck, it was opening day and, in David's mind, the Babe Ruth commissioner had to look alive and halfway human if at all possible. He went down into his law office in the finished side of the basement and sat at his desk to put his team batting lineup together for opening day. His office had two other desks, one for Annie and one for Christy. All three often worked at night in the office, which made for bonding, according to Annie, though each had come to know a bit too much about each other's business.

The papers on David's desk were strewn about like a pile of unshuffled cards. They all concerned the baseball league.

His team, the "Choppers," was named after a local custom motorcycle shop named Cycle Chopper.

David looked at his watch. It was 7:25 a.m. and he was running out of time. First game for the day was at 9:00 a.m. David had to be there by 8:00 a.m. as Babe Ruth commissioner to open everything. The teams would start to warm up at 8:15 or so. He had prepared the field the previous night to buy some time in the morning. David climbed the stairs two at a time to the kitchen and made a move for the refrigerator, when he spotted her dressed in her robin-eggblue pajamas sitting in the dining room and sipping on a cup of juice.

"Good morning, Annie," he said.

No response. She finished sipping her juice. Her sandy-blond shoulder-length hair glistened in the sunlight. She pushed the hair over her eyes away and then combed the rest of her hair back with her fingers as she tried to look presentable.

"Does it really start today?" she asked softly, putting her cup down and staring off into space.

David reached for the orange juice in the refrigerator and contemplated his answer. "If you mean baseball, then yes, it starts today."

"Shit," she said under her breath, removing the cup from her lips. It wasn't in her nature to swear. She set the cup down and looked at the chips in her nail polish, which she had put on for their anniversary last week. She rarely ever wore any makeup. When David finished law school with loans to pay off, Annie jokingly advertised herself to David as an attractive, "all-natural and debt-free" bachelorette.

He shook the almost-empty carton and contemplated drinking from it to finish it off, until Annie gently reminded David to use a glass.

He reached for a cloudy glass out of the cupboard as if he never intended to drink from the carton in the first place. "What's the weather today?" he asked, looking to change the subject and knowing that she had been watching the Weather Channel upstairs.

"Shit," she whispered as the memories of baseball from last year's season awoke. She enjoyed the actual games, but the behind-the-scenes work that David did before, during, and after the season bordered on obsession as far as she was concerned. She looked at the scab that had formed over a cut to her index finger from working in the garden the day before and wondered if she should put a bandage on it.

David decided he wasn't going to react to Annie. He already had two strikes on him and was quite content in taking a third so as to avoid revisiting the longstanding argument over the time he spent on baseball. He had to leave in a few minutes; that argument could last all weekend. He pretended not to notice her effort to engage him and took her weather forecast at face value. "I don't know about that. The sun's out. Looks pretty good."

She rotated her index finger around the cup's rim three times. "There is a one hundred percent chance that I'm a baseball widow starting today," she said, looking at him directly for the first time with her chocolate-brown eyes.

David decided to try and skip the argument and go right to the resolution. "I'll try and do better this season, Annie."

Annie took another sip from the cup and then barely peeled her lips away from it before she spoke. "Last night, I read *that* e-mail," she said through the bottom of her cup.

David sighed. "I asked you not to read my e-mails."

"I hadn't since you asked me last year, but I was cleaning your desk and this particular one was open and staring at me on your Jumbotron of a monitor down there. I couldn't help but notice it. That guy's a lunatic. He says you're acting disturbed. What is he talking about?"

David took a gulp of juice and put it down on the counter. "He's got a couple screws loose," he tried to say matter-of-factly while admitting to himself that Barkus may have a point, since he'd almost shot him dead an hour earlier.

"How long has this been going on?" she asked.

David crossed his arms and leaned back against the kitchen counter. "Annie, I wish you didn't look at my e-mails. This really shouldn't concern you."

"It shouldn't concern me?" she said, raising her voice. "Your e-mail box is full of stuff from Rob Barkus. I saw it. I feel like he's in our house. I don't like that feeling. He says terrible things about you and then CC's everyone. I have every right to be concerned about that."

David didn't say anything. He drank his orange juice and stared into the backyard through the kitchen window. It was a deep backyard that went into a field. In the rear of the yard there was a batting cage. David had built it a few years earlier for Christy and his friends. In the cage was David's prize possession, an ATEC Casey Pro Pitching machine, otherwise known to him as his artillery piece. He'd seen the machine used at Mets training in Florida two seasons ago and wanted one. It could pitch a ball over ninety miles per hour. It could throw every type of pitch conceivable. It could hurl a ball a distance of over four hundred feet in the air when its trajectory was adjusted. Amazing, David thought as his mind broke away from the topic of conversation.

"Did you hear me?"

"Yes, Annie, I heard you."

"What do you say to that?"

"Nothing to say other than what I've said already. I can take care of Barkus."

"Well, will you take care of all the people in town that will have nothing to do with me anymore?" Annie worked as a human resources trainer for a large corporation, where she taught employees at every level to get along with one another.

David looked at her sad brown eyes. "What do you mean?"

"I thought it was me, something I did, but now I see what's going on."

"What are you talking about?"

"All the people CC'd on the Barkus e-mails. When they see me around town, they shun me."

Her eyes were welling up. David walked over and hugged her from behind while she sat in the chair. "I'm sorry, honey. I didn't know." He kissed her cheek.

"David, this is all about the field, isn't it?"

"It goes beyond the field."

"I read the e-mail. Barkus wants to use the field like he did last year. Can't you just let him use it?" Annie thought that if she could solve multifaceted human conflict situations at a Fortune 500 company, surely she could solve problems in a youth baseball league.

David sighed and pulled away from Annie, then sat down beside her.

"The Barkus teams can play on the two school fields."

"So why does he want the Babe Ruth field then?"

"Because it's the best field in town."

"I don't understand," she said, wondering if what all these parents needed to get along was a training seminar that taught them Dr. Donahue's five core principles of behavior: lead by example, think beyond the moment, make things better, maintain the self-esteem of others, and focus on the issue, not the person.

"Good, that means you pass the sanity check," David said.

"David, I feel I'm going to lose you again like last season. I feel like an outcast in my hometown."

"Annie, I promise to try and do better this season. As far as those people go, they're not worth your friendship. Most of these folks aren't the 'five tool players' that you are used to dealing with at work." David used baseball's five tools terminology (running speed, arm strength, hitting for average, hitting for power, and fielding) to describe people who embodied Annie's core principles.

Annie went back to circling the rim of her cup. She stared into it, looking for answers, as a tear ran down her cheek. Christy and David were around the house in between practice and games, but the topic of discussion always seemed to be baseball related and, if the topic wasn't baseball, David would somehow steer it in that direction eventually. Annie had come to learn that she, at best, was second to baseball during the season. She had come to associate baseball with loneliness outside of the games. David got up and got her a tissue, then sat down beside her and dabbed the tear away.

He pushed her hair from her eyes with one hand and touched her chin with the other to bring her eyes to his. "Annie, I have to get going to be at the field for the first game. Please know that I love you."

"I know. I love you too," she said, trying to smile.

"I'll be back before Christy's game. We play at noon. We can talk more then if you'd like."

She stood up and kissed him on the cheek, then went upstairs to take a shower.

David checked his watch again. It was now 7:45 a.m. and time to leave for the field to make sure the 9:00 a.m. game went off well. David didn't want any opening-day issues—he knew Barkus and his allies were looking to seize any opportunity to pressure him.

David flew out the door. When he got to his car, he spotted a dent on the trunk from a foul ball. He had not seen it before. Butterflies danced in his stomach. Annie didn't need to see that dent; that was the last thing she needed to see. The Mustang was a present from her and the idea that a baseball, of all things, had damaged it would upset her to no end. Fortunately, no paint had been chipped from the car and it was a nice round dent. He opened the trunk and pounded underneath the dent with his fist and popped the dent out. *Good as new*, he thought as he drove off to the field.

3

MEESON'S SKIRMISH

David's mind wandered on the way over to the field. On the eve of the first day of battle at Gettysburg, General Buford and his junior officer, Thomas Devin (known as Buford's "hard hitter"), were reportedly sitting around a campfire discussing the day's events and Buford's defensive plan. Devin expressed confidence that Buford's forces could easily withstand anything the Confederates could throw at them the next day. Buford said in response, "No, you won't. They will attack you in the morning and they will come booming—three skirmishers deep." David tried to ready himself for whatever opening day—his first day of battle—would throw at him.

David entered the parking lot and drove past the field and to the farthest point away from home plate. He didn't need any more dents from errant baseballs. There were people roaming about and a man took note that he had arrived by staring and pointing at the car. David pulled the car into a spot far away from the field where there were no other cars parked. He turned the ignition off. He got out of the car and looked up.

There stood Mrs. Angela Meeson, hover mother of Jackson Meeson, the supposed future first baseman for the New York Yankees, at least in the opinion of Mrs. Meeson.

"Good morning, Mrs. Meeson, where did you come from?" David asked.

She pushed her waist-long black hair away from her face as she flicked her head back, revealing the makeup job of a rodeo clown. "Over there, by the burial mound," she said.

"Oh, you don't say," David responded without emotion, noting that she had bought into the burial ground myth like all the carpetbaggers in town.

"I won't stand for it this year," she rasped, standing with both hands on her hips. She flicked her head back again and her mane fell back behind her shoulders.

Ambush! David thought while looking away toward the bare flagpole. He wondered where he had stored the flag last fall.

"Stop trying to avoid me," she said, and scolded David with her index finger. His attention turned back to Angela.

"I'm standing right here listening to you, Angela."

"Yeah, but you're looking over there."

All of a sudden, David felt something biting his right ankle. He looked down and pulled his pant leg up to reveal a tick engorged in his flesh. He pulled it out while admiring the perfection of Angela's pink polished toenails flashing from her open-toed heels.

"It's opening day, Angela. I have a lot on my mind."

"I think you're trying to ignore me."

David looked at her bulbous hips, her skinny upper torso, and could only think of the replacement lightbulbs he forgot to buy for the women's rest room.

"Angela, I'm standing here talking with you. What more do you want?"

"I want you to pay attention to me," she said, wagging her finger as her softball-sized breasts bounced in rhythm. It was like she was the director of a marching band and her breasts were the French horns bobbing around in perfect rhythm with one another. He thought that her breasts looked bigger this year. *Maybe they underwent some off-season surgery?* David thought. He recalled the plastic bags of nacho cheese in the concession stand he had handled the night before in preparation for opening day and he wondered if that's how silicone implants felt. He looked at Angela's breasts again. Then it hit him. The real reason they looked larger was because she was braless. Her breasts swung freely with every hand gesticulation under her tight black V-neck sweater. It was, he thought, a new strategy of hers to get what she wanted, and her breasts were aimed at David like artillery shells. He understood that Angela would stop at nothing to promote her son's baseball stature, to ensure he'd be one of the chosen few to play for the school and the Elite Travel Baseball League teams.

"Angela, I couldn't avoid you if I wanted to."

"What do you mean by that?" she said, flicking her hair back.

"Nothing, except that, if anything, you are persistent. Angela, please, I've got a lot to do." David looked at the breasts bounce and his baseball instincts took over—he wondered if he should put a fielder's glove on to catch them before they hit the ground.

Angela got closer to David. "You're a commissioner and I have a complaint." He could smell it on her breath, the scent of hard liquor.

"Angela, your son plays at the Cal Ripken age level; the Babe Ruth level starts at age thirteen. I'm commissioner of Babe Ruth, not Cal Ripken."

"Well, I have been doing a lot of thinking about the situation and—"

"I'm sure you have. Is this the same complaint you had all last season?"

"—and I have some thoughts," Angela said, ignoring David's question.

David could not take an opening-day round of Angela's crap. He had not seen her since last season and she was picking up right where she had left off. He cringed at this déjà vu moment. David felt like he was in the midst of a midlife crisis of sorts where time marches on but things never change. He wanted a fresh start for the battles he planned to fight this season. He was determined that this year would be different.

"Look, I'm sorry Jackson did not make the all-star team, but I think we covered the topic in all the conversations we had last season."

"I don't want the same thing to happen to Jackson *this* year."

"Like I said last season, I don't make those decisions. The all-star team coach does."

"But you are a commissioner. You have a say."

"No, I don't. Jackson and the coach have a say. You and I don't."

"How does Jackson have a say?"

"Did Jackson do any off-season work? Does he plan to practice hard now that the weather has turned?"

"Oh, come on now, you and I know it is mostly politics involved in picking the all-star team."

"You think so? Well, talk to Arnold then. Have him work it out for you." Arnold was her husband and was a board member. Their older son, Alex, played for three separate teams: the freshman school team, the Indigo Valley Babe Ruth League team, and the Elite Travel Baseball League team. He was one of two freshmen boys who played Babe Ruth baseball. Even after adjusting for their age difference, Alex was far more gifted athletically than Jackson.

"Arnold's a good-for-nothing."

David was not going to get between Arnold and Angela. He looked over her shoulder and spotted Wayne Duffel, the high school athletic director, walking toward them from the other end of the parking lot. David's stomach dropped. Duffel was dressed in a black suit and a beige trench coat. *Was this the guy that was with Barkus?*

David eyed Angela. "Look, I have to get ready for the game, so unless you want to tag along and help me set up while we talk—"

"I don't have time," she said as her breasts and hands waved about.

"Suit yourself." David turned and began to walk away from Angela. *Typical parent,* he thought, *plenty of time to complain but no time to volunteer.* If he hung around, he knew he would end up saying something to upset her and she would ride him and try to break him all season long. It would, he thought, be too much like his recurring dream, the dream when he steps in dog shit and can't get it off his shoe. It was a dream born from experience, as people like Barkus used the ball field as a toilet, their dogs laying mines that went off when David worked on the field every morning. Dog poop and David had a magnetic relationship and he hated stepping in it almost as much as he hated Angela Meeson.

"You know, I can go play in the Elite Travel Baseball League," she called to David.

David kept walking. *She must be under the mistaken impression that I give a shit,* he thought. He knew the drill: parent does not get her way; parent threatens to leave. Arnold already had one foot out the door with Alex. David figured Arnold hung around on the board to see if he could get the Babe Ruth field for the freshman team and for Barkus.

In any event, David appreciated that the Elite Travel Baseball League had one incidental benefit. He was more than happy to ship problems like Angela Meeson to their doorstep, even if it meant one less player in his already dilapidated league.

Angela cupped one hand around her mouth to project her voice toward David. "You know, you really should give the field to them," she said, standing on her toes as she wobbled in her heels.

David ignored her. Angela had joined the enemy ranks in his mind. It only made sense that she would try to get the Babe Ruth field if she were on her way out the door.

Angela typified what to expect from the enemy. Like Buford at Gettysburg, there was no need for David to go to the enemy. David understood that the enemy would come to him as sure as sharks were drawn to blood because he had possession of the prize—the Babe Ruth field—and he was only one man. One man stood between the pack of crazy travel baseball parents and the feeding of baseball to their young. David knew that in their estimation, one man could be had by virtue of their strength in numbers. The Babe Ruth field had become the chosen field of the Elite Travel Baseball League parents. It was their field of dreams en route to the Promised Land of scholarships and major league contracts.

4

DUFFEL'S CHARGE

Wayne Duffel has assumed a position between David and the ball field. When David walked and veered in one direction toward the visitors' field entrance gate by the third baseline, Duffel mirrored his move and got between him and the field again. Just for fun, David changed direction to the home field entrance gate on the first base side of the backstop, just to see Duffel hustle in that direction. Duffel obliged—nothing would deter him from his mission.

Wayne Duffel was the newly hired athletic director for Indigo Valley High School's fourteen hundred students. He was a tall, thinly built, middleaged man with a balding, square head, and pointed chin like the back of home plate. He was wiping his brow with a washcloth as he walked toward David. *Not a good sign*, he thought. He knew Duffel perspired like a fountain when agitated.

He looked at Duffel and wondered again if he was the man he had seen with Barkus earlier that morning. Duffel didn't have the power-red tie that David had seen. He wasn't wearing a tie at all. He looked down for the flashy ring he had seen on the man's hand but couldn't see his fingers.

David knew there was a battle developing on Duffel's front and this was one that had to be fought in his estimation. Duffel positioned himself directly in front of David and stood his ground.

"Hey, we need to talk," Duffel said as David approached.

"Good morning to you, Wayne. What brings you out ¹ day?" David said while walking toward Duffel. He knew f coming.

"You know the freshman team has historically had acc͟ Ruth field for practice and for their home games, right?" Duffel asked.

"Yeah, that's my understanding," David said, stopping in front of him.

"I heard that this year *you* won't allow us access. What do *you* have to say about that?"

You, David thought. The choice of that word intrigued him. David didn't have authority to deny the freshman team access to the field even though he was the Babe Ruth commissioner and directed the league's day-to-day operations. He could be overruled by the board. But Duffel didn't seem to know this or he thought David had board support. A good field general knows better than to remedy the missteps of an enemy, and so David decided to play Duffel's misperception to his advantage to buy himself some time.

"That's correct," David said matter-of-factly. "That's what was decided," he added for good measure. He walked around Duffel and headed for the field again.

"What's going on?" Duffel asked, turning around as David walked by.

David stopped and turned to look at Duffel. "How many players from the freshman team are playing in our in-house Babe Ruth baseball program?" he asked.

"How am I supposed to know?" said Duffel, raising his hand to wipe his forehead.

David looked at Duffel's hand and saw a large wedding ring. He wasn't sure if this was the ring he saw earlier in the morning.

"Try the number two. That's two out of fifteen that are playing in our program. I hear that the other thirteen are going around school saying that Babe Ruth baseball sucks. They think they're too good to play Babe Ruth in-house baseball. But evidently, they don't think they' re too good to use the Babe Ruth field."

Duffel unbuttoned his suit and pushed his jacket and coat to the sides, putting his hands on his hips. "You mean you won't support our high school athletes?" he said.

David didn't see any blue lanyard around Duffel's neck, though he noted his fly was open. He thought about telling him.

"I would love to support the school baseball program," he said. "There's nothing more I'd rather do right now than to give you my full support. I graduated from this high school thirty years ago. High school sports were very important to me. It helped shape who I am. Heck, I would like my son to have the same experience. But I'm not going to support your program at the expense of the community program. Life is a reciprocal arrangement, you know. Bottom line is that your freshman team needs to support the Babe Ruth program before we consider giving them access to the field. So far, the team is batting the equivalent of .130 in supporting the Babe Ruth program. Now what do you do with a player batting .130? You bench him. So consider the freshman team benched from using the field."

Duffel's voice grew louder. "You guys have given the freshman team access to the field for years and now you're taking it away?"

"We gave the field to the team because they all participated in our program years ago. Now they don't."

"That didn't seem to matter until this year."

"It's about time someone stood up and took note of what is going on here with our field," David said. "Former board members happily gave you the field for use, which in turn gave them an assist, or so they thought, in getting their boys onto a school baseball team. Would you expect them to say no to such a request even if it meant hurting *our* league?"

"You know something," Duffel said, "you have your baseball program to worry about and I have mine."

At that point, David caught a glimpse of Duffel's open fly once more and decided that he had his fly to worry about and Duffel had his.

"I don't get it," David said. "You live in the town, so why not take pride in our town league. It's your league too. The programs are not independent of one another. Your success is dependent on our success and vice versa. We are your feeder program—we provide you with your baseball players. I don't think you understand that at all."

"Look, what I don't understand is why we can't use the field like we've done in the past."

"Why? Because you're not supporting our program. At one time, the freshmen players participated in our Babe Ruth program. But that's not happening now. And there are no players here from the junior varsity or varsity levels. I'm not taking the field away from you and your parents and kids. They are losing it because they don't support our program. Using our field is a privilege, not a right."

"What do we have to do with your enrollment numbers?"

"Nothing. That's the problem. You aren't exactly encouraging players to participate in our program."

"That's not our job."

"That's ridiculous, Wayne. Our program *is* the community; the community *owns* the school district. It's in the board of education policies that the district is supposed to support programs that support the community. Read them on your website. Other school districts encourage participation by their players. Why not you?"

"You obviously have to do a better job with your program to get the kids interested. You must have field time available for us."

"You have got to be kidding me. The only reason we may have any field time is because you aren't supporting us. And on that basis, you think you are entitled to use the field? Unbelievable."

Duffel wiped his brow. "Look, our parents have to make choices for their kids and maybe they thought it was too much baseball, playing both in the school program and Babe Ruth with homework and all their other activities."

David laughed while shaking his head. "Well, you tell me then why eighty-seven percent of the baseball-playing kids in this town can't play both Babe Ruth baseball and school baseball when just the opposite is true everywhere else in the area? Don't our kids like baseball as much? I have to imagine our kids can handle school and baseball. Are you saying our kids can't handle both?"

"What do you want me to do?"

"You could start by encouraging players to play Babe Ruth; you could start by supporting your community program."

"Parents are going to do what they want to do."

"You know there is not one school district in the region, maybe even the state, which has such a low participation rate. It is as if there is almost a prohibition against playing both in the school program and in our league."

"A prohibition? So there's some sort of baseball conspiracy at work here, is that what you're saying?"

"I think I have it figured out, Wayne. You also think the school players are too good to be playing Babe Ruth."

"You, ah, have quite an imagination, David."

David knew what was going on. Babe Ruth had an in-house or recreational component that called for all boys to play in a league with one another in their own community in order to be eligible to try out for an age-specific all-star team from that community.

The Elite Travel Baseball League had no in-house component. They didn't have to play with other boys from Indigo Valley. They were pure travel baseball teams made up exclusively of school players to the exclusion of other boys in the town. They only played teams outside of Indigo Valley. David understood that Duffel wasn't going to admit that he thought the school players were too good to play with the Babe Ruth boys. That would be a politically explosive statement; it would not help him get access to the field.

David pressed on. "That's a shame, really. This is the last community sports program left for teenagers in town, the last program that gives teens, all teens, an opportunity to play a sport regardless of skill level."

"That's very touching, but it has nothing to do with letting us share the field."

"Are you listening to me, Wayne? Our numbers have been cut in half since the Elite Travel Baseball League started taking the school players. I'm not sure there will be a league in a few years if we don't take appropriate steps."

"That's too bad, but that seems to be the trend for programs like yours."

"It's too bad for *all* of us. Would you rather see these boys bustin' a baseball or bustin' into your house? Don't you understand that we provide a positive outlet for kids and that makes them less likely to get into trouble at school or around town?"

"Just stop it, will you? You're saying kids are going to be breaking into my house over baseball now? God, I just came to you to talk about field time."

"Wayne, I think we're going to use our field to spread the interest in our baseball program, to provide more opportunities to the players that are left, to try and increase enrollment, to try and improve the program and attract other boys. We need to grow our numbers to survive if the school players won't play with us. Besides, you have two fields and four teams including the modified team. I have got six teams and one field to schedule them on, with more teams coming later on. I think you can manage with two fields. If anything, I should be coming to you for field space since I have more teams and only one field."

"Hey, you can apply for field time through our office."

"Sure, Wayne. I have a better chance of winning the state lottery lucky seven jackpot than getting time on the school fields."

"What are you talking about?"

"It seems like the Elite Travel Baseball League teams are scheduled to use them even when they aren't."

"What?"

"You heard me right."

"I don't get it."

"Yeah, you sure don't. But if you are being straight up with me about not knowing what's going on with your fields, maybe you want to invest some time and figure that out for yourself."

David knew what was going on even if Duffel didn't. In years prior, the Indigo Valley Baseball League had access to the two full-sized baseball fields owned by the school district so scheduling was easier. But now, since the school coaches had sided with the Elite Travel Baseball League to field its summer baseball teams, David had been prevented from accessing the fields by the school athletic office. The assistant athletic director was a friend of Barkus. The assistant did all the school field scheduling and David had long ago given up on being able to use those fields. Whenever David requested a time slot on one of the school fields, the assistant told him that the slot had been reserved by the Elite Travel Baseball League. One day he went into the assistant's office and requested a half dozen time slots and was given the usual line that the Elite Travel Baseball League had reserved them for those times. When those games were supposed to be played, David would drive over to see if the fields were actually used. The teams played games there twice, while the field went unused during the other four times he requested. He got the message: the school did not want to provide fields to the Babe Ruth kids.

And so David had stopped asking to use the fields and neatly boxed up the anger he felt. *Out of sight, out of mind*, he would tell himself.

Duffel stood there, speechless. He was caught off guard by what David said about the school fields.

"Look, Wayne. I've got a 9:00 a.m. game here. I've got to help get things ready. Think about what I said."

David turned away. Duffel realized he could not exactly push for use of the Babe Ruth field if the school fields were not available to David. Duffel scrambled to find some snappy comeback as he watched David stride toward the field. Then it was too late.

David believed that his skirmish line of arguments had confused the inexperienced Duffel, and he was pleased that he had at least bought some time on this front. In his estimation, Duffel would have to pull back and regroup before coming after the field again.

David believed that he was rightly shaking things up in the town baseball community. He understood that he was challenging entrenched beliefs and assumptions and that he was making people at least think about how things were done in the past. He felt as if he were defending baseball, the right of teenagers to partake in an athletic endeavor, the only sport offering left in town that was open to all teens regardless of skill.

David walked toward the Babe Ruth concession stand, which was located behind home plate and overlooked the field. As he rounded the corner to the front of the stand that faced the field, he saw one lone man by the closed service window. It was Rob Barkus.

5

CARNIVAL BARKER

David considered trying to avoid him. But it was too late. Barkus had spotted him. "What does a guy have to do to get a cup of coffee here?" he asked, painting on a broad smile.

David felt badly about the events earlier that morning. He was ashamed that he let his emotions get the best of him. He wanted to make amends. "Stand doesn't open until game time, but I'll see what I can do for you."

"Thank you."

He's thanking me, David thought while breathing a sigh of relief. Gratitude wouldn't be the sentiment of a man who knew he'd been David's shooting target a few hours earlier.

Barkus hadn't changed his clothes; his charcoal slacks camouflaged the shit splatter. Though he figured Barkus wanted something more than coffee, probably the field, David wanted to spend some time with him to make sure he knew nothing about the events of early that morning.

David went around the side to open the concession stand door and entered. He went over to check on the coffee he had timed to brew for the morning crowd the day before. The steel slats banged against each other as he opened the steel security window blinds to the outside to reveal the concession stand counter. On the other side, there stood Barkus and Angela Meeson—a likely couple in the making—perfectly framed for David's viewing pleasure.

Angela was a bit startled by the noise of the steel curtain. She glanced at David, while Barkus didn't miss a beat.

"Angela," Barkus said, "I have seen Jackson play, and I have to tell you that he is a ballplayer with a growing skill-set, a young man with great potential."

David looked over Angela's shoulder and recognized the distinct limp-arm throwing motion of Jackson Meeson. "Yes, and I see Jackson warming up over there with Alex outside the fence of the Cal Ripken field."

Angela and Barkus turned around to see all two hundred pounds of twelve-year-old Jackson Meeson stuffed into a five-foot-eight-inch frame.

"He looks sharp," Barkus said, before Jackson threw one into the ground twenty feet in front of Alex.

The three watched, waiting for Jackson to redeem himself. But every third or fourth throw spiked down into the ground and ran past Alex. He held the ball too long, maybe because of his plump hands. While Alex chased the ball down, Jackson went back to the bleachers and took another bite of some grease-drenched fast-food breakfast sandwich that made Jackson's face shine like a piece of waxed fruit.

"He's not in playing shape yet," Angela said to Barkus.

"Of course not," Barkus said, knowing better than to criticize a potential client. "It's to be expected."

When Jackson had a bad streak of three balls going into the ground well short of Alex, Angela had seen enough. "Jackson, you need to keep your elbow up," she yelled over to him, not knowing what that meant, but recalling that's what Arnold said to him sometimes when he made bad throws.

Jackson heard his mother embarrass him in front of the other kids on the field and stared her down a second before waving Alex off and heading to the stands to finish his sandwich and then gobble down his hash browns.

"David, did you hear what Rob said?" she asked, glancing at him.

David was working the coffee machine, getting ready to brew another pot. "I heard it, have heard it, and undoubtedly will hear it all season long."

David knew there was nothing he could say to change what was happening even if he wanted to try. Arnold Meeson had taken the initial step to remove his oldest son, Alex, from the league. Jackson would be following in his footsteps after he had played through the Cal Ripken program.

"Angela, don't pay any attention to him," said Barkus.

"I'm not. I already told him that Jackson should have made the all-star team last year."

"What? Jackson did not make the all-star team?" Barkus looked at David. "Are you kidding me?"

David didn't say anything as he poured Barkus a cup of coffee. He knew that paying a series of compliments to parents about their sons' baseball talents was part one of the sales pitch.

"That's what I told David," Angela said.

"Arnold is on the board and Jackson didn't make the all-star team?" Barkus asked.

They both looked at David, waiting for a response. David put a plastic lid on the coffee and placed it on the counter. Barkus reached for it while David held the palm of his hand over the lid.

"That'll be seventy-five cents, Rob."

Barkus whipped a crisp bill out of his stuffed wallet. "Can you break a fifty?"

"Rob, we haven't opened up yet. That's about all I have in the register."

Barkus smiled and took out a ten. David went to the register to make change.

"Angela," Barkus continued, "with all the potential that Jackson has, I'm not sure he should be playing rec ball anymore. He's too good to be playing with *those* players."

It wasn't that Barkus believed any of his spiel; it was just that he wanted to do Arnold a favor so he would help him out on the board, maybe help him get the field.

"Really?" said Angela.

David returned and placed the change on the counter. He hated this part of the pitch the most. This phase required Barkus to plant the seeds of baseball snobbery in the town, to create two classes—the "haves" and the "have-nots."

"He's only going to get better playing with better players from better teams outside of town," Barkus said.

David sat down on a stool. It was a great act of salesmanship, a beautiful con, a show perfected over the years, and David was repulsed by it while at the same time he admired its effectiveness.

"If Jackson keeps working hard with the right players and the right league, he can even win a college scholarship," Barkus said, reeling her in now, working that pole like a deep-sea fisherman with a Goliath grouper on the hook.

"You think so?"

"Alex looks to be headed in that direction. Why not Jackson?"

Nice touch there, David thought. What parent would say yes to one son and no to another?

"You're right," she conceded.

Time to get out the landing gaff, David thought.

"Good, he'll be ready for the school team then," Barkus said. "I've got a lot of pull with the freshman coach. I'll tell him about your son."

Silky smooth, David thought, *bringing the freshman coach in on the close*. At the same time though, David's threshold for admiration had been exceeded by disgust. "Did you tell her about the costs, Rob?" he asked.

Barkus spoke though his clenched teeth. "I was *going* to tell her, David."

"Don't let me stop you then, Rob."

"Angela, like the all-star team, playing in the Elite league will cost some extra money," Barkus said.

"Oh, okay, I didn't know. Arnold pays the baseball bills."

Barkus glared at David. He did not want to put a number out there in front of him. No need to give the enemy ammunition. "Arnold knows the details," Barkus said. "Talk to him."

David sensed an opportunity. "Aren't you going to give Angela the Ivy League school line now? Isn't that what comes next?" he asked.

"I'm done, David."

"Let me take it from here then, Rob. Angela, please understand that organizing all this great baseball with other great players from all around the area takes a lot of work. Just like the tuition at an Ivy League school, it can be expensive."

"How much?" she asked, before lifting her head up and twitching her nose. "God, what smells so bad?"

Barkus backed away from Angela. "I don't know," he said, trying to remove his shit-stained slacks from consideration while at the same time looking around for something else to blame.

With that, David was fairly sure that Barkus had no idea what happened that morning. "Yeah, something really does reek," David said. "Anyway, the cost really doesn't matter. You'll pay it, just like you are for Alex."

David understood that some parents raised questions among themselves about where all the money paid to Barkus went, but that this was merely an annual ritual that preceded the eventual signing of the check. Since all the other "haves" in town were paying up, who were they to deny their son a place among the great ballplayers in the area? It was mob behavior at its best. The parents were easy marks and always ended up reaching for the checkbook despite the grumbling.

"Rob, do you know what percentage of high school players receives any college scholarship money for baseball?" David asked.

"I don't know, but I'm sure a large number of our players get scholarships."

"Less than three percent of all high school ballplayers get an athletic scholarship and the average amount is a little under six thousand dollars per year."

"Nah, that's not right. Don't listen to him, Angela."

Barkus's two older boys were attending private colleges because Barkus thought state schools were inferior, the same way that Babe Ruth baseball was inferior. The fact that state schools were less than a third the cost of private colleges was of no consequence to many Indigo Valley parents like Barkus who did not want to suffer the embarrassment of having to admit to other parents that their child was going to a lowly state school—an institution of perceived lower learning. For Barkus, the tuition bills were mounting yearly, as his three boys were only one year apart, with his youngest scheduled to enter college next year. The way out of this pickle, in the mind of Barkus, was for his youngest to get a large baseball scholarship, maybe even a full ride, and the facts were not going to stand in his way. His last great hope could hit the ball all right, but the fact that he had issues throwing from right field did not seem to register with Barkus. It never dawned on him that college scouts might be looking for fielders that could both hit and throw, and maybe even run.

"Don't worry, Rob," Angela said, "I know David doesn't know what he's talking about."

"Show's over," David said, before closing the steel curtain. There was no need for David to go on and explain to Angela that there was 182 times more money available in the form of merit scholarships for college assistance than through baseball, or that there was nine times greater chance of an applicant receiving a merit scholarship than any baseball money. David knew that Angela wasn't going to let some facts stand in the way of doing exactly what everyone else was doing in pursuing a baseball dream for their beloved and talented children. Nothing was going to stop the baseball parents of Indigo Valley from investing the time and effort required to have the great privilege and high honor of playing a golden lottery ticket.

David opened a drawer and removed a plastic grocery bag. He stuffed it halfway into his rear pocket and opened the creaky screened door and walked out of the concession stand. He picked up a rake along with a shovel leaning against the building wall and headed toward the field entrance gate.

As expected, Barkus trailed behind. "Hey, Thompson, wait up. I need to talk with you."

"I don't share that need," David quipped over his shoulder as he continued toward the field.

"Hey, you did a nice job on the field. That's what I want to talk to you about."

"Walk and talk then, Barkus. I've got things to do," David said, looking off to one side. Barkus tagged along one step back.

"The field looks real playable," said Barkus.

Playable, David thought as he cringed inside. He stopped and turned toward Barkus.

"My teams need some field space," Barkus said. "As a town-owned field, I think we're entitled to use it. Of course, we would pay for its use."

David now looked Barkus in the eye. "Maybe if you did not play so many games, you would not need so much field space," David said.

"Hey, you got to play a ton of games in order to get better," said Barkus, grinning.

"Yeah, I guess so, as long as they aren't in-house games with other boys from the town, right Barkus?" David turned and entered the gate behind home plate and walked to inspect the pitcher's mound.

Barkus followed. He needed the field. He wasn't going to be shown up by David. He did not want to signal weakness to his followers; he did not want to lose the field after so long. He did not like to lose at anything. Losing face was unacceptable. A defeat, he thought, would signal to his followers that he did not run baseball in the town any longer.

"Look, we will pay you fifty dollars per game, no more."

"Are you going to stop sending the hate mail then?"

Barkus stroked the fatty folds on the back of his neck. "What hate mail?" he said.

There was silence. David laid down his tools and walked on the mound to look for any soft spots in the pitcher's landing area by pushing his toes down in the mound. The anger inside him was building and he was about to explode. *Calm down*, he told himself. The footing felt firm and good enough for the upcoming game. *Deep breath*, he told himself, as he would tell any pitcher he coached when he was getting too emotional on the mound. David stepped on the rake tines and drew the rake handle up so it slapped against his hand. He thought, *Annie would say to focus on the problem, not the person.* He took the rake and cleaned up his footprints and then looked to the rear of the mound and saw the paw prints. David turned to Barkus and stared through him.

"Do you see this?" David asked.

"See what?"

David pointed down. "Those paw prints. What kind of asshole unlatches the gate and lets his dog run around messing up the baseball field."

Barkus shrugged his shoulders and looked at the players warming up for the first game in right field. "Are you sure they're dog prints? Maybe they're bear prints."

"There are no bears around here. Besides, bears don't open gates to let themselves in to run around and then close the gate on the way out." David looked toward home plate. "Look, the dog messed up the batter's box too." He scanned the infield. "Look over there by second base. He was everywhere. Look at the first baseline. What kind of person lets his dog run on the ball field?"

Barkus shook his head and looked down. "I don't know."

"*Disrespectful* is a word that comes to mind—disrespectful of the field, disrespectful of the game."

"Look, too bad about the field. I'll pay you fifty dollars per game. You guys can work the concession stand to make even more money."

"Barkus, this may be town property. But we have a lease and as a tenant we have certain rights. We have the right to the *exclusive use* of the premises from April through November. That means we have a right to say what is on and off our field during that time frame. Your parents chose to leave our program with your help and, when they left, the field did not go with them. It stayed here with us. Now why would we give our field to an outfit that is taking the so-called best baseball players from our league and telling them not to play in-house Babe Ruth baseball?"

"Wait just a second there. We don't tell parents not to play Babe Ruth."

"No, you just tell them that Babe Ruth and its players suck and that their boys are too good to be playing Babe Ruth. Same thing. And after saying that, you want us to work the concession stand to serve your program and your parents? Are you kidding me? Do you think we're your slaves or something?"

David started to consider the similarities between working in the concession stand for Barkus and the institution of slavery during the Civil War, before Barkus spoke and made him lose his train of thought.

"So you're saying it's not enough money then?" Barkus asked.

"It's not about the money."

"It's always about the money. How much is it going to take to get the field? Remember, I said you could make more money if you worked the concession stand."

"The only reason our parents work the concession stand is to benefit our program and all of its kids. Now, after you took kids away from our program, the community program, away from their friends, you want to use our field and you want our parents to work for you too? Go fuck yourself."

"No need to get nasty. I would be careful what you say to me."

"You're telling me not to be nasty? Who pitches countless nastygrams to my e-mail box every day and CC's everyone in town on them?"

Barkus felt perfectly comfortable sending his vicious e-mails to David, but they weren't something he felt comfortable discussing face-to-face. "You need the money," he said, changing the subject. "Everyone knows the league has problems."

"We're doing just fine," David said, "no thanks to you. You still haven't paid for when you used the field last fall."

"I'll talk to Fog about it," Barkus said. Darryl Fog was a lackey for Barkus. "I'm very busy right now."

"Yeah, busy counting all your registration money."

"What is it with you, Thompson?" Barkus said angrily. "What exactly are you insinuating anyway?"

"Nothing, except that players pay a lot of money to your outfit. I've heard numbers ranging from five hundred to eight hundred dollars per player for games alone. That could total anywhere from six to twelve thousand dollars per team depending on the roster size. That's a nice chunk of change. At an average of nine thousand dollars per team, with three hundred teams, you are grossing about $2.7 million per year. Where does that money go, Rob?"

"We have expenses."

David noted that Barkus did not contest his calculations. "Yes, I bet payroll is a big expense."

"It's none of your business!"

David was hitting close to home with Barkus. He knew the cost of running a team from his experience operating the Babe Ruth program. He understood the huge profit margin that the Elite Travel Baseball League cleared. He had now put Barkus on notice that he knew; David wanted to put the fear of being exposed in Barkus. "All I know," David said, "is that I am a volunteer here along with other folks. We work long hours with no pay for the benefit of *all* youths in our town."

"Our kids are from the same town!" Barkus said, raising his voice.

"You took them from the town program! *Your* parents have contracted with *you* to have their sons play baseball. So go find them a field! You've certainly got the money."

At that point David and Barkus shared the same vision in their heads: a picture of Barkus in the early-morning hours of a hot and humid summer weekend, the day after heavy summer storms, sweating profusely while following behind his mower. Cutting the long, wet grass in the swamplands of the school fields, his mower choking on it and coughing up large chunks of it all around the field. Barkus raking and lifting the piles and putting them in barrels, then pushing the puddles back and forth with his sand rake upside down, trying to make the water disappear on the infield. The mud sucking on his shoes like a million leeches while the weeds all over the infield dug in and laughed.

"Our parents worked hard in *your* baseball program in their early years," Barkus said. "We helped to build this field. This is a town field and we pay taxes on it. They should be able to use it."

"Your teams don't even have tryouts."

"That's not true. We use the school tryouts."

"That's not good enough. You're denying some teens an opportunity to play on those teams who don't want to play on the school team. You're discriminating. What you run are private teams. If we did that, we wouldn't be allowed by the town to use this field. There is no reason to allow you to do what we can't."

"Do you know who you're talking to?"

"Yeah, some guy who runs private teams but has no private field. Private golf clubs have their own course. So go buy yourself a field. We'll try to grow our program and use all of our field time for the development of that program so that baseball is available to every kid in this town. That is our responsibility and it is the right thing to do. Your private teams shouldn't be allowed to use the school fields either, but you've got two of them. I'm happy for you. Now leave us alone."

"I don't think you understand, Thompson."

"I understand perfectly what's going on."

"I'm making you a very generous offer."

With coffee in one hand, Barkus slowly reached into the inside breast pocket of his jacket to pull out a cigar, revealing a thick gold chain around his neck that was buried deep in his chest hair. He brought the cigar under his nose and inhaled before placing it between his plump lips.

"So what are you like the godfather of baseball in this town?"

Barkus pulled out a gold lighter from his side pocket. He lit his cigar with a long flame and puffed on it. "Some have called me that," he said, exhaling smoke in David's direction.

David thought to himself how much he hated the odor of that cigar. Barkus had a habit of leaning over the fence near the dugout while watching in-house games. That's how he did his recruiting. That cigar fragrance would drift into the dugout and was the tell-all to David that Barkus was around. It wasn't enough that Barkus was always in his ear about his league, whether in person or via e-mail, but now David had to smell his presence as

well. There was no getting away from Barkus. It really angered David that the sanctity of his dugout had been violated. It was the one place he thought he could be free from the Barkus aura, if just for a little while.

"You're full of shit, Barkus."

"You have already told me to fuck myself this morning. Now you say I'm full of shit. You really should treat a man like me with more respect."

David ignored him. "Speaking of shit, where there's been a dog, there's shit to be found." David picked up his shovel and began surveying the field for it, knowing full well where it was located.

"There it is," David said, pointing. He began walking toward the first baseline with his shovel and rake in hand. Barkus finished his coffee and followed.

David found the mess left by Barkus. He removed the plastic grocery bag from his back pocket and laid it on the ground. With one hand, he slid the shovel under the crap and with the other he raked any leftovers onto the shovel as best he could.

"Respect?" David asked, continuing the conversation. "What do you know of respect? You never treated the field with respect when you had it."

"That's not true. We made it playable."

"There's a difference between making a baseball field playable and caring for it," David said. "You think if there's one blade of grass on the field, then it's okay to play ball on it." David recalled that he had first learned of that expression when he overheard one of his Cycle Chopper players use it.

"I don't get it."

"Right. Baseball is a business to the godfather and nothing more."

"Business makes the world go round, Thompson."

David stood up. It was 8:30 a.m. It was time for the visiting team to take the field for its fifteen-minute pregame practice. He waved to the visiting team coach, who was waiting by his dugout on the third base side. "You can take the field, coach, whenever you're ready."

David looked at Barkus puffing on his cigar. "Things are changing quite a bit and you need to keep up with the times, Barkus."

"What are you prattling about now?"

David began walking toward the gate and Barkus followed alongside. "The town passed a no-smoking ordinance for all of its parks in the off season. So I suggest you put that thing out now."

Barkus slowly inhaled deeply and let out a billow of smoke in defiance.

"Is that so? I don't see any signs around."

"Well, if you don't believe me, you take your cigar to Chief McNeal over there who is directing traffic at the entrance. You can discuss the existence of the ordinance with him while puffing away." David knew Pete McNeal would not be friendly to Barkus. His sons played Babe Ruth baseball but were not interested in playing on the school teams. McNeal knew vaguely that Barkus had something to do with the baseball problems in the town.

Barkus looked over to McNeal and then back to David. "So you guys gave in to the anti-smoking Nazis." He started laughing. "Next thing you know, you guys will be serving fruit and granola bars at the concession stand and you'll ditch the fryer." Barkus laughed harder still until it caused him to start coughing.

"We won't bag the fryer so long as you're stuffing your face with our fried mozzarella sticks," David said.

Barkus tried to suppress his raspy cough.

"Those mozzarella sticks slide right into your arteries, like fingers sliding into a glove. I'm not sure if the sticks or the cigars will kill you first. We can't sell you the cigars, but we can clog your arteries with mozzarella. You are a cardiologist's dream and a great league revenue source all wrapped up into one."

"Bite me," said Barkus.

"Not a chance."

"Thompson, I think you've lost your mind. Duffel told me you are not giving the freshman team the field either. Is that true?"

"None of your business."

"You'll never get away with that."

David ignored Barkus and walked through the gate. He didn't know that Barkus knew Duffel. He wondered again if it was Duffel he saw on the field earlier that morning with Barkus. He looked over his shoulder and he saw Barkus extinguishing his cigar on the field.

"Hey, Thompson," Barkus hollered so everyone around the field could hear him. "We'll see what your board says about our teams playing on the field!" Faces turned toward Barkus from the stands and the parking lot. Some players warming up on the field looked over. Barkus had an audience now and he played to it. "Sleep well, Thompson!" Barkus yelled. "Yep, we'll see what the board says! Sleep well, Mr. Commissioner!" Barkus started to laugh.

David ignored Barkus in front of everyone. He made sure they all understood his resolve and that he would not be intimidated. He walked toward the concession stand.

David knew that it was a matter of time before Barkus maneuvered the board against him. Unlike Duffel, Barkus understood from his prior experience on the Indigo Valley board that David was just one vote. If it came up for a vote, Barkus knew he had people in place to override David and get the field. David knew it too. But that was another battle to be fought on another day. In the meantime, David was going to make Barkus fight to get it. There would be no surrender. Barkus would have to endure some pain himself if he was going to take the field, and David was only too happy to dish it out.

Everything was in place and the teams for the 9:00 a.m. game were arriving. Late boys stumbled out of their parents' autos wondering if they were the home or away team that day. He took a minute to lean over the fence to take in the scene. Slowly, the popping of balls in gloves from boys warming up could be heard around the well-dressed field. The ping of metal bats followed in the nearby batting cages. And as the game got closer, more and more chatter and laughing could be heard from the boys and parents. Spectators started to take their places in the stands. Parents had opened the concession stand and David could smell the cider doughnuts and coffee. The symphony of youth baseball had begun for the season. David soaked it all in. For a moment, everything seemed right in his world. But he couldn't savor that feeling. It was 8:45 a.m. and David knew he had to get home.

NEW RECRUIT

D avid knew Annie would be waiting for him with a new attitude when he arrived. It was the rhythm of how things operated in the household during baseball season. Christy would be up and Annie wasn't going to display the full range of her feelings about baseball in front of him.

She knew the game was important to Christy and that he might not make the school team. Without Babe Ruth baseball, Annie feared that Christy would be another teenager set adrift in a town where alcohol and drugs were readily available, where too much leisure time often proved to be the handmaiden of trouble. Annie knew from her days at Indigo Valley High School about the number of kids that drank alcohol or did drugs in some teen-constructed fort in the woods, in some kid's basement, or on some golf course during the warmer months.

At some point, depending on the sport, you were either good enough to make the Indigo Valley school teams or you had to find something else to do with your idle time besides sports. Intramural sports in the school district were nonexistent for the rest of the kids who didn't play high school sports. Right at the time when kids needed an athletic outlet the most, there were none available.

But in Indigo Valley, baseball was the exception to this state of affairs, and Christy had played since he was five years old. Annie appreciated baseball for what it had to offer. She saw it as a positive outlet for Christy and the other boys, a way to get them outside to enjoy the outdoors and each other's company. She saw the camaraderie in the dugout, the smiles, the sheer joy of the boys doing something they loved. She tolerated David's time commitment to baseball as a cost of providing for Christy's happiness and well-being.

Annie heard the Mustang's engine from the dining room window when he rolled into the driveway. She got up from the table where she was balancing the checkbook, the scorebook as she called it, with neat pencil strokes. She opened the door to greet David.

"Hi, babe," she called out in a perky voice. Her hair was still damp from the shower, but she was good to go. Her running suit attire advertised that fact. She didn't need a caffeine jolt. From that point on, she would be in perpetual motion for the rest of the day.

"Good morning, Annie," he said, admiring her restored sprit. "What's the good word?"

"Christy is awake and having breakfast. He's looking for you."

David kissed her good morning. He walked into the dining room. "Glad you could join the living before noon," David said to Christy, who was sitting at the kitchen table reading the sports section of the newspaper.

"Hey, cupcake," Christy said.

Annie had started calling David cupcake a few weeks ago, and Christy thought he had the right to tease the man that had given him a girl's name.

David was munching on some cereal and reading the sports section of the paper.

"So are you ready for our first game?" David asked.

"Can't wait."

"Did you notice that we don't have any school players on our team?" Though there were only two freshmen that played in the league and no junior varsity or varsity players, there were a number of seventh and eighth graders that were on the modified school team that played Babe Ruth. Like their predecessors, many were destined to leave and play on the freshman team and the Barkus teams.

"Yeah, I saw that at practice this week," Christy said. He knew his dad had a reason for drafting that way; he always seemed to have a reason for doing anything. "So, why did you do draft that way, Dad?"

"To make a point, hopefully. I wanted to prove that we could compete as a team without school players."

The modified school players were viewed as the better ballplayers by all the adults, including parent coaches. Right after the draft, the other Babe Ruth coaches noticed they had four or five modified players on their teams —more than their fair share. When they discovered David didn't have any, all of the coaches privately reveled at their good fortune. Some of them openly snickered at David.

"At least we have a lot of boys from last year's team playing with us." Christy said.

"Yeah, nobody wanted them in the draft," David said.

"Well, their loss is our gain. We did pretty well last year."

The Choppers struggled during the regular season but thrived during the playoffs, before they were eliminated in the semifinals. After getting a bowl of cereal and a glass of milk, David joined him at the table while Annie went back to the dining room to work on the checkbook. Christy looked up from the paper.

"Dad, I meant to tell you about something that happened at tryouts yesterday."

Christy had decided to try out for the school's modified baseball team. He hadn't tried out the previous season when he was first eligible.

"Oh yeah? What's up?"

"Well, you know that Coach Singleton is holding the tryouts, right?"

"Sure. Singleton is the modified coach, right?"

"Yeah, and Coach Powers is helping him during the tryouts."

"Coach Powers is the freshman coach, right?"

"Yeah. So anyway, we were in the locker room before tryouts began and Coach Singleton is nowhere to be found. In walks Coach Powers and he tells us to get dressed and sit down on the benches so we could have a meeting. So we did as we were told. Coach Powers tells us that he's coaching a summer team. He said that anyone who makes the modified team gets invited automatically. He says his team plays the most competitive baseball in the area and if we are invited to join, we should play on his team."

"Did he say that it was the Elite Travel Baseball League?"

"Yeah, that's what he called the league."

David could not believe what he was hearing. He dropped his spoon in the cereal bowl and put his hand to his forehead and rubbed it back and forth.

"Dad, are you okay?"

David was silent. He started stroking his chin and stared off into space. His mind was racing as he sorted through the ramifications of what was happening.

"Christy, do you know when this team starts playing?"

"He said it starts after school ball ends and goes right through the summer."

"Well, this is just fine and dandy. His team plays right in the middle of the Babe Ruth in-house season. So how are those modified boys going to play both in-house baseball and on his travel team? There will be conflicts for boys who sign up and play in both leagues. And who do you think these parents will have their boys play with when there is a conflict between our league and the team of the freshman coach?"

"I would guess with the freshman coach," Christy said.

"You betcha. Parents want their kids to make the freshman team next year and what better way than to play for him the previous summer. Why the heck is a school coach recruiting kids from our own program to play with him in a competing league?"

"I don't know, Dad. It was weird the way it all happened. Coach Powers hadn't said one word all week long during tryouts. He was just kinda hanging around and helping out. And then all of a sudden there he is telling us about his baseball team and Coach Singleton was nowhere around."

David reflected a bit and said: "This has Barkus written all over it."

Annie was half listening to the conversation while doing the dishes, but when the name Barkus was mentioned her ears perked up. "Why don't we have him over for dinner?"

"You're kidding," David said.

"Nope, I'll give him his last meal and then I'll beat him up," Annie replied. Christy blew milk threw his nose when he heard this and started laughing along with David.

"What's so funny?" Annie asked.

"You, Mom."

"A threat doesn't sound right coming from you," David said, laughing. "I don't think threats are one of Donahue's core principles of behavior."

"I could take him, you know," Annie said. "Isn't that how you men talk?"

"It might sound more manly, Mom, if you said you would kick his ass."

Annie shook her head in disapproval. "Such foul language." She thought for a second while David and Christy cleaned up the milk splatter with napkins. "I don't understand. If this coach was so intent on coaching a travel team, why doesn't he coordinate a team through you and the town baseball league? Why doesn't he coach an all-star team?"

"Barkus is behind it, that's why. He always brags about how he has the freshman coach in his pocket. I'm sure Barkus sold him a bill of goods about his program."

Annie scrubbed a bowl, trying to remove some crusty, day-old oatmeal. "You would think the freshman coach would figure it out that he is pulling kids out of the community program, the same community that makes up the school district."

David rolled up the wet napkins and arced a long shot into the garbage can. Christy high-fived him. "Barkus thinks for the coach," David said, "and Barkus isn't going to run a program through our league where he can't make a buck."

"David, maybe you should meet with them and try to work it out," Annie suggested.

"Work what out? They both think their players are too good to be playing Babe Ruth. Barkus could care less about our in-house baseball program. We're in trouble, deep trouble now."

"How is that, Dad?"

"They're going to take the modified school players from the league. There will be conflicts between our league and the Barkus league. And so parents will have to make a choice between playing in our program or the Barkus program this season. Like I said, parents will play with the freshman coach and they'll drop out of our league one or two years earlier, and our Babe Ruth enrollment numbers will go down even more."

"Don't the kids have any say in things?" asked Annie. "I thought you said that boys liked playing in-house games, Christy."

"Mom, there are school players that love playing in-house. But parents schedule their lives. I have had school-team kids that come up to me and say they want to play Babe Ruth but their parents won't let them."

"Yep, the parents control their lives through their purse strings," said David. "In any event, when the conflicts happen, they will feel compelled to play with the freshman coach. This Babe Ruth season will be a mess and next year's modified players won't even bother with Babe Ruth."

The three of them took it all in for a minute. Annie returned to balancing the checkbook. Christy munched on his cereal and went back to reading the sports section. David sipped his juice and stared at the table until it hit him.

"Barkus wants to kill our baseball program," David said.

Annie stopped. Christy put the paper down and looked to his Dad.

"What do you mean, David?" asked Annie.

David' s forehead crinkled as he massaged it with his index finger and thumb over and over. His face turned a shade of red.

"What on earth are you talking about, David?" she asked again.

David started shaking his head. "They started taking players years ago at the varsity level. Then it was the junior varsity players, then the freshmen and now the middle school. They are working from the top down."

"I thought you said that he could care less about Babe Ruth," Annie said.

"He doesn't care about it. He wants the field. By killing us, he knows he'll eventually get the field as the only other baseball program in town."

"Why can't you have a league without the school players?" asked Annie.

"There wouldn't be enough players left in the town to form a league with multiple teams. We'd run into a numbers problem. We have a numbers problem already on the Babe Ruth field. If the modified school players leave, it will be the end of the league."

Annie and Christy looked at one another. David took a sip of juice and contemplated the situation.

The town had held a charter to play Babe Ruth baseball dating back to 1957, but David did not know how much longer that would last. At that moment, David wished that he had shot Barkus, shot him dead. He thought maybe he could get off on the grounds of self-defense . . . defense of his hometown . . . defense of baseball. He'd figure out a defense after the fact.

David stood up, like he was fighting gravity, his knees stiff from working on the field. "This could be the end of baseball for our town." He jerked his head back, tipped the cup, and finished the last drop before slamming the cup down on the table.

Christy understood now that kids defined one another starting in elementary school. By the time middle school arrived, everyone had been more or less categorized and you sat with your fellow group members at lunch. At the extremes, there were the nerds and the jocks; then there were the popular kids and the outcasts. Somewhere in between there were the wannabe jocks and wannabe popular kids. The druggies began to emerge as a group toward the end of middle school.

Andrew Golder was most definitely an outcast. He had once picked his nose in kindergarten and had perfected the skill by picking it straight through the fourth grade, earning himself the nickname "Gold Digger." Kids didn't know nor could they understand that Andrew's rhinotillexomania was prompted, most likely, due to the general anxiety he felt in seeing his parents fight, and ultimately divorce, leaving him with a stepfather who expected more from him than his own dad. It also didn't matter that Andrew hadn't picked his nose for over four years, because Andrew would probably be forever known as "Gold Digger" to his schoolmates, even at his fiftieth high school reunion, even if he won the Nobel Prize.

Christy had begun to understand that your grouping defined your station in life and it carried through middle school, then high school, and perhaps beyond—and there was little you could do about it. But Christy knew that baseball offered a rare opportunity to redefine himself.

Christy's claim to fame was that he was the first kid in kindergarten to wear eyeglasses. Instead of picking some fashionable glasses, David and Annie bought the same type of round, wire-rimmed glasses that David's grandfather had worn while teaching Latin at Fordham University in the early 1900s. Over time, Christy became a nerd in the eyes of the other kids. He didn't think much about occasionally being called "four-eyes" or "professor" in grade school, as he could take it and dish it out with the best of them.

But when his grade school friends started saying he had a girl's name (thanks to Mrs. Cheswick's music class), and then they stepped up their name calling to include some impressive alliterative qualities, like "four-eyed fag" or "four-eyed fuck," Christy saw his future being defined as both a nerd *and* an outcast. That was too much to handle. Before the baseball season started, he asked for and received contact lenses from his parents.

Baseball in Indigo Valley involved kids from all the five public elementary schools, two middle schools, some private schools, and even the home-schooled. Baseball gave kids one of the few opportunities in life to establish new identities for themselves, to make new friends, to break free of the reputation that preceded them in their daily lives. Christy was afraid that the loss of baseball would make his life miserable.

Christy said, "So what you are saying, Dad, is that Barkus is a jerk."

David gave Christy a thumbs-up out of sight from Annie and grinned ever so slightly, but not enough to trigger her radar. Christy stared into his cereal bowl, jabbing his Cheerios with his spoon. Annie shook her head side to side, closed the checkbook, and then got up to walk to the kitchen window to look into the backyard. The grass was overgrown with lots of bare patches; wild violets and dandelions had poked their heads above the grass line. "David, don't you think you should cut our lawn before the game? Why can't our lawn look as good as the Babe Ruth field?"

"Okay. Maybe it's time that Christy started cutting the grass around here?"

"He has to do his homework before the game," said Annie. "I talked with him about it before you came home."

"Dad, looks like you got the lawn today. But I'll trade you. If you want to do my homework, I'll cut the grass."

"What's your homework in, Christy?"

"Algebra."

David chuckled as he got up from the table. "Where's the mower?"

Christy laughed.

David's cell rang and he picked it up. Annie could tell by the tone of David's voice that it was a baseball call.

"I understand," David said into the phone. "Sure, that should be fine. Where and what time?"

David saw Annie roll her eyes as he scheduled the meeting. She knew what was coming. Oh, sure, there would be a few meetings, phone calls, and e-mails in April, but the pace would quicken in May as the day-to-day problems of running a league would grow: rainouts, fights in the stands, ejections on the field, illegal use of pitchers, illegal rosters, broken baseball equipment, complaints about certain umpires and coaches, injuries to players, broken car windows from foul balls, shortages of field supplies, problems with the concession stand deliveries, and vandalism to top it off. At first they would happen one at a time, but then they would happen in pairs and then three at a time. But in June—the crazy month of June—when the inhouse season was about to end with a championship tournament, everything would align to hit their lives all at once and in full force, like a tsunami of baseball shit.

"Sounds good. I will see you then," David said, closing his clamshell phone.

"So here we go again with the endless baseball meetings like last year," Annie said.

"Annie, that was Brad Summers, state commissioner of Babe Ruth on the phone. I don't think that's a meeting I could blow off."

"I suppose not. State commissioner? What does he want?"

"Heck if I know. I didn't ask. He wants to meet."

"I don't understand why this baseball has to be *so* complicated," she said, shaking her head. "I hope cutting the lawn is not that complicated for you. All you have to do is get your lines straight."

David had learned long ago to take the baseball jab from Annie. It was going to be a long season and he understood the importance of picking his battles.

"Christy," David said, "did I ever tell you how marriage is like baseball?"

"I don't think so," Christy said.

"Oh don't you start now, David Thompson," Annie said. "It's too early in the season for all of your baseball comparisons." Annie knew full well that by the end of the season, David would be discussing everything in terms of baseball, like he was looking at the world through a catcher's mask. By last June, when Annie shared a story about work at the dinner table, David was breaking it down into baseball terms for Christy, like he was calling a play-by-play.

"Just like in baseball," David said undeterred, "if you don't do what you're told and touch all the bases, you'll be called out."

Christy chuckled and Annie held back a smile.

"Very funny," Annie said. "Now go cut the lawn before I throw you out."

Christy started to laugh at the exchange and Annie turned to him. "Don't get him going, Christy," Annie said. "You know your father is easily distracted by baseball this time of year."

"You know I do love you guys," David said.

"I know you do, David, but I think you love baseball more some days."

"I can love both," David said, walking to the door. "Christy, we have a noon game, so be ready to go at 11:00 a.m. sharp."

David swung open the door and did first what he always did when going outside during baseball season. He looked up to the sky to check the weather to the west. It was sunny. Popcorn clouds changed shape while blowing to the east. He recalled lying on his back as a boy, watching the clouds roll by and shape-shift into animals or people. He felt in harmony with nature then. As a kid, he would react to the weather and adjust his plans depending on what the weather brought. He had a comfortable relationship with the weather. Nothing beat racing a summer storm home, trying not to get wet as the rain chased him down the street on his bike. But as Babe Ruth commissioner, he was forever battling with the weather, trying to force baseball games to happen when nature said to do something else that day. But like with all baseball seasons beginning anew, he could not help but feel hopeful that the weather would cooperate. With all the work and headaches of getting the season started, he hadn't had the time to entertain the idea of playing actual baseball with his team and with Christy. He zoned out while he cut the grass and he looked forward to watching his son play baseball like any other dad with a son in the league.

7

THE FIRST GAME

David barely finished the front lawn before 11:00 a.m. There was no time to do the back. He ran upstairs to put on his uniform. Unlike other coaches in the league, David wore a baseball uniform at games, the same uniform as his players. But David's jersey didn't have a number, though. Like the players of his time, Christy Mathewson didn't wear one and so neither did David.

After David got dressed, he knocked on Christy's bedroom door.

"Christy, time to go."

"I'm coming, Dad."

Christy had a history of moving in slow motion when he had to be someplace, like time and the game would wait for him.

"Now, Christy."

"Okay."

"Annie, are you coming with us?"

"No," she said from upstairs. "I've got some errands to run. I'll try and make some of the game afterward."

"All right, I'll see you later then."

David went to his Mustang and loaded the catcher's equipment, baseballs, and Christy's bag into the trunk. Christy walked out the door to the house and saw David trying to slam the trunk closed. It kept bouncing open because there was too much equipment.

"Hey, I remember that thumping sound," Christy said.

Trying to close the trunk had been a pregame ritual every year since David had been coaching.

"Sounds like baseball season to me!" Christy added.

"Get in the car, wise guy."

"Okay, Dad." Christy had put his feet in his cleats without first untying them, so they didn't fit—his heels were riding on top of the back of the shoes. His balance was impaired as he walked like a woman in high heels to the car.

"Christy, when do you think you'll learn to put your cleats on? By the time you're twenty?"

They both got in the front seat. Christy put one foot on the dashboard and undid the laces so he could slip into the shoe.

"Get your cleats off the dashboard," David said. "Last thing I need in this car is cleat marks on my dashboard. This car takes a beating every season. Let's try to make an effort this year."

"All right, Dad. Nice uniforms this year, by the way."

"What do you mean?" David said, half smiling.

"We're wearing red jerseys with grey numbering—the school colors."

"Glad you noticed. Do you see any irony in it?"

"I'm not sure what you're getting at."

"We're dressed in school colors but have no school players on our team."

"Oh, yeah. How did you get those jerseys?"

"Well, I was first to reserve them. Being Babe Ruth commissioner has one or two perks."

David started backing the car out of the driveway. There were two large oaks on either side opposite one another and the driveway narrowed in half on account of them toward the end. Not one season had passed without David scraping against the oaks at least once. He had repaired the Mustang but the trees still showed their scars. David parted the oaks successfully and headed for the ball field. "I am officially one for one this season."

"Just a matter of time, Dad. Ticktock, ticktock. You want to bet you hit one of them once before the season is over?"

"I don't like those odds, Christy."

Christy laughed. "Hey, aren't these uniforms the same colors as the Elite Travel team's also?"

"Yeah, imagine that," David said, grinning.

"Hey, Dad, I think I want to play for the Elite team this year," Christy said.

"Yeah, right. Well, you had better first make the school team. Otherwise you don't have a chance." David wanted Christy to play school baseball just like he had played high school sports. But he didn't want Christy to play on any Barkus teams because of what he represented.

"You want to know why I'm playing in the Elite Travel Baseball League this year, Dad?"

"Okay, I'll bite."

"Did you know that ninety-five percent of all Elite Travel players receive college baseball scholarships?"

"What? Says who?"

"Some kid in my earth science class who plays on the team."

"What did you tell him?"

"Nothing. I just laughed."

"I guess you don't have to worry about your grades if you play for the Elite Baseball League."

"I guess not."

"Yeah, just play baseball with them and you'll get a free ride to college. Maybe Elite should set up its own private school and just funnel the boys off to college on free rides."

Their laughter tapered off to silence as they both thought about the upcoming game.

They pulled into the complex and made their way back to the Babe Ruth field. It was 11:15 a. m., the time David had told the team to be at the field. He started to unload the car with Christy by hoisting the equipment bags and a bucket of baseballs over the fence by the home team dugout on the first base side. He saw much of the team already there walking in and out of the dugout. David thought to himself that this was a good sign. When boys arrive on time, they want to play baseball.

"Good morning, gentlemen," David said.

A chorus of "Coach" or "Hey, coach" was heard from the boys.

"Go run out and the touch the 360-foot marker in center field. Come back and do your stretching as a team. Then find a partner, get a ball, and then throw along the first baseline in right field. You know the drill," David added. Most of the boys had been on his team last year.

Christy jumped the waist-high fence to right field and began running. A few groans and complaints were heard as the other boys joined him.

David turned to a husky boy walking lazily out of the dugout with his hat brim turned upward and called out to him.

"Hey, Skit, you can lead the team in stretching with Christy."

"Okay, coach," said Skit, cracking a smile.

"I expect you to run out and touch the marker, though. You can't lead in stretching if you can't lead in running." The smile disappeared. Skit didn't like to run unless it was during a game.

"I'm going." He continued his walk from the dugout.

"You *do* know what the word *run* means, right?"

Skit started to jog.

"Game starts in forty minutes, Skit. Hope to see you back here by then."

Skit started to run as he mumbled some cusswords.

"I can call you a cab if you think that would help," David said.

Skit shifted it into overdrive and began to pass other players.

His real name was Sammy O'Connor. He was a broad-bodied, heavyset teen. The boys gave him the name Skit after the colored bite-size candy he ate in the dugout during games. By the end of each game, his tongue and face would be stained with food coloring.

David walked into the dugout. He found a roll of duct tape in the bag and posted the lineup on the dugout wall with it. He sat down and looked out at the infield. The other team was warming up.

David's Cycle Chopper team was playing against the team sponsored by Babson Concrete Block. He counted the number of school baseball players on the other team. Out of thirteen players, four played on the modified school team and one on the freshman team. Like all teams in the Indigo Valley Babe Ruth League, Cycle Chopper and Babson were composed of thirteen-to fifteen-year-olds, plus the twelve-year-olds that made the modified school team. David had only nine players on his team. He let the other teams draft more because the school players were likely to miss a number of games and David wanted them to be able to field a team.

The Babson coach was hitting balls from home plate to various infielders. Their work looked crisp, no errors.

He looked out to right field and saw his team stretching in a circle with Skit and Christy leading in the center.

Andrew Golder pushed aside his long bangs and wiped his nose with his sleeve like any other kid. He had told his mother that he wanted to try playing for a coach other than his stepfather, Nick, who coached a Babe Ruth team where his biological son, Joe, played. David had drafted Andrew after one of the coaches said he was always picking his nose when he had him on his team in third grade.

Andrew was one of the taller boys on the team and was as skinny as the foul pole he guarded in right field. Christy told David before the draft that Andrew was a nice eighth grader who could, at least, catch in the outfield, perhaps because he wore his father's oversized glove. He did so well in practice that the boys on the team started calling him "Gold Glove."

The players kept glancing over to the infield to size up the other team. A few shook their heads. Grim faces all around. David could imagine what they thought about the matchup. He decided to stem the tide of any negative thinking by talking to the team. And so he began his walk out to right field to meet with them before they broke off and started throwing to warm up.

After exiting the dugout, David abruptly turned around and headed back into it. He had forgotten his fielder's glove, an item he had learned to carry after a number of errant throws last year. He slipped it on his left hand and resumed his walk. The Babson team was doing infield work and throwing to first. As he walked out past first base toward right field in foul territory, a ball soared by the first baseman toward David's head. He saw it out of the corner of his eye and raised his glove to catch it while in full stride. After he caught it, the coach at home plate from Babson said, "Heads up!"

It was Oscar Poser, board member and a Barkus toady. He was head coach of the team. David now saw Arnold Meeson by the dugout working on the scorebook. He was the assistant coach and David now understood why Angela was at the field earlier that same day.

The first baseman turned around. Like all the school players, he had a red and white windbreaker marked by a white semicircle panel that dropped from the collar halfway down the back. "Indigo Valley Baseball" was embroidered on the front along with "Tony Poser" on the other side. David wondered why they chose white for their jackets instead of gray.

"Sorry, coach," Tony said with a smirk as he strutted over. "You gotta be careful out here, coach." David could see that he wasn't wearing his Babson Concrete cap; he was wearing his high school cap instead.

"No problem. I came prepared," he said, showing his glove. "Hey, that's a nice jacket."

"Thanks," Tony said, adjusting his Oakley sunglasses, the same brand worn by Coach Powers. Tony was the King of Swag, at least in his own mind.

David walked the ball over to him. "I'd throw this ball back to you but I don't want you to miss it again and get that nice white jacket all dirty."

Tony scowled.

"You know," David added, "your jacket looks like what they wore when I went to Indigo Valley High."

"Really," Tony said, feeling a dose of swag run through his veins.

"Yes," David said, lowering his voice as he placed the ball in Tony's glove. He whispered to Tony: "The football cheerleaders looked real cute in them." Tony's jaw dropped and David turned to jog toward his team.

The Choppers continued to stretch while sitting on the ground. They tried not to look at the other team. Every now and then, David saw a few of them take quick glances during stretches.

As he got close to the circle he started talking. "Now, boys, listen up as you stretch. I see you guys looking at the other team and I know what you're thinking. You're thinking that we don't match up well."

"Okay, time to get up and touch the toes," said Christy.

It took Tim Minnifield a couple seconds longer to get up due to his disability. Piriformis syndrome, which causes pain to the buttock area and upper thigh, hindered his running. He was tall as a tree and when he ran he could only take very short, shuffled steps; his knees hardly bent, like he was running on a pair of short stilts. The boys called him "Roots" because it was like he was pulling his roots out of the ground with each step he ran. "Coach, a bunch of those boys play for the school," he said.

"Don't hit me with those negative waves so early in the morning, Tim," said David.

"Negative waves?" said Roots. The rest of the team exchanged puzzled looks.

"*Kelly's Heroes*. Movie made in 1970. Donald Sutherland was great. Oddball was his character's name and that was his line. His point was that negative thoughts in tough situations don't help, so don't bother with them. I don't care if they have a number of school players and neither should you."

"Dad, we *do* have a school ballplayer."

"What are you talking about, Christy?"

"Bullwhip here told me while running that he made the junior varsity team this year. He wanted me to tell you."

"Is that so, Bullwhip?"

Bullwhip nodded. He didn't talk much. Bullwhip's real name was Billy Wilson. He was a high school sophomore and a pitcher and had never played school baseball before this year, nor had he been on an all-star team. He had developed as a pitcher through playing in-house baseball during the previous season.

"Congratulations, Bullwhip," David said.

David was happy for Bullwhip but knew immediately what it meant for his team. The junior varsity coach would not want Bullwhip pitching for the Choppers during the school season. It made sense from a safety point of view if he was going to pitch for them.

"Dad, can he pitch for us during the regular season?"

"Probably not until the school season is over, but at least in time for the playoffs," said David.

"You're kidding," said Skit.

"I am starting to feel those negative waves again," said David. He realized that the boys were smart enough to know what missing Bullwhip on the mound would mean. While Bullwhip was an excellent pitcher and good fielder, he was inconsistent at the plate. With Bullwhip in the lineup but not able to pitch, he was a liability to the team. "Look," David said, "I had the opportunity to draft a bunch of school players and I didn't. I don't care if you guys play on the school team or not. I think you guys have the talent or the potential to develop the talent to compete with the team over there, or any other team."

"Coach, do the other teams have a lot of school players too?" asked Skit.

"Yes, some of the other teams have four or five school guys." Some boys groaned. "Now that we have this out in the open, can we please get over it, boys? For the guys who were not with the team last year: we struggled during the season but come playoff time, even as the last seed, we made it to the semifinals."

"We rocked during the playoffs," said Skit.

"You bet we did," said Christy. The faces on the boys came to life with the memories of last season.

"Now that's more like it," said David. "And there is one more thing you should know. I drafted every one of you for one common reason. You guys all have heart. I'll take you any day over a team of talented drones who don't love the game half as much. Now get a partner and spread out along the first base foul line and start throwing and get ready to play. Hustle up!"

With that the boys jumped up, got a baseball and a partner, and began throwing. David turned around and headed back to the dugout in foul territory. As he approached, another baseball sailed toward his head, intended for the first baseman. He stopped and extended his glove to where his head would have been had he kept walking. The ball popped in his glove as he shook his head from side to side. Instead of flipping the ball to the first baseman, David crow-hopped and threw a laser to the catcher himself. The catcher hadn't expected a throw from David, and certainly he didn't think it would get there that quickly since he had to rush to raise his glove to his chest. His feet were not positioned well to receive the throw. The ball popped into the catcher's mitt, right between the numbers, forcing him to take a step back and bump into Poser. The players on the infield stared at David.

"I don't believe it, coach. You could have hit me with that ball!" Poser said.

David didn't break stride for the dugout. "What I can't believe is that a fifty-year-old coach can throw better than your team can. What's up with that?" David then entered the dugout and contemplated his defensive options for the game while Poser motioned for the ball from the catcher so he could fungo another grounder.

When it was David's turn to give his team infield practice, he stood up and assigned positions. The boys hustled out. David did not have any five-tool players on the team. Some could run but couldn't hit; some could hit but couldn't run; some had holes in their gloves; others could field but had arms of glass. At most, any player had three of the five tools. If David could combine the skills of all nine players, the most he had was three complete players. It was like he was coaching the Island of Misfit Toys from the 1964 *Rudolph the Red-Nosed Reindeer* Christmas special.

But the warm-up would be for naught as the winter had chilled their throwing arms, though the few practices held before the season began were enough to elevate the team a notch from "suck-to-the-max" status to "plain suck" status. The school players, on the other hand, had started their season by throwing and hitting in the gyms. They were in much better playing shape than any Babe Ruth player and were more athletically inclined. The Choppers jogged back to the dugout and got their fielding assignments. They were the home team and would take the field first.

Last season, David had Roots mostly play in right field. The strategy was a simple one. David played Roots where he thought the least amount of damage could be done defensively by his presence in any given inning. But he was not so sure this year as a ball hit to the outfield past Roots last season turned into a potential triple. Roots wanted to play second base anyway, and David thought that at least he would have an outfield to back him up on any balls that got past him.

"YES!" said Roots when David announced he would play second base. He grabbed his glove and eagerly took the field. It would take three errors on pop-ups and grounders over three innings to convince both Roots and David that this may not have been a good idea. Roots went out to right field later in the game and through good fortune no balls were hit in his direction.

Skit did not help the cause either. He was thrown out trying to push a single into a double and trying to steal a base where he was not given the steal sign. Skit always wanted to make the big play. This extended to the defensive side of the game too. Skit played catcher and tried one inning to make the big pickoff play at third base. Trouble was that the third baseman could not catch the ball and it went out to left field, allowing a run to score. To add insult to injury, this happened when there were two outs.

While David admired Skit's spirit, his lack of discipline was not helping. And to top it off, his temper was bringing the team down. When Skit failed in his efforts, he would cuss under his breath in the dugout and throw things. David had to pull him aside during the game to settle him down and get him focused.

In the end, the team lost 14–3. After the game, the team gathered in right field along the first baseline for a team meeting. As David began to walk from the dugout to right field to meet with his team, he smelled the foul odor of cheap cigar. He turned and saw Barkus leaning on the fence, smoking a cigar as fat as one of the folds in his neck.

"You see that score up there?" Barkus said to David, gesturing to the scoreboard with his cigar. "You got your ass handed to you. My boys don't need rec ball."

David walked over to the waist-high fence. "We call it in-house baseball. We don't call it rec ball. Besides, it's one game, the first game of our season."

"Call it what you want," Barkus said. "Who cares? You might as well call it wreck ball with a *W* because it is a wreck. Some of your kids couldn't find home plate unless you pointed it out to them."

"They'll get better with practice now that the weather has turned. When you and your buddies coached here—before you bolted the league—you never had any practices for the non-school-boys and then you complained that they sucked. What did you expect? Did you expect these other boys to learn baseball through osmosis?"

"Hey, some boys don't have what it takes athletically, Thompson."

David took a deep breath and calmed himself before continuing. "Part of our mission here is to try and make boys the best ballplayers they can be and teach them some life lessons along the way. Maybe some boys just don't develop as soon as others or maybe they just need some attention. Some of these kids come from homes where there is no father presence and mom doesn't play baseball. Anyway, you won't catch bad baseball habits by playing with them. A little integration in major league baseball back in the 1940s didn't hurt anyone."

"What? Are you calling me a racist or something?"

"No, you're more like a baseball snob as far as I can tell. You think your Elite players will become infected by playing on the same field as the Babe Ruth players."

"I don't like the direction this conversation is taking."

"Okay, fine, I'll end it here then," David said as he plucked the cigar from Barkus's hands and then stomped on it before walking away toward his team.

"You'd better watch it, Thompson," Barkus said loud enough for the parents to hear.

As David approached, he told the boys to take a knee. He looked at the disappointed faces as he summarized the game. "Plain and simple, we beat ourselves today, gentlemen. Errors and unearned runs were the nails in our coffin."

"Sorry, coach," Stretch said.

Barry "Stretch" Anderson was six foot four inches tall and pitched for a good part of the game. He was a good pitcher if he located the ball at the knees. He did not have an overpowering arm, but if the ball arrived at the knees, players had a hard time hitting anything but grounders. Trouble was that Stretch was leaving the ball higher in the strike zone—waist-high and right over the plate—and the Babson players were feasting on them.

"Stretch, this loss isn't on you. We made plenty other mistakes out there that caused us to lose. Win or lose, we do it as a team."

David surveyed the team and made eye contact with Mark "Steady" Prior. David saw his face beaming with a comforting smile. Mark was a lefty pitcher who played center field and first base. They called him Steady because at the end of the day, nothing seemed to get him down. He was always positive and hustled and was eager to play. And David long attributed this quality to Steady's religious upbringing and strong family. "Coach," he said, "I think we can get better."

"I agree," David said. "I think what we need to do is practice more. Let's face it. The school boys have been practicing for quite some time now. We have some catching up to do. It was the same way last year at this point. It's a long season and this is just our first game. So let's not get down about it. Let's learn from it and then do something about it. We will have some practices next week. Let's bring it in and call it a day."

All the boys circled up and put their hands into the middle.

"Choppers on three," said David. "One, two, three," and the boys responded with "Choppers" before breaking the huddle to return to the dugout to pack up and go home.

While David was returning to the dugout, Jake Fletcher, left fielder for the Choppers, had already packed up and was outside the fence at the rear of the backstop while all the other players were still in the dugout looking for their gear. Jake was a sprinter on the track team and they called him "Flash" for his speed in doing everything both on and off the field. He talked fast, ran fast, and had an attention span that came and went fast. Flash was attention deficit disorder dressed as a ballplayer in the outfield. He'd sometimes get under a fly ball so fast that David wondered if he might forget why he was there before catching it.

David saw Flash's dad, Jim, standing beside him, calling and motioning for David to come over. Jim Fletcher was an attorney friend dating back to law school who had a solo white-collar criminal practice in downtown Mohawk City. He walked over to the gate to greet David.

Jim extended his hand and almost shook David's hand off. "David, so good to see you."

David touched the sleeve of Jim's tailored dark gray pinstriped suit as he pulled away from his grasp. "Jim, you're dressed in your lawyer's uniform, on a Saturday?"

Jim chuckled. "I've been busy, real busy. You?"

"Same here, though I've been less of a lawyer and more of a sports administrator lately."

"So I've heard. What's going on here anyway? I hear a lot of things. I don't know what to believe."

David thought Jim, if anyone, could appreciate the craziness of what he was going through and could maybe even help.

"Yeah, it's quite a story," David began.

Another parent walked by and patted Jim on the back while heading for the parking lot. David stopped talking while Jim acknowledged him and then turned back to David.

"You were saying?"

"I've got this guy, Barkus, who thinks he's the town godfather when it comes to baseball—"

Suddenly Flash was between them. "Dad, can I have some money for the concession stand?" Jim whipped out his wallet and gave him a five dollar bill.

"I've got this guy, Barkus, and the school looking to access our field—" Jim's cell phone went off. "Hold that thought, David." He picked up the phone and talked in a hushed tone with one hand cupping the receiver. After ten seconds, David heard him say, "I'll call you back," and he closed the phone.

"Sorry, David, things have been nuts for me. I called you over because I could really use your help."

"What's going on?"

"You have heard about that Moss case in Mohawk City?" Moss was a Mohawk City School District employee who was booked for rigging bombs on the cars and at the homes of people who crossed him or his friends.

"Yes, it's all over the news."

"Well, I got a call from Moss's attorney yesterday and he asked me to take the case because he had a conflict of interest and had to withdraw."

"Wow, that's quite an opportunity for you. Are you taking it?"

"Yeah, I talked with Moss and he's good with it. But I need help at least at the beginning and that's where the favor comes in. I need you to sign on as co-counsel for now. The criminal case is mushrooming against him and I can barely keep up with all the other matters I'm handling. I need you to do some investigation and preparation for trial."

"Has the grand jury sent up an indictment yet?"

"In a few weeks. They keep wheeling him from one jurisdiction to another at this point to face charges so they can keep him in jail."

"What do you want me to do?"

"Go down and meet with Moss. Talk to him. Get anything you can from him about his involvement. Give me your appraisal of him. Maybe you can get more out of him than I have. I don't think I'm getting everything. You have this way with people."

"Is Moss good with it?" asked David.

"Yes, he seemed fine with it when I saw him yesterday. But he wanted to meet with you first."

David was reluctant. The season was about to begin and he was short on time himself. But he owed Jim and wasn't about to turn down the prospect of a paycheck, even it was earned outside his newly declared specialty of positive law.

"Okay, I'll go down and talk with him."

"Great. I'll have my secretary run copies of my files over to you," Jim said, while flicking his thumb around his cell phone screen. "I'll operate as lead counsel. Call me with any questions. I'll take care of billing; just keep track of your time. Let me know what you think after you talk to him."

"All right, Jim."

Fletcher's cell phone went off again. "Thanks, David. You're the best."

David was frustrated. Unless Indigo Valley's baseball story was available for viewing on a handheld device, Jim Fletcher didn't have time for it. If Jim didn't have time for it, David figured that nobody else in Indigo Valley had time for it either.

The question, in David's mind, was no longer whether baseball would die, but how it would meet its death. David figured it would die the way the wild indigo crops had died in Indigo Valley hundreds of years ago. It was then that the settlers tried to grow it in hopes of producing a dye. Other than reporting the conception of the idea to plant wild indigo, history never recorded anything about the undertaking, leaving one to surmise that the results were so awful that the settlers wanted to forget the entire episode and move on. David expected baseball would meet a similar fate and that the details of its undertaking and demise would fade, never to be discussed again, forever lost to history. Death seemed to be a constant companion to David and he was sick of it.

8

CHARTER JEOPARDY

S unday arrived and David rolled into the Tick-Tock Diner parking lot a little after 11:00 a.m. He walked in and saw Brad Summers in a booth facing him at the far end of the diner. There were no other customers in the area. Brad waved. David waved back and walked to the booth. They exchanged greetings and David sat down across from him.

A waiter came by and gave him a menu and asked if he wanted coffee. Brad was already sipping a cup.

"A glass of orange juice would be fine." They both ordered breakfast. Brad was a tall man with an athletic build who did not look his age of fifty-five years even with his black-rimmed glasses. His black hair was neatly combed over and parted at the side. He wore a navy-blue dress shirt with a power-red tie and his black slacks were perfectly creased. He sat with his right leg crossed. It was bouncing in the aisle, revealing his black wingtip shoes, but no skin, since his socks ran high up his calf. Everything about Brad was neat. He looked and smelled like he just came from church. He played the role of New York State Babe Ruth commissioner well. He had once been president of his local league before being promoted to state commissioner, a position he had held for five years.

"I saw your friend Barkus yesterday and he sends his regards," David said.

"Jesus Christ, what was he doing there yesterday?"

"One thing he was doing was bitching about you being a highly compensated executive from Babe Ruth league."

"You have got to be kidding. Is he at that again?"

David laughed. "Yeah, that's part of the script."

"That guy is fucking unreal."

"You should really get the word out and let people know you're a volunteer."

Brad pushed his glasses up his nose. "I don't want to stoop down to his level and engage in any kind of discussions with him or Frank Morgan, the other guy he's in bed with. To recognize them is to legitimize them."

David interlocked his fingers and placed his hands on the table and leaned forward. "I think it may be time for a change in approach for you in some respects, Brad. I mean, come on now, they have three hundred teams in the area and have a huge web presence. They have been around now for over a decade. I don't think you can pretend that they don't exist. Besides, there are guys on our board that believe what these clowns have to say. You know, these guys are e-mailing us with this stuff—about you being some kind of hired body broker from Babe Ruth."

"You're kidding me."

"No, I'm not. They're e-mailing the entire board every day, it seems. It's like Barkus and Morgan are in our freaking boardroom. And many board members are buying into this crap. Our board is under the spell of these guys. Did you know that half our board now has their boys playing in this Elite Travel league?"

"Oh, come on now. Are you serious?"

"Yes."

Brad tapped the table with his index finger. "These board members have a conflict of interest then in being on your board and not participating in the Babe Ruth–sponsored programs and choosing to go elsewhere."

"I know, I know," said David. "It's like they're on the McDonald's board of directors but they eat all their meals at Burger King."

Brad clenched his coffee cup with both hands. "You said they're *invited*?"

"Yes, they're invited."

"No tryouts? You mean an invitation-only team?"

"You got it. So if some kid doesn't make the school team he will not get invited to play on the Elite league team, with rare exception."

"So the school program teams and the Elite league teams are one in the same?"

"Yes, that is the way it is in our town. They just wear different uniforms in the summer."

"Incredible. I don't know of any other league that has this problem."

"Yeah, well, this causes them some problems in requesting use of our field."

"How so?"

"We are supposed to give all kids an equal opportunity to play in our league under our lease in consideration for the town renting the field to us for one dollar per year."

"And no tryout means no equal opportunity?"

"You nailed it."

"What does Jack have to say about all this?" Jack Masters was the town league president who oversaw baseball at the Cal Ripken and Babe Ruth levels. All three of his boys played at the Cal Ripken age level so they weren't old enough to play on the Barkus teams. David reported to him as commissioner of Babe Ruth. Jack Masters was the reason David was on the board. David had lost the election the previous year as Babe Ruth commissioner to Darryl Fog, a crony of Rob Barkus's. Jack found David another spot on the board, and when Fog resigned as commissioner, Jack appointed David into the position and the board then confirmed it.

"Look, Brad, Jack worked hard to get me on the board. Looking back, though, I'm not sure he was doing me any favors. Jack will give me occasional support but the truth is that he is friends with some of these guys who play for the Elite Travel Baseball League. He won't show any one of them to the door because then he would have to show all of them the door. And Jack's real worry is that if they leave, he won't have anyone to do the work to make the Cal Ripken league run smoothly. I hear you on the conflict of interest issue. As a lawyer, I understand that point and agree with you fully. But the reality is that I'm outnumbered. And when push comes to shove, Jack sides with the greatest number and the greatest number on the board happens to be those who play in the Elite league."

"You're not painting a very pretty picture. I don't envy your position in the least."

"And it gets worse. I just got word that the freshman coach will now be fielding a team in the Elite Travel Baseball League."

Summers's eyes bugged out as he put his coffee down and looked to David.

"What the hell is going on in your town? Why in God's name would the school put up a coach in competition with its community program? What the hell are they thinking?"

"Obviously, they aren't thinking at all. I can't believe it either. I think this has Barkus written all over it. He must have sold this idea to the school coaches. This Barkus scheme has become the school machine."

"I'm not sure they can do that with the out-of-season coaching rules. Each state has its athletic association which regulates high school sports. One of the rules in some states is that a school coach is prohibited from or limited in having out-of-season contact with players."

"So does New York have an out-of-season contact rule?"

"Not any longer. But the Suburban Council league, where your school team plays, has those rules. So you may want to look at them."

"Thanks, I'll see if I can get ahold of a copy."

"I have to ask you, David, do you plan to have any all-star teams for thirteen-, fourteen-, and fifteen-year-olds this year? This has been a real problem to me in your league. Part of our charter requirements is that you place an all-star team into each of these age groups."

"I don't think there are enough interested boys left for an all-star team at every age level this year."

"I think you're running out of time."

"What do you mean?"

"Your in-house enrollment numbers are rapidly declining. A few years back, you were at one hundred and fifty players between the ages of thirteen and fifteen at the Babe Ruth level. Now your numbers are less than half that."

"I know. I'm trying to stabilize the numbers, but the freshman coach has thrown a wrench into the works—"

"The magic number is forty-eight. That is four teams of twelve. You really cannot have a league without at least four teams."

"Excuse me?"

"If you fall below forty-eight, we are going to have to look at revoking your Babe Ruth and Cal Ripken charters."

"What, no more baseball for our town?"

"Either that or combine your program with another program, probably one that's adjacent to your territory, like Mohawk City."

David knew the program was at risk, but he wasn't aware of the specifics. "You've got to be kidding me. We don't want to have to travel someplace else to play baseball. We've had a charter since 1957. That's over fifty years. Doesn't that count for something?"

"It's not only your numbers, though. Like I said, you haven't fielded any all-star teams in years."

David shook his head and rolled his eyes. It was enough that Barkus and the school wanted to shut down the town baseball program, but now the state commissioner had the same thing in mind. David caught a glimpse of the trench coat hanging from one of the coat hooks by their booth. A thought flashed in his mind: he wondered then if Brad was the man he saw with Barkus the other morning. *Maybe Barkus is paying him off to sink the program?* David thought, before considering whether this was a far-fetched idea.

"Look, Brad, I'm not Superman," David said, realizing just then that Brad looked a lot like Clark Kent. "I can't make people play Babe Ruth or all-stars when they're being lured away from our league. They go to the Elite Travel Baseball League at the direction of Barkus and the school. How am I supposed to fight that?"

"David, please understand that pulling your charter is one of the last things I want to do. I'm not sure how it would all work out with your league and another league merging, if that is the route we took."

"Aren't there any other options?"

"Yeah, there is another option. I could pull the Babe Ruth charter and dissolve your board altogether. I would appoint an interim president from out of town who would place men and women on the board who were dedicated to the Babe Ruth ideals of a community baseball program."

"Now that sounds like a plan to me. That's a surefire way to get rid of the conflicts of interest and give me some people to work with."

"It sounds easy enough but there will not be experienced people on your board to run the league. And at first, the entire idea would be met with great resistance and upheaval. It would be a mess for years before the ship was righted. As a result, this would be an option of last resort to me, but one I'm willing to take."

David stared at the table and turned his head away from the conversation. He was unsure if Barkus had gotten to Brad. He was going to clam up until he was sure that Brad was dealing from the top of the deck.

Brad sensed his dismay. "Look, maybe I could buy some extra time given your situation here. But that doesn't change things. At the rate you're losing kids, you will be at forty-eight within two years, maybe one year. Like you said, that freshman coach will only make things worse for the program. Have you given any thought about a plan on how to deal with this situation?"

David looked up and into Brad's eyes. "Why do I need to come up with a plan? Why not go to Jack and ask him to come up with a plan? He's the fucking president."

Brad took a sip of his coffee and set the cup down. "You're in charge of Babe Ruth and seem to have a better handle of what's going on here. Plus, you're a lawyer and I think this requires a legal mind. Jack has to run the entire league. We don't have problems with the younger age groups in your Cal Ripken program. Everything is going fine there."

David had to make sure of Brad's alliance before he shared any thoughts about a plan. He stared out the window to the parking lot and brought up his index finger and pointed. "Hey, there is a green Taurus parked out there with a Babe Ruth decal on the bumper. Is that your car?"

"Yeah, that's mine."

"I've been shopping for a new car. How do you like it?"

"It's been a good car."

"How does it do in the snow?"

"Not the greatest."

"Do you use another car for the snow then?"

"No, my wife's car is a Taurus too."

"No SUV then?"

"No, why do you ask?"

"Well, some couples have a basic car like the Taurus and a snow vehicle like an SUV."

"No SUV for us."

"Okay."

David leaned back in his seat and was relieved that Brad had nothing to do with Barkus.

"So let me get this straight," David said. "You want me to come up with a plan to increase our numbers and field all-star teams? Is that right?"

"I'm searching for answers along with you, David."

"I can't focus on *answers* or *plans* these days. I can only face the problem that is right in front of me, one at a time. My head is spinning; I feel like I'm in a whirlpool waiting to get flushed down the vortex. My wife, Annie, doesn't understand how running a simple little town baseball league could prove so complicated and time-consuming. And I can understand her point of view from the outside looking in. To people on the outside, to parents just like Annie, all I do is arrange a series of fucking playdates for two teams under the supervision of umpires. And, like Annie, they ask themselves what's the big deal? And now I am asking myself the same question. And I have to ask myself, why shouldn't I just run my son through this program and leave this entire mess behind like everyone else has done before me? Obviously, it took years of neglect to get this program where it is today. And it's going to take years to clean this up. I'm only one person. I have already left my law practice behind to work on this more than sixty hours per week and now you are looking to me to invest even more time into this sinkhole as a volunteer to develop a plan to make it all better? This is nuts."

Brad's eyes opened wide. "My God, David. I'm sorry. I had no idea what this was costing you in time and energy."

"It's a full-time job and then some. Let me ask you this, Brad. You have been around the other leagues in the area. How many board members are assigned to the Babe Ruth program in those local boards?"

"I don't know, maybe fifteen on average?"

"Do you know how many are assigned to the Babe Ruth program here in our league?"

"No, I don't."

"One, and you are looking at him. There are no other board members assigned exclusively to Babe Ruth. You want to know who the groundskeeper is for this field? You're looking at him. Do you know who does the scheduling of more than one hundred and fifty games per season? It's me.

Do you know who schedules the umpires? Tag, I'm it again. Oh, sure, being the Babe Ruth commissioner sounds impressive until you realize that nobody is assigned to help me. It's a joke. Barkus and his cronies set it up this way. They outsourced our baseball program to the Elite Travel Baseball League so they really didn't need more than one person to keep things going on our board. And now that the Babe Ruth league falls on my shoulders entirely, they hope that I quit in frustration so they can come in and take the field."

The waiter came back with breakfast and set the plates down along with two glasses of water.

"Thank you. This looks good, real good," said Brad, throwing a napkin down on his lap.

David looked at his plate and saw typical diner fare. "Yes, thank you," said David.

Brad looked up while trying to cut his sausage with his fork. "David, I've had similar problems in other leagues. But nothing even close to what is going on here. What you just said is quite telling. You know, youth baseball is all about the control of the fields."

David swallowed his eggs and felt the grease coat his throat on the way down. He reached for his water and took a few gulps. The grease lingered.

"You're right," David said. "Barkus and his followers want the best field in town—the Babe Ruth field—because they think they field the best baseball teams in town. Brad, they think they're *entitled* to that field."

"Yes, the parents think their sons are special and that they deserve special treatment," Brad said.

"Right, their baseball is born of privilege and arrogance," David said. "These Elite players are nothing special, just like all who have come before them. They're not real ballplayers; they're impostors and they are exposed for what they are upon graduation when there is no scholarship offered and they drop out of baseball for the rest of their lives."

"I'm not sure I'd go so far as to call them impostors," Brad said. "I think they're definitely misguided."

"Okay, fair enough, but I have one question for you, Brad, which gets to the heart of the matter. Where have all the real ballplayers gone? Where? I'm not talking about a physical skill set here; I'm talking about a mental makeup. Where have the boys that don't play for their parents or the scholarships gone? Where are the ones that play sandlot ball on their own? Where are the players that don't need a school uniform or a promise of a payoff as a reason to keep playing? Where are the ones that respect the game and play to improve themselves and to forge friendships? Where are the ones that aren't robots, the ones that play with a passion and a love and respect for the game? These are the real ballplayers, Brad, and they're tough to find because we live in a world where pretenders, their parents, and promoters, are driving the real ballplayers from the fields."

Silence. Brad had wondered why the quality of baseball in the local leagues had diminished in the past decade and been replaced with something else that he couldn't quite put his finger on or, perhaps, something he refused to recognize. His Babe Ruth territory had been losing teams to the Elite Travel Baseball League at an alarming rate all over the region, and other boys were dropping out of baseball too.

Brad's sausage was as tough as a catcher's mitt. It was burned on top and he couldn't cut it with his fork. He picked up his dinner knife and started sawing away. "I admit I don't have an answer for you," he said. "Besides, that's in the past. I need to look at the here and now and to the future. I admire you for reclaiming the field," he added.

David took another bite of eggs. "The field is the one thing we have that they want." He again reached for his water and gulped it empty. "I don't understand why Barkus and his followers don't play on the school fields and leave us the hell alone. I mean, why not spend their time and effort on fixing those school fields up and just leave us alone?"

"They feel threatened by you and want to hold on to what they have."

David motioned to the waiter to come over to the table. "Threatened? Threatened by growing our program and giving other boys the opportunity to play baseball? Oh my God, Brad, what's the world coming to? Barkus and his cronies must be terrified. And the school, they must be panic-stricken by the notion that more boys are playing baseball and might even try out for their school teams."

Brad had a victory over the sausage and held a piece to his mouth. "That's not the way they view the world." He put the piece in his mouth and began chewing in earnest. It sounded like he was chewing on sand.

"Right, Barkus and his cronies want a world of haves and have-nots and I've upset their happiness by giving other boys the opportunity to play more baseball on the Babe Ruth field."

The waiter came over and David asked for another glass of water and a steak knife.

"As for the school," David continued, "they seem to think they can pick the best baseball players at age twelve, play them on the Elite summer teams, and ride those kids to a state championship when they play on the varsity team. The other boys in the town, the ones that develop after age twelve, can drop off the face of the earth for all they care."

Brad laughed while still working over the sausage in his mouth. "How has that plan worked out for them?"

"We're the only school program out of the original Suburban Council teams that has never won a New York State sectional championship in fifty years."

Brad nodded. "Fucking brilliant. I think reclaiming your fields is a good first step to your plan."

"You give me too much credit, Brad. You keep talking as if I have a specific plan. I'm making this up as I go along; all I've done so far is hit a hornet's nest with a bat."

"It had to be done."

"Maybe so, but now I have two choices. I either run or get stung something terrible."

The waiter returned with another glass of water and a steak knife for David. David quickly cut his overdone sausage into a tic-tac-toe pattern. At that moment, Brad recalled his father telling him to always choose the right tool for the job. He looked at David and wondered if he was the right tool.

David rested his hands on the table while gripping his utensils so tight his knuckles began to turn white. "I can't run. That's not an option. I need to show the bastards that they will all sting themselves to death before they bring me down. So every day I have to wake up and look at my e-mails to see how Barkus is stinging me before the entire board. The latest is that 'Thompson has driven a permanent wedge between the school baseball program and our league. He is acting in a disturbing manner.' I will tell you where I would like to drive a wedge—right into Barkus's ass. But do you know what I do in response? Do I send a stinger back? No, I take the Jackie Robinson approach and just turn the other cheek and take it. There is no other choice. It's tough for them to argue with silence. They look foolish after a while."

Brad thought that David had the determination to maintain a fight. The last thing that Brad wanted was someone bailing on him if he elected to take a stand. "You're right, David. That's the right strategy. Keep it up."

"Easier said than done," David said. "Easier said than done," he said again with some resignation. "I don't know how much more I can take. It's not in my nature just to sit back and take endless bullshit, to fight with silence. I

just blow things off and try to make our league better with every defama-
tory e-mail Barkus sends me. I go out and have college coaches come in to
do clinics or I have semi-pro teams here to conduct camps. I take all of the
Barkus negative energy and try and create something positive from it so I
can shove it down his throat in an announcement that goes to the entire
board that inevitably ends up in his hands. He hates it when the have-nots
have more and better opportunities to play baseball than his players. It
makes him look foolish in front of his parents. At the same time, I'm
working to attract more kids to play baseball in town so we can keep out
program afloat. So it's a win-win approach as far as I'm concerned."

"I like your approach—making something positive out of a negative. It's
a winning strategy." Brad was elated that David had found a way to posi-
tively combat Barkus. He could back this approach as state commissioner.

"If you like what I'm doing, then support me and promise me that you
won't take our charter away," David said.

"I can't do that. I am here to give you a heads-up to try and avoid that
situation. Look, I can help you out—"

"Unless you can catch bullets for me, I'm not sure how you can help,"
David said, poking the food on his plate. He looked up at Brad. "I don't sleep
anymore, Brad. My wife thinks I' ve lost my mind to baseball. I'm being
hounded by men who take our boys, our players, and then want to use our
field. I feel surrounded and can only fight on so many fronts. I'm getting it
from all sides, including you now. And you want me to grow our numbers
in this environment? In case you haven't figured it out, I'm on defense here,
Brad. I'm fighting a defensive battle, just trying to hold my ground, trying to
hold on to the field, like General John Buford on the first day of battle at
Gettysburg."

Brad's lips opened and closed like a goldfish but no words came out.
What was he to think? He had dealt with every kind of volunteer over the
years but this one took the cake. He had a guy right in front of him who
thought he was fighting at Gettysburg. But what intrigued him was that
metaphor made sense to him, the imagery gave clarity to the situation. Brad
realized then that David was the right tool for the job, the only tool for the
job; now the circumstances had presented themselves where he could draw
a battle line.

Brad was not one to take on a fight lightly. As a commissioner that
oversaw dozens of leagues, he had to pick his fights carefully. He couldn't

afford to be consumed by one, but this was one that had to be fought. He was losing too many teams. With David leading the way in Indigo Valley, he could establish a foothold there and draw a line in the sand for other leagues to witness.

"Maybe you need to take some time off from baseball, give yourself some distance to gain some perspective," said Brad.

"I can't. The season is just starting. You know how it is. It doesn't stop until the end of July. If I turn my back for a second, I could be out and they could be on the field."

Brad put down his utensils and dabbed his mouth with his napkin. He stuck his index finger under his dress shirt collar and moved his head to place his Adam's apple underneath his top button. He straightened his tie a bit and, with the confidence of a corporate chieftain, he offered his best operative. "Like I said, I don't know what's going on in your town. This is as bizarre as it gets. But I have an idea on how I can help you out. There's a guy who might be able to help. You have to do me a favor, though, and remember that he is not on my staff. He doesn't report to me. And so what he does, he does on his own."

David thought for a few seconds about Brad's offer. The last thing he needed was a new item on his to-do list. But giving this guy a call couldn't hurt. He had nothing to lose at this point. "I'm not sure I understand your up-front disclaimer. I suppose I could call him."

"Great. His name is Johnny McFadden. He used to run the Babe Ruth program right next door to you. That program almost went bankrupt before he turned it around into a model program. In the process, he coached four straight state championship teams, including one that went to the Babe Ruth World Series. I think he can give you some good ideas."

"I don't need ideas; I need manpower."

"McFadden is a one-man army."

David looked at Brad's face. He was dead serious. The insanity of the situation took hold in David's mind. *Great*, he thought, *instead of sixty versus one it's going to be sixty versus two.* He wished that Christy didn't have such a passion for baseball; he wished he had taken up another sport. He wanted to be rid of the entire mess. But he knew that he couldn't bail. It was not in his nature to quit and he wasn't going to give Barkus that satisfaction. He couldn't let Christy and the other boys in the league down. Where would they play baseball in the coming years?

"I guess some things have changed since Babe Ruth started in our town way back when," said David.

"Yeah, our country gave birth to a multibillion-dollar youth sports industry," said Brad.

"And it seems that a part of this juggernaut wants to roll me over to get what it wants. When does this madness end?"

Brad stirred his coffee. "The madness ends when parents stop feeding the beast."

David finished his meal and wiped his face with a napkin and laid it on the table. He looked at Brad.

"So, do you really think we can change the collective mindset of these people?"

"You have a strategy. You are taking all of their negative energy and using it to improve your program; in turn, you're forcing the Barkus parents to consider what you can offer."

"Come on, Brad, these Elite parents aren't coming back."

"Maybe not, but the parents behind them might."

"Yeah, all is good if we don't fold as a league before then. It's a race against the clock."

"You leave that to me. You just execute your strategy. I'll do anything I can to support you."

"Right, and in the process of executing this plan, I'll be punishing my family. How are you going to support my family through this ordeal, Brad? Will you pay my legal costs after Annie files for divorce?"

Brad broke eye contact with David and looked down at the table. He didn't have a ready answer for David. He himself had scarified his family for baseball over the years. Now he was finally going to take a stand against the Elite Travel Baseball League, a decision that would not exactly create bliss in his household either.

David didn't miss a beat and stood up. "I have to go now. You can start supporting me by picking my tab up here, Brad. It may be my last meal if I don't get home to Annie in short order."

Brad stood up to shake David's hand. "I want to thank you for meeting with me today, and thank you for all you have done for Babe Ruth."

"Yeah, no problem. Look, I'll think about what you said."

"Thank you again, David."

With that, David looked at his watch and hurried out the door.

9

HERE'S JOHNNY

Monday morning rolled around and David was up before anyone else to research the Elite Travel Baseball League on the Internet. It took about two hours before he fully digested the ridiculousness of what he discovered. When it hit him, he had to say something, even if only to himself.

"Bullshit," he blurted out loud. "I cannot believe this crap!"

He heard rumblings in the house upstairs. He checked his computer clock. It was a little past 7:30 a.m. Soon the door to his office opened up.

"David, are you okay?" Annie said from atop the staircase.

David walked over to the bottom of the stairwell. There stood Annie in her bathrobe.

"I'm sorry, did I wake you?" he asked.

"No, I was just lying in bed, watching television, and I heard you say something."

"I'm sorry if I startled you. Is Christy awake?"

"He's in the shower. Is something wrong?"

"I . . ." He caught himself before bringing up the forbidden topic, but it was too late.

"It's about baseball, isn't it?"

"I'm . . . I'm afraid so."

"David, I thought you were doing real work down here."

"Annie, you've got to hear this." He figured that an explanation of his findings would prompt her to ignore his meandering. "You're not going to believe this but the Elite Travel Baseball League does not exist as a viable legal entity, nonprofit or otherwise, in New York State."

Annie put her hands on her hips and sighed. "What do you mean they don't exist? Don't they play over on the school fields? Do you think there're ghosts playing over there or something?"

"It is a made-up name of a make-believe organization."

"Doesn't this baseball stuff ever end, David?"

"Maybe there is an end to it here."

"How does it end *here*, David?" Annie said, crossing her arms.

"I think there is enough to take this to the New York State attorney general at this point. The Elite Travel Baseball League looks to be misrepresenting itself by stating in its constitution that it is an IRS 501(c)(3) nonprofit corporation and giving that appearance on its website. It's not. It's a front. The attorney general may have cause to shut the outfit down."

Annie looked at David and began shaking her head. "Oh, now that's a great idea, David." She threw her hands in the air. "Now you'll be known as the man who took baseball away from innocent kids that play in this other league. I'm sure the Elite parents will be glad to come over and play in your Babe Ruth program after you ruin their season. Do you think that move will bring them to your side? I think they will be burning crosses in our front yard before that ever happens. You'll be known as David Thompson, the man who took baseball away from their kids. And don't think that the Barkus PR machine won't be running full tilt to make you look like some evil, maniacal man who killed baseball. What about Christy? Did you ever stop to think about him?"

"Christy has nothing to do with this."

"Oh yes he does. He is under enough pressure from the Barkus players at school. They know you are trying to keep them off the field. That's all they know and all they have to know to make Christy's life a living hell. Wait till they find out you want to close down their league. Christy will have to wear a bulletproof vest to school."

"Christy hasn't said anything to me about the kids at school."

"He doesn't want to upset you. He's tired of seeing you get upset about baseball stuff."

David felt awful about Christy. "What do you think I should do then?

Should I just ignore all this? These guys are running their baseball league like the mob."

Annie sat down on the top step. "Parents won't understand the situation, David, and even if they did, they won't care. That's the sad truth. In their worky-worky, busy-busy lives they just want to know where and what time to drop off their kids and then what time to pick them up. The rest of the stuff is beyond them."

"Annie, there's absolutely no way we can compete with a for-profit outfit. We're volunteers. If Barkus and his cronies have a financial stake in their league, they will say and do anything that keeps the money flowing." He climbed the stairs and sat on the step below Annie. "I think we're going to lose our charter, Annie. I'm not sure baseball will be available to every boy in this town anymore."

She put her hand on his shoulder. "I'm sorry, David."

"Annie, we may be one of the last community sports program open to all teens in the town. You know, kids need an outlet to avoid getting into trouble. The school is cutting back on their offerings due to budget cuts. I've got a number of troubled kids in our program. Their problems are not necessarily of their own doing either. They may need to leave home if just for a few hours to play ball. Annie, we provide that outlet for them, our dugouts are safe houses for them. Baseball has been precious to our town for over fifty years and we're on the fast track to losing it. Isn't this something worth fighting for?"

"David, I love your spirit. But you are going to have to change your strategy if you are going to be effective. You might want to take a page from Jack Masters's handbook."

"You mean Jack's waffle recipe page? One day he supports Babe Ruth and the next day he's looking to give up and just cave in to the never-ending pressure from the Barkus machine."

"Yes, but don't look at his waffling alone," Annie insisted. "When he is on your side, look at the techniques he employs to support you even if they don't last. He is much more politically savvy than you are, David. You aren't afraid to take on anyone directly. That's just a part of your personality. One of Jack Masters's techniques is to find a fall guy to support his goals so that he doesn't look like the bad guy."

David thought for a few seconds. "I'm not sure what you mean."

"Just the other week, when some lady was asking if an Elite team could access the Babe Ruth field and Jack said no in an e-mail, not because he objected to them using the field personally but because the town would have to approve the arrangement. He saw no way that the town would support that use. The town was his fall guy and he deflected criticism away from himself. Do you see what I mean?"

"Why do you read my e-mails?"

"Someone has to look out for you."

"You are a funny one."

"Why do you say that?"

"On the one hand you think I spend way too much time on baseball, but on the other hand you seem to be spending a considerable amount of time on it yourself. I think deep down inside, you feel the same way as me about what's going on."

"David, I think your heart is in the right place. But I worry about you losing your head in the process and causing more problems for all of us. Don't forget, Christy and I have to live in this town too. Anything you do impacts us. So anytime you can achieve the same goal without confrontation it is a good thing. Often your message gets lost because of the emotions you generate. Don't forget, I've been involved in human resources for over twenty years. I think I know a bit about human behavior."

"I understand. You think I need to find a means to keep the Elite teams off our field without me personally saying no to them."

"Right. People on your board will be more receptive to what you're trying to do if you're not confrontational."

David squirmed. "Yes, Mrs. Thompson."

"You're too much."

"I'll tell you one thing. Many on the board don't want to confront the school, that's for sure. They're afraid of the repercussions."

"Try not to be so harsh, David."

David began rubbing his forehead with one hand. "Annie, I am sorry about all of this. You have no idea. It's just something I feel passionately about and sometimes I can't help myself. I appreciate your help, I really do."

Annie reached down and hugged him. She kissed him on the cheek and continued to hug him until Christy came into the kitchen without saying a word.

"You all set for school today?" asked David.

"Bite me," said Christy, finding the box of doughnuts and grabbing one.

"Christy Thompson, how about a 'good morning' from you?" Annie said.

"Uh-oh, does someone have a test today?" asked David.

"Sorry, Mom. Good morning. No tests today. The final modified base-ball cuts are tomorrow." Christy was nervous. One of his earliest memories as a child was of his father's trophy case in his office filled with awards from his days of playing football and running track at Indigo Valley. He wanted to show his dad he could make the team. He knew baseball was his best chance to play a high school sport because he had been playing it forever.

"Oh, I didn't know that," said David.

"Yeah, I'm not sure if I'll make the team."

"Just do the best you can and don't worry about it," said Annie.

"Coach Singleton is a fair coach," said David. "If you do well and show a positive attitude, that's all you can do. There'll be plenty of baseball for you no matter what happens."

"Okay, Dad," Christy said. He was relieved his dad wasn't pressuring him to make the team.

"Good luck," David said. "Have a great day at school. I made your lunch. It's in the fridge."

"Thanks."

David retreated back down to his office. He wanted to research the out-of-season coaching rules that Brad Summers had mentioned. But he couldn't locate them on the Internet.

He thought about the name Brad Summers had given him and decided to give Johnny McFadden a call to see if he could help. He picked up his office phone and dialed the number. There was an answer on the first ring.

"Hello."

"Hi, Johnny, my name is David Thompson. I'm calling from Indigo Valley Baseball. Brad Summers gave me your name and suggested I call you about some problems we're having over here. Do you have a few minutes?"

"Sure, David, I've got time for another baseball call. I've only had ten already this morning and it's only 9:30 a.m. My boss is going to fire me but it doesn't matter at this point so long as baseball is saved. Baseball must be saved!"

David didn't know what to think. "I'm sorry. Maybe I should call back at a better time for you."

There was silence on the other end of the phone for a few seconds. "Gotcha!" Johnny said, laughing. "I'm busting on you."

"Really, I can call back if you'd like," said David.

"I said I was just kidding. I mean, I've had ten calls this morning but my boss can't fire me."

"I don't understand."

"I'm my own boss. Don't get me wrong, I have fired myself several times but I always end up hiring myself back. Seems like despite all my faults, I'm the only guy who can get things done."

David laughed. "What do you do for a living?"

"I am a door-to-door salesman."

David laughed again. "No really, what do you do for living?"

"I just told you," Johnny said flatly.

David paused. "You're not kidding then."

"Nope."

"I didn't think anyone did that line of work anymore. What do you sell?"

"High-quality meat products. Hold on. I'm driving up to Mrs. Reynolds's house. I see the Jaguar in the driveway. Hopefully Mr. Reynolds left the checkbook home with her. I have a few minutes, though. Brad called me about you last night. What can I do for you?"

"Oh, okay," David said, a little surprised the two had already spoken about him. "Let me ask you this. I'm trying to locate the Suburban Council athletic guidelines for out-of-season contact. We have the freshman coach planning to manage a team of twelve-and thirteen-year-olds in the Elite Travel Baseball League. It may be in violation of those rules."

"I can get you a copy."

"Just tell me where to find them. I don't want to bother you."

"You can't find them. They're not published. You've got to know people to get them."

"Rules that aren't published? How does the league work without published rules?"

"The athletic directors write them and they have them. That's all that matters to them. I'll get you a copy."

"Oh, okay. I was wondering if I could meet with you to discuss things."
"Not today. I've got appointments. I can get you a copy of the rules in about

two hours. You're on my way to see some customers in Indigo Valley. I can drop them off to you. I have your address. We can meet tomorrow."

"How do you know my address?"

"I have a computer console in my truck with an Internet hookup."

"Neat," David said, thinking to himself that this was quite a setup for a man who sold meat door-to-door.

"I'll be there at 11:00 a.m. sharp."

"Thanks for your help."

With that David hung up the phone. He had done a lot of thinking. If he could stop the freshman coach from having a team in the Barkus league, he might be able to stop the exodus of players. He dialed up Wayne Duffel to talk with him about Coach Powers and the Elite team.

"What's the Elite Travel Baseball League?" Duffel asked.

"You don't know about it? It's the league run by Rob Barkus?"

"Who is Rob Barkus? Why should I know about this league?"

"Because all of the high school players play on teams in that league during the summer on the school fields. In fact, your freshman coach plans on starting a team in that league and was recruiting players during modified tryouts."

"What? He was there during modified tryouts? I'm going to check that out." Duffel seemed confused and concerned.

"Look, I want to talk to you about this in private. Does 2:00 p.m. work for you?"

Duffel hesitated but then agreed to meet.

David hung up and was encouraged by his conversation. Duffel seemed taken aback at Powers's actions during the modified tryouts.

David went into the kitchen to fix some tea. His mind was racing. He wondered how much Duffel knew about what was going on. The baseball program was just one of many sports programs offered by the high school. There was a good chance that he was being spoon fed all of his information by someone. But Duffel said that he did not know Barkus. David thought about who else might be involved. He thought that the missing link may be Coach Braxton, the varsity baseball coach.

Annie came down from upstairs with her hair wet. She was wearing some bright activewear with new walking shoes. She started to bounce around the kitchen like Tigger from *Winnie the Pooh*.

"Good morning, Annie."

"Hello again, you baseball nut," Annie said kiddingly.

"There was a time when you were a baseball nut too, if I recall."

He was thinking about the time she had told him they needed to talk after they had been dating for long time. Annie's tone was very serious and

David thought they were going to have the commitment talk, a discussion about getting married. But when they sat down, Annie astonished David by wanting to have a heart-to-heart conversation about the infield fly rule. He couldn't help but fall more in love with her at that moment. Then when she started scoring each Yankee game perfectly on sheets of lined paper she had boxed into a score sheet with pencil herself, David knew he had found his future bride. He gave her an official scorebook as a wedding present.

"That was BC," Annie said, "before Christy."

"So are you off for a run this morning?" David asked, in search of a lighter moment. He knew full well that the last time Annie went running was on black Friday at a sale at Macy's.

"No, I'm just getting breakfast before heading to work downstairs."

"I'm your office mate today. Aren't you happy to have my company?"

"Sure."

"I can keep an eye on you to make sure you don't get eaten up by that silly little baseball league of yours. Maybe, just maybe, you'll start thinking about practicing law again."

"I am practicing law; it's called baseball law."

"Does it pay anything?"

David thought for a second. "It's like an investment in Christy and our community, so there's a payoff of a different kind."

"You're impossible. You know what I mean. You were such a fine elder law attorney in your day. I don't understand you now."

"I got tired of trying to manage people's deaths and the disposition of their stuff. Everyone around me was dying all the time and sometimes they were dying horrific deaths. It was getting depressing. With baseball, I feel like I'm trying to give life to something. I couldn't save my clients. I felt helpless. But maybe I can save baseball."

Annie thought David might be going through a midlife crisis of sorts. "David, you need to think about your life beyond baseball."

"I'll figure it out eventually," David said, looking away. He had begun to understand that the very thing that was giving him hope for renewal was causing Annie consternation. He felt bad, but he didn't have any answers at this point except to try and see the baseball situation settled before taking on his future.

"By the way," David said, "I'm going over to the high school to meet with Duffel this afternoon to try and work this out."

"Really?" Annie said, sensing that reconciliation with the school might get David's head out of the clouds. "What's your plan?"

"I'm going to try what you said. I'm going to be nonconfrontational and see if we can come to an understanding."

"Oh, I'm so proud of you," Annie said.

David felt the guilt fall from his shoulders as he, perhaps, found a way to redeem himself in her eyes.

"Please be careful," she added before embracing him.

"Okay," he said, hugging her back. "I will."

Their eyes met. They exchanged looks of affirmation over the armistice they seemed to have reached on the topic of baseball, at least for the remainder of the day.

David went downstairs to the office and researched issues relating to the freshman coach on the Internet. He wanted to see if the school district had a policy about supporting community programs. Sure enough it did. So he printed out a copy and went about preparing for his meeting with Duffel. Annie came down and joined him and began her work for the day.

The doorbell rang. David looked at his watch and then looked to Annie. It was exactly 11:00 a.m. Annie was on the phone. David motioned to her that he would get the door. He went upstairs and looked through the door window but there was nobody there that he could see. So he stepped outside to get a better view. He saw a pickup truck idling in the driveway with a freezer unit mounted on the bed. He then spotted a man pacing back and forth in the driveway with his cell phone pressed to his ear.

Johnny McFadden motioned David to come over with the papers he was holding in one hand. Johnny was a stocky man of average height with larger-than-life forearms. Put him in a baseball uniform and he was a catcher. He was dressed neatly with his green matching Dickies shirt and pants separated by a brown leather belt with a big gold buckle. His brown hair was combed from front to back perfectly, like he had dried it in a wind tunnel, and his bristle-like mustache provided what his slightly receding hairline could not. The 'stache provided symmetry to his granite face; it was hard to imagine him without one.

David walked over and Johnny handed him the papers while he continued to talk on the phone. David started reading the papers while half listening to Johnny's conversation.

Johnny flashed David the just-one-minute finger before his hand went into wild gyrations as he talked. "Joe, don't give me that line. I know why you want to play in the Elite Travel Baseball League. You want to be able to schedule shitty teams. You want to win a lot of games so your parents can feel good about themselves and have a reason to party throughout the season."

There was a pause as the person on the other end could be heard yelling at Johnny. Johnny held the phone away from his ear and looked at David while pointing to the phone. When the voice at the other end stopped, Johnny got back on and continued. "I'm sorry, but you have to play the good teams too in the Babe Ruth travel program. This isn't like professional wrestling; we run a baseball league. Until you figure out what that means, don't bother calling me." With that, Johnny closed his cell phone and turned his attention to David.

"David, so how are you?"

"You must be Johnny McFadden," David said, reaching for his hand. "Nice to meet you. Thanks for bringing this over."

"No problem."

"Hey, I couldn't help but overhear your telephone conversation. You seem to know a lot about the Babe Ruth travel program."

The Babe Ruth travel and all-star programs supplemented the in-house or recreational league of each community. The more skilled players were given the opportunity to play teams outside of their community so long as they continued to play baseball within their community in the in-house league.

"I should. I've been running the Babe Ruth travel program locally for five years now."

"Oh, I didn't know that."

"Actually, my wife does a lot of work to help run the league. I couldn't do it without her."

"Do your boys play in the league?"

"No. My boys are in their twenties. They're too old."

David paused for a second. "Wow, I have to hand it to you."

"How's that?"

"You don't have a kid in this program and yet you're still volunteering your time. That's admirable."

"Well, I get something out of it. Baseball keeps me out of trouble. But that's another story for another day. You said you wanted to meet? How about tomorrow night at the Yellow Ribbon Diner at seven?"

"Okay."

With that, Johnny shook hands with David, then got into the cab of his pickup truck. David could see the "McFadden Meats" sign on the side of the freezer unit mounted in the bed as he backed out into the road and hurried off.

10

TWO ON ONE

D avid looked at the out-of-season contact rules that Johnny had given him. He read them and reread them. They were written poorly and had typos. They seemed to prohibit Coach Powers from coaching the Elite Travel Baseball team because that would constitute out-of-season contact with the incoming freshman school team. David thought if he could convince Duffel that the out-of-season contact rules were being violated, he could prevent the outflow of players to Coach Powers at the modified level. He had some other arguments in his toolkit as well and thought he could at least buy the Babe Ruth league some time. It was worth a shot. David mounted his Mustang for the ride over to meet with Duffel at the high school.

After Indigo Valley lost its wild indigo crops, the town did move on to raise corn. But in the 1900s, the cornfields were replaced by homes and then housing developments, and that's when raising suburban children became the main crop of the town—planted in the elementary school, nurtured in the middle school and harvested in the high school.

Indigo Valley High School administrators had always described the school as the "focal point of the community" and, to the extent that people stared at the school's architecture in a state of bewilderment, this was an accurate statement. Built in the late 1950s in an architectural style known as "California design," the school was mostly a one-floor maze of open-air, connecting breezeways; courtyards; and large windows throughout that thumbed its nose at the winters of the Northeast. On the outside, it looked like a one-story brick version of Frank Lloyd Wright's *Fallingwater* but without the charm of the water, the surrounding forest, and anything else that might soften the edginess of a school drowning in right angles. Over the years, the school endured over a half dozen construction projects that offset many of these design features while adding new ones, creating a distinct architectural style known as "Indigo Valley sprawl." The newly discovered style was highlighted by an ongoing debate concerning the location of the main entrance given the multitude of possibilities—like a maze with a number of solutions.

The 2003 addition was considered by some to be the main entrance, at least for a time. It housed the new swimming pool, a new fitness center, and Wayne Duffel's new office.

David passed through the 2003 entrance and opened the door to the reception room adjoining Duffel's office. It was a cramped space filled with papers stacked on tables around the perimeter. There was a closed door off to one side that had Wayne Duffel's name marking his office. Under the glare of cool fluorescent lighting recessed in the suspended ceiling tiles, Duffel's secretary sat clicking a keyboard. There were a few students sitting in a row of chairs against the wall near the entrance to the reception area. They were talking to the secretary when David entered.

David greeted the secretary and she pointed to a chair against the wall opposite the kids and told him to have a seat. Near his chair was a lostand-found table piled high with clothing: Nike and Under Armour shorts, a couple of sweat bottoms that said "pink' or "love pink," a North Face polar fleece, some Aéropostale shirts, and a pair of Ugg boots.

David's chair was pinned in from either side by a table stacked with papers, files, and notebooks. He had to scrunch his shoulders to fit between the tables. He felt if he moved, the towers of papers would fall on him and trigger the collapse of the staggered painted cinder blocks that encapsulated the room.

The students, three boys and a girl, sat facing David. They were chatting away among themselves and with the secretary about the goings-on at school. The door to the athletic office opened and the students looked up. In walked a man with a whistle dangling from his neck.

One of the boys looked up and said, "Hi, Coach Braxton," and then the other boys followed with a similar greeting.

"Hello," Coach Braxton said to the students.

"Good afternoon, Coach Braxton," said the secretary.

"Hello, Mrs. Downey." His smile revealed shallow dimples on either side of his mouth. He was tall, muscular, with long hair so blond it stood in stark contrast to his skin, which looked the color and consistency of an old, dried-out football. He wore a red polo shirt with a gray "I" for "Indigo Valley" on his breast pocket that matched his gray slacks.

David had never met Coach Braxton but knew that he was the varsity baseball coach. David sat off to the side and looked like a piece of office furniture set back between the two stacked tables. Coach Braxton didn't acknowledge him. David started to feel uncomfortable sitting there with everyone else in the room engaged in conversation. He pulled out some papers he had brought and began thumbing through them.

"This is going to be a challenge," said Braxton to Mrs. Downey, rubbing his chin with one hand.

"I did the best I could, but adding Coach Powers's team into the mix makes it difficult," said Mrs. Downey.

David realized they were talking about the field schedules for the school baseball teams. Now he felt even more out of place as he pretended to read the papers he'd brought with him. He wondered if Duffel had told them he was coming and they were staging a woe-is-me act for his benefit. He hadn't asked for Coach Braxton to be at the meeting with Duffel.

The door to Duffel's office swung open and out came a field maintenance worker.

Mrs. Downey got up and poked her head into the office and then turned and said, "Mr. Duffel can see you now."

David had to turn sideways to slide out of his seat. Coach Braxton continued to look at the papers Mrs. Downey had given him. As David passed him on his way to Duffel's office, Braxton put the papers down and began to follow David inside. David entered the office and extended his hand to Duffel.

"Hi, Wayne, thanks for seeing me this afternoon."

In came Coach Braxton, who closed the door behind him.

"David, have you met Coach Braxton?" Duffel said as David was about to sit down.

"No, I haven't." He swung around and stood upright and extended his hand to the coach.

"Nice to meet you, coach."

"Sure," he said, extending his hand. They shook hands and David felt his knuckles crack under the pressure of Braxton's grip. He looked at Braxton's eyes. They were red. He had puffy coffee-colored bags under his eyes that, unlike the rest of his face, were wrinkle-free, as if they had been injected with Botox.

Duffel moved past them as they shook. He closed the blinds to the large glass window that looked out on the busy hallway, then moved back to his chair and sat down behind his desk facing David and Coach Braxton.

"What brings you here, David?" asked Duffel.

"Well . . ." David felt ill at ease in the unexpected presence of Braxton. He asked Duffel on the phone to meet with him privately yet here was Braxton. "I first wanted to talk to you about the perception in the baseball community that in order to make the school baseball team, you have to play on the Barkus teams in the summer—"

"Hold on right there," Braxton said. He leaned forward and put a pad of paper on Duffel's desk and with one stroke took out a pen and clicked it ready to write and put it to paper. "I want names," he said, raising his voice. "Give me names of people who think that!"

Duffel leaned back in his swivel chair and clasped both hands behind his head and looked at David. David saw that Duffel was going to sit by and watch Braxton go on the attack. Any concern that Duffel had about the situation during their telephone conversation had disappeared.

"I'm not sure what is going on here," said David. "I just came in to see Wayne here to try and address a situation caused by Coach Powers the other day during modified tryouts."

Braxton was insistent. "I want names! Give me names right now!"

David tried to keep calm. He had come in with the idea of being nonconfrontational, as Annie suggested. It seemed, though, that Braxton's plan was to be confrontational.

"The names?" David said. "You can find the names on the rosters of the Elite Travel teams. Although a few of the school players participate in the Babe Ruth in-house program, none of them play in the Babe Ruth travel program or in the all-star program."

"Parents make their choice on where to play," said Braxton.

"Look, at this point no parent is going to choose for their son to play in a league other than where the freshman coach is participating," said David.

"That's not my problem," said Braxton.

"Well, coach, you're part of the problem as I see it."

"What is that supposed to mean?"

"Your sons play with the Barkus teams. Parents follow you. It reinforces the perception that kids have to play on the Barkus teams in order to play school baseball."

Duffel brought his hands out from behind his head and wheeled up to his desk, then crossed his arms and leaned forward. David's eyes met his. Duffel squinted as he wagged his index finger at David. "I have no control over what a coach does in his time outside of his coaching job with the school," he said.

David looked back at Braxton. "Nobody said it was your problem alone, coach. It's really a school district problem."

"Didn't you hear what I just said? We have no control over what anyone does with his own free time," said Duffel.

David looked back at Duffel and leaned forward and lifted his own index finger as if to mimic the man's gesture. "The school district should not allow someone in the role of coach to promote an outside for-profit travel league to kids on school grounds. It is a pure conflict of interest with his role as a teacher here and his role as a coach."

"I don't understand what the big deal is here," said Braxton.

"Well, do you allow any teacher or coach or administrator to sell anything they want here on school grounds to the kids? Doesn't the school district have a policy against solicitation on school grounds? Or are kids a captive market for school personnel products and services?"

"I'm sure there are a lot worse things being sold in school than a baseball program," said Braxton, laughing a bit. "Right, Wayne?"

Duffel squirmed in his seat at that response, as he was also the director of health for the school. Braxton didn't deal with the drug, tobacco, and alcohol problems of Indigo Valley High School except when one of his athletes was involved. Duffel attended the regularly scheduled administration meetings and public meetings and these problems were always a topic. Still, he managed to offer a halfhearted smile in support of Braxton as he rocked back and forth in his chair.

David filled the void. "Look, I've done some research and the school board has passed some community relations goals." He shuffled through some papers and pulled out one. "It says right here that one of those goals is to quote, 'encourage community participation in activities and organizations that support school programs,' unquote. Now it seems to me that our Babe Ruth program has been supporting the schools goals of providing kids with an outlet, a positive physical activity since this school was built. So what are you guys doing to support us?"

Duffel leaned back in his swivel chair and paused for a second as he put one hand to his chin. Then he rocked forward again and put both hands on the desk and began softly tapping his index finger on the surface. "Maybe what would help you is to have the opportunity to tell the modified kids about your Babe Ruth league."

David paused to gather his thoughts. "You shouldn't have to make that offer. I mean, really, do you think the solution to having your coach sell and endorse Coke is to have the guys from Pepsi come in to try and sell their product? Not that we're Pepsi or anything; we're volunteers working to serve everyone in this community, as we have done for decades. As such, we're the *only* choice."

"Like I said before, what Coach Powers is doing by coaching this travel team is none of our business," said Duffel. "He's doing this on his own personal time."

"It is *your* business as much as it is *his* business. You're allowing him to sell his team to the kids on school time, on school grounds in his role as a school coach. There is no tryout for this team; it is invitation-only. And you give him the school fields to play on. It sounds like a school-endorsed program to me. You might want to let your insurance company know that you are fielding school teams in the summer, though."

"These are not school teams," pleaded Braxton.

"If it looks like a duck, acts like a duck, quacks like a duck, it's a duck," David said.

"These teams have insurance as far as I know," said Duffel.

"Are you sure, Wayne? Do you have the certificates of insurance on file for those teams? And even if you do have certificates of insurance for those teams, do you have proof of insurance for the Elite Travel Baseball League? It would be a neat trick if you did because it doesn't exist as a viable legal entity. I doubt any insurer would underwrite them, since there is nothing to underwrite."

Duffel exchanged a glance with Braxton. Braxton's hands became fists. "Look, don't destroy what we have here," he said as he gaveled one fist to Duffel's desk. "Don't destroy what we have here," he repeated with a raspy, exasperated voice.

"I don't know what you mean, coach. According to Wayne over here you guys don't have anything going on. Wayne says this is all something that the freshman coach is doing on his own and the school has nothing to do with it."

Braxton opened his hands and began rubbing his thighs back and forth as he talked. "Stop laying into Coach Powers. He's a good guy. He does a great job with the kids."

"If you say so, coach. But this has nothing to do with Coach Powers as a person. I am sure Barkus sold him a bill of goods and he just became a part of the Barkus money machine."

"Are you saying that Coach Powers is getting paid?" asked Braxton.

"I have no idea if he is getting paid. But someone is collecting some green. There's lots of money changing hands."

"I will have you know that Coach Powers is a volunteer. He doesn't get paid," said Braxton.

David paused for a second. "I think it's great that he wants to volunteer his time to help boys play baseball. I wish he would consider helping the program that has been helping boys in this town forever as opposed to supporting an outfit that seems hell bent on destroying it."

"Look, what you don't understand is that the Elite Travel program has helped us get closer to winning the sectional title in the playoffs," said Braxton.

"Really? At what cost though, coach?" David asked.

"What are you talking about?" Braxton quipped.

"I like to win as much as the next guy. But my philosophy is to win at minimal costs. I don't want to forget about what we are trying to do here, in our program at least. We're trying to provide all teens with a positive athletic experience. We want to steer them away from the unhealthy options that are out there. Whether you know it or not, you have adopted just the opposite philosophy as far as I'm concerned. You are about winning at all costs."

"Stop right there," said Duffel. "Coach Braxton is concerned about the welfare of his players. He would never sacrifice the well-being of his players just to win."

David's voice grew louder. "That is not the cost that I'm talking about. *We* are the cost. Our Babe Ruth baseball program *is* the cost. My son, Christy, is the cost. All the boys that don't play on the school baseball teams are the cost. If Coach Powers takes players from our program and steers them to the Elite Travel Baseball League, our numbers are going to go down and these boys won't be able to play baseball because there will be no league. And the sad part is Powers could coach travel baseball through Babe Ruth and its program while the boys also played Babe Ruth in-house too with the other boys in town."

"Why does it matter to us where *our* boys play so long as they are skilled?" asked Braxton.

"There's more to this town than the boys that play on *your* teams," said David. "Don't those boys matter? Or do we create a crack and let them fall through it? There's a team larger than all your school teams combined: it's our town, our community."

Braxton rolled his eyes.

David decided to use another line of argument. "You know, the board of education's wellness policy requires that you offer intramural sports open to everyone. What do you offer?"

Braxton and Duffel exchanged glances. David knew the high school offered none.

"Why not think of the Babe Ruth league as your intramural offering?" David asked. "Why not support us? By the way, have you checked yournumbers lately, coach? What is the number of boys that try out for thevarsity team?"

"We had twenty-three last year," Braxton responded. "What of it?"

"You're missing twenty to thirty players," David said.

"What on earth are you talking about?" Duffel asked.

"You have fewer kids trying out than many other schools," David said. "Bethlehem had fifty-five try out. South Colonie had fifty-six try out. LaSalle had sixty-six."

"We have a lacrosse program that is nationally recognized that takes kids from baseball," Braxton said. "Kids are recruited to play lacrosse. That's why our numbers are low."

"At the younger ages, maybe you have a point," David said, "though the other schools have lacrosse too. But I can't think of one player at the age of twelve on up that you lose to the lacrosse program from baseball. When they leave baseball, they don't go to lacrosse. They just drop out of baseball and never return to any spring sport. So when you take kids from our league to play elsewhere, you actually damage your own program because we lose kids that could push your kids to make them better through our league. And with fewer players for you to draw from at the school level, there is less competition for a spot on your varsity teams. Of those few kids that tried out, how many did you cut?"

"A few . . . ," Braxton said.

"Right, there weren't any other kids really pushing the ones that normally make the school teams."

"Like I said before, there is nothing we can do. What Coach Powers does outside of coaching the freshman team is his own business," said Duffel.

"What about the Suburban Council out-of-season coaching rules?" asked David. "Don't they apply?"

"They don't apply to a coach for age thirteen and under," said Duffel. "Coach Powers will have a team of boys at age thirteen and younger."

"Really. I didn't see that exception when reading those rules," David said. "But then again since they're written in gibberish, I suppose anyone can read anything into them. Who decides what these rules mean or don't mean?" David asked.

"The Suburban Council meets as a board and every year a different athletic director is chosen to chair the board on a rotating basis," Duffel said. "Who is chairing the board this year?" David asked.

"It's my turn," Duffel said with a smirk.

"Why doesn't that surprise me?" said David, shaking his head.

Braxton fired back. "You know, I really have to question your integrity for making such a big deal about what Coach Powers is doing. You're taking this too far."

David's eyes became like lasers as they looked at Braxton. He felt a rage build inside him and he did all that he could to try and control himself.

"I have to ask you, coach, on what basis are you challenging my integrity? We haven't met before today. You don't know me at all."

"I have my reasons."

Duffel rocked back and forth in his swivel chair like he was on a porch watching the sun set.

"Has Barkus and his cronies fed you some line of crap about me?"

"I don't have to tell you anything more."

"Sure, coach. Whatever. You know, athletics meant a lot to me when I attended this school long before you started working here. I used to be a proud alumnus of this school. That is, up until this point."

Duffel and Braxton exchanged glances.

"Wayne, I was under the impression that you had an open-door policy here," David said.

Duffel stopped rocking. "You're here, aren't you?"

"Oh, I get it. The door is open but after it closes, anything goes."

"What are you talking about?"

"I came in here to voice a concern as a community member. I tried to be respectful of you and your coaches in a very difficult situation. Your varsity coach here yells at me that he wants names like you're conducting some kind of inquisition. Then he questions my integrity for reasons unknown and you sit there and make no effort to try and mediate. Instead, you sit there and do nothing. Nice one-eighty from when I talked with you on the phone earlier."

Duffel went back to rocking. "Coach Braxton is well respected in this school."

David stood up. "Look, you guys play a good circle-the wagons game and your two-on-one intimidation act is not bad either. But I've got things to do."

David gathered his papers. Duffel and Braxton rose and each looked to the other to say something. But before they could, David looked at Braxton and continued.

"You're the head football coach at the varsity level as well, right?"

"Yes I am," Braxton said proudly.

"You're amazing. I don't know of any coach in the area that is the head coach for two major sports programs."

"Coach Braxton is an amazing individual," said Duffel.

"So it seems," said David. "You know, I started on offense and defense in football and on special teams when I was here. I weighed 155 pounds on a good day. Many players on the other side thought I was an easy mark because of my size. They thought they could intimidate me. But they soon learned that they could not."

David picked up a football from the shelf and started flipping it. "It is ironic, you know, that the very qualities I learned here at school on that field out there are the same ones that will drive me to fight the good fight if the school doesn't change its ways."

David flipped the ball to Braxton. "Hey, I don't want to wear out my welcome here anymore than I have. Thanks for letting me come in today." David shook Duffel's hand and then shook Braxton's and left the office.

David walked out to the parking lot and his mind was racing. *Some alma mater*, he thought. He looked over to the football field and the running track that surrounded it.

Ever since he graduated from high school, David would make it a point to run around the track on warm and sunny days. There was no thought process to running around in circles on the track as opposed to running on the roads: no cars driving around, no potholes in the street. He would just run and let his mind wander. He'd think of all the football games and track meets he had there, all the good times, all the good memories. He would lose count of the number of laps he had run. No matter, as he thought he could run forever and sometimes his mind would go blank and he would be conscious only of his body movement and his breathing. The sweet smell of freshly cut grass would embrace him from all directions. He would take off his shirt and the sweat would trickle down him but would soon evaporate in the breeze that blew across the fields. With any luck, the lawn sprinklers would turn on and he could run through them to cool off. It was a place of memories, relaxation, and reflection; his runs there helped reconnect him to his soul.

But when David looked over that day to the track and the football field, he did not feel anything. He was numb and his stomach was queasy. A shiver ran up his spine but it was warm outside. He looked away from the field and started to jog toward his car. He recalled his beloved football coach and the distinguished athletic director that founded the department at the high school. They had long since retired. Things had changed. No longer did he feel a bond to what had been his high school, and he wondered what Christy's experience would be there over the next four years. A piece of David died that day and suddenly he felt old.

11

THE FIRST CASUALTY

It was midafternoon when David returned home from his meeting with Duffel and Braxton. He walked through the door with the idea of heading straight down to his office. He saw Annie in the kitchen having a late lunch. He was in no mood to talk.

"Hi, Annie," he said as headed toward the office.

"Hi, babe. How did your meeting go?" she said before he could touch the office doorknob.

Twenty years of marriage had caused Annie to develop a radar detector that could pick up on anything amiss with him. And as much as David might try, he knew he couldn't jam that radar for any length of time.

He turned toward her. "It was an interesting meeting. I will have to tell you about it later." He grasped the doorknob to go downstairs. The last thing he wanted to do was upset Annie about anything related to Christy or baseball.

"What's wrong, David?"

Damn, I think she's on to me, he thought. He released the doorknob and faced her.

"Did something go wrong in the meeting?" she asked.

David knew she would not let up until he offered her something. He decided to cast an overview in her direction to see if that would suffice. "As expected, they couldn't hear what I was saying."

"I'm sorry, David."

"Yeah, me too. Hey, no biggie. I gave it a try."

David stood there, frozen in time, hoping that explanation would do it. He didn't want to tell Annie how bad things actually were.

The drive home had given him occasion to think about what had happened. All the while in Duffel's office he was aware of the impact he was having on Christy's ability to play on the modified team. But once Braxton openly challenged his integrity, he realized it was too late. No matter what, Christy was not going to make the team. If these men had no problem ruining an entire community baseball program, they wouldn't give a second thought to rolling over on Christy.

Annie would flip if she got wind of this fact. David realized he simply did not have the energy to argue with Annie about that now. He was drained and felt horrible that Christy was not going to play for the school because of him. David had held the Babe Ruth field at all costs, but the first casualty of war was Christy.

He felt an incredible guilt. David had taken school baseball away from Christy. If he didn't save the Babe Ruth league, most likely there would be no baseball for Christy or any of his friends starting next season.

David knew he had to sort it all out in his mind. But he didn't want to do it in front of Annie. He did not want to say something to her now he would later regret. David had already hurt his son over baseball; he didn't want to hurt his wife over baseball too. No need to go for the daily-double with her. It was time to retreat and regroup in silent mode. And David viewed his office now as offering asylum.

"Were they nice to you?" Annie asked.

David realized that this was a loaded question and carefully crafted his response. "I think they were as nice as they could be given the circumstances from their point of view."

Annie's radar was hard at work. "That is a cryptic response if I've ever heard one."

David considered wrapping himself in the aluminum foil on the kitchen counter to deflect her radar. "What time is Christy due home from tryouts today?" he asked, hoping to change the topic.

"He said this morning that he would be catching a ride home with a friend and would be here around 5:30 p.m. What are you going to do now?"

David wasn't sure what Annie meant and he didn't want to ask for clarification. He turned and began to slip down the stairs to his office before Annie could read him fully. "I'm going down to my office to shift gears."

"That's a good idea. Maybe you can focus on bringing in some income for the family. You're going to have to find some new legal work eventually. The money you saved over the years isn't going to last forever. Baseball isn't paying any bills."

Ouch, David thought. But she was right and he knew it. David had been letting the black hole of baseball eat up much of his time, yet he felt good now having something in his back pocket for Annie.

"I'm going to do some legal work for Jim Fletcher on a case and I'll get paid for it," David said. He didn't bother to mention that the case was about Stan Moss.

"Oh, that's a good start," she said. "You know, there is that Norman Rockwell drawing hanging in the office that your parents want to sell. Why not sell it and take a commission for your efforts?"

"Okay, Annie." And with that David sat in his office chair and began to rock back and forth while looking at the Rockwell drawing on the wall.

The drawing was a study done in preparation for an illustration. Rockwell completed the illustration in 1946 for the *Saturday Evening Post* and entitled it *Maternity Waiting Room*. David's grandfather received the drawing as a gift for posing in it and for finding other models to pose in it.

In the drawing, ten men wait for their blessed event. The men all show different levels of anxiety. Five sit on a couch that's as long as a stretch limousine. Two pace in front of the couch while three are seated in chairs on either end of the couch. David's grandfather sits in a chair on the far right, his body split in half at the edge of the drawing. His face studies the other men in the room while he nervously rips pages in a magazine.

David's grandfather had passed away and the family thought it best to sell the drawing since they couldn't really share it among different households.

David had mixed feelings about selling it. He enjoyed looking at it in his office. He liked having his grandfather's company. He liked the symmetry of the work—how the number of characters were fairly balanced across the artwork. He had come to know the other characters in the picture as well, since the models' names were written in pencil beneath their portrayals.

David searched for the phone number to the Normal Rockwell Museum in Stockbridge, Massachusetts, about an hour away from his hometown. He thought they might be interested in buying it. It would be a win-win if they purchased it for their collection: he would have sold it and generated some income and anyone in the family could still enjoy viewing it if they wanted.

He spoke with Cary Shannon, curator for the museum, but was told that the museum was short on funds due to the recession and couldn't buy the drawing. But she did invite him out to show the drawing at the museum to help generate some interest in purchasing it. She also invited him to a Friday-evening lecture about Rockwell where he could network among potential buyers. David thought a trip out of town would do him good, and so he agreed to attend and to show the drawing at the museum.

David hung up and a second later the phone started ringing. David picked up. "Hello."

"Hey, David. It's Nick." Nick Antonio was a Babe Ruth coach for one of the six teams in the league. Nick's son Joe played on his team while Nick's stepson, Andrew Golder, played on David's team. Andrew had an older brother, Jacob, who had quit baseball years earlier.

"Hi, Nick. What's up?"

"I just wanted to, ah, tell you about an incident yesterday on the Babe Ruth field." Nick's voice was a bit shaky.

"Incident? What happened?"

"You know Darryl Fog, right?"

"Yeah, sure, he is Barkus's right-hand man. What about him?" Nick knew of Barkus, though it was nothing more than a general awareness of his doings.

"Well, yesterday afternoon, he came over to the field with a bunch of boys from the high school teams that play on the older Barkus travel team. I was there practicing with my son, Joe. Fog comes up to me and says his team is there to practice. I asked him if he had permission and he said he didn't need it as it was a town field and anyone could use it. He then told me that I could have my boy practice with his team. But if he did not want to practice with them, he told us we should get off the field because they were taking it. Then while he's confronting us, he goes into this spiel about him not wanting a confrontation, about how he hates confrontations. Well, this guy sounded like he had most of his screws loose, David, and I wanted nothing to do with him. So I just took Joe over to the batting cages and did some work with him there. Is this guy nuts or something?"

"Sounds like a skirmish," said David.

"Huh, what do you mean?"

"Oh, just ignore my ramblings, Nick. It's the Civil War buff in me talking." David knew it would take a long time to explain all that was going on to Nick and he might think that his Civil War take was a bit off the wall, maybe even crazy. Nick knew just enough to know that Barkus and Fog were nuts, and that was good enough for David.

"Speaking of the Civil War," Nick said, sensing an opening, "are you going to have the Babe Ruth coaches play that old-fashioned baseball game again this year?"

"I hadn't thought about it."

"Do me a favor, David, and don't think about it."

"Really? I thought teaching the kids the Knickerbocker Rules was a good lesson on the history of baseball."

"Let *them* play Civil War baseball for a day then. My kid hasn't stopped laughing since I tried to play ball last year."

"There's an idea," David said, before drifting off into thought. David believed that the Barkus strategy was to send skirmishers like Fog forward to occupy the field and to gauge his willingness to fight. David realized that he had made a tactical error in advertising to the enemy when the field would not be occupied. The Babe Ruth field calendar was up on the website for public viewing. Barkus could determine when the field was being utilized and when it was open.

"Are you there, David?"

"Sorry, Nick," David said. "I think I have an idea on how to keep Barkus and Fog from bothering you again. Leave it to me."

Before ending the call, Nick asked David how Andrew was doing and David let him know he was doing fine.

David logged on to the league website as an administrator and removed the calendar from public view. Coaches would be notified of their game schedule or anything related to their team, but they wouldn't know when the other teams were scheduled to be on the field. Barkus would now have to guess and there was too much room for error in guessing, especially since David now planned to have the field booked at all times with clinics, practices, or anything else he could arrange.

It was a little after 5:30 p.m. when David heard the entrance door open upstairs and Christy walked in.

"Hello?" said Christy in a tired voice.

"Hi," said Annie.

"Hey, Christy!" David said, trying to sound cheerful from the office. There were footsteps to the top of the stairs and the door to David's office opened. "Dad, I'm sorry, I have some bad news . . . ," Christy said, trailing off.

"Oh really, come on down and tell me about it," David said, trying to sound unfazed as his heart dropped through the floor.

Christy came downstairs hanging his head and took a seat at his computer. He looked up. "Dad, I got cut today."

David inhaled deeply once to gather himself. He did not want his emotions to show. He wanted to maintain a positive attitude. "I'm sorry, Christy. I know this must be tough on you."

Christy started to rub his forehead with his thumb and index finger so hard it looked like he was trying to strike a match. He quickly caught himself and his hands fell to his lap.

"Did Coach Singleton give you any reasons?" David asked.

Christy leaned back in his chair, and with fingers on both hands intertwined, he brought his hands to the back of his head to act as a headrest. "Yeah, I suppose, but it was strange."

"What happened?"

Christy bit his lower lip and shook his head. "Weird," he said, "real weird."

"How so?"

"I'm the last of the players to go in Coach Singleton's office and he tells me to sit down. He tells me my hitting was a little weak, which is true, even though I nailed a double today. Then he says my fielding was awesome. Then he starts telling me about Coach Powers and what he said—"

"What?" David said. "What did Coach Powers have to do with this?"

"Coach Singleton said that Coach Powers said that I was a . . . 'substandard' fielder. I think that was the word he used."

"Well, I thought Coach Singleton said you were an excellent fielder?"

"He did. He said I was the best at tryouts."

"What am I missing here?"

"Coach Powers was talking about last season."

"He has never seen you play, though." Then a light went off in David's head. "Barkus!" he spat out.

"What are you talking about, Dad?"

"Maybe Barkus told him this and Powers is parroting this information to Coach Singleton."

"Why would he do that?"

"To make sure you didn't make the team."

"Why?"

"It has nothing to do with you, Christy," David said, dropping his head. "They're doing this to get to me through you. I'm sorry, Christy."

Christy sat there for a moment and put his hand on David's shoulder. "Dad, it's okay."

"You aren't upset with me?"

"No, I'm just surprised that a coach would do such a thing. That's mean."

"Welcome to the world of youth baseball, son."

Christy sighed. "I'm not sure I like this world."

David rose and put his hands on Christy's shoulders. "Me and you both, son. Me and you both. What else did Coach Singleton say?"

"He said he was surprised that Coach Powers said this because he thought I was the best. That's about it."

"Okay. Christy, you need to realize that no matter how well you did, you weren't going to make that team. Coach Powers saw to that."

"Some guys on the team said I should have made it."

"I'm sorry, Christy. More than you know." David was trying to conceal how upset he was on the inside.

"I gave it my best shot, Dad."

"I am sure you did, but this was out of your control."

"You're not upset with me then, Dad?" Christy asked. He wanted to make the team. He wanted to show his dad he could play high school sports just like him. But if his dad wasn't upset, he wouldn't be upset either because he really didn't like most of the kids that made the team. They were the ones who badgered him during tryouts because of his dad's efforts. He had little interest in being harassed by these guys all season long during practices or games when he would likely ride the pine.

"Absolutely not."

Christy was relieved. "I can still play Babe Ruth with my friends."

"Yes, you can. You have a great attitude, Christy. Do me a favor, though."

"What's that?"

"Don't tell Mom about what Coach Powers did when you go upstairs and talk with her. Spare her that detail. I don't want to get her upset at what he did."

David knew Annie would get upset with Coach Powers if she heard that story. But that was the least of it. David knew that while she may be upset with Powers, she would be livid at him when she figured out that he might have been the cause of it. He couldn't take that now.

"Okay, Dad. Will do."

David stood up and held his hand out to Christy. Christy put his hand out and David pulled him up from the chair.

He held Christy by the shoulders and looked into his eyes. "Are you good?" David asked.

"Yeah, I'll rub some dirt on it and I'll be fine," Christy said, smiling.

David laughed. "Yeah, nothing hurts after you rub dirt on it."

Christy headed upstairs. David looked at the time and picked up the phone and dialed up Duffel, hoping to catch him before he left the office for the day.

"Hello, Wayne Duffel," said the voice on the other end.

"Hi, Wayne. It's David Thompson."

There was a pause. "What's up," Duffel blurted.

"My son Christy was just cut from the modified team. Stuff happens, but I thought team selection is about what happens *during* these tryouts."

"Yes, absolutely."

"I understand Coach Powers told Coach Singleton that Christy is a substandard fielder during tryouts."

"Well, maybe your son didn't have a great tryout."

"That's the thing. Coach Singleton said he was the best fielder there."

"How does your son know what Coach Powers said about him?"

"Coach Singleton told him that when he cut him. What's going on, Wayne? Sounds like Coach Powers is bad-mouthing my son."

There was silence on Duffel's end for a second. "I will have to look into it and get back to you."

"Do you think you can get back to me before hell freezes over, Wayne?"

"What did you say?"

"Never mind. Have a good evening, Wayne." David hung up.

He went over to the wall where all his high school athletic awards hung above his trophy case. He picked up a plaque from the wall and read it to himself as his hands began to tremble. He turned around and spotted the wastebasket next to his desk. He walked over and threw the plaque in it and paused for a brief second to gauge his feelings about what he had just done. It felt good, real good. Then he turned back to the wall of fame and removed as much as he could carry, then tossed it all into the wastebasket. Then he dragged it closer and cleared the rest off the wall and from the trophy case without hesitation, until the wastebasket was filled. He lugged it upstairs and it thumped against every step he climbed. He got to the top of the stairs.

"Annie? Annie, is it garbage night tonight?"

Annie heard him from the third floor. "Yes, it is. Why are you asking?"

"I have a load of stuff I need to take out."

"Oh, okay."

Christy saw him hauling the wastebasket by him as he was having a snack in the kitchen. "Dad, what are you doing?"

"Spring cleaning," he said abruptly as he moved toward the front entrance.

"What's the matter, Dad?"

"Nothing a little spring cleaning won't fix. I'll feel better after I take out this trash."

Christy rolled his eyes, not knowing what his dad was throwing out. He knew his dad was impulsive when it came to cleaning. His dad was perfectly comfortable with papers piled on his desk and around his office. But every so often, he would go on a cleaning binge that could last hours, sometimes days. One never knew in advance when it was time for a cleaning cycle to kick in, but Christy knew when it did kick in that his options were to help or to hide. Christy went up to his bedroom.

David had topped the garbage can with so many trophies and plaques that they overflowed. A car slowed as the driver took a glimpse of the metallic pile of silver and gold, the plaques and pictures piled over the can's rim with some ribbons and metals hanging down the side. He took it all to the curb, turned around toward the house, and never looked back.

12

THE PLAYER

That Monday night, Jerry Conway, principal of Indigo Valley High School for eight years, sat in his bed resting against two propped-up European goose down pillows that were sandwiched between his back and the bed's mahogany headboard.

His face was the shape of a thimble and his flat-top blond hair thrust upward like the bristles on a shaving brush. His face had traces of dimple lines on either side of his mouth that seemed to have faded with the onset of middle-age bloat that infected his head and his wide, athletic upper torso.

He might have been concerned with the articles on the front page of the newspaper covering the rash of high school student suicides in the bordering Mohawk City School District, which now numbered four. But his full attention was fixed on the sports section and an article covering the upcoming NFL draft. After all, Mohawk City Schools was a whole different world to Conway, a world of violence, substance abuse, and overall urban decay. Suburban Indigo Valley had no open sores along these lines. Yet for every generation to pass through the school system, there was a substance abuse incident at the high school that would make headlines in Mohawk City's *Daily Gazette*. Like clockwork that article would soon be followed by an editorial cartoon mocking the students, parents, and administrators, or at least two out of the three. The entire episode would ultimately conclude with a stream of angry letters to the editor from the offended. In time, the topic would fade, burrowing itself into the ground for a future generation to unearth in, say, thirteen years, like the life cycle of the Indigo Valley cicada: a few months of loud, unbearable screeching followed by years of silence.

Conway removed his silver Rolex from one wrist and a diamond-cut white gold bracelet, the thickness of a boy's belt, from the other and placed them both on the nightstand next to his two cell phones.

He was thinking about Josh Cribbs, the Cleveland Browns kick and punt returner sensation who was looking to renegotiate his contract. Conway wondered if he, like Josh Cribbs, had outperformed his contract with the school district and was entitled to a new one.

Then the *Mission Impossible* ringtone went off and he reached for his school cell phone. Edwin's name was flashing on the caller ID. Conway wondered why his boss, the superintendent, was calling him at eleven on a Monday night. He sighed and thought about ignoring the call. But the payoff in taking it and perpetuating the game was too big. He turned down the volume on the television and picked up the phone.

"Hi, Edwin, what's on your mind?"

"Sorry for the late-night call, Jerry. I couldn't sleep."

"What's bothering you?"

"I'm getting heat from a few on the board of ed."

"What's the problem?"

"You're the problem."

He had to shift the phone to his left ear. His right ear was sore from pressing his phone against it so much. "What did I do?"

"We're getting those letters again."

"What, more anonymous ones about me?"

"Yes, and what you're doing—"

"Edwin, we've covered this ground before—"

"Don't cut me off, Jerry. Listen, you need to keep our name out of it. We don't want our name associated with your doings. The district has a reputation to uphold. Jesus Christ, if I had known years ago what you were going to do, I would have, we would have . . . well, you know . . . . "

"What would you have done differently, Edwin?"

"I don't know . . . but I would've done something."

Conway knew that Edwin's words were empty. He knew Edwin would do nothing because he wanted to be liked. Edwin wanted to be thought of as

one of the boys and not some buzzkill at a party. Besides, Edwin was in too deep. His fate was tied to Conway's now. Conway knew he would outlast Edwin, just like he had with the previous superintendent, just like he would outlast the superintendent after Edwin.

"Look, Edwin, I've been trying to keep the district's name out of it—"

"If you had done a better job, we wouldn't see so many letters then."

"Edwin, don't worry, these letters never amount to anything."

Conway knew that parents in the know would look the other way long enough to see their kids graduate. He knew they would never emerge from the anonymity of their letters to do anything to jeopardize their child's high school experience and their futures.

"They're still some board members who think there's a conflict of interest in what you're doing," Edwin said.

"Doesn't matter. They don't have the numbers to do anything."

Over the years, the board of education had become accustomed to doing nothing in the face of these letters, as doing something would involve too much effort and too much conflict. Instead, the board and the school district were determined to produce the usual pat-on-the-back press releases announcing the excellence of the Indigo Valley School District as determined by some media outlet analyzing its performance on state-mandated tests. Nobody bothered to check beneath the surface to see if graduates were being placed in comparable college programs at a rate in line with other high schools in the region. That would be too much like meaningful work. Appearances, as marked by standardized test scores, were the only thing that mattered to those who believed that David's hill was an Indian burial mound.

"Yeah, well, Carl Strock is kicking the tires again and asking around," Edwin said. Strock was an investigative reporter for the *Daily Gazette*.

Conway's other cell phone was buzzing now. He picked it up and looked at the caller ID. He grimaced and wanted to hang up with Edwin to take the call. Conway didn't care about Strock. He figured he'd outlast him too. Like Edwin, Strock was getting on in years. "Okay, well, thanks for the heads-up, Edwin—"

"Don't be flip with me, Jerry; this doesn't look good. Strock is damn good at what he does. He could blow the lid on this. He's causing me all kinds of headaches."

"Okay, I'll try and keep the district's name out of it. Anything else?"

"Yeah, where were you during the varsity basketball game Friday night when those kids were caught with alcohol in their water bottles?"

It was too late—the other call dropped to voice mail. Conway closed his eyes and tossed that cell phone on the bed. "I had some personal business to attend to—"

"You and your personal business. What personal business was so important that you couldn't be at that game?"

"Edwin, I told you never to ask me about my business."

"Okay, hotshot, whatever you say. Anyway, it doesn't look good when you're not at the school when the shit hits the fan. What if something happened at school while you were traveling on business?"

"You know you can always reach me. I always pick up your calls."

"Yeah, you're good about that. Well, I hope nothing happens when you're away from the building on your personal business. We're screwed if it does. It'll rain lawsuits."

"Edwin, you need to relax. This isn't Mohawk City, you know. It's not like there's a crisis every minute. Besides, my assistant principals will cover for me. Look, these things are going to happen. I can't keep kids away from alcohol. They're going to find it."

"Just keep it out of the school. We can't have it in the school. Anyplace but the school."

"How about your front lawn?" Conway joked, hoping to change the subject.

"Very funny. Did you hear about that?"

"Yeah."

"Goddamn kids throwing beer cans on the lawn late at night. My wife called the cops. She's afraid they're going to try and break into the house now."

"Why are the kids picking on you? Do you have any idea where this is coming from?"

My wife thinks it has to do with the article that was run recently, and how much I make in relation to all the other superintendents in the area. Who the fuck knows? Kids . . . ."

Edwin's cussing always seemed out of place to Conway. Cussing just didn't go with Edwin's bow ties and fancy degrees; he sounded like a schoolboy trying too hard to fit in with the cool crowd.

"Tell me about it," Conway said.

"Do you know any of the kids caught at the game?"

"I looked at the names and I don't know them—"

"You never seem to know them. Don't you know any of the kids at school?"

"Hey, you told me on day one when you came in as superintendent that my job was to report to you and manage the building. Anyway, I know them by their faces, pretty much—"

"Sure, sure. Whatever you do, you know not to bring the police in on it. I don't want the hassle from the parents and the press. Keep it quiet."

"I know the drill, Edwin."

"I'll call you tomorrow." And with that, Edwin hung up.

Conway sat there. He didn't like being pushed around by Edwin; he didn't like being pushed around by anyone.

He put his feet on the floor and stood up, his pajama bottom cuffs flowing down his hairy, skinny calves to his ankles as he slid into his slippers. Conway's knee was stiff from an injury dating back to his football days. He picked up the television remote from his bed and walked over to the computer on his desk. He looked at the monitor to read something. His face cringed like a prune as his head recoiled back from the screen. He leaned back in his chair. His index finger and thumb stroked his chin as he thought. His other hand brushed his crew cut. Conway wanted to respond to what he saw on his screen. But he didn't know if he might be crossing the line. It was late and he was tired, and so the line was blurry and grew fuzzy as the night wore on. He wondered if he should wait until morning to do something about it. Maybe he would wake up with a new perspective. But as he sat there, the anger did not subside. It ate at him and Edwin fueled the fire. He wanted to do something: he wanted to show this son of a bitch that he was watching and that he was a man not to be messed with. He vacillated between waiting until morning and doing something right there so he could go to sleep with a sense of satisfaction, a reaffirmation of his status as a big shot.

He picked up the remote and turned the volume up. *Godfather II* was on the screen. Conway continued to stroke his chin as he leaned back to watch, gently swiveling in his chair. Fredo Corleone and Michael Corleone were arguing:

Fredo: I'm your older brother, Mike, and I was stepped over!

Michael: That's the way Pop wanted it.

Fredo: It ain't the way I wanted it! I can handle things! I'm smart! Not like everybody says . . . like dumb. I'm smart and I want respect!

That's all Conway needed to hear to push him over the edge, to set him on his task. There was no hesitation as he rolled back up to his computer and started banging on his keyboard. Though he had been on the panel of a school anti-bullying conference just a few days earlier, that didn't bother him in what he was about to do. All that bullshit applied to kids, not to important men who should be shown respect. Yes, Fredo had said it all. It was all about getting respect. The e-mail he was about to send would serve notice not to mess with him:

Peter,

Who the hell are you? You know me???

If you did, you would know that my marketing days are in the rearview mirror.

You should focus on your thriving law practice and scribing of current briefs before you comment about me.

Regards,

J. O. Conway President, J. O. Enterprises

Conway did not reread the e-mail before pulling the trigger. He was sure of it. He pressed the send key and off it went like a night train to its destination. Ignorance and apathy in Indigo Valley had given Conway the freedom to dream and to dream big, to dream of being more than an unknown principal of a nondescript suburban high school in an unknown upstate New York town. His salary was good at $118,000 and climbing. He had great health benefits and a generous pension in the works and all he had to do was punch the clock and go through the motions. But Conway wanted to be more than a caretaker to a bunch of kids. He wanted to make a name for himself; he wanted to achieve fame and fortune; he longed to be feared and revered; he wanted to be a player.

13

THE GODFATHER

The next morning, David checked in at the Mohawk City jail and was led to a small, private visitation room to meet with Stanley Moss. The odor of sweat, urine, feces, and Pine-Sol was busy peeling the institutional green paint from the walls. He entered and saw Moss sitting there in his orange jumpsuit.

"My name is David Thompson," he said, reaching out to shake Stanley Moss's hand. Moss took it and squeezed hard and, for a second, was reluctant to release his grip. His eyes locked on David's.

"Stan Moss," he said. "Glad you're on time," he grumbled. "Most lawyers are late."

David let the hostility slide. Anyone in jail for the first time was allowed to be cranky. "I do my best," he said.

Moss sat down on one side of the small table. David waited for him to sit down before seating himself.

Moss had a chiseled face with a reddish-orange complexion that complemented his bright orange jumpsuit. He was of medium build, below average height. No wrinkles on his face. He looked younger than his age of sixty, though his obvious rug suggested he was trying to hide his years.

David had reviewed the file that Jim had sent over to him. Moss was a thirty-five-year employee in the grounds and maintenance department of the Mohawk City School District. He was the facilities manager and a union boss at the Mohawk City school system. He had been arrested a week earlier and faced a number of charges from more than a decade-long crime spree aimed at people who crossed him on his job or who crossed his friends. According to the file, the grand jury had met numerous times and heard nearly fifty witnesses. Although the indictment had not been handed down, Jim had written down what he expected in formal charges: arson, terrorism, counts of criminal mischief, criminal possession of weapons, attempted coercion, and more. David knew if the district attorney were to bat a mere .250 in convictions, Moss would be lucky to ever see the light of day as a free man.

"Jim Fletcher asked me to serve as co-counsel. I assume you have discussed this with him?"

"It was my idea to put you on the team."

Jim had indicated to David that acting as co-counsel was his idea, not Moss's. He did not know what to make of it, but decided to play along. "Do I know you?" he asked.

"No, but I know about you. I make it my business to know about everybody. I know you are friends with Jim. Read it in the *Daily Gazette* a few years ago when you guys were given some lawyer award for helping out that homeless family."

"Oh, I didn't know that was in the newspaper."

"Yeah, it was a small article in the local section, about halfway in, toward the bottom of the page. You didn't see it?"

"I don't read the newspaper often."

"I do. Every morning down at the office. Need to know what's going on, who's doing what."

David smiled; Moss reciprocated with a bigger one.

"I came down here to review the case with you," David said, reaching for his satchel.

"Yeah, okay, but I got to tell you that you're not on the team yet."

"I don't understand. Do you want my help or not?" David said, while pulling out the file Jim had given him.

"Maybe, depends how the interview goes."

Moss now grinned ear to ear, eyes again locked on David. David thought his demeanor was out of proportion to his dire circumstances.

"So you're interviewing me?"

"Yep."

David set the file folder down on the table and leaned back in his chair, crossing his arms.

"What's wrong?" Moss asked.

"Jim didn't indicate that there might be a problem with me serving as cocounsel."

"Well, that's because I didn't tell him there might be a problem. You might as well learn right now that I call the shots."

David picked up his pen and started rolling it between his fingers and thumbs below his chin, trying to assess what he might have gotten himself into. He looked back at Moss, who hadn't taken his eyes off him.

"What do you want to know about me?" David asked.

"You live in Indigo Valley, right?"

"Yes, I do," answered David. He wondered where this was going.

"Me too. I live right down from Indigo Valley High School, a couple blocks away. I got a lot of friends in Indigo Valley whose kids go to the high school. I know a lot of guys in the custodial department there from me being president of my union unit."

David wanted to take the conversation back to Moss's background. "I understand you had a dual role as union president and facilities manager for the school system."

David knew he was being kind in terming it as a "dual role." He viewed it as a conflict of interest that placed Moss in a powerful position. When the union workers had a complaint against management, it was Stanley Moss they were complaining to or about, the same man who happened to be their union president, the same man who would allegedly become their worst enemy upon learning of any complaint against him as manager. This conflict of interest between the two positions allowed Moss to effectively silence employees and gain power with the administration as their problems disappeared.

"Yeah, in those two positions, did you know I reduced the number of grievances from dozens down to zero?"

David replied, "So I understand." In David's mind, everyone in Moss's unit had come to understand the consequences of complaining to Stan about Stan.

Moss went on. "The administration loves me for taking them to zero. Here's a funny story. The director of human resources gave me a photo of Marlon Brando, the godfather, during a staff meeting." Moss broke out into laughter. Then he suddenly stopped. "They think I'm like Don Moss or something. One day I even get a call from this guy in labor relations and he tells me that the union higher-ups see me as the godfather too and are scared shitless of me."

David sat silently and twirled his pen and thought about Barkus. *Two godfathers within a few days*, he thought.

"What do you do with your spare time?" Moss asked.

David wondered why Moss was so intent on wrestling the direction of the conversation from him. Moss leaned forward over the desk and rubbed his lips together. "Tell me," he said.

David leaned forward himself and put his pen down. "Okay, if you need to know, I help with a baseball program in the town. That takes up a great deal of my time."

Moss sported a huge smile. "That's nice. You help kids. Good sign of character. It takes up a lot of your time, you say?"

"Yes."

"Do you think you have enough time to work my case?"

"I'll do what I have to do to make time. Jim and I are a good team."

"Fair enough. Your son must play ball then?"

David picked up his pen again. His cobalt eyes locked on Moss. "How did you know?"

"Well, I just assumed your son played. Why else would you be involved?"

"No, that's not my point. You said 'son,' not 'sons.' You assumed I had just one son."

"Did I? I didn't mean anything by it, thought you had at least one boy playing then."

Moss started to speak faster. "I'm tired. You know, they keep passing me from one court to another, arresting me again and again in different juris-dictions so I can't get out on bail easily. I understand they're planning to file a trumped-up terrorism charge to deny me bail, to keep me in jail."

Suddenly, his veins popped out of his neck, his face as red as a cherry bomb. "Listen, I'm no fucking terrorist!" he said, his eyes bulging. "Jesus Christ, I didn't fly no plane into the World Trade Center. I served my country in Vietnam in combat and was given an honorable discharge!" He pounded the table. "It's not like they say that I killed anybody or anything. Shit, I never hurt anyone! I've got a clean record. I deserve to be out on bail. I'm entitled to that right. "

David recognized the entitlement argument from his dealings with Barkus. David opened the redwell file and flipped through some papers. He knew what Moss said was true, that he didn't kill or hurt anyone physically, though he easily could have. His mode of operation was different. His aim was to get into the minds of his victims, to instill fear by acts of vandalism and bombings accompanied by suggestions that he was behind it all. It was psychological warfare at its best.

"Can we go over your case now?" David said while reading the file. Moss's color began to turn back to its normal reddish-orange hue; his veins subsided.

"Our discussion is protected by attorney-client privilege, right? I mean, you're not officially on the team yet, understand? I don't want what I say to be used against me."

"You're right, you're protected," David said.

"We understand each other then?" Moss said with his eyes fixated on David.

"I think I just agreed with you," David said, looking up from his papers briefly.

"Good. Let's talk about the DiNapoli charge."

DiNapoli was the athletic director at Mohawk City High School. Moss's reign of terror allegedly was not limited to his workers.

David turned a page in his file. "We can get to that in good time. It might help me to understand things better if we did this chronologically."

"I want to talk about the DiNapoli charge."

David stopped and looked up at Moss. He wondered if this man was going to be an uncooperative client. He pulled the DiNapoli folder from his file. "What's on your mind then?"

"DiNapoli is full of himself. He thought he was better than me and better than others in the district." Moss looked for a response from David.

"What's your point? Are you saying he got what he deserved?"

"He crossed the line."

"I read your e-mail to him where you said exactly that." David flipped through his file. He located the e-mail and started reading from it: "'You have crossed a line with me. I am not a tolerant person to begin with. I'm even less tolerant of people who show me disrespect.'" David looked up. "Do you like instilling fear in people?" he asked Moss.

Moss leaned back in his chair and folded his hands behind his head. "With a little fear, you get a certain type of respect."

David picked up his pen and started spinning it again. "I think with a little fear, you respect that person's ability to hurt you. Nothing more."

"Works for me. How else was I gonna talk to these people? I have one hundred and ten employees under me and we're not talking about a bunch of educated, refined people. They're like me; most of them have no degrees or anything. You got to talk to these people in a certain way, a way they understand, a way that gets the job done with the least amount of bullshit in return. I don't have time for bullshit 'cause I get flak from all directions. I got these administrators and teachers, like DiNapoli, who look down on me and they want to be treated differently. Well, that's not me. I treat everyone the same. I can't change."

David's eyebrows rose. "Weren't you withholding keys and codes from DiNapoli so his coaches could not access the athletic facilities?"

"I had problems with people giving out keys and passing them around, so I couldn't keep track of who had what. It was a security risk. But that's not the point. It doesn't make any difference. He should have come to talk with me man to man, worked it through the chain of command."

"You shouldn't rat on the godfather, right?" David said, testing the waters of Moss's mindset, knowing full well that the chain of command had a Moss backer at the top with the superintendent, and Moss's boss beneath him in the role of assistant superintendent.

"That's right. He went over my head to the superintendent, questioned my authority, and showed me great disrespect. I got thirty-five years' time at the district and he thought he was better than me. He was being a wise ass by going to the superintendent. I don't like punks and wise guys; they should get what they deserve."

The veins on Moss's forehead popped for a second as he continued his rant. "So DiNapoli goes to the administration and says it was me who did his house and he also wants his keys and access. They say it's a police matter and tell him to forget fighting about the keys and codes and all; they tell him not to fight it 'cause what's the point if he's going to retire in six months and, besides, he can't win anyway. At the end of the day, the administration backs me and does nothing."

David put his pen down. He rested his chin on his hand with his elbow on the table to support it. He looked at Moss. "The DA indicates that they have someone who will testify that you called them that night looking for DiNapoli's home address. Then the next morning DiNapoli found his tires slashed and a bomb under his windshield wipers."

"So what, there is no proof that I did that stuff. They got no, what do you call it, forensic evidence. Enough of DiNapoli. Let's talk about you. What baseball ages are you involved with?"

Here we go again, David thought, pushing himself back in the chair. "Look, I've got a lot to cover here—"

"Hey, did you forget? I'm interviewing you."

David sighed. "Ages thirteen through eighteen."

"Do you play on a major-league-sized infield at thirteen?"

"Yes."

"You must play on the Babe Ruth field, over in the town park."

"Yes, you know of it?"

"I've been there."

"You've seen games there then?

"No, I've seen the lights on early in the morning a few times when I was up and about. I wondered what the heck was going on there at 4:00 a.m. 'cause those lights cost money. I know that from my work."

"That was probably me working the field. It's my second home during the season."

"Really? Why are you there so early?"

"Probably couldn't sleep. Can we talk about your case some more?"

"Are you there that early often?"

"Yes, Mr. Moss, can we please focus on your case?"

"Okay, let's talk about the White charges."

"All right," said David. It wasn't the item that David wanted to discuss but it at least moved them off the topic of his personal life. David located his folder on the White charges and opened it on his lap.

"Now, White is a backstabbing jerk," Moss said. "He worked in my unit. His wife wrote a letter to the boss in my union saying I was running my shop like a gangster movie and saying I could not be head of my unit and a manager at the same time."

"Wasn't the letter anonymous? How did you know she wrote it?" David asked, thumbing through his papers.

"It's my business to know."

David started reading from his file. "Okay, the DA says you vandalized their home a few months later—spray painted 'Rat' on their house on all four sides with red paint, and sprayed their vehicle as well."

"They got what they deserved," Moss said, staring at the ceiling.

"Is that all you have to say?"

Moss looked at David. "No, the lesson to the story is that you shouldn't rat on your boss or justice will catch up to you."

David began rubbing the back of his neck with his head tilted back. "You mean street justice?"

"Sometimes the only justice is street justice. I'll always believe in street justice. Anyway, there is no proof I did any of that."

David returned to his file. "Then, the DA says, you had a van of ten of your employees drive over on work time to see the vandalized home the day after."

"So what?"

"You did it on district time and in district vehicles? Didn't the administrators care?"

"Not really. They back me. And I don't rat on them."

"The DA says over the course of the next few years you vandalized the White vehicles several more times."

"He can say all he wants. Too bad their lives have been miserable. Did you know they installed some security cameras at their house and White slept with a shotgun under his bed? Imagine that."

Moss hit a nerve. It was easy for David to imagine that. Sometimes he slept with his Sharps carbine by his nightstand or under his bed.

Moss went on. "He and his wife have some drill they go through when they hear a noise 'round the house at night. White sneaks around the house like he's back in Nam and the Vietcong are outside. They wonder every night if someone is coming to bomb them or set their house on fire. Can you imagine living like that? Can you imagine you're so afraid that you sleep with a shotgun under your bed? Can you?"

David knew this feeling too well, but he wasn't going to share this with Moss. "How do you know what the Whites do?" David asked.

"It's my business to know. But I got to tell you, whoever did this was smart."

David decided to go along with Moss's implicit denial of involvement. "How so?"

"It's fear when you find out someone can touch you at home. There's no other fear like that. You come to realize that you are only protected so far no matter how you cut it. There's nothing more fearful than knowing you're not safe in your own home. You wonder if the guy who hit your house is out there every night. Is tonight the night that he burns your house down? Is tonight the night he blows your car up? Your mind plays tricks on you; every sound you hear or imagine could be him. You get exhausted being on watch night after night. You become your own worst enemy. Thinking or knowing some guy was at your house or even in your yard, that's an icky, awful feeling, don't you think?"

Moss was leaning forward with the fingers of both hands interlocked, placed on the table. David looked up and met his face. Moss's eyes were wide open; his forehead was furrowed.

"I guess you're right," David said, noting to himself that Moss's elucidation on the topic pointed toward his involvement.

Moss leaned back in his chair with a grin on his face. "You know, they're treating me like I'm the most dangerous man in New York State. They don't look at the bigger picture; I'm all about helping people. You know what also hangs in my office besides a picture of the Godfather?"

"No."

"A picture of the Lone Ranger, which everyone can see. I've given jobs and saved jobs for lots of people. I do favors for people all the time. I take care of my friends. I want you to understand that. Do you hear what I'm saying?"

"I think so," David said. He knew that a few of the vandalism strikes were allegedly done as favors for his friends. One of them took place in Schodack. He wasn't sure if that's what Moss was talking about or if he was saying something about his own character in general. He decided to try to discuss the Schodack incident.

"You do know that in Schodack the DA has said that they've lifted some DNA from a cigarette used as part of a fuse device. They are suggesting that it's yours."

Moss leaned forward and made a steeple with his hands as he set them on the table. "They also say I'm a terrorist. They can say what they want to say, and they'll say anything to keep me in jail without bail. Proving it in court is another matter. I'm done with this interview."

"What do you mean?"

"I've got nothing more to say. My interview is over."

Moss stood up and looked toward the door. "Officer," he called. "Officer!" The door opened and two officers entered. "We're done," Moss told them. They began to escort him back to his cell. He turned to David as he walked out. "I'll get back to you if I want you," he said, smiling as he left the room. David sat there in total disbelief.

14

AT WIT'S END

David was in a foul mood when he rolled into the Yellow Ribbon Diner a little before 7:00 p.m. on Tuesday. His jailhouse meeting with Stanley Moss had been as productive as Detective Starling's first meeting with Hannibal Lecter in *Silence of the Lambs*. David had spent the remainder of the afternoon writing an e-mail to Jim about it.

When David entered, Johnny was already seated in a back-corner booth —the largest one in the diner—chatting with a waitress. David walked down the aisle of booths and checked the faces of folks to make sure he didn't recognize anyone from Indigo Valley. David chose the Yellow Ribbon Diner because it was in Mohawk City and most people from Indigo Valley rarely ventured there, especially after dark and on a weeknight.

If you imagined a cider doughnut—a favorite treat baked at the local orchards—Indigo Valley and the other surrounding suburban communities were viewed as the sweet, sugary outside while Mohawk City was viewed as the hole in the middle—a shadowy, vacant space where danger lurked. Despite the valiant efforts of the city to change its perception through renewal efforts, avoidance of Mohawk City had been a trait passed down from one generation of Indigo Valley families to the next as they cycled through the school district.

David wanted to make sure that anything that might be overheard in the diner didn't travel to the town baseball rumor circuit. He didn't see anyone he knew when he walked in, and Johnny had found himself a private booth away from the dinnertime crowd. They exchanged greetings and Johnny introduced the waitress to him as Susan. She poured them coffees, a cup of decaf for David and a cup of high-test for Johnny. "You know her?" David asked, taking off his windbreaker. "I went to high school with her mother. She's a cute girl, isn't she?"

"Yeah, sure. She has no connection to baseball anywhere, does she?" Johnny watched David fumble to hang his jacket on a hook beside the booth. "No, none that I know of anyway." David looked around the diner once more. Nobody was within easy earshot. "Geez," Johnny said, "that's a strange question. What's wrong with you anyway?" David leaned over to Johnny across the table and spoke softly. "I feel like

I've been dealing with the mob this past week." "What's going on?" "One of Barkus's toadies kicked one of the Babe Ruth coaches off the field." "Did they push the coach around or anything?" "No, it didn't escalate to anything physical." David's eyes darted around the diner and out the window. He brought his hands together and clenched them on the table. "Okay then," Johnny said. "They took the field. What are you going to do about it?"

"Nothing."

"Nothing? I would have gone over to the field and kicked them off and cracked some headlights with a bat."

"It might be that I don't want to get disbarred over baseball if I can help it," David said. "I want to pick the time and place of battle. They wanted a confrontation there and then; it's not in my nature to give the enemy what they want, when they want it."

"Okay then, so what're you going to do about it *now*?"

"'I can do nothing with the enemy save observe him,'" David said, recalling these exact words as written by General John Buford during his frustrating pursuit of Lee's army after Gettysburg.

"Nothing? Is that your middle name or something?" David responded, "What's there to do now? Complain to my board? I feel surrounded by guys that are plotting my demise. Did you know a majority of our board's kids play for Elite Travel?"

"That's not right," Johnny said.

"Yes, it's a conflict of interest. They are supposed to be promoting Babe Ruth baseball and instead they are promoting something that undermines it."

"I suppose you can't remove them from the board."

"I'm afraid I'm only one vote, and that won't get the job done. They're not going to vote themselves off the board. Our president, Jack Masters, tries every so often to set them straight but acts more often like a stack of waffles—"

"Can't make up his mind?"

"One day his head is as clear as glass; the next day it's as clear as mud. He's got a hundred things on his mind due to work and his family and he's got the entire league to run and not just the Babe Ruth component. So he is in a LIFO state of mind when it comes to this situation."

"LIFO?" Johnny asked, looking for clarification.

"Yes, LIFO means 'last in, first out.' It's an accounting term. Whatever position Jack heard last from someone is the one he has at that point in time. There are a bunch of vocal guys on our board whose kids play in the Elite Travel Baseball League and who want access to the field. And that's not even counting Barkus, who is not on our board but influences votes on account of his big mouth and his e-mail blitzes. Odds are that Jack has heard all day long from these guys that Elite Baseball should be allowed on the field. That's all he hears except from me. The only way to counter that is for me to be with Jack all day and night, to remind him of right from wrong. I can't move in with Jack and be with him twenty-four/seven. People would talk, you know."

Johnny started laughing.

"I'm glad you find such humor in my misery," David said.

"You have to be able to laugh when you do this line of work or it will eat away at you," Johnny said. "These Elite guys really take the cake. You don't know the half of it, though."

"What do you mean?"

"You only know what's going on from your perspective, in your town. Multiply what you have experienced times thirty, because that is the number of leagues in the region that are being impacted by the Elite Travel league. I'm at my wit's end with this." Johnny's head drooped. "There's only so much I can take or do. I'm on the phone all day trying to do anything to keep our Babe Ruth leagues from getting eaten alive by Elite Travel."

Johnny looked out the window. The sun was setting. It had been a good day for playing baseball. Johnny looked down at his hands resting on the table and began opening and closing them like butterfly wings. David could see the whiteness of dry skin and the calluses on his hands, calluses now derived from packing and unpacking endless boxes of meat as opposed to swinging a bat. Johnny looked up. David saw that Johnny's complexion looked yellow in the sunlight, like he was jaundiced. For a second, David thought he saw the passing image of a ghost. Johnny leaned forward out of the light and his face flushed with a new thought. A grin came over his face. "So I've decided to make a life-changing decision."

"I'm afraid to ask what that might be—"

"Time to hit the bottle and do some drugs," Johnny said.

David chuckled. He didn't know what to think except that Johnny seemed to enjoy keeping him off balance.

Johnny's eyebrows fluttered. "You think I'm kidding?"

"I don't know what to think anymore. My head just spins day after day."

"Has baseball made you reach for the bottle yet?"

David was hesitant about where the conversation was heading but decided to go with the flow. "Sober as a choirboy for now."

"Well, I used to drink and do coke. I've snorted a boatload of snow in my life."

"Am I supposed to find comfort in your revelation?" David asked as he squirmed in his seat.

"It's true. Drugs and drinking were an obsession at one point in my life. I have had some run-ins with the law."

"The drinking and drug use caught up with you then?" David said, wondering what he had gotten himself into with Johnny.

"No, it is what I did while drinking and on drugs."

David sat up and elongated his neck while his eyes darted around the diner one more time. He realized that his world had now become about thugs and drugs. Johnny McFadden might as well have been Stanley Moss at that point. David's instinct was to leave Johnny and his world behind.

"What are you doing?" asked Johnny.

"I'm looking for the nearest exit in case I have to make a quick getaway."

Johnny laughed.

"I am glad you find humor in all this."

"You don't have to worry any. I don't drink or do drugs anymore."

"Oh, I'm happy for you," David said sarcastically, wondering if the volunteer work Johnny did for Babe Ruth was part of some kind of work-release program. "So you say you're no longer a crackhead?" David asked.

"Technically, I *was* a cokehead. But no longer. Quit cold turkey."

"How did you manage that?" David asked, looking out to the parking lot.

"I found that the best cure for one addiction is to replace it with another. I'm addicted to baseball now."

David sipped his coffee and tried to gather his thoughts. He was partly relieved to discover someone who seemed to be crazier than him over baseball, but at the same time, he wondered if there was any boundary to Johnny's craziness, or if he lived his life totally outside of fair territory.

"Don't you feel," David said, treading carefully, "that any addiction might prove unhealthy?"

"Not with baseball. You know, the rhythm of a baseball game is soothing. It's a game of ones: *one* pitch, *one* out, *one* inning, *one* game at a time." Johnny spoke slowly and gestured with his hands as if he were performing a poetry reading. "But at the same time," Johnny added before biting his chapped lower lip, "baseball is drama, it's war in the form of a game. It heightens the senses and commands your attention. The rhythm and the drama make you forget whatever had you feeling worried, sad, or angry. Baseball softens life's edges and keeps you engaged in a story that's being told with every pitch. Baseball *is* good medicine."

David looked at Johnny and wondered how such eloquence flowed from a man so rough on the surface.

"How long have you been helping with Babe Ruth?" David asked.

"I don't know," Johnny said, "must be going on ten years now—ever since I stopped snorting coke. You know, I coach Babe Ruth baseball and live it when I'm not trying to make a living. When I was a kid, I played Babe Ruth. It was important to me then in dealing with my life; now it helps me deal with my adult life."

"Tell me, Johnny, what's your title with Babe Ruth anyway?"

Johnny thought for a second and ran his hand over his slick hair, front to back. The smile was gone. He clenched his teeth. "Why the fuck do I feel like I'm being cross-examined by Sylvester Shyster here? What's in a title? Do you think this is some kind of Fortune 500 outfit? We're a bunch of volunteers for Babe Ruth. There's Brad but there are others too. Our kids have aged out of the local leagues and we share a common interest to try and keep community baseball going in our area, outside of our hometowns."

David was taken aback by Johnny's mood swing. "Sorry, Johnny. I'm sorry I upset you. It's just that Brad made a point of saying you weren't on his staff and so I was trying to figure out your role. I thought your title might be a good indication."

"Why would I want to be on his staff?" Johnny asked.

"I give up," David said. "You tell me."

"The answer is that I don't want to be on his staff."

"You two don't get along or something?" David asked.

"No, we get along just fine," Johnny said.

"So, why are you giving me this attitude then about being on his staff?"

"Look, you may think we are dealing in just youth baseball, but we are dealing in so much more," Johnny said. "We're dealing with the dreams of dads to see their sons play in college or the big leagues. We are also dealing with a bunch of very large egos either running the leagues or coaching teams. And they all aren't necessarily dads of the kids playing baseball." Johnny lifted his coffee and took a few sips.

David cupped his head between his hands and rubbed his cheekbones. He pulled down the skin around his eye sockets to reveal his red eyeballs. "Now what were we just talking about?" he said. "Oh, yeah . . . so what does all this have to do with being on Brad's staff?"

"Well, if you wait a minute, I'll get there," Johnny said, putting his cup down. "Now, sometimes these guys get out of control and do crazy things that are not in the interest of Babe Ruth or their leagues or their teams. You see, we need some way to deal with these people. We also need some way to reward all those that are loyal to Babe Ruth. Sometimes we need to do things that Babe Ruth and Brad shouldn't be involved in directly."

"What is this, the mafia or something?" David said. "God, I'm tired. Two minutes ago I was talking to a crackhead—"

"Cokehead."

"Whatever," David said, lowering his voice. "And now I feel like I need to check to see if your friend, the waitress, is wired."

Johnny looked half amused and half surprised as his bushy eyebrows did a double take up his forehead. "You're nuts."

"Am I? That's how they arrested Moss in Mohawk City, you know." David took a sip of coffee. "Do you know about him?"

"Yeah, I read the papers."

"They had a cop wired and he all but confessed to the bombings."

"What does Moss have to do with baseball?" Johnny asked.

David sat quiet. He didn't feel like explaining to Johnny that he had met two godfathers in the past few days in Barkus and Moss, especially since he thought that Johnny sounded like a third.

"You're paranoid," Johnny said. "But we can check the waitress for a wire if you want." He spotted her a few tables away. "Hey, Susan, could you come here?"

Susan turned from the table she was serving. "I'll be there in a minute, Johnny."

"Now you're the one who's nuts," David said. "I was just making a point. You think I'm nuts? Check the mirror."

Johnny laughed. "Who's the one who came in casing the place looking for anyone with a baseball cap who might be suspicious?"

"Was I that obvious?"

"Yeah, and then you asked if Susan had anything to do with baseball. You're checking to see if you're in a den of spies yourself."

Susan walked over. "What can I do for you guys?"

Johnny did a double take with the eyebrows again and smiled. He tilted the coffee cup up and finished it, then set it down.

"I'd like another cup of coffee," said Johnny. David was relieved. "And then my friend here would like to check you for a wire." David spat out what coffee remained in his mouth as he put down his cup. Johnny started laughing. Susan looked bemused.

"I think my friend, David, here also needs a bib when you get a chance," Johnny said. "Maybe one of those lobster bibs."

"Don't listen to him. He's nuts," said David.

"Johnny, are you up to no good again?" said Susan with a deadpan look as she cleaned up the spat coffee up with a dishrag. Then she lifted a pot of fresh brew from a nearby burner to fill David's cup.

"Afraid so, Susan."

"I am just going to ignore you then, hun." Off she went to another table.

"So what were we talking about?" asked Johnny.

"We were talking about your short-term-memory problem—"

"You're a funny guy. Oh, yeah, so there are things that need to be done sometimes and Brad shouldn't have anything to do with those things as state commissioner."

"Right, any good covert operation needs plausible deniability at the top," said David, recalling Admiral John Poindexter's testimony in the Iran-Contra affair in the late 1980s.

"Plausible deniability?"

"Yeah, it's the ability of the top dog to say he knew nothing about what the rest of the pack did. The pack acts as enforcers, soldiers, and hit men doing all the dirty work while the head man stays clean and above it all."

"Wow, you said it better than I ever could," Johnny said seriously.

David laughed. "Yeah, but I was just kidding."

"I'm being serious."

David sat there flummoxed. He wasn't sure who was crazier at this point: Barkus or Johnny. "You mean to tell me that youth baseball has become like a covert operation? So what do you do then? Do you break legs and make people disappear all in the name of youth baseball?"

Johnny laughed. "No, no . . . we have our ways, though, through more subtle, nonviolent means."

"I'm afraid to ask what that involves."

"One word: *control*. First off, there's the control of all the district and state tournaments. We award those based on a league's loyalty and support of our efforts. We can also achieve a lot when we control a team's schedule in our league: quality of the opponent, amount of travel, date and time of game. We can basically make or break a team's season right there. We can arrange no-show games where the other team doesn't show up. Then we can give teams exactly what they want and screw up their season that way."

"How does giving them what they want mess with their lives?"

"When they request something and we just give them what they want, knowing full well that things will not work out for them. If they want to play too many games or travel to a shithole, we just give them what they want without saying a thing."

"You're an asshole."

"Yes, but I'm an asshole with good intentions, a benevolent asshole if you will."

"Must be nice being God."

"Right, I'm God and I drive a meat wagon." Johnny savored that thought for a moment before letting out a burst of laughter.

"You need some serious help, Johnny."

"I'm not sure anyone can help me in a way that I need. If I'm God, then Barkus and Morgan are the devil. We're losing our Babe Ruth travel teams to these clowns all over the place."

"So these guys are not just our town problem?"

"No, they're everyone's problem. And we are at the breaking point."

"What do you mean?"

"Well, you get to a point where so many teams are leaving that the ones left look around and see that they're only one of a few remaining. So they think their season will be no more than playing the same five teams over and over again. They look at the Elite Travel Baseball League and see all the teams over there. The remaining teams leave in one flush within hours of one another, leaving you with a vacant league. We're at that point now—"

"Oh, that's wonderful news," David said, rolling his eyes at the ceiling. "I'm a fool then."

"What's wrong?"

"If you guys are about to raise the surrender flag, I have just launched the equivalent of Picket's ill-fated charge at Gettysburg. I'm telling the school that they should support our Babe Ruth travel and our in-house program, but now you're telling me that its travel program is about to fold. Beautiful."

"Dude, I have fought for over five years to keep this boat afloat. I can't take it no more. My business is going down the tubes because the economy sucks. My wife, Joan, who does the scheduling for Babe Ruth travel, is currently disabled. I don't even know my daughter. . . ."

"I'm sorry," David said. "I didn't know."

David sat silent and sipped his coffee, lost in thought, while Johnny stared out the window. This guy, this meat salesman, and his disabled wife had taken a stand in their lives to help teenage boys play baseball and keep the communities intact from the ravages of travel baseball. David looked at Johnny's forehead. He had a scar that began at his hairline and disappeared in his thick brown hair. There were other scars too. David thought he must have gotten them in fights. Johnny picked up his coffee, took a sip, and continued to stare out the window.

"Just ignore me," David said. "I'm mouthing off to you because you're probably the only one that will listen to me. My board just talks over me and my wife cuts me off midsentence when I start talking baseball. I'm sorry about your wife, your family."

"It's okay. We just need to get Joan some help to repair some nerve damage she suffered." Johnny leaned back in the booth and put his arms up on either side of it and grabbed the dividing spindles mounted on top. "Youth baseball can make you laugh and cry so much; it's like riding an emotional roller coaster. It can bring out the worst in parents, particularly dads, and makes them vulnerable. They stew in their dead-end jobs all day going through the motions, afraid to take chances out of fear of being shown the door. But when they are out coaching on the field or playing baseball politics, it's like a jailbreak of emotions that exposes them for who they really are underneath it all. Sometimes guys can find real meaning in the local baseball leagues and contribute far beyond what they do in their real jobs and really help some teens. Those guys are the heroes. But oftentimes, it is just the opposite and a tyrant or a nut job is released and some will do things they would never think about doing at their jobs or under the watchful eyes of their wives."

"I'm feeling like one of those nut jobs these days."

"Nah, you're trying to set things right in your town so that baseball is available to everyone."

"My life isn't much better. Sometimes I'm not sure what's worse: the dying clients in my elder law practice or this baseball underworld I seem to have stumbled upon. I have the athletic director, varsity coach, my baseball board, and some baseball crazies all mad at me just because I want to make sure baseball is available to everyone. The state commissioner is thinking of pulling our charter. My son has every right to be mad at me because I messed up his school baseball career. On top of it all, my wife wonders if I'm forever stuck in the muck of a midlife crisis."

For a minute, nothing was said between the two of them. David sipped his coffee; Johnny checked his cell phone for messages. They looked down or around the diner. Johnny looked out the window into the parking lot. Two young boys in baseball uniforms and their parents were getting out of a car. They had smiles on their faces as they approached the diner entrance. Johnny smiled as he looked at David.

"Hey, do you see those kids out there in the parking lot?" Johnny said, motioning with his head in the direction of the family.

David looked over his shoulder. "Yeah, I see them."

Johnny's eyes opened wide. "That's what it's all about," he said as he tapped the table with his index finger.

David looked stoically out the window. "Yes, I know it's supposed to be about the kids. I hear that line usually right before the discussion becomes all about the adults."

"Yeah, you're right, but you are missing the point. What do you *really* see out there? Drop the cynicism for a moment."

"Two future pawns in some guy's fantasy travel baseball team," David said matter-of-factly.

Johnny laughed. "Funny guy, you are. Try and look at the entire package, though."

"I'm just focusing on the problem at hand. I don't feel like taking a trip down some tangent to nowhere."

"Sometimes it's difficult for us to step back because we are so heavily involved," Johnny said.

"I, myself, am worthless," David said, echoing the same words that John Buford had written to his superiors after Gettysburg in pursuit of Lee in the hot summer of 1863. "I'm exhausted," David continued, "and can only deal with the here and now. Cut to the chase."

"Well, here is a family and now it is time to recognize what this is all about. At the end of the day, we are about families and giving them a common thread that holds them together."

"I guess we have to remember that the crazy travel baseball family is probably in the minority," David said.

"Exactly."

"Too bad my board is made up mostly of travel parents."

"That happens."

Johnny's face grew sullen as he looked down at his coffee while turning the cup in his clasped hands. The pace of his speech slowed down to a crawl. His voice cracked as he spoke. "I guess deep down inside my point is a personal one that just hit me like a train when I saw that family. It's just that when I was a teen, baseball, Babe Ruth baseball, was the thread that held my family together. Times were tough and my family situation could get out of control. My good times always revolved around baseball. But there's more to the story now. . . ."

David looked at Johnny's eyes water at the edges. He tried to imagine what Johnny could be talking about. If only the scars on Johnny's face could talk. David held back from prying—no need to cause a cry-fest. It wouldn't help either of them. Johnny had made his point and his passion for the game was deep as much as it was pure.

"You know, I have thought this Elite Travel Baseball League thing through time and time again," Johnny said, "and while in my head I know this is probably a losing battle, I can't let it go."

All of a sudden it hit David. Johnny needed baseball on another level. It wasn't just the memories of good times playing baseball as a kid. Johnny was really using baseball to manage his coke addiction. If Johnny were a heroin addict, baseball was his methadone. Babe Ruth had said once that without baseball he would either be in the penitentiary or in the cemetery. *That's Johnny*, David thought.

"It seems you and I are two peas in a pod," David said, trying to comfort Johnny. "Look at me. I can't let go either. But it has nothing to do with my experience in baseball as a teen. I didn't play then. I was involved in other sports. But for Christy and his friends, baseball is everything outside of school. And now Christy won't play for any school team after I went to the athletic director to try and set things right. If our league folds, baseball won't be in the lives of Christy and these boys."

David explained what happened when he went to Duffel's office and how Coach Powers went out of his way to badmouth Christy during tryouts. Johnny just shook his head in disbelief.

"I've always tried to teach Christy right from wrong," David added. "He knows what the Elite Travel Baseball League is doing is wrong. If I don't do something about this situation, how am I going to look my son in the eyes? I couldn't face him. I don't want to teach him to walk away from things."

"You're a good father," Johnny said. "Long after this is done, he will carry this lesson through his life. Baseball teaches lessons beyond the sport itself; it teaches life lessons."

The two men looked at one another. Johnny smiled. David looked away and pulled a sugar packet from the condiment holder. He started spinning it around on the table. "But who is to say the Elite league will not destroy Babe Ruth baseball in our area altogether?" David asked.

Johnny said, "I think travel baseball is about to uproot and replace community baseball in our region. The best players will always have a place to play; the less talented players won't." Johnny's eyes met David's. "So do you want to fight them?" he asked.

"I'm not sure either of us has a choice anymore," David said. "We've come too far. Might as well see it to the end."

"I'm with you," Johnny said. "I have to go down fighting. I guess I don't know any other way."

"Yes, the scars on your face would seem to agree with you," David said. They both smiled.

"Now we just need a plan," Johnny said.

15

HATCHING A PLAN

D avid said, "I think we need to first reassess the strengths and weaknesses of our position to develop a plan of attack."

"Agreed. One of our weaknesses is the name. The Babe Ruth Travel League won't work here any longer. We need to rename it."

"Why?"

"Marketing issues. You know, Babe Ruth is known for its in-house baseball programs worldwide, where every boy is given an opportunity to play. But some people like to be considered part of something special. They don't want to think their son is some everyday sandlotter playing cruddy baseball in Babe Ruth."

"Yeah, the word around our school now is that Babe Ruth and Babe Ruth Travel suck. Barkus led that campaign and it has been effective."

"He and Frank Morgan ran the same campaign with other leagues too. Yeah, it's been effective. No problem. We can just give our league a different name. Rebrand it."

"So you're looking to give it snob appeal?"

"Yeah, whatever works. You got to give people what they want. If they don't like the old name, give them a new name. Let me tell you a story. One time, I called on an old meat customer. Her name was Delores. Nice older lady. She orders a variety of steaks and seafood from me. She also orders ground round and proceeded to tell me how much she disliked the ground round sold by Lodo Supermarkets.

"Flash forward," Johnny continued. "I get a call from Delores one week later looking for delivery of her order. I check with my warehouse guy and everything is in except for the ground round. But she wanted the entire order delivered that day. I panic and go out to Lodo and buy her ground round order and bring it home and rewrap it in fancy butcher paper and print up a couple of labels and call it 'Excelsior Ground Round.' I deliver it all to her that day. One week later I get a call from her. I wonder if I've been found out and so I avoid the call. She calls again the next day and leaves a message. Finally, my boss hears about all her calls and tells me to call her back. So I give her a call and she answers. She had called to tell me that her and her sister Lydia thought the ground round made the best meatloaf they have ever tasted. I got off the phone and rolled on the floor laughing. Simple repackaging did the trick. True story."

David started laughing. He couldn't remember laughing so hard. It felt good.

"And you know what the kicker is to this story?" asked Johnny, beginning to laugh himself.

"No, tell me," said David, slowing the rhythm of his laughter to catch his breath.

Johnny paused to contain himself. His eyebrows lifted as he blurted out: "I charged her three times my cost." David busted a gut and Johnny followed. Johnny tried to catch his breath. "And . . ." He couldn't contain himself. He tried again, "And . . ." Then David laughed louder and Johnny couldn't finish. After a bit, Johnny tried again, "And . . . she is placing orders for Excelsior Ground Round to this day!"

The laughter reached a higher level and then subsided as they returned to drinking their coffees.

David thought for a second. "Let's call it the Empire State Baseball League."

"Nice! We want to cover at least the entire state and that name does the trick. It's a solid name."

"And a solid name demands solid pricing," David added.

"You bet. And we will price it high enough for people to accept that we have a quality product to offer but less than the Elite Travel Baseball League. Listen to this story. One day, this guy from East Greenbush asks me how much it is to play in our league. I tell him it is $650 per kid. He says, 'Wow, that's expensive. It must be a great baseball league.' I tell him, 'Yeah, it's a great baseball league and I can give it to you at more than half off!' 'Half off,' he says, 'how do I sign up?'"

They both laughed again.

"You think this guy would have signed up if I first told him the price was half that of the Elite league?" Johnny asked.

"No, probably not."

"Right, he would have thought I was pushing an inferior product."

David thought Johnny could probably sell ice to an Eskimo.

"I think," David said, "the biggest advantage we have is that Babe Ruth leagues have primary access to the best fields in the region because of their nonprofit status. We need to spread the word to the local governments that the Elite Travel Baseball League is a for-profit and that it is undermining their community baseball program. You can't play baseball without a field, and so we need to keep the Elite Travel Baseball teams off our fields. That is one prong of our attack."

"Maybe you should meet with your town officials," Johnny said.

"Now you're talking," David said. "Come to think of it, I think Mayor Reed's son is thirteen years old and starts playing Babe Ruth this year. I'll go and see him. Meanwhile, we need to spread the word to other towns and cities as well."

"I've got connections from baseball around the area. I can take care of that angle."

"Great," said David. "We'll tell everyone that Elite Travel Baseball League plays on crappy fields. If they want to play on the best fields in the area, they'll need to play with the Empire State Baseball League through Babe Ruth."

"Marketing 101."

"Yep, now where is the best baseball played in the area? Is it played on our pristine fields or in the swamplands of the Elite Travel Baseball League?" asked David.

"Now that's an easy sell. A crappy field equals crappy baseball."

"And you know what you find on crappy fields?"

"Do tell," said Johnny.

"Holes . . . We'll call them craters for effect," David said, starting to laugh.

"Craters can cause leg injuries. We'll need to find or make these craters and then get pictures of them."

"Right," Johnny said, starting to laugh. "And we can start rumors about players disappearing in the craters."

Johnny's face started to turn red from laughter as a thought crossed his mind. It was contagious; David laughed louder. The laughter from the two of them grew so loud that a few people in the diner started looking over. Johnny tried to contain himself in order to speak. After two failed attempts, he was able to talk. "Yes, and we can videotape parent testimonials: 'I dropped Billy off to play baseball and he dropped off the face of the earth.' "

Both of them cracked up at the thought. They both started wiping tears from their eyes. At this point, more people in the diner started to look at them with some curiosity.

Johnny didn't care. He was having too much fun. "And we can put their pictures on milk cartons. 'Have you seen this boy, Billy? He was last seen on an Elite Travel baseball field.' "

"Stop it! You're killing me!" pleaded David.

People in the diner began smiling at David and Johnny laughing out of control. Susan, the waitress, looked over and started to chuckle at the two. They tried to regain some composure but failed. Eventually, their laughter gradually subsided. The people in the diner gradually looked away and went back to their meals and conversations.

"One more thing: there's no way we can compete against Elite Baseball without paying some of our staff. An all-volunteer outfit working in its spare time can't compete with a paid organization that works forty hours per week plus to grow its business. That's the reality of it all," David said.

"Yeah, you're right," Johnny said. "We really don't have a choice at this point."

"Our hand has really been forced. Unless we change the way we do things, the local Babe Ruth leagues will be gobbled up by those with a vested interest to promote their baseball businesses."

Johnny looked at his cell phone to see what calls he had missed. "Money makes the world go round, I guess."

"Yes, the sad fact is that if we can't keep the Empire State Baseball program running, the Babe Ruth leagues will start folding like lawn chairs after a summer concert."

"I wish there was some other way."

"How long has Joan been doing the scheduling for Babe Ruth Travel?"

"Five years now."

"And she has not made a nickel, right?"

"True."

"All that time and effort to support Babe Ruth is about to go to waste," David said. "That's not fair to you guys and it will not help Babe Ruth survive in our region."

"I know—"

"Look, volunteer organizations like Babe Ruth have natural turnover. As kids age out of their local programs, their parents tend to leave as well. And all that accumulated knowledge about how things work or ought to work leaves with them."

"I never thought of it that way, but you're right."

"Yeah, well then there is the other side of the coin too: the Elite Travel Baseball League has no turnover. Morgan and Barkus have always been a part of it and will always be a part of it so long as there's money to be made. So they lie in the weeds and watch and learn what we do and how we do it. Then they seize upon any weakness in the local league structure. Weaknesses develop when there is turnover. The rookie board members coming up don't know as much and are gullible to the Barkus pitch. Then Barkus and his henchmen might try and put his cronies on the local Babe Ruth boards."

"Like with your board?"

"Exactly. Fog was placed on the board to do the bidding of Barkus after he left. Now Poser and Scully have taken Fog's place."

"And your league is not the only one," Johnny said. "There are others too. I hear stories of graft and corruption in other leagues."

"They want those Babe Ruth fields to put their teams on and they will stop at nothing to get them."

"And we let it happen!"

"No more," David said. "The next time you have an unofficial chat with Brad Summers, please reinforce the idea that ignoring weeds in your garden just invites more weeds to grow. They don't disappear."

"You are preaching to the choir. But I think you and I can keep these clowns at arm's length at this point."

"Not for long and certainly not forever, and certainly not the way things are now. We'll both end up in the poorhouse and divorced."

"Tell me about it."

"That is why we need to institutionalize and finance our efforts so there is support for you, me, and Joan and whoever follows in our footsteps to make sure Babe Ruth leagues are never threatened again."

"Okay. But I hope there is some fun to be had in all this work. All work and no play makes Johnny a dull boy."

"Yeah, you have shown me your fun side a few times already."

Johnny's eyes twinkled and he started to laugh out loud again, but suddenly a serious look came over his face. He explained to David that he would have to be quick on his feet to pull this off, and that he would need to sound like he knew what he was talking about at times even though he might not. Johnny stressed above everything else that David could not care about what people thought of him.

"You will not survive a day of this if you care about what others think," Johnny said. "People are going to hate your sorry ass when we start to fight back. And you had better develop a thick skin about it because your name will be as good as shit until we have won and are done. And that is no sure thing. There is no getting around that with Barkus biting your ankles with every step. You are going to be messing with his happiness. And so when you put his panties in a bunch, he will come back at you as sure as I am sitting here. So you have to be prepared to live this way. Otherwise, you won't last."

David sat there speechless. He knew Johnny was right. "I have done okay so far," he said. But then he thought about Christy and Annie. *How will they take it? How will it impact them?* He didn't have an answer.

"You've done okay," Johnny said. "But the stakes just got higher. We're not just going to hold the bastards at bay. We're going to turn it around on them and beat them back into their holes."

"All right, all right, I get the point. So you want to have some fun, eh?"

A grin came over Johnny's face. "Might as well."

"We could take the 'Elite Travel Baseball League' name to make a point."

"I don't get it. Barkus and Morgan are using that name."

"I've checked and they haven't registered their name with the secretary of state. You see, they represent themselves as a nonprofit organization on their website but they have not registered their name as a nonprofit. This is not some oversight. It has been going on for years. So the name is available as far as the secretary of state is concerned to any citizen of the great state of New York."

Johnny rubbed his eyes and chuckled to himself. "Aren't the elite of this country supposed to have brains? Even the mob knows to run its operations behind phony corporations."

"I think we can reserve the name to make a point. When we hold a reservation for that name in hand bearing the seal of New York State and show it to every parent and league board member, even the brain dead among them will think that something is not right. They will understand that Barkus and Morgan are not who they say they are."

"Now that should be a real wake-up call."

"I'm not so sure the idea will be anything close to an epiphany for them, but at least it might stick in their gray matter for more than five minutes with that approach. Maybe they will even take it home with them to discuss it with their spouses and friends before the idea falls out of their heads."

"Great idea," Johnny said. "Oh, and of course we will need a website. We will need a beautiful website just like the one that the Elite Travel Baseball League has to show off to attract parents."

"Funny," David said, "the last time I checked, you can't play baseball on a website."

"Yeah, they probably dress up their website to compensate for the fact that their fields suck."

They both laughed and finished their coffee, then said goodbye to Susan. David grabbed the check and Johnny took care of the tip.

Walking out of the diner, David felt better about things. In Johnny, he had someone he could talk to about the problems he faced. He had an ally. He was not alone anymore. He felt alive.

But he was out of his element and he knew it. As a lawyer, David felt most comfortable when he had a handle on the facts, and in this respect, the handle was greased. David had become accustomed to dealing with dead people and he was of the firm opinion that they were always easier to handle than those that were alive and kicking. These baseball people were not dead or on their way out like he had been dealing with for over twenty years. These people were alive and on the move and he had to react to and anticipate them. If he failed to anticipate, he had to be quick on his feet like Johnny said. This was a new experience for a lawyer usually stuck behind a desk divvying up of assets, a lawyer who had only been to court once in all his years of estate and elder law practice. With baseball, every day a new element was added to the mix and he felt challenged and engaged in fighting for its survival. But things became darker with each step he took. The end seemed nowhere in sight, but he felt he couldn't turn back.

While driving home, David thought about Johnny. Joan and he had sacrificed so much in order to make baseball available for boys. He was amazed by their generosity with their time in light of their limited resources. He was touched deeply by Joan's efforts given her medical condition. She still managed somehow to work for the benefit of boys she did not even know. David shook his head. It wasn't only about Christy and his friends anymore. David felt he had to help these people out. It was the right thing to do; it was the only thing to do. He could not turn his back on these good people. And he could not turn his back on Christy and his friends.

It was 10:30 p.m. when David rolled into the driveway. He took his carbine out of the trunk. The house was dark but Annie had left the entrance light on for him. David opened the door and locked it behind him. He checked every lock in the house to make sure they were secure. He usually turned off the outside lights but thought it would be a good night to leave them on. David went to his gun safe in the living room and opened it. He removed about a half dozen rounds and squeezed them in his pocket before heading upstairs. He turned on the hallway light and tried to make as little noise as possible.

David opened Christy's bedroom door. The light shined in from the hallway and framed a life-size poster of Cal Ripken. He checked the bed. There was no head resting on the pillow. The covers lay neat. His stomach dropped for a second. But then he discovered that Christy was sleeping upside down with his head at the foot of the bed and his feet under his pillow at the other end. David tried to move him by lifting him but he was too heavy. He gave up and took the pillow covering Christy's feet and slipped it under Christy's head at the other end. He covered his feet with the quilt and left the room.

When David opened the bedroom door, the hallway light revealed the outline of Annie sleeping soundly under the covers. He walked into the room and checked the backyard through the bedroom window. There was a full moon that lit up the yard. David's mind was awash with the day's events. He asked himself if he was being paranoid but did not have an answer. Above all right now, he needed peace of mind. He needed to get some sleep. David turned off the hallway light and used the moonlight to guide him to his side of the bed. His carbine's barrel glistened in the light as he laid it under his bed. He took the rounds out of his pocket and placed them on the nightstand. David thought about loading it, but decided to draw the line there. He got undressed, slipped into bed, and trailed off to sleep.

16

SPYING ON THE ENEMY

T he warmth struck David's face first. The morning sunlight had crept up the bed and was poking him in the face. He sensed the light through his eyelids but it did not cause him to wake up right away. Instead, the sun crept into his dream, a dream about the Babe Ruth field no less, a dream in which he sat in a chair with his Sharps atop his hill overlooking his ballpark as the sun slowly peeled away the hill's shadow over the field. It was 10:00 a.m. and David had slept for more than five hours for the first time in over a month.

Christy had long since left for school and Annie was awake and about. The sun persisted and penetrated David's consciousness. He opened his eyes and realized from the sun's position in the room that it was midmorning.

David popped out of bed, put both hands at his side, and straightened his back. He stumbled to the bathroom like he had just gotten off the tilt-awhirl ride at the local fair. He looked in the mirror and saw his wind-burned face and hair sticking straight up.

"Oh, geez," he said out loud.

Annie was downstairs at the kitchen table pecking away at her laptop. "David, what's the matter? Are you okay?"

"Yeah, fine. I just look like an Indian, that's all."

"What?" Annie got up from her chair and walked over to look up the stairs. She shook her head with a half grin. "Why, David Thompson, you look like a Mohawk going off to war. But I thought you were partial to Mr. Lincoln's war? So are you going to play war today with the boys as a warrior or as a Union soldier?" Annie liked to tease David about his Civil War infatuation.

"Give it a rest already, Annie."

"It don't matter none to me, good sir. You just take the job that pays you the most and you won't hear a thing more from little old me."

"See ya," David said while closing the bathroom door and thinking that this making a living stuff was getting in the way of baseball. He shaved, showered, got dressed, and went downstairs to the kitchen.

"Annie, I have an errand to run. Be back in a few."

"A few what?"

"Um, a few hours."

"Hours?" Annie crossed her arms. "What's going on?"

"Nothing, just a few things I need to take care of this morning."

"Baseball?"

"A bit. But I got some other things too."

"There you go again!"

"Okay, I hear you."

"Can you at least drop by the pharmacy to pick up a prescription for me?"

"Sure," David said. He knew from experience if he would agree to run some errands that Annie might cut him some slack on the baseball front.

David went to his office and printed out some incorporation forms for the Empire State Baseball League and then he printed out a name reservation form for the Elite Travel Baseball League. He took the papers over to Johnny's house and they signed all of them before David took them down to Albany for filing.

As he returned to his car, David dialed up Johnny on his cell phone.

Johnny picked up and said, "What's up?"

"Hey, it's David. Papers have been filed. They should show up on the secretary of state's database within twenty-four hours."

"Good job."

"Anything going on at your end?"

"I spoke to Brad Summers and he is going to support us."

"What's he going to do, catch us when we fall?"

"Ha, actually he's going to ask the local renegade Babe Ruth leagues to support Empire for travel baseball or go somewhere else for their in-house baseball program."

"You mean they'll lose their Babe Ruth charter if they don't support us?"

"Yeah, it seems that way."

"Well, that ought to get them squawking. Wait until my board gets wind of that. They'll squeal like stuck pigs."

"Are you going to spread the word about town that we have registered the Elite name?" Johnny asked.

"Yeah, I'm making some phone calls this afternoon. I'm going to tell the mayor too."

Johnny laughed. "I've got to run. If Joan finds me on the cell talking baseball again she will run me out of the house."

"Yeah, I know that feeling all too well. I'll talk to you later." David hung up and drove off to Canfield's Pharmacy to pick up Annie's prescription.

Canfield's was located on Main Street in a cluster of a half dozen shops that made up the old business district of Indigo Valley. There were other businesses scattered throughout Indigo Valley, but they were mostly located on the periphery of town, away from the unfavorable zoning ordinances that protected the developer-created neighborhoods. The other businesses consisted mainly of chain drug stores, banks, pizza parlors, grocery chains, and a Starbucks.

Canfield's was an old-fashioned pharmacy with a soda fountain that doubled as a lunch counter with six stools and no tables. The eating area was off to one side of the store and was shielded from the rest of the store by an aisle of dated books, magazines, and a few half-empty revolving greeting card racks. During the weekdays, locals would come in and socialize while grabbing a bite to eat.

It was 2:00 p.m. when David opened the entrance door. It was well past the lunchtime rush and the store was fairly quiet. As David proceeded to the prescription pickup counter in the rear of the store, he saw the backs of two men eating at the end of the lunch counter. He recognized the one with a bowling ball of a head and butch cut as being none other than Barkus. As soon as he realized that, he had the other man pegged as Darryl Fog, a tall man so thin that he could enter a room through the crack of a closed door.

The two men were sitting there yammering away at each other like a pair of gossiping busybodies. David slipped into the books and magazine aisle and walked to the back of the store to the pharmacy pickup counter.

He did not want an encounter with these two and was glad that he had maneuvered his way to the back of the store without detection. David wasn't afraid of them. He just had no need for a scene. There was nothing to be gained and he didn't want to say anything that could be used against him.

But while waiting in the pharmacy line, he had the idea of picking up a magazine in the aisle and pretending to read it while eavesdropping on Barkus and Fog.

He paid for the prescription at the pharmacy counter and sauntered down the aisle and aligned himself with the top of Barkus's head on the other side. He picked up a magazine and began to thumb through it. He could hear the two talk as they turned their heads to one another at the lunch counter. At first they were talking about their sons, but then the topic turned to the baseball fields.

"I got a call from Morgan the other day. He says our season is going to begin a week earlier this year. On May 16," said Barkus.

"What day of the week is that?" asked Fog.

"Let me get my cell calendar out."

David looked down the aisle in both directions to see if there was anyone around. It was all clear.

"It's a Saturday," said Barkus.

"Crap," Fog responded. "Are we home or away?"

"Morgan says we are the home team," Barkus said. "The other team doesn't have a field."

Fog said, "That's not going to work. May 16 is Indigo Valley Day. The school ball fields are used by the town that day. One is used for crafts tents and the other is used for fireworks."

Indigo Valley Day was the annual spring festival celebrating the town's heritage that was marked by a parade, crafts, games, and fireworks.

"Are you sure?" Barkus asked.

"Yeah, my wife is on the steering committee. That's the way it's been done for years. We won't be able to use those fields."

David turned a page and waited for them to continue.

"Hey, I know of one field we can use on Indigo Valley Day," Fog said, laughing.

"Where?"

"The Babe Ruth field. I saw on the website that there are no games being played on the fields in honor of Indigo Valley Day."

David knew Fog was right. He had put that up on the website calendar before taking it down when he learned that Fog had taken the field with his team for practice a few days back. It was a mistake, but a forgivable one. David wanted to make it known that, unlike Fog and his predecessors, he would not allow baseball to be played on Indigo Valley Day. He thought the town kids should be encouraged to participate in the parade and festivities.

"Thompson is such a sap," Barkus said. "Do you think we can get away with it?"

"He didn't do anything when we took the field the other day," Fog pointed out.

"That was funny. I wished I could have seen the look on his face."

David turned a few pages quickly as his hands clenched the magazine, putting a few wrinkles in the cover. He wanted to go over and kick Fog's pencil-thin ass.

"Good point," Fog conceded. "I can have one of the guys on the board make sure there are no practices then."

"Morgan wants a start time for that game," Barkus said.

"Tell him 10:00 a.m. It has to start then," Fog insisted. "The Indigo Valley Day parade starts at 10:00 a.m. Everyone in Indigo Valley will be up there at the parade. That will give us good cover."

David had heard enough. He wanted to go over there and get in their face and tell them they would get the field over his dead body. But he restrained himself and decided it was time to go before he was spotted. He put the magazine back and walked out of the store.

He calmed himself down. As far as espionage goes, the day and time they planned to take the field again seemed like good intelligence to have, but he had no plans to use it. His most immediate concern was to check the holes in his line of defense and the mayor came to mind. He got in his car to drive to the town mayor's office. David wanted to drop in to see him and make sure that flank was covered.

17

READING REED

I van reed had been elected mayor the year before and prior to that he had been a state assemblyman. In his discussions with him, David thought he had developed a bond based upon their common legal backgrounds. In the back of his mind, David thought Ivan Reed would understand the legal absurdities underlying the Elite Travel Baseball League and that he would have an ally.

David walked up the staircase to town hall and spotted Ivan in his fishbowl office on the second floor. Ivan was sitting at his desk reading some papers with pen in hand. David had dropped in to talk with him on occasion to discuss topics relating to the baseball league. Ivan always made time for David and was very helpful in providing town assistance to maintain and upgrade the baseball facilities that it leased to the Indigo Valley Baseball League.

David greeted Ivan's secretary outside of his office and Ivan heard David's voice and invited him in. Ivan was a tall man with thick dirty-blond hair. Ivan stood up to walk over to greet David from behind his desk. He was wearing a matching teal green suit, yellow tie and chestnut-brown wing-tip shoes. Ivan looked like a walking cornstalk.

They exchanged greetings while shaking hands. Ivan invited David to sit down and David made himself comfortable in one of the upholstered chairs.

"I see you are getting scorched in e-mails from Rob Barkus," Ivan said, now sitting in his swivel chair. "Just saw one a few minutes ago."

"You're kidding. Was it written to you personally?"

"No, he CC'd me."

"I don't understand why you're involved," David said.

"It started a few days back," Ivan explained. "He came in a few days ago and I told him that I was a nonvoting member of the baseball board. Since then he has been copying me on stuff."

"He was here? What did he want? Oh, no, don't tell me. Let me guess. The field, right?"

"Good guess."

"What did you tell him?"

"I told him the process in the lease is that the baseball board has to approve any use by teams outside of your league first and then we as a town have to approve the usage."

"Yeah, well, there are some things you should know about Elite Travel Baseball." David proceeded to tell him that the league did not have a legal identity. He told him he had reserved the name of Elite Travel Baseball from the Department of State to prove his point. David advised him that the Elite teams probably owed money to the league for using its field.

"I want to thank you for bringing this to my attention," said Ivan.

"Sure thing. What's your take?"

"My take is that someone is operating a nice business for themselves."

"Good read. Any thoughts about us giving them our field?"

"What you guys do is your choice, but if the matter ever got to the town level, I don't think we could approve it. We would need the Elite to have nonprofit status and it would probably have to be certified as a nonprofit by the IRS."

David was thrilled with Ivan's take. He thought now at least he had his flank protected should the league board fail him.

"Yes, I agree," said David.

"But I wouldn't like to see this get to us for a decision. We have a few town councilmen who might not understand this as well as I do. And Rob might be applying pressure to them as well."

David heard him but wanted a commitment from him. "I'm sure you would do everything in your power to make sure our field was protected."

"Sure."

David got his commitment. Not much else he could do except hope that

Ivan would honor it. He considered this visit with Ivan as a victory for the good guys and was really appreciative of his support.

David thought to ask about Ivan's son and prepared to exit stage left. "I understand your son, Harry, is Babe Ruth age this year. What team is he on?"

Ivan stood up and put his hands into his pockets. "Um, Harry's not playing this year."

"Oh, no, don't tell me that he's dropped out of baseball." Age thirteen was the age many kids dropped out, as the big field's size appeared intimidating to them.

"No, no, that's not it. He's playing for the Greenbush Hornets."

David could not believe his ears. "You know that is an Elite Travel Baseball Team?"

"Is it? I wouldn't know. My wife takes care of these things."

That didn't make sense to David. Baseball was usually the husband's responsibility in any household he knew about, if there was a husband still a part of the family equation.

"I don't understand. Why wouldn't you have your son play in our program?"

Ivan took a few steps back toward his desk. "It's not my decision, really. My son wants to play with his friends and his friends are playing for the Greenbush Hornets."

David was forgiving of parents on the Elite league's fringe, like Ivan, who used their son's fancy to play with their friends as a justification for playing outside of the town league. Jack Masters, the league president, would approve of such a maneuver inasmuch as the boy was being used as a shield and deflecting blame from the father for playing there, almost to the point of making the boy into the bad guy. And Ivan, to his credit, had taken the dodge to a higher level of gamesmanship by taking cover behind his wife as well as a second line of defense.

But, as David realized, Ivan was no typical parent. He was the town mayor and this baseball program was, in essence, *his* baseball program. And David thought that the town mayor would be inclined to take a stand for his program and try to recruit the other parents to play in his own league, to represent his town. And, if that failed, David thought that he might try and persuade his son to play in the town league anyway, giving his son the opportunity to make a new group of friends.

David couldn't believe that the mayor's own son was playing for the enemy. At that moment, the realization that Ivan was not going to take the high ground and defend his town's baseball program hit him. He wondered how he could feel more passionate about the town and its baseball program than the mayor.

David decided not to press the topic with Ivan because he wasn't going to risk losing the only ally he had in town, and he certainly didn't want to manage yet another conflict.

"Well, it's still not too late to sign up," David said, standing up. "Let me know if you guys change your minds."

"Okay, thanks, David. Thank you for trying to fix things here."

"I'll see you around," David said while backing out of the office and giving a two-finger salute to the mayor. He turned around, walked out of the office, and said goodbye to Ivan's secretary. He scampered down the stairs to the lobby below.

He reached for his cell phone and dialed up Johnny while walking to the parking lot. Johnny picked up.

"Hey, the town mayor is on our side," David said. "I think he' ll help keep Elite Baseball off our field."

"That's good news, Mr. Thompson."

"Yes, in a way. We got somebody on our side officially, but not personally."

"What do you mean?"

"His son just turned thirteen and is playing over in East Greenbush for an Elite team."

"What? The town mayor doesn't want to have his son play in his program?"

"He said his wife handles baseball matters in the house and he said his son wanted to play with his friends."

"So this guy is your town leader, your captain?"

"I hear you, but at least he is supporting the program in his official capacity."

"He's like everyone else. They always say that by doing what their kids want they are doing what is best for their kids—blah, blah, blah. Truth is, these guys are not acting like responsible parents. A responsible parent has his son support the community program so that everyone can play in the town."

"I'm hoping he comes to his senses and comes back. He said he didn't know that the Greenbush Hornets were an Elite team. Maybe he'll figure it out after thinking about it a bit. At least he isn't planning to play on the Barkus teams in town. At least he's not playing on Coach Powers's team."

"Ha, I think you are on to something and don't know it."

"What are you talking about?"

"Maybe your town leader ends up on the Powers team after all."

"That's not what he said to me."

"What he says to you and what he does could be two separate things. He's straddling the fence and playing both sides. You think he would tell you he was playing for Powers? No, it is much easier for him to say he is playing in East Greenbush for now. Saying he's playing in East Greenbush to you is like a trip to Switzerland to him. It keeps him out of the fray."

"I hope you're wrong. He seems like a nice guy who is very supportive of our league."

"Yeah, and I hope to win the lottery this week. Get a grip and face the fact that he might be playing you."

"I don't think so, though I have to admit it's more difficult to sell a community program when our mayor is avoiding it."

"You are either part of the problem or part of the solution. Pick a side because there's no middle ground. And your town mayor has decided to be part of the problem."

"Tell me about it."

"Why are you guys such wusses over there? What do they put in your town water?"

David got to his car and leaned against it. "I don't understand what is going on here either. You know, I can't find anyone who gets it and is capable of doing the right thing. It's very disheartening. I don't feel like I belong here. Imagine that. I feel like an outcast in my own town."

"Get used to it. I never said this was going to be easy, remember?"

"Yeah, I remember. There's one positive. At least Ivan is not in favor of letting the Elite league on our field. At least I think we can expect his support on that front."

"Come on now, David. Didn't you hear what I just said? That guy is playing both sides of the fence. Did you ever think he might be telling

Barkus something different? Maybe you are the one being played and maybe

he promised Barkus that he could have the field."

"I don't think so."

"Why not?"

"Because I overheard Barkus and Fog talking about taking the Babe Ruth field earlier this afternoon. They want to play a game on it in the middle of May. "

"What? How did that happen?"

"Long story. Anyway, they wouldn't be plotting to take the Babe Ruth field if Ivan was going to give it to them."

"What did you do? Bug their phones?"

"Let's just say I was at the right place at the right time."

"Okay," Johnny said. "I talked with Brad a few minutes ago for the second time today and his campaign to get leagues on board with our program is working well."

"Good to hear," David said. "Okay, I had better get home."

"I hear you, man. I got meat to sell. Later."

David slipped into the front seat of his car. He found two baseballs on the driver's side floor. On the passenger side, there was a spilled bucket of balls. David lifted the bucket and put it on the passenger seat and reached over to fasten the seat belt around it so it didn't fall over. It was 3:00 p.m. and time to get home. Christy would be getting off the bus in a few minutes.

18

A CALL FOR EXPULSION

David walked through the door and called out for Annie. "Hi, Annie, I'm home." There was no response. He called out again. "Annie?" Still nothing. He looked out in the driveway and could see her car, so he thought she must be at home. He walked into the kitchen and looked out the window on to the backyard. Nothing but the trees dancing in the afternoon breeze. The sky was clear. The scheduler in David emerged as he searched the horizon for clouds. *Looks like a game tonight*, he thought. He looked around the first floor but did not see Annie. He went upstairs to the bedroom. *Maybe she's resting.* But the bed was made with covers taut and no sign of a body occupied the bed. David moved toward the bathroom. The door was wide open and there was nobody in there. Down the hallway, Christy's room was all clear as well.

While standing in Christy's room, he heard Annie's voice calling his name. But it was not her usual cheery voice. It was a weak voice. She was not on the second floor but he could still hear her voice in the distance. He went out to the top of the hallway steps and looked down. The voice was not traveling up the stairs. It was coming from someplace else. He could hear it coming from their bedroom too, but he could not pinpoint the location. He went into the bedroom and heard her voice again softly calling his name. It was coming from the heating ductwork.

David bent down to the register. "Annie, can you hear me?" He waited for a response. Nothing. "Annie, are you all right? Where are you?" He heard her sobbing in the ductwork.

"I'm in your office," she said in between sobs.

David took off down the stairs from the second floor and then rumbled down the carpeted steps into his office in the basement. He saw Annie sitting at his desk in front of his computer. He sat down beside her and took her cold hand. Tears welled in her eyes and then slid down her cheeks. He grabbed a tissue from his desk and gave it to her. She wiped her eyes and her cheeks and then blew her nose.

"Honey, what's the matter?"

She gave David the used tissue. David gave her a fresh one. "Have you seen these e-mails from Rob Barkus and your board?"

"No, you know I don't check my e-mails when I'm out."

"It all started with this one from Barkus. He said some terrible things about you. Just awful. He said you are acting in a distressing manner in not sharing the field. He said you were a selfish man and that all you cared about was Christy and getting him on an all-star team."

"I'm sorry, Annie, but please don't look at my e-mails."

"Somebody has to protect you."

"Annie, please don't worry about me. I'm a big boy. This will all straighten itself over time."

"Over time? How much more of this do we have to take? Did you see who he CC'd on this e-mail?"

"No."

"He sent this to Jack Masters and CC'd your entire board, the athletic director, Coach Powers, Coach Braxton, and Mayor Reed. He CC'd people whose names I don't even recognize. These people are probably forwarding it all over Indigo Valley. Who knows who is reading this on their computer screens?"

David remembered what Johnny had told him about not caring what others thought or said. "Annie, we are going to have to be tough about it."

Annie wiped her eyes and her face turned scarlet red. "Easy for you to say, David. You stay in here and plan baseball all day. You go back and forth between home and the field and that's it. I go out. I have friends outside of baseball. I don't spend day and night on the baseball field. I have a life. Now how can I go out in public with this out there?"

"I'm sorry, Annie," David said.

"Forget about me, David. How about Christy? Did you think about how this would impact him? You know parents are going to spoon feed some of this to their kids and it will get back to Christy at school."

David had not thought about how this would impact Christy either. "Let me see the e-mail," he said, turning the computer monitor toward him. A scowl came over his face as he began reading it.

He had not anticipated this e-mail attack by Rob Barkus. David had no time to anticipate; he had barely enough time to react to all that was going on around him.

"I'll save you the time of reading the rest, David. Barkus goes on to say that you're an angry man who is intent on hurting the school players and their families because your son is not on the school team. How can he say such things about you in front of everyone?"

"It is all part of his plan."

"What are you talking about?"

"He wants me to resign."

"David, he's not waiting for you to leave."

"What do you mean?"

"Don't stop at that e-mail, David. Look at what came in response." David scrolled down and saw that within two minutes of the Barkus e-mail, two board members had called for a special meeting to consider removing David from the board. Under the league bylaws, any two members could request a special meeting. Jack Masters, as president, had sent an e-mail later scheduling the meeting for the next evening.

"David, they obviously want you off the board. What's going on?"

David could feel his heart thumping in his chest. He started breathing heavily. His muscles tensed up. He didn't know what to do, if anything.

"David, what are we going to do?" Annie asked.

David tried to contain himself. He took a deep breath and exhaled slowly, then got up to stretch. He sat back down and rubbed his face. David thought about the walnut stock of his carbine, the straight grain, the smooth finish, the absence of gouges or even nicks, the soft chestnut brown, the shine of it glistening in the sunlight, and it calmed him. The carbine was a comfort to him. It was as beautiful as it was functional. In fact, it was superbly functional and that was an especially attractive quality to David at this point in time when nothing seemed to function around him.

"David, are you okay. Say something!"

"I don't know what to say."

"Are you going to write these people back and set them straight?"

David paused. "I don't think so. I don't think I can win by writing back. If I respond and defend myself, it will just lead to more e-mails aimed at me. It would give them an opportunity to work themselves up into a frenzy and it would get me upset and give them the satisfaction of seeing me upset. This was all planned. Look at the time stamp of those two e-mails from the two board members, Scully and Poser. They were both sent within two minutes of getting that Barkus e-mail. You mean to tell me it was just coincidence that these two Barkus toadies were reading their e-mail accounts at the same time Barkus sent his e-mail? No, this was all staged and right now they are all sitting in front of their computer screens waiting for me to respond to their nonsense. Let them wait. I'll just wait for tomorrow night."

"Do you know what you're doing?"

David thought for a second and gathered himself. "Why give them the satisfaction of seeing me upset? These chuckleheads have been yapping on the phone with one another, planning this all out. If I say nothing, they might imagine that I have folded, that I won't show tomorrow night. I can try and work that to my advantage."

"How could he say all those things about you? This is crazy. My God, this is about kids playing some baseball."

"You're right. It is crazy."

"Are you are going to let Rob Barkus drag our name through the mud then?"

"Annie, you're upset. So am I. But do you really think we are going to change their minds by writing them back? Not a chance. If anything, we will add fuel to the fire. Come to think of it, I'm doing what you asked me to do."

"What are you talking about?"

"You told me the other day to be nonconfrontational; you told me to be more like Jack Masters."

Annie was taken aback by David's point, as it rang true. She tried to distinguish what she said the other day from what was going on now. "Yes," she said, "but that was all about how to find someone or something else to shield you from blame for making a decision."

"Same general, nonconfrontational idea," David said. "Just call me Jackie Robinson, call me Gandhi."

Annie was torn. If David was removed from the board or resigned, they would be done with baseball and life would return to normal. But she realized then that she did not like the idea of her husband being fired from such a public position. She became concerned about what other people would think, what other people would say. "You don't get it. If you don't do anything, they are going to throw you off the board."

"I don't think so. But if it happened, maybe it would be a good thing, right?" That's the last thing David wanted, but if saying this would keep the peace, so much the better.

"I thought so, but now I'm not sure," Annie said.

"Well, whatever happens, happens, okay?"

"I guess so. This doesn't sound like you, though. What are you really thinking?"

"I haven't totally thought it through yet."

They both heard the squeaky brakes of a school bus stopping in front of the house and looked at one another. David checked his watch. "Christy's home."

Annie picked up some tissue and cleaned herself up. "Not a word of this to him," she said as she hurried upstairs.

"Okay."

David took Annie's seat in front of the computer to do some legal research on potential strategies. He had an inkling of a plan but needed to confirm it was viable. But he could not focus on the task at hand.

David told himself to calm down and to approach the situation rationally. It had been a roller-coaster day; it had been a roller-coaster week for that matter. And he was wondering how another day could pass by with him totally consumed by baseball. Yesterday, he and Johnny had figured out a plan to try and fix things. And in less than twenty-four hours, everything was about to fall apart. If the school and Barkus took the field and he was off the board, it would all be over. A part of him now wanted that to happen. He could say to himself and anyone who cared that he had given it his all; he could return to the safety and isolation of his law practice, perhaps start a new one in a different area of focus. As state commissioner for Babe Ruth, Brad Summers would be forced to take the charter away from Indigo Valley and the board would be reorganized under his supervision. David began to calm down when he thought about it that way. There was no shame to be had.

He thought to himself that the community baseball program had been neglected for years, long before he had arrived on the scene. The mess, he thought, was just too large for him or any one man to clean up and, certainly, he had done more than anyone else to fix it. It was beyond repair. It was a total loss. Perhaps, he thought, when the town baseball program was finally gone it might be missed, and people would finally do something about it. If not, then in the eyes of the community, the town baseball league wasn't worth keeping, and its death sentence—no matter how much David disagreed with it—was its fate. He could not revive it for more than a fleeting moment if the community did not support it. Even if David stayed on the board defending the field, he could not stay forever. Heck, Annie was close to leaving him now and Christy was not going to be playing Babe Ruth baseball forever. *People eventually get what they deserve in running a youth sports program*, David thought. That was the natural evolution of things. And there was nothing he could do to change it. Without community support, the best he could hope for would be to delay the inevitable. David kept telling himself not to worry about things he couldn't control, and this surely was one of those occasions. He tried to compose himself and did so for a while. But it didn't last.

The thought of the program's inevitable demise gnawed at his core. It did not taste right. Perhaps all his community needed was a little leadership, someone to point them in the right direction, someone to get the ball rolling for the next generation.

The townspeople did not have the inducement to do anything about the situation so long as the program still existed. Their cares were satisfied in that their boys were still playing baseball, at least for now. Like the landfill mound that embraced the baseball field, everything looked fine on the surface to them. And that was all that mattered. There was no immediate need to dwell about what was underneath.

David thought of Annie and the impact his removal would all have on her. He had assumed Annie would stand by his side even though she was growing tired of it all. And then there was Christy. David did not know what was going on at school as a result of his actions. Some days when Christy would come home, he would appear upset. But when questioned by David he would deny it and go and talk to Annie instead. David would hear whispers between the two of them. Annie would later tell David that something had happened at school but that Christy did not want to talk about it with David because he thought his father had enough baseball to worry about without dealing with his school problems.

Christy told Annie that he could handle the kids at school. Christy had grown a thick skin, like Johnny had asked David to do. But was it fair to Christy to have to live with the legacy of a father who is thrown off the baseball board? Surely that is what the Elite kids would say to Christy at school every day until high school graduation.

Then David began to think about his relationship with Christy, his son, going forward. He had seen older youth in the town drift away from their fathers after high school and he did not want this incident to come between him and Chrisy; he did not want to forever look at his son in his later years, knowing that he had failed; he did not want Christy looking away from him, acknowledging his failure. *Let my failure be something else other than baseball,* David thought, because baseball had at least been a bridge between the two of them, father and son, where so few opportunities for bonding existed.

He thought about Joan and Johnny and how they had sacrificed so much for the sport. He had made a commitment to Johnny. He would not be able to fulfill that commitment if he was thrown off the board.

The more David thought about the events, the more he realized that he had come too far to let things run their course without a fight. The more he thought about it, the more uneasy he became, until there was no calm to be had as anger pumped through his veins. He realized that he was about to be run out of town—his town—by a bunch of carpetbaggers. There was only one guy on his board, Avery Bransen, who had any roots in Indigo Valley. Neither the athletic director nor any of the school coaches had any roots in Indigo Valley. If David were kicked off, he would be the outsider forever more. It would no longer be his town; it would become their town.

That was a legacy he did not want to live with. If he was removed, every day he lived in that town would remind him of that failure. And that would be an unbearable existence as he planned to live the rest of his life in Indigo Valley. A shiver ran through him as he turned his attention back to the computer screen and his legal research.

David realized that he had set into motion a chain of events that could not be reversed. He had risked everything by taking a stand and there was no turning back.

19

TARGET PRACTICE

On Thursday morning, David talked with Christy before he got on the bus and told him that some men were going to try and kick him off the baseball board that night.

"What are you going to do?" Christy asked.

"Make sure it doesn't happen," David said. He was searching for a silent killer: a means by which he could defeat those calling for his removal without setting in motion a new wave of wrath directed at him. It was a delicate balancing act. "I want to give you a heads-up in dealing with the kids at school. They may come at you with this today."

"Thanks. Appreciate it," Christy said.

"Need any advice on how to handle these guys?" David asked.

"I think I've got it covered. I've dealt with them so far." Christy wanted to spare his dad all the crap he had to put up with at school. The Babe Ruth boys, especially the boys on the Chopper team, had stood by his side at school and made life tolerable there. He knew his dad did not have that kind of support network in dealing with the baseball board.

"Do you know why I'm fighting this, Christy?"

"Yes, you're trying to save baseball for me and the Babe Ruth boys."

"Okay."

"You know, I want you to fight for us, Dad. You're the only one who can."

"I guess you're right," David said. "I appreciate your support, Christy."

Annie was still asleep when David said goodbye to Christy and took off in his Mustang with his Sharps.

By the time Johnny had arrived at the Rod and Gun Club later that morning, David had already shot thirty rounds. He had been shooting at a man-sized target fifty yards from the firing line. He fired one more time as Johnny walked up behind him. The shot echoed throughout the range and the gun recoiled against his shoulder. The fifty-two-caliber bullet hit the upper torso of the target and made it shimmy.

"Nice shot," Johnny said.

"Yeah, not bad."

"Who was that guy who played the lead in *The Rifleman* in the sixties?"

"Chuck Connors?"

"Right, that was his name. Are you like Chuck Connors with that repeating rifle of his? Boy, I loved the opening of that show—forget the show itself. At the opening, he would let about twelve shots go and then he would twirl the gun. Man, that guy was cool. Then he would look right through the camera as he reloaded and the theme music cued. Is that you, Thompson? Are you Chuck Connors?" Johnny laughed.

David shook his head. "This isn't a Winchester repeating rifle like he had. This is a breech-loading single-shot carbine."

"Yeah, whatever that means."

"It meant a big advantage during the Civil War."

"What are you talking about?"

"A soldier with a musket could fire two or three times a minute. This gun could be fired ten times per minute by a capable soldier. This type of gun allowed General Buford to delay the Confederates and to take the high ground of Cemetery Hill as a defensive position."

"Good for him. Why the hell are you out here all alone?"

David glanced over his shoulder and saw that his car and Johnny's car were the only ones in the lot. "I find firing the Sharps to be very relaxing," he said.

"You got an interesting way of cooling off."

"Yes, I'm doing my absolute best to stay away from the bottle or from doing lines."

"You're quite the comedian, David. You said you wanted to talk to me?"

"I received some e-mails yesterday informing me that they are calling a meeting tonight to try and throw me off the board."

"Wow." Johnny looked at David twiddle with the carbine saddle ring. "What is it with your town and e-mails anyway? Doesn't anyone talk face-to-face over there? Or does everyone need to hide behind a computer terminal?"

"I don't know. Do you think I should recommend some group therapy for my board?"

"I think your board is beyond help. I guess it shouldn't surprise me that they want you out. After all, you have managed to piss everyone off at the same time. If you had pissed them off one at a time and gave each a chance to cool off or get distracted by some other crisis in their lives, you wouldn't be in this position."

"You have got to be kidding, right? I've got enough to worry about on every front, including the home front, to try and control exactly when these guys get pissed off at me. It's baseball season and they all want the prize. They all want the field."

"Okay, okay already. What's your plan?"

"Have to see how they come at me. Hit them with some divide and conquer; maybe a little rope-a-dope. The law is on my side so I can hit them with some legal razzle-dazzle. If that doesn't work, I'll take W. C. Field's advice: 'If you can't dazzle them with brilliance, baffle them with bullshit.' You got any thoughts?"

Johnny sat down in the shooter's chair, which was behind the shooting table. David set his unloaded gun on the table. Johnny picked it up.

"Sounds like you have lots of rounds to hit them with tonight. What time is the meeting?"

"Jack set it for 6:00 p.m."

Johnny picked up the carbine and sighted it. "First thing I would do is push back the time to 7:00 p.m."

"Why?"

"It is one less hour they have to roast your ass. Tonight is a Thursday, a school night, and they have to work tomorrow. That's in your favor. Those bastards will be dog tired from work and the last thing they want is a late-night dealing with you."

"Good idea."

"Just give Jack some excuse to move it back to 7:00 p.m." Johnny put the carbine back on the table. "Shoot with a musket tonight, though."

"What do you mean?"

"You have to outlast these guys tonight. Shoot once and take your time reloading. Take them out one at a time. Don't piss them all off at once." Johnny handed the gun back to David.

"Good idea. Hopefully, only a few show. It will make less work of it."

"It would, but I wouldn't count on it. You're more entertainment than anything on television tonight. Everyone enjoys a lynching."

"Nice image there, Johnny. Me swinging by a rope. Thanks."

"Are we having fun yet?"

"I'm not sure this is the type of fun I envisioned."

"You can have fun with this if you want. First, like I said before, sound like you know what you're talking about and let it flow from there. You're a lawyer for Christ sake. You've been trained to sound like you know what you're talking about. Who was the guy that said that all war is deception?"

"Maybe it was Chuck Connors," David joked.

"Fuck you."

David smiled, picked up his gun, and put it in its leather case. "Close—his name was Sun Tzu."

"Right, that's the guy."

David gathered his unspent ammunition and put it in his cartridge box.

"What kind of funny bullets are those?" Johnny asked.

"What do you mean?"

"They have a paper on the outside."

"Yeah, they have a paper casing to hold the charge."

"Those look like they are right out of the history books. Where did you get those?"

"I made them."

"You made them?" Johnny said in disbelief.

"Yeah, you make a dowel to fit the barrel, treat some linen paper with some saltpeter so it burns up on firing, cut with scissors, get a glue stick to hold it all together, load it with powder, do some twists and tucks. Load the bullet first and then the charge. And then you are good to go."

"Sounds like a good arts and crafts project for a Sunday afternoon. You're starting to worry me."

"It's no big deal."

"Yeah, that is what has me worried about you. You have a gun fetish and don't even know it. Do me a favor there, Daniel Boone."

"What's that?"

"Leave the gun home tonight."

David's upper lip shifted to one side and his eyebrows lifted.

"Why would you think I would bring the gun with me tonight? Do you think I'm crazy?"

"In case you hadn't noticed, you're a bit of a gun nut. Next thing you'll tell me is that you make your own bullets."

David picked up his gun case and cartridge box and the two started walking toward the parking lot. "Well, I have been known to pour some hot lead into a bullet mold now and then."

Johnny looked at David and shook his head. "Remind me to never get on your bad side. Now I've got to go out and buy a Kevlar vest to wear when I'm around you."

David laughed and took out his cell phone. "At least I haven't been in trouble with the law. If I had been, you might have reason to be concerned." David winked at Johnny.

"You're somewhere between obsession and addiction with that gun of yours. Who are you calling on the phone?"

"Jack Masters." With that, he dialed up Jack and got the meeting pushed back until 7:00 p.m. Jack didn't have much choice. It was tough to have a lynching without a victim.

"Okay, Jack is going to set it back to seven," said David.

"That's a good first step."

"I'll let you know what happens. Wish me luck."

"You got it. I'm only a phone call away if you need me."

"Thanks."

David and Johnny shook hands and parted.

20

HANG 'EM HIGH

It was twenty minutes before the appointed execution time of 7:00 p.m. when David rolled into the town hall parking lot. Christy and Annie were at home watching a baseball movie together.

The irony and humor involved in being fired from a volunteer job did not escape David and it had him in a chipper mood.

Jack Masters had reserved the second-floor conference room for the meeting. Normally, half the board would arrive late to meetings but tonight was an exception, so it seemed. David could see the lights on in the conference room and, when he slowed, he recognized some board members sitting and standing in the room.

David thought about waiting until exactly 7:00 p.m. to make his appearance. But it seemed that almost everyone was already there, except for him, which made it likely that they had arrived early to plan his demise, or so David thought. In David's mind, there was no need to give them that advantage, and so he parked his car and walked into town hall and up the stairs to the conference room.

He saw Benny Melotti standing in the hallway outside the conference room talking with Arnold Meeson.

Melotti, father to a pair of talented boys, was built like a pitcher. He had a slicked-back black mullet that just touched his shoulders in the rear. With his mustache, he looked a little like the Hall of Fame pitcher Dennis Eckersley. Back from his annual janitorial supply convention in Florida, Melotti sported a tan on top of his olive-toned skin. He wore his usual five o'clock shadow that evening and was upset that he had to leave the Mohawk City Off-Track Betting parlor early in order to make the meeting.

Arnold Meeson was of medium height and build with perfectly parted and combed blond hair. He was dressed like he had just finished a round at the private Iroquois Golf Club, where he was a member through the real estate company he worked for as a broker. His short-sleeve Tiger Woods golf shirt exposed his pasty white complexion.

"Arnold, Benny," David said when he saw them. They both stopped talking immediately and looked at David and nodded, acknowledging him without a word.

"Don't let me interrupt," David said as he passed them on his way to the conference room.

He opened the conference room door. "Gentlemen," he said as their talking came to a halt. It was as if he had walked into the opposing team's dugout. The rest of the board was there, a total of twelve men, including David.

David saw Jack Masters sitting at the middle of the conference table with his small belly pressed up against the edge. Jack was a muscular man of medium build with a layer or two of winter fat on top to help smooth things over. He was a handsome redheaded man who appreciated his own good looks and made it a point to get his hair trimmed every three days and his hands manicured weekly. Jack owned a jewelry store and had to close early in order to attend the meeting.

Jack placed his thick hands against the edge of the conference room table. He pushed his chair back and rested his hands, fingers interlocked, on his stomach, as if trying to hold it from falling onto the carpet.

"Nice suit," he said to David.

Street clothes were the usual dress attire for board meetings and David had decided to overdress for effect. He had shaven again before the meeting and sprinkled himself with a dash of Derek Jeter cologne. He looked dapper in his navy-blue suit, white pressed shirt, and blue tie. David hated suits and kidded clients that he would charge more per hour if he had to wear one. But a sharp appearance was part of his strategy. Jim Fletcher always told his clients to wear a suit to court, and David took the advice now to make a different, if not better, impression on the jurors in the conference room.

"Thanks. Sorry I'm late," David said, looking at his watch. "Oops, my watch must be broken. It says six forty-five."

Jack smiled and said, "Your watch is fine."

"Oh, you guys just got an early start then. No problem."

"We haven't called the meeting to order yet," said Jack.

"Okay," said David. He searched the table for an empty chair and saw a few but chose the one at the end of the table that faced the door. He unbuttoned his jacket, sat down, and placed his satchel at his feet. Oscar Poser and Paul Scully were seated on either side of him. Melotti and Meeson were still in the hallway.

Oscar Poser, the vice president, stood up from his seat and started walking toward the door. "I've got to go use the head," he said. Poser was one of the two board members who e-mailed the rest in asking for David's removal. He was a tall, athletic man who owned an electrical supply company and had never met a hair dryer he didn't like—he blew his brown hair up like he was an extra in *Saturday Night Fever*. Oscar was used to being in charge at his company and thought that everyone in the baseball league worked for him. Everything was a crisis to Oscar and he was forever in crisis-management mode. There was no filter between his thoughts and his mouth. His wife spent a good deal of time around the baseball fields trying to smooth things over with people whom he might have offended. It was becoming a full-time job.

Poser's oldest son of thirteen was playing on the school's modified team. He was a borderline player that Oscar thought needed extra help in order to make the freshman team the following year. Oscar had done his best to make good friends with Rob Barkus. With Coach Powers, the freshman school coach, having been recruited by Barkus to run the thirteen-year-old Elite team, Poser was now excited as a puppy with a new bone to help out Barkus and Powers in order to ensure his son's placement next year.

A minute later, Paul Scully also got up from his seat next to David and headed for the exit. Scully was a tall, wide-body man with unkempt curly hair who had to turn sideways to exit any doorway. He always rubbed his hair at the meetings and looked at the table, like he was back in high school and clueless about what was going on in class. He was the other board member who had e-mailed everyone asking for David's removal. Scully was a gopher for a home renovation company. He knew how to take orders and follow people around.

Scully had contracted Praisehim-Trashim Syndrome when his son was eight. An attack could come at any moment and there was no known cure. Scully's symptoms manifested themselves as the predictable and annoying tendency of praising (Praisehim) his own son's baseball talents for minutes on end and, immediately thereafter, trashing (Trashim) some other boy's baseball skills for what seemed an eternity. It was the one-two punch approach to one-upmanship that caused the experienced witness of such an attack to disregard Scully's attestations to his son's greatness completely, and to instead focus on guessing the identity of the boy that would be trashed. If it were possible to call a time out after Scully praised his son during an attack, the league could have taken bets on the name of the trash victim and raised enough money to buy the Babe Ruth field from the town a dozen times over.

Scully's son, like Poser's, was now thirteen. Scully had followed Oscar's lead in developing the same friendly relationship with Barkus. He too now aspired to be Powers's servant at large so that his son could make the freshman team. It was rumored that Scully did all sorts of handyman favors for Barkus and Powers.

David was in no hurry to get the meeting going; time was on his side. The longer things dragged on, the more likely he would survive the night. So he engaged in chitchat with the remaining board members while waiting for the four who were outside the room to return. David was joking with them and tried to show them that he was unconcerned with the proceedings that were about to get underway. He turned on the charm so that maybe some of the remaining seven board members in the room would not be so dead set on removing him.

It was 7:10 p.m. when Meeson and Melotti returned. Ten minutes later, Poser and Scully returned. They left the door open and sat on either side of David at the long conference table.

Jack called the meeting to order. "Okay, this special meeting was called by Oscar and Paul here to consider the removal of David from his duties as commissioner of Babe Ruth. Is there a motion on the table?"

David saw an opening. "Yes, Jack, before we begin I would like to motion that we move to executive session."

"What's that?" asked Scully.

"It is part of the session that is held in private," Jack said.

"Aren't we meeting in private now?" Poser asked. "I mean, we're in a conference room and nobody else is in the building. How much more private can we get?" A few of the men chuckled.

Jack sighed. David was right and he knew it. "I think it is customary that personnel matters be held in executive session," Jack said.

"Okay, let's go into executive session then. Let's get going," Scully said, tapping his pen tip on the table.

"Maybe we need to shut the door and close the drapes too," Melotti joked.

Jack smiled and shook his head. "A motion has been made to go into executive session. We need a second."

"I'll second," said Scully. "I don't get why we have to do this."

"Is there any discussion?" Jack asked. Only the creaking of some swivel chairs could be heard. "Okay then, all in favor?" Jack asked. There was a weak chorus of "Aye"; some men chose to raise their hands instead. "Anyone opposed?" Silence. "The motion carries unanimously then," Jack announced.

The secretary, Chuck Spittle, scribbled all the happenings down on paper.

Chuck Spittle looked like he had just got off the bus from the Woodstock festival. He wore 1970s tinted glasses and sported a beard the length of his long brown and silver frizzy hair.

"All right, can we move this along now?" said Poser.

"Yeah, sure," said David. "So long as we understand that discussions in executive session are confidential."

There was a pause. "So what does that mean?" said Scully.

David explained, "It means that if you discuss what takes place in executive session with anyone outside this room, you could be the subject of disciplinary proceedings, or possible expulsion."

Spittle's leg started to bounce up and down like a jackhammer, Melotti's eyes rolled, and Arnold shifted in his seat. They all understood that David was making reference to Scully and Poser's eagerness to tell Barkus everything that would take place that night.

"Where are you getting this stuff from?" asked Poser.

"*Robert's Rules of Order*," said David calmly.

Jack tried to explain it all. "*Robert's Rules of Order* is a part of our league constitution," he said.

This was news to all of them, as Jack didn't use *Robert's Rules*. Jack wanted to be one of the boys, and enforcing rules at a meeting was not a part of that persona. Instead, as in many leagues, there was very little order at Jack's board meetings. No one ever had the floor, so people would talk over each other. There would also be many private side conversations going on during business discussions. The board would often wander off topic and no effort was made to get back on. Tangents led to tangents on tangents. Male bonding trumped substance at all points. It was no wonder that an average meeting exceeded three hours. If these men had brought sleeping bags and made a campfire out of the conference room furniture, they would have made an overnighter out of it.

Jack continued. "Personnel issues are generally discussed in executive session."

"You've got to be kidding me," Poser said.

"This is a waste of time," Scully said. "We want you to resign."

David wanted to rip Scully a new one. He wanted to tell him to go fuck himself. But Annie had trained David in Dr. Donahue's five core principles of behavior. She was talking through David to Scully. "Help me understand why I need to leave," said David, separating the problem from the person. Annie had a disarming way of addressing potential conflict. David knew the numbers were clearly stacked against him, so Annie's approach made better sense. There was always the chance that some board members would be more sympathetic to David if he kept his calm. "What are the charges?" he asked.

"You know what the charges are, David," Poser said as he put both hands on the table, leaned forward toward, David and stood up.

Scully followed Poser's lead. "Don't act like a dumbass. You know what's going on here."

David sat back in his chair and looked at Jack. "I don't think talking to me in such a manner is appropriate under *Robert's Rules*, right Jack?" Annie, David thought, would have been proud of him for not getting upset and for defending himself in a polite yet firm way. David was looking to Jack for some help to keep order. That was his job as president.

Jack was writing something on his legal pad and did not look up. "Ah, guys, try and tone it down a bit," he said. Masters did not want anyone to get upset with him if he could help it. When push came to shove, he went with the flow. If board members went at one another, that was fair play unless enough objected, and nobody was going to object to David getting slammed.

Melotti said, "Hey, David, screw you and *Robert's Rules*."

Jack continued to write. David looked at Jack for a response to Melotti's comment. Nothing. There were some uncomfortable smiles around the table. Seconds passed and a tacit agreement was made among the board to ignore what Melotti had just said.

"Benny," David said, "it would appear that Jack agrees with you." Melotti relished his victory by flashing his porcelain-white veneered teeth.

Jack looked up to consider saying something but was content to let Poser go back on the attack. "You know *why* you're here!" Poser said.

"You want me to resign," said David. "I get that much. Your e-mail did not give any reasons, so I'm left to guess."

"David, you stole the name of the Elite Travel Baseball League," Poser said.

David was surprised that word had spread so fast. He looked Poser in the eye. "I'm not sure how this is at all relevant to our league. Besides, the name was available to anyone in New York State. How could I steal something that did not belong to anyone?"

Scully's eyes squinted as he looked at David. "Don't be a wise ass. You know what Oscar means. Rob Barkus thought of the name first. He put it on his website."

"You know, Rob Barkus and the Elite families want to know why you did that," Poser said.

"I am not sure I understand," David said, trying to remain calm. "What does Rob Barkus have to do with our league? He isn't on *our* board. His son does not play in *our* league. He is running an outfit that competes with *our* program."

Poser rubbed his chin. "Okay, I'm asking you as a board member of this league, why did you register the name?"

"I did it to make a point," said David.

"What point was that?" Scully asked.

David looked down the long table at the faces. Meeson had the same stupid grin on his face that he had when David first saw him in the hallway. Spittle had his nose to his pad of paper trying to figure out what to note as secretary while his leg was drilling a hole through the floor. Melotti put a cigarette between his lips and was about to light it.

Henry Maxwell was staring at Melotti, eyes wide open from across the table. Henry, an auditor, was a stickler for rules but only when they impacted him. "Benny, there's no smoking allowed here," he said.

"Aw, nobody else is here 'cept for us. They all went home. Who's gonna know?"

"I'm gonna know," said Maxwell. "I can't stand cigarette smoke. My dad died of lung cancer, you know."

"Put it away, Benny," said Jack. "All we need is for the smoke alarm to go off."

Melotti put the cigarette away while shaking his head. "I'm gonna need a smoke soon. I hope this doesn't take long."

"David, will you please answer the question already?" pleaded Poser.

"Look," said David, "there has been some confusion about what the Elite Travel Baseball League represents." Annie liked the word *confusion* since it did not assign blame to either side. David continued. "The Elite Travel Baseball League portrayed itself as a nonprofit organization. You can see it on its website. But if I now own the name as a nonprofit corporation, then it raises some questions."

"Yeah, like how do you have *so* much free time on your hands?" Scully joked.

"I try to make time to do the *right* thing," said David. "Anyway, I think there is some confusion about what the Elite Travel Baseball League is all about. As I was saying, many people thought it was a nonprofit organization, a program authorized by the Internal Revenue Code like its website suggests. But if I'm the one who has the name reserved as a nonprofit corporation because it wasn't taken, then what exactly is the Elite Travel Baseball League? If it's not a nonprofit organization, it looks like it must be a for-profit outfit."

"So what? Who cares?" asked Scully.

David locked Scully in his sight. "Well, Scully, you obviously don't care. But it might bother some people that there is an outfit misrepresenting itself as a nonprofit that wants our baseball field. It might bother some people that they are volunteering their time while someone else is profiting off their labor."

"Why can't we just play baseball?" asserted Poser. David knew that the just-want-to-play-baseball appeal would find the lips of some board members before the evening was out. It was a favorite rallying cry of board members when faced with issues they wished to avoid as either too complicated or too controversial. It was offered now as a chant to unify the men in looking the other way on the issue. And David sat patiently in his chair and waited for the "amen" chorus that would almost certainly follow.

"I'm with Oscar on this," said Melotti. "Who gives a shit? Give me a field and a schedule to play and leave me the fuck alone."

"Amen," said Scully.

David could always count on Scully to come through with an "amen." David looked at Melotti sitting next to Poser. "You may not give a shit, Benny, but the town might—"

"Screw the town," said Melotti.

David eyed Melotti. "Easy for you to say, Benny. You don't even live in this town."

David had called Benny Melotti out. Over the years, rumors had circulated that he lived in another town. But nobody dared question him about it. David had done the research and confirmed that he lived in an adjacent town and in that town's school district. Evidently, Melotti used a relative's address in Indigo Valley to access the schools there for his children without paying the higher school taxes. More important, he lived outside the boundaries of Indigo Valley baseball. He and his son should have been playing ball in another town.

Melotti was surprised that David was calling him out and stood up and started waving his arms frantically and spitting saliva. "I don't have to put with this bullshit. Mind your own business."

"Take it easy, Benny, and sit down," said Meeson. "This meeting isn't about you."

Before Melotti could sit down and before anyone could say anything more, David proceeded to make his point. "Look, the town doesn't lease us the field for one dollar per year so we can offer it to a for-profit outfit to use for its own gain. They give it to us to use as volunteers to provide baseball to all the kids in town."

Melotti sat down and began to swivel from side to side.

"The Elite families live in this town," Poser said. "Why can't they play on the Babe Ruth field? They can pay the league to play here."

"Right, like last year?" David countered. "Show me the books and show me where the Elite paid us any money. There was some oral agreement for them to pay us, but show me where it paid us one dime. Besides, we shouldn't be in the business of supporting a program that competes against us, a program that undermines community baseball."

The treasurer, Eddie Reddick, woke up at the end of the table. "I haven't been able to reconcile the books from last year. They were not in order when they were given to me. I didn't see any record of payments."

Eddie Reddick was a slender CPA who was elected treasurer last autumn. Poser and Scully had roped him into it about the same time his son joined an Elite Travel team.

"Quiet, Eddie," said Poser.

"Look, I was just saying—"

"Did you hear what he said?" asked Scully. "You know, when it was my first year on the board, I kept quiet and I learned a lot. Try it."

Eddie picked up his pen and started twirling it like a baton from one finger to the next.

"Take it easy, Paul," Jack said. The last thing Jack wanted was a resignation from the board, especially the treasurer. That wouldn't look good. It would mean work for him to find a replacement and he just wanted to make it through the season and deal with any residual problems afterward.

David kept his focus. "It's not just the money, though. It's the principle too. The Elite teams do not have any tryouts. They are invitation-only teams made almost exclusively for the school players. It is not open to all kids. Under our lease, we are supposed to provide equal opportunity for youth to participate in our baseball programs. How are having teams without tryouts providing equal opportunity to all youth in our town? How can we allow these teams to use our field? Look, these are private teams with their own rules. And people have a right to participate in them just like they have the right to join a private golf club and socialize with people of their choosing." David now looked directly at Meeson. "But we are not a private baseball league. This is a public field and we have been entrusted with it to provide baseball for all kids in this town to play as one. Just like private golf clubs own their golf courses so they can do what they want, the Elite teams need to buy their own field. The Babe Ruth field is *not* for sale."

Poser stood up and started pacing on one side of the long conference table. He stopped and looked down at David. The veins in his forehead and neck started to bulge as his face turned red. He puffed out his chest and stuck out his lower jaw. "You just like to find ways to fuck us over, don't you David?"

Now Scully stood up. He was the mirror image of Poser as he looked down at David. "Is this how you get your kicks, Thompson?"

The room went silent. David thought Poser and Scully were going to jump him at any second. He readied himself by backing his chair away from the table and stared them down, one at a time.

Poser went back to pacing and Scully joined him, but on the other side of the table. Poser tried to calm himself down. "Look," he said loudly, and then he paused. He lowered his tone and said, "Look, they don't want to *buy* the field, we just want to *share* it and pay for our use of it. Now that is a reasonable request, right David?"

David looked down the table. All eyes were on him. There was no need to point out that Poser had mixed "they" with "we" in the same sentence. It didn't matter to these men. He closed his eyes and pinched the upper part of his nose with his thumb and index finger. "*Share?* You want to *share* the field? Let me explain to you what your idea of sharing has done to this league. Five years ago, we had twice the number of kids participating in Babe Ruth in-house ages thirteen to fifteen. That has been cut in half since you guys started to share the field. And guess what? At the rate this is going, in a year or two there won't be enough players left to have a league in this town. Can you imagine that after having Babe Ruth baseball in this town since 1957, we are about to lose our charter because we don't have enough kids left to play baseball? We are already close to losing the charter now because we did not field an all-star team at ages thirteen through fifteen last year because all you cared about was fielding these Elite baseball teams where most of your kids play. You don't believe me?

Go ask Brad Summers, our New York State commissioner. Bottom line is that your idea of sharing has almost killed Babe Ruth baseball in this town."

Poser and Scully stopped pacing and glanced at one another quickly.

Arnold Meeson sat up in his chair and looked down the table at David. He dabbed his brow with a tissue and pulled his golf shirt V-neck down with his index finger, revealing his large Adam's apple. It was time for the smooth politician to go to work.

Arnold had called David several times over the course of the previous year to lend support and encouragement to the changes he was making to the program. He realized that there was something deeply wrong with baseball in the town. His conscience caught up with him. Yet Arnold would never talk to David on the phone with his wife Angela around. Whenever David heard Angela in the background during a call, Arnold would rush to cut it short. On the field, Arnold would seek David out to talk with him so long as no other Elite parent was around.

At board meetings—where his Elite buddies could see him—Arnold was unwilling to back David on any issue, though he had supported David just a few days earlier when he made one of his frequent phone calls to him. Instead, Arnold would sit in the boardroom and say absolutely nothing except to offer some backslapping comment to a fellow Elite parent. He was one of the good-old boys when he was placed in the boardroom. After a few goarounds, David no longer took or returned Arnold's phone calls. He thought Arnold might be better served by seeing his priest for confessional services.

Arnold cleared his throat and said, "David, I hear what you're saying and I support your efforts. You know my son is playing Babe Ruth this year. Surely, you have *some* field time to offer the Elite teams in the summer? You could not have scheduled the field for this summer yet? I mean, it's April after all."

David heard Annie whispering in his ear. He heard her telling him to be nonconfrontational, to provide an excuse for his action, to deflect blame away from himself. "Arnold, we only have one field, whereas similar programs of our size have two fields," he said. "We don't have any access to the high school fields, so we are forced to cram all of our programming onto one field."

If Barkus and his followers could say that they didn't have time to play Babe Ruth baseball, David was content to say that he didn't have any time available for them to play on the Babe Ruth field.

Arnold clasped his hands and rested his milk-white forearms on the table. "But you said that the program was now half the size it was five years ago. There must be some room for us."

"Yeah, he's right," Poser said.

Spittle's leg stopped jackhammering for a second. "He has a point."

"He hit the nail on the head. There's gotta be room for us," said Melotti.

"There has to be room for us," echoed Scully.

"David, is there room for them?" asked Jack.

David could not believe his ears as he leaned back. The reason that the in-house enrollment had been cut in half was because these clowns were too busy promoting and accommodating the Elite Travel league at the expense of the Babe Ruth community program. And now they sought to use that fact as justification to take the field. But these guys either did not see that or didn't care. They wanted access to the field, period.

David looked at Jack. "I think there is a misunderstanding here," he said. Annie also loved the word *misunderstanding*. Like *confusion*, it did not assign blame to either side and aimed to defuse a situation. David continued. "I think we may have forgotten what our mission is here under our constitution and lease."

"Oh, geez, here comes the legal mumbo jumbo," said Scully, still pacing. "I can't stand lawyers."

Poser let out a laugh in stride.

While David ignored the pacing antics, some board members eyed Poser's and Scully's pacing back and forth like they were watching a tennis match.

"You're going to give the Elite teams field time!" blurted Scully.

"They are not part of our organization," David said. "Besides, there is no real field time to offer. The field time is booked by our own teams and programs."

Poser stopped his pacing and shouted, "Oh come on now! How can there no open field time in July when the rec season ends in late June?" Back to pacing.

David stood up and faced the board. "While we may have free field time for the summer now in April, we need to allow for Babe Ruth travel teams and all-star teams to form with the kids that remain. We'll run clinics and camps on the field after school ends in June to energize our program. If you guys won't play with us, we'll try and separate other kids from their game consoles to play. The field will be fully utilized. Our community baseball program has been severely damaged and is on life support. We need to give it an opportunity to recover so that it can flourish in the years to come. Besides, the Elite teams already use the two school fields. It is not as if they have no place to play."

"It's a lot of work to cut the grass on those fields," said Poser. "The school doesn't cut the grass in the summer, you know."

"Might I suggest that you pay someone to do it then," said David. "You pay enough money to Barkus and company to play baseball. You put some of that money toward cutting the grass. Why can't you leave our program alone?"

Arnold took out his tissue and wiped his brow.

Melotti leaned back in his chair and clasped his hands behind his head. "You say we are going to lose our charter because we don't got enough players and we don't field no all-stars teams, right?"

"Yes, that's correct," David said.

Melotti leaned forward and bellied up to the table. "I say I'm sick of this Babe Ruth charter bullshit."

"What do you mean, Benny?" asked Jack.

"We don't need the Babe Ruth charter. We can get a charter from the Elite Travel Baseball League and be done with this Babe Ruth charter bullshit for good."

Almost before Melotti was finished, Meeson said, "Now there's an idea." At that moment, David understood what the two had been talking about in the hallway before the meeting.

David sat down and leaned back in his chair. "You would have to change the constitution and take out all the references to the Babe Ruth charter."

"So what?" said Poser.

"It would require a two-thirds vote of our board," said David.

"It's a lock," said Scully.

David looked down the table at the other board members who not had said anything that evening: Sam Waterman had one elbow resting on the table with his hand propping up his forehead while engaged in a staring contest with the table's surface; Avery Bransen was slumped over hypertexting someone on his

BlackBerry; Steve Harrison was doodling geometric shapes on a pad of paper; and Rich Cox was yawning while creating origami from a league handout.

David thought Avery Bransen was paying the least attention. "Avery, you played Babe Ruth baseball here as a kid, what do you think about that idea?"

Bransen was startled and set down his cell phone. "Ah, um, sorry, I was texting my daughter."

David smiled. "Avery, what do you think of the idea of dropping the Babe Ruth charter after fifty years?"

Bransen put down his phone and sat up. "I'm sorry, where did this come from? Why would we do that?"

"Good question," David said. "I know the town would ask why we are surrendering our charter with a national nonprofit organization to go with some local, for-profit outfit."

Poser stopped and turned to pace the other way. "Why can't Elite Travel Baseball League register as a nonprofit too?"

Henry Maxwell spun his chair around and faced Scully. "I think that name has been reserved already."

Scully puffed out his chest and stopped his pacing. "Yeah, you could say that Thompson stole the name!" Back to pacing.

Without looking up from his doodling, Steve Harrison commented, "If it was their name in the first place why would the state give the name to David?"

Rich Cox was trying to get his origami boat to sit on the table without falling over. "I think Elite's claim to that name has the same problem as my boat here. It doesn't float."

Sam Waterman nodded. "I have to agree with you there, Rich."

David's plan was working. By reserving the name of the Elite Travel Baseball League and telling folks, board members were faced with Elite's nebulous status. If David had reserved the name as a nonprofit corporation, what exactly was the Elite Travel Baseball League?

"They can file as a nonprofit under another name. Big deal," said Poser.

"Let's get real here," David said. "Why would they file as an Internal Revenue Code–certified nonprofit after all these years? The gravy train has been on the express track and you think they are going to derail it?"

"Could you speak a little slower," said Spittle, stroking his beard with one hand. "I'm trying to get this all down in the minutes."

Poser stopped his pacing and looked in disbelief at Spittle. "You don't have to write this down. This meeting isn't about Thompson's opinion of things." Back to pacing.

Meeson was ready to make his move now. "What about the freshman team?" he asked. Meeson's son played on the freshman team and he had made his political calculation: the best way to get in good with Coach Powers was to get him the best field in town. He would gladly sacrifice the Elite teams, if needed, in order to be the hero who secured the Babe Ruth field for the freshman team.

"What about them?" asked David.

"There should be room for them," said Meeson.

"Have you ever been a scheduler at this level or any other level, Arnold?" David asked.

"No, it hasn't been one of my jobs."

"So what makes you qualified to say that there should be room for them?"

Meeson was determined. "You said our numbers are down. So you should be playing less baseball games overall. So there should be room for them. We've let them use it before. Is there room for them?"

"Not really. The boys that we have left will be playing more baseball this year to revitalize the interest in the league to draw more kids in to play."

Meeson tried another angle. "I support what you're doing, David. I really do. My son is playing Babe Ruth and school baseball. Knowing that, can't you make room for the freshman team?"

"If you want me to make an effort to support the freshman team, you need to make an effort to get more freshman kids to play in our program. So far, there are two of you. You need to talk to the freshman team and get more players like your son to support us."

"Some of these parents think that it is too much to be playing rec in addition to school baseball."

"In-house baseball is what we call it."

"Whatever you want to call it is fine by me."

"Why is it that all other leagues in the area have eighty to one hundred percent of school players playing in-house baseball in addition to school baseball and we have a tough time getting past single digits?" David asked.

"I don't know," said Meeson.

"Well, I will tell you what I think, Arnold," David said. "I have to agree with Rob Barkus on this point. At least he is being straightforward on this front. He says flat-out all the school boys are too good to be playing in-house baseball. You don't want to say that because politically it would not come off well. You know that attitude is not as likely to get you the field. Instead, you say it is too much baseball, which is code-speak for saying that you are too good to play with us."

Meeson sat speechless while reaching for his tissue to wipe his forehead. Poser had to jump in to the rescue. "You are out of order! How dare you accuse a fellow board member of lying."

"Those are your words, Oscar, not mine," David said. "What is it about inhouse baseball that is so terrible? Is having fun playing baseball with other kids from the same town so awful?"

"Baseball is about having fun while getting better," Poser said. "Playing rec ball does not benefit the better athletes. You have to play with better ballplayers to become better yourself."

"Oh, so that is how you want to define *benefit?*" David asked. "You sound like Barkus. Let's talk about it your way then. In the job market, are you better off with one skill set or two skill sets? The more skills you have the more you are able to land a job, right? Does anyone disagree with that?"

"Makes sense," said Spittle. Others nodded while some sat frozen in time.

"When you play in-house baseball," David said, "you get to play positions that you would not otherwise play in school baseball or on a travel team where you generally play only one position. You can catch if you want to try. If you have never pitched, you could try that too. Who knows? You might be good at some other position. And if you're skilled at another position, you are more valuable as a player to a team. What happens if all you've ever done is catch in high school and travel ball but your college team already has a catcher and needs outfielders? You're out of luck then. With experience in other positions through Babe Ruth in-house, you are infinitely more attractive to all those colleges. You also get some additional at-bats too if you play Babe Ruth in-house baseball. If you sit on the bench during school or travel ball, at least you are getting some at-bats when you play in-house baseball where all kids play. You can experiment. You can try to bat left handed if you are a righty. So right there are some of the benefits defined in adult terms."

David was on a roll. "Take it one step further for all the bottom-line dads and you could say that playing in-house baseball increases the chances of landing that college baseball scholarship. In fact, I know of just such an example over in Colonie. Kid didn't pitch on the school team or travel team and continued to pitch in-house until he got better at age sixteen and then got a ride to college as a pitcher."

"Those are good points, David," said Meeson. "Those are some of the reasons my son plays rec baseball."

"Glad you agree," said David, though he cringed as Meeson called it "rec" baseball again. "Now, instead of wasting time here in trying to secure the field for the freshman team that does not support our program, go back to the parents and spread the gospel to them, get them to sign up, and then we can see what we can do about supporting the freshman team. You can have them sign up now and we can waive the late fee. We just started the season and so we will get them placed on a team. What do you say, Arnold?"

The room was silent as the board members looked at Arnold. "I don't think the parents are going to change their minds. They are too worried about schoolwork."

"Schoolwork? I thought all these players were getting athletic scholarships?" kidded David.

"You're asking us to play a lot of baseball," said Meeson, gripping his tissue.

"Really? You think so? Let me tell you a story. I've got this player who is playing both school baseball and in-house Babe Ruth baseball. The player goes to school in Cohoes and the parents are divorced with one living here in Indigo Valley and the other in Cohoes. The player lives in Cohoes and plays for the school modified team—seventh and eighth graders. The Babe Ruth program over there was destroyed by the Elite teams, as they took many of their kids so there were not enough to form a league. The player's family was able to register for our in-house Babe Ruth program here because the father lives in the town. Funny how this Cohoes player can manage both school baseball and Babe Ruth baseball. There must be something in the water over there in Cohoes. Oh, did I mention to you that the player's name is Melissa, Melissa Meade?"

And with that vignette, David had pitched the ultimate low blow to the egos of the men in the room. A *girl* could handle both school baseball and Babe Ruth baseball, in two different towns no less. A *girl* could do both and the Indigo Valley freshman boys could not? It was the kind of checkmate argument that ends discussions among men and causes them to hang their heads in shame. For these men and their major-league-bound boys, there was nothing more embarrassing than losing to a girl in anything, but in baseball? Baseball was a man's sport in their minds; this was the domain for burly men and their teenage sons on the verge of manhood.

Girls played softball, not baseball; mothers worked in the concession stand, not as coaches and certainly not as board members. Girls and women were supposed to be spectators in the sport of baseball, not players.

In *A League of Their Own*, Tom Hanks's character said that "there's no crying in baseball." But the look on the faces of these men tested that line. There was a genuine sadness in the room.

The absence of any conceivable comeback line to David's attack on manliness was unsettling to the men. They looked at one another. Poser sat back down in his seat and Scully followed. They all longed for the silence to be broken by something, anything, anything at all. Someone needed to find those eloquent words that would unite the souls of these men and lead them back to battle. They searched in vain until Benny Melotti, wordsmith of the Elite Travel Baseball League, delivered his best effort.

"Fuck you and this girl," he said.

The men wanted to rally around this cry; they were desperately looking for something, anything, but was this it? Some men looked at each other with puzzled expressions. They were looking for affirmation from someone else in the room that this was the cry to rally around. But there was no second to Melotti's counterattack. Something just did not feel right to them about Melotti's call to arms, and something especially did not sit right with Arnold Meeson.

Arnold Meeson's teenage daughter played travel softball and months earlier, her male coach was arrested for statutory rape after having sex with one of the girls on the team. It was all over the newspapers and Arnold kicked himself for not sensing there was a problem with this coach before the incident. If there was one single driving motive to everything that Arnold Meeson did in life, it was to protect his children, to protect his daughter from lowlife, to protect his sons from baseball politics.

Before the rape incident, Arnold's children, even as teenagers, were not allowed out of the house in the parents' absence even though their neighborhood was safe by any standards. Since early childhood, the kids' outdoor play time had always been structured by and supervised by Angela and Arnold to keep the kids safe.

Meeson and parents like him did their best to kill outdoor free playtime in the 1990s, forcing pedophiles to abandon their cars and opt for a direct marketing approach through a computer terminal to reach the kids. But it wasn't the computer or a stranger that had pierced the veil of security that Meeson had cast over his family. It was someone the Meesons had known for years. Arnold Meeson blamed himself for failing to detect a problem with this coach; rekindling that memory at the meeting caused Meeson to have a systems shutdown.

David knew about the rape incident; he saw Meeson wavering. Meeson needed one more push to get him out the door. Since Melotti was doing such good work of it, David wanted to give him every opportunity to finish the job. "Benny, what did you just say?" David asked.

Some of the men at the table cringed at the thought that Benny was up to bat again. "You heard me right the first time. Girls don't belong on the baseball diamond. You know, the only diamond a girl should care about is the one on her finger when she marries."

Nice finishing touch, David thought. He could always count on Melotti to say something stupid and Melotti had come through again in the clutch. David leaned back and waited for Melotti's poison to flow through Meeson's veins.

Meeson's face became flush and he began to perspire again. He took out his crumpled-up tissue and wiped his forehead as his hand tremored. But the tissue, soaked with perspiration from the night so far, disintegrated as it passed over his brow and little flakes fell onto his Armani slacks. He wanted to give Benny Melotti a piece of his mind. He wanted so desperately to set him straight, but he sensed his emotions had gotten the best of him; he was afraid he would lash out and regret what he might say, and that it would somehow come back to haunt him or his sons. Meeson's longing to say something to Melotti had been squelched by a political calculation.

In his younger days, Meeson was an enthusiastic young man whose ideals led him to do good deeds and to speak his mind. But he had grown older and had become the consummate politician—a spineless middle-aged man who had been consumed by an overwhelming desire to protect and to promote his children.

He would name-drop to people, who would listen, that he was friends with all these men in the room, including David if it helped his cause. Meeson understood that Benny Melotti, as well as the other men in the room, were not true friends. He understood that Melotti, like the others, was an ally whose interests meshed for the moment. Meeson viewed everyone as a potential sports acquaintances to be used and discarded once they had served their purpose of benefiting, in some way, his children.

Meeson was so upset with Melotti that he could not focus on David anymore; he could not, at that moment, come up with anything to effectively counter David. He checked his Movado gold-trimmed watch. The time was 8:15 p.m. but that did not matter to him. Meeson was leaving regardless of the time. It was the gesture to the group that counted. Arnold held the watch up to his face for an extra second, just to make sure that everyone in the room saw him look at it, and to make sure everyone had an opportunity to admire its distinctive black face. He gathered himself together, as best he could, and said, "Guys, you will have to excuse me. I need to get to another meeting now."

Meeson collected his belongings and walked to the door. Melotti looked at him and knew something was not right. Meeson surely would have told him before the meeting if he was going to leave early. He touched Meeson's forearm as he got up and drew an angry stare from him. Melotti removed his hand and looked away as Meeson walked out the door.

Poser stopped a few feet away from David. "Cut the crap," he said, motioning his hands like an umpire ruling a runner safe. "Are you going to resign?"

"Be careful what you wish for," said David.

"What is that supposed to mean?" asked Scully.

"Who is going to do the scheduling if I step down?" David said. "Who is going to arrange for the announcers? Who is going to handle the umpires? Who is going to oversee the field maintenance? Who is going to oversee the in-house coaches? Who is going to make sure the concession stand is staffed? What's your plan?"

David knew the deal, even if some board members had not thought it through. If they wanted the Elite Travel Baseball and school teams to *share* the field, they would need to take on a huge workload and serve the inhouse program, the very program which they despised.

"We'll figure it out," said Poser.

"Let's summarize your plan and think the timeline through," said David. "So it's going on the end of April here and the Elite Travel Baseball League season begins one month from now. So within the next month, Barkus is going to see the light and file as a certified nonprofit corporation under a different name and, consequently, put a halt to his gravy train. Now, do you think Barkus is going to give up his charter for his new enterprise and give it to our league, which is the equivalent of giving up the financial control and the income of his operation?"

Nobody said a word.

"Okay, let's assume that happens. You guys are then going to approve the new charter as a board. Then you are going to rewrite our constitution and remove all Babe Ruth provisions and hope we don't lose our Babe Ruth charter for in-house baseball in playing a game of chicken with the state commissioner. And then you are going to get the approval of the town for this new arrangement after you tell them that these Elite teams don't have tryouts, all within thirty days. Does that about sum it up?"

David understood why the board wanted him removed instead of just voting to approve the Elite's use of the field. If they chose to just approve the Elite's use of the field at the meeting and not deal with David, they knew that David would fight them at the town level while he was still on the board. With David gone, they could just allow the Elite teams on the field without mentioning it to the town, just like they had been doing for years.

Maxwell immediately spun his chair around and faced Poser. He had heard enough. "Look, it's getting late and I promised my wife I would be home soon. The Elite Travel teams have the two school fields, right Oscar?"

"Yeah, they have them."

"Okay, let me know how you work this out then. I have to go." Maxwell stood up while grasping his notebook and headed quickly out the door.

"Hold up," said Cox, "I'll walk you out. I have to get going too." With that, he rolled up his origami boat into a basketball, shot into the wastebasket, and followed Maxwell out the door.

David looked out the window and long enough to see Arnold Meeson's mocha-colored Dodge Grand Caravan minivan exit the lot with its five stick-figure decals representing the family affixed to the rear window.

Poser clenched his fists and placed them on the table and leaned his tall frame over David. "Are you going to resign or are we going to have to vote you out?"

"Vote me out? You can't vote a director out."

"You're crazy," said Scully.

"Sorry, Paul," said David. "New York law says you can't vote a director out without cause unless our bylaws allow for it and they don't."

"Oh, here he goes again with the legal crap," said Scully.

"Hold on a second," Jack said, "I think David may have a point."

"You're kidding," said Poser.

"He's at least got one part right," Jack said. "But *Robert's Rules* is part of our bylaws and, if I'm not mistaken, it provides a way to remove a director and board member."

"You're right, Jack," David said.

Melotti's neck and forehead veins ballooned as he eyed David. "Didn't you get me the first time? Fuck your stupid rules!" He stood up and paced, zigzagging sideways, moving little by little backward to the open door as he spoke. It was like watching a piece of debris resisting the force of a vacuum that was the doorway. "I've been sittin' here listenin' to this crap all night. There is this rule and that one. There is this constitution or bylaw or whatever. Someone has got a charter; someone is going to lose a charter. I can't stand it no more. I just wanna play baseball. Whatever happened to playing baseball?" Now Melotti took a few steps back toward the table and slapped his hand on it. "You know what you can do with your *robber* rules or whatever they're called? Do you?" he said, shaking an index finger at David.

David said calmly, "*Robert's Rules* is what we have; a league without rules is no league at all."

"You brought all this up first," Melotti said. "It's your fault. If you would just fuckin' leave, we could all go play some ball." He turned around and retreated a few steps as the doorway sucked him toward the threshold.

In that instance, David recalled the first time he had seen Melotti act this way. It happened in a game a year ago where he and Melotti were both coaching town teams that were competing in the semifinals. Melotti had three boys in the bottom of his lineup who could not hit. So he had them all wear oversized jerseys that were pulled out in front so that they would virtually hang out over the plate when the kids were at bat. The kids didn't so much try and hit the ball with the bat as they tried to hit it with their jerseys. They wanted a hit-by-pitch call from the umpire so they would be awarded first base in position to advance and score when the top of the order was reached. After a few of these hit-by-pitch calls, David asked the umpire to direct the kids to tuck in their jerseys. The umpire agreed and Melotti went ballistic, pacing the first baseline and wagging his finger at the umpire while having a tantrum until the metal dugout door swung open and some assistant coaches managed to capture and cage him in the dugout to save him from ejection.

Melotti could not stay in front of David any longer because David now represented authority in Melotti's mind; Melotti had a problem with authority of any kind, and the force of the doorway caused him to move toward it. For a few seconds, Melotti was unsure if he should continue to resist as he paced side to side in limbo near the door threshold.

Avery Bransen was texting someone yet again. His son played on Melotti's travel team and Bransen had experienced Melotti's antics firsthand on several occasions. But his son was a borderline player and he did not want to say anything to Melotti that would jeopardize his son's standing on the team. Bransen would mumble one-on-one to folks about Melotti behind his back, but he would say absolutely nothing with Melotti around.

But Bransen had a daughter too. He felt the sting of Melotti's outburst. He stood up before Melotti could continue. He realized he would not be saying anything to the group in front of Melotti. That could spell potential confrontation, something that was not in his nature. Instead, he decided that he would express his feelings by walking out and hoping someone else would set Melotti straight. "Sorry, guys. I have to get going," he said. "My *daughter* needs to be picked up from drama practice at the middle school." With that, his cell found a respite in the phone holster hanging from his belt. He walked past Melotti on the way out with his eyes fixed on the exit.

Melotti turned and watched Bransen leave. He could sense that Meeson and Bransen—two allies—were not enamored with him for some reason. All Melotti knew was that if they had left abruptly, it was time for him to go as well. But Melotti wanted to go out with a bigger splash so that he could one-up Meeson and Bransen and then brag about it to them later.

"You know what?" Melotti said to the room as he broke into a little Hughie Jennings jig. "I'm outta here; I'm outta here for good!" A smile came to his face. "You can blame it all on Thompson here, him and his stupid rules about this and that, like who really gives a rat's ass."

"So you are resigning from the board then?" asked Jack.

"You're goddamn right I am. No more of this bullshit for me. I just wanna play baseball." Melotti pulled out a cigarette and lit it as he let out a new round of obscenities that made the likes of Poser and Scully look like amateurs. He turned and headed toward the doorway, puffing and cursing some more, and he disappeared into the smoke haze and bright lights of the hallway. His cursing echoed throughout the building.

Poser and Scully looked at one another and searched for words.

"It's your fault," Scully said, looking at David, "you made him quit."

"You're kidding, right?" said David. "Nobody could make Benny do anything."

"Are *you* going to resign already," asked Poser.

"No, I'm afraid you guys will have to force me out," David said firmly.

"David, I don't know where you get your fight from," said Jack, shaking his head.

David bit his tongue as he wondered if Jack had taken a stance on anything of substance in his life. "Jack, I'm fighting for the right of all kids to play baseball in their own town, on their own field," said David. "What's so hard to understand, Jack? You know this is the right thing to do."

"Jack, how do we get him off the board?" asked Poser.

"I'm not totally sure," Jack said, shrugging his shoulders. "I know there are procedures under *Robert's Rules*."

"Perhaps I can help you guys out," said David, reaching down into his satchel to pull out a small, thick golden paperback edition of *Robert's Rules*. David referred them to chapter twenty, entitled "Disciplinary Procedures," and reviewed, in great detail, the steps necessary to properly rid themselves of him. He indicated that they first needed to appoint an investigative committee through a resolution before the board. If approved, the committee needed to perform an actual investigation. If the investigation failed to exonerate him, David pointed out that they needed to propose a resolution that specifically charged him. If approved, a trial date would be set and David said he was entitled to a reasonable time to prepare his defense and could secure an attorney. He then told them that witnesses could be called by each side at trial and they would be followed by arguments from both sides before there was a vote to determine his guilt. He told them there were specific procedures for each step and, if they were not followed to the letter, David said he was within his rights to sue the board members for damages.

"Did you get all that, Chuck?" David asked.

Spittle was furiously trying to write everything down that David had said. "Yeah, I think so. Wow, you said a mouthful."

Poser rolled his eyes.

For the first time during the meeting, Sam Waterman removed his head from its hand support, took his elbow off the table, and sat upright with his arms at his sides. "That seems like a lot of work," he said as he rocked back and forth in his chair.

Steve Harrison dropped his pen on the table and pushed his doodles aside and looked at Waterman across the table. The two made eye contact. He swung his chair and faced the rest of the men at the table. "How long does this process take?"

"A few months at least," said David. "It should at least last all through the summer to about the time we are all up for reelection anyway in the fall."

Waterman's eyes grew large as he looked at Harrison for a moment. He looked at his watch. "I have got to get going or my wife will kill me." Waterman came to life as he rocked forward and sprung himself out of his chair.

Harrison pushed his chair back and faced the rest of the members. "It's about time I got going too." He quickly rose and walked with Waterman toward the door. He turned back and looked toward the men that remained. "Whatever you guys decide is fine by me."

Waterman looked over his shoulder and said, "And by me too." And with that, they both were gone.

David rolled his chair to a position where he could see the driveway outside the conference room picture window.

Poser stood up and stretched and faced the window. Spittle, Masters, and Reddick remained seated along with David. Scully leaned back in his chair and wondered if he should stand along with Poser.

Poser stopped and turned to face David. In an almost pleasant voice he said, "Hey, David, some parents I know are trying to make plans for Indigo Valley Day. Is it true you are not going to schedule games on Indigo Valley Day?"

David kept his eyes fixed on the driveway and said, "No, there will be a host of makeup games played that day due to rainouts. Some teams also want to get on the field to practice."

Poser and Scully exchanged puzzling looks. Poser shrugged his shoulders and Scully rolled his eyes.

Jack pointed at the copy of *Robert's Rules* lying on the table by David. "David, can I borrow that book for a few days?"

"Sorry, Jack, it's the only copy I have and it looks like I'm going to need it."

Scully looked to Jack. "What's the next step? Let's get this back on track."

"I'm not sure," Jack said. "David says we have to form a committee, an investigative committee. Isn't that what you said David?"

For a second, David was amused with the fact that he was the one outlining the process for his own expulsion. But discussing the process at length served his purposes now, as he was stalling for time. David said, "Chuck, why don't you read back your minutes on that topic."

"All right," said Spittle, who was happy to be included in the meeting, even if it was done at the invitation of David. Spittle began reading the entire procedure that David had outlined. About halfway through, David saw two more minivans drive out of town hall onto the roads of Indigo Valley. He knew they belonged to Waterman and Harrison. A sense of relief came over him as he realized that the nonsense he had endured was about to come for an end, at least for now.

David stood up and packed up his papers and the book and put it all in his satchel. He had made it to the finish line and it was time to go home.

Poser walked over to David and scowled. "Where are you going?"

"I'm going home to see my wife and son," said David.

"You can't," said Scully.

"Why not? How come the others can leave and I can't? Am I being held prisoner here?" asked David, throwing his satchel strap over his shoulder.

"Because this involves you! That's why," said Scully.

"This is your doing, not mine," said David. "Besides, you guys are going to do what you want to do anyway. I'm one guy; I can't stand in your way." David began to walk toward the door.

"He's right," Poser said, sitting down. "We don't need him. Let's get this committee formed."

"We need a motion from the floor," said Jack.

David turned around and faced the group. "I think you need a quorum in order to conduct league business, right?" The men exchanged glances with one another.

"Yes, that's correct," said Spittle.

"And with Melotti quitting, six is a quorum, right Chuck?" asked David.

"Yeah, I think that's right."

"But I'm leaving," said David, "and so that will make five."

Scully realized then that David had control; he could end the meeting by walking away. His eyes bugged out of his sockets and his face looked like a red balloon. "You're staying here, Thompson!"

"You guys are going to have to decide if you want to prosecute me or if you want to play baseball," David said. The room was silent, as David had taken their I-just-want-to-play-baseball plea and shoved it back down their throats.

"I'm going to give these kids a great baseball season they'll remember," David said. "Just keep in mind that by the time you are done ousting me, the baseball season will be long over and it won't matter one bit, and you could be faced with a lawsuit for all your trouble." With that David turned and walked out the conference room door and into the hallway.

"Get back in here!" yelled Poser.

"You're going to regret walking out!" Scully added. "You're a goddamn coward!"

David stopped in his tracks; his eyes popped wide open. Annie was walking toward him in the hallway. "Annie, what are you doing here?" he asked. She stopped to kiss him and said, "I'm here to protect you." Then she turned and marched into the conference room.

David could see the men at the table get up when she walked into the room. They were shocked that a woman would walk into their dugout. She stood in front on the conference table and looked at all the men, one by one, as she spoke.

"My husband might be some things, but he isn't a coward. He's got more guts than the lot of you combined. Nobody, I mean nobody, talks to my husband that way. Anybody who does will have to answer to me every day for the rest of their pathetic lives. You'll be my Eddie Waitkus; I'll be your Ruth Steinhagen. You get the picture?"

The men looked at one another, wondering if Annie had overheard the entire meeting, wondering if she had heard the comments about girls and baseball.

Chick Spittle whispered to Jack, "Who is Ruth Steinhagen?"

Annie heard him. "She's your worst nightmare. She's the stalker who was obsessed with Phillies player Eddie Waitkus and shot him in the chest. Do you get the picture now?"

The men looked at one another, not knowing what to make of Annie before she turned and walked out of the room with as much purpose as she had entered.

She walked to David and grabbed him by the hand.

"Let's go home, David," she said. They walked hand in hand down the hallway.

David looked at Annie, not knowing what to make of her. "Annie, how did you know the story about Ruth Steinhagen and Eddie Waitkus?" he asked.

"I was watching *The Natural* tonight with Christy on the movie channel. They discussed the history of the movie before it started and talked about the incident." Annie had thought about Robert Osborn's introduction while watching the movie. She was struck by the possibility that Donahue's five core principles of human behavior might not apply in a world where nobody was aware of or interested in Donahue's rulebook.

David and Annie didn't say anything more before they stood in the parking lot by Annie's car. David pulled her toward him. "Annie, are you okay?" he asked.

"Never felt better," she said.

David hugged her and felt how warm she was against his body. He could feel her heart beating fast like she had run up to town hall from home.

"I don't know what got into you tonight," he said as he touched her chin and pushed back her hair. Her face was radiant.

"I guess life finally caught up with me," she said before kissing him.

21

NORMAN ROCKWELL'S VISION

I t was a sunny Friday morning and David found himself sitting alone on a backless bench in the center of the Norman Rockwell Museum in Stock-bridge, Massachusetts. All of the other museum visitors had congregated in the meeting room down a hallway where Angelo Wrighton, noted Rockwell scholar, was about to make his presentation.

David held his family's glass-framed *Maternity Room* drawing under one arm as he spun around to take in the octagonal room. Four Norman Rockwell illustrations surrounded him in the heart of the museum on four separate walls divided by hallway entrances that branched out to other gallery spaces in the museum. The sun cascaded through the high-domed glass ceiling of the room and splashed around the dome walls. This was the heart of the gallery, the core of Rockwell's artistry, designed specifically to enshrine Rockwell's illustrations of Franklin Roosevelt's Four Freedoms: *Freedom of Speech, Freedom of Worship, Freedom from Want,* and *Freedom from Fear.*

David's family modeled in several of Rockwell's illustrations. He recognized Mead Schaeffer posing in Freedom from Want and he felt like Schaef (that's what Norman called him) was inviting him into the dining room to enjoy Thanksgiving dinner with the rest of the family there.

David's eyes rested on *Freedom from Fear,* the last freedom enunciated in Franklin Roosevelt's 1941 State of the Union address. In it, a husband and wife are tucking their two sleeping children into bed while the father holds a newspaper with World War II headlines. The painting reminded David of when he tucked Annie and Christy into bed after a long day of dealing with —perhaps Doubleday best described it—his "trifling difference of opinion" over the state of baseball in his town, his state, his America.

"Sir, excuse me sir," said a voice over David's shoulder.

David turned around on the bench and saw a security guard standing over him. "I'm sorry," David said, "I was just admiring the painting."

"No apologies necessary, sir. That's why we hang them up," the guard said, smiling. "I just wanted to let you know that the talk is about to begin in the west gallery meeting room if you would like to attend."

"Thank you," David said, and he got up with his drawing and moved to the meeting, where he took a seat on a bench in the rear.

Cary Shannon, the lady who had talked to David over the phone, introduced Mr. Wrighton to the audience, and then he began his talk.

"I want to welcome you the Norman Rockwell Museum," he said. "This is my first visit here and, I must say, I am stunned by the elegant simplicity of this museum in its classic town-hall design. It is a fitting home for Norman Rockwell's work and it is a great starting place for us to begin discussing what it meant to be an American to Norman Rockwell. Like the town-hall design of this gallery, Norman Rockwell's work focused on the community. Most of Rockwell's works focused on family, friends, the community at large and their interrelationships. His works, in general, downplayed individualism for its own sake— there are very few works that have only a single person as the subject. Today, all over America, from the Guggenheim earlier this decade to the Smithsonian at the end of this decade, people are in the process of reexamining Rockwell's work and looking deeper into what people used to think was corny or hokey. They are discovering that there was something more there, something that was overlooked at the time, and they are accepting that it is all right to be a fan of Rockwell. Rockwell realized full well that what he portrayed was not real as much as it was an ideal. In his 1960 book, *Adventures as an Illustrator*, Rockwell said, 'The view of life I communicate in my pictures excludes the sordid and ugly. I paint life as I would like it to be.' Rockwell's upbringing and his personal life were far from perfect for sure, but he painted to express his ideals of what we are when we are at our best. And to Rockwell, we are at our best when we realize that quote, 'everybody has a responsibility to everybody else.' "

Those last words hit home with David and he considered them as his mind wandered from Wrighton's talk. What he lacked in his baseball universe were parents who felt connected, who realized they had a responsibility to everyone else and not just their own son, who understood that baseball was a community sport, and who cherished the notion that kids from all different walks of life and skill level could get to know one another and enjoy playing baseball in their hometown.

David rejoined Wrighton's talk as he wrapped up. "In summary, I have to agree with C. F. Payne, famous illustrator, known as the modern Rockwell, when he said, 'In baseball, one name stands alone: Babe Ruth. In illustration, our Babe Ruth is and will always be Norman Rockwell.' Thank you."

The audience applauded and Cary Shannon proceeded to take questions for Mr. Wrighton.

David put the drawing of the *Maternity Room* on his lap. He tilted it backward to get a good look at it. No longer did he see a waiting room scene; he saw his baseball board meeting from the night before instead. The two men pacing in front of the long waiting room couch were Paul Scully and Oscar Poser. He had seen the same body language and the same facial expressions the previous night at his board meeting. The only difference was that the other men in the drawing sat on a long couch and on a few chairs at either end as opposed to sitting at a conference room table. All of a sudden, the anger David felt toward the men at the baseball board meeting was overcome by a sense of compassion and then pity for them. Nothing had changed for them in all the years since they first became fathers; they were still concerned over protecting their sons even as they entered their teen years. But more than that, the men in his baseball league never connected; they never saw the greater good in being able to provide baseball in their town to every kid because it had become all about their kid. In Norman Rockwell's words, they failed to understand and embrace the idea that everybody in a community has a responsibility to everybody else.

"Excuse me," said a woman's voice. "Hi, I'm Cary Shannon. Are you David Thompson?"

"Yes," David said, standing up and extending his hand. They shook. "Nice to meet you," he said.

"Glad you could make it," she said.

"It was a great talk. Hey, I brought the drawing," David said, turning it around for her to see.

"Oh, my," she said.

David handed her the drawing and she held it at each end while looking it over. "It is absolutely stunning," she said. They talked about some of the characters portrayed and labeled underneath: the "frightened novice," the "distraught executive," the "believer in the worst," the "pacer," the "chain smoker," the "hearty salesman," and the "magazine shredder" as portrayed by David's grandfather.

"Thank you for allowing us to share it with everyone else here at the museum," she said.

"My pleasure."

"I'm going to take it back and place it in our vault for safekeeping until we can create an exhibit space for it."

"Sounds like a good idea. Thank you for inviting me to the talk."

"You're welcome, Mr. Thompson. We're having a reception in the other room and you're welcome to join us."

"Thank you. I will."

And with that she summoned a security guard and the two walked away back to the administrative offices with the drawing.

David had some refreshments and looked at the other works in the museum, but he was eager to get back home to see Christy and Annie. He said goodbye to Ms. Shannon and began the winding walk to the parking lot. David reflected on the day. It felt good to get out of town and go to a new environment to help put things in perspective. He felt refreshed and reenergized. Wrighton's talk was uplifting and infused him with optimism. Maybe, he thought, there was hope in his situation where he had seen none before. Maybe, he was too much a part of the situation, too close to it to realize the existence of other possibilities and options that might straighten the baseball mess out. Surely there must be someone else who could help lead the men away from the Elite Travel Baseball League money machine and instill them with a sense of tolerance and cooperation for the good of all. This Rockwell ideal of community used to be part of baseball in Indigo Valley.

David's cell phone rang as he approached the car. Johnny's number flashed on the screen.

"Hey, what's going on?" said David.

"What are you doing?" asked Johnny.

"I am out in Stockbridge, Mass, doing some work."

"Did you survive last night?"

"Yeah, I survived. Who knows what they plan to do next." David then proceeded to tell Johnny what happened.

"You did a good job holding your ground," Johnny said. "You won that battle."

"Yeah, chalk one up for the good guys. Anything else new?"

"Brad has really been helping to align Babe Ruth leagues with the Empire concept. They are signing up to participate."

"That's great news!"

"Yeah, well, maybe the news is too good for us."

"What do you mean by that? How can it be too good for us?"

"The scuttlebutt is that Barkus and Morgan are going nuts over losing teams."

"So what? Let them go nuts then."

"I'm talking *really* nuts. Bat-shit nuts as in they're going to do something crazy to get back at us."

"Like what?"

"I dunno. Just be careful."

"Okay." David did not want to dwell on that prospect and ruin his day. "Hey, I have an idea."

"What's that?"

"You know Wayne Duffel, the athletic director, doesn't understand what's going on here. But he's new and that's to be expected. But our high school principal has been around awhile. So maybe he can help fix things." David had memories of the two prior principals and they were both engaged fully in the lives of the kids at school. "Duffel reports to the principal in some fashion, so maybe he's the guy that can step in to help straighten things out, to give our community direction."

They both agreed that David had nothing to lose by seeing him. With Christy then in his last year of middle school, David didn't know anything about the high school principal. But he thought there was an opportunity with him that he should not overlook in trying to prevent things from getting out of hand. He felt he had a responsibility to fully explore this option, to smooth things over, to reach an understanding with the principal and, ultimately, to make things right in the baseball community. David liked his positive, constructive approach. Annie would be proud of it.

When David returned from Stockbridge that afternoon, he called the high school, found out the principal's name, and made an appointment with his secretary to meet with him on Monday morning.

22

SHOW ME THE MONEY

The next Monday, Jacob Golder, Andrew Golder's older brother, leaned against the wall by the auditorium at the intersection of the two main hallways of Indigo Valley High School, a place aptly called the "Crossroads." His hands were in his pockets and he had one foot extended outward on the floor and the other foot up against the wall under his rear. It was the typical guy stance at Crossroads, a stance handed down from one class to another since the school opened in 1957.

Jacob had the stance down pat but it masked the turmoil going on within him. He was a senior in his second semester and everything around him was subject to question as he considered where he had been, where he was going, and what that meant, if anything. He had applied to Brigham Young University in the fall and had received an early acceptance so he hadn't bothered to apply anywhere else. But over the past few months, his religious beliefs had changed and he wondered if Brigham Young was a good fit for him anymore. Jacob was trying to sort it all out. Brigham Young had a religious presence on campus that embraced a belief in God and, for now at least, he didn't believe in God any more than he believed in the tooth fairy or the Easter bunny. His religious beliefs consumed him so much that he felt compelled to share them in the *Cornhusker*, the school newspaper. The article had been published three months earlier but this morning he had gone a step further on his blog by putting the church on a list of things to hate and by declaring a boycott of God. He thought he might find some sort of peace in the written expression of his religious beliefs, but that didn't happen; instead, he moved on to question other facets of his life.

Jacob's friends thought he was way too serious; they were too busy celebrating the end of high school.

Jacob looked at the swarm of students changing classes; the crowd grew outward from the center of the intersection until it was almost on top of him. He acknowledged some friends and acquaintances when they walked by as he thought about what he would write about next for the *Cornhusker*.

It was then that someone tripped over his extended foot. Jacob saw the backside of a man dressed in a suit almost fall to the floor. The man righted himself as he looked over his shoulder.

"Sorry," Jacob said to the man.

"I didn't see your foot there," the man said. "You need to be more careful, son."

"Yeah, I'm sorry," Jacob said to the man again, though he thought maybe the man should take his own advice. He recognized the man as someone who worked in the school. He had no idea if he was a teacher or administrator.

Jerry Conway grabbed his lapels and straightened out his gray pinstriped suit jacket. He was running late and was immersed in his own thoughts when he tripped over Jacob's foot on his way to his office. He was wondering then about how to handle Correll Buckhalter's situation. He turned away from Jacob and continued his purposeful strides, dodging the kids around him like he was running a football practice drill. His mind wandered to the e-mail he'd sent Peter. He wondered if his e-mail to him would shut him up or whether he would have to do something more. He entered the school's main office and didn't notice the crowd of students waiting there at the service counter as he sought out his secretary seated at her desk outside his office door.

"I don't want to be disturbed," he said to her.

"But Mr. Conway, you have an 11:00 a.m. appointment."

"Damn it," he whispered out loud. He glanced at his watch. It was 10:45 a.m. Conway was waiting for a call on his business cell and he didn't want to have to miss it. "Who is it?" he asked.

"David Thompson." "Who is he?" "Some guy who wants to talk with you about a baseball player or some thing baseball related."

"Right, now I remember. Let me know when he's here," Conway said as he walked into his office. He closed the door behind him.

David rolled into the parking lot at that point. There were a total of three parking spots that had signs mounted on posts that said "Visitor" on them. David spotted an empty visitor space, one sandwiched between a Buick and a shiny black Lincoln Navigator that was backed into its space. David tried to negotiate his Mustang into the space but had difficulty fitting as the Navigator had been parked with the passenger side tires resting on top of the painted parking line adjacent to David's space. After a few back and forth maneuvers, David was able to squeeze his car into the spot. As he pulled his keys from the ignition he saw a school district groundskeeper in the middle of a grassy island planting flowers by a flagpole and monument located in the center.

David slipped out next to the Navigator, making sure not to hit its side-view mirror. He saw a cell phone amplifier antenna the size of a fishing pole protruding from the Navigator's roof and noted the shiny chrome hubcaps.

The groundskeeper was on all fours and looked up at David. "Mighty tight fit there for you," he said while planting some pansies.

David approached him. The worker was a slender middle-aged man dressed in forest-green coveralls. He was black, which was remarkable only because Indigo Valley did not have many blacks. He had massive hands that were out of proportion to the rest of his sleek features.

"Yeah, that is quite a barge I parked next to there," said David.

The man laughed and said, "Funny, I have never heard anyone call it *that* before."

David asked, "Oh, you mean you've seen that vehicle here before?

"Every day."

"Every day?" David echoed.

"Yeah, that's what I said and I always mean what I say."

"I don't get it. You mean the guy who drives that thing—I assume it is a guy—visits here every day?"

The man laughed as he glanced up toward the school, then looked to either side. There was nobody else around.

"What's so funny?" David asked.

"You said 'visits.' You could say he *visits*. You are right, it is a *he*, though," he said. The man looked up and squinted at David. "Hey, haven't I seen you at the town baseball fields before?"

"Yeah, you might have seen me there. I run the Babe Ruth program for teens. You have a son playing ball there?"

"Yes, I do. I have a son who is starting to play Babe Ruth this year." The man stood up and wiped off his hand, then extended it to David. "My name is Eric. Eric Washington."

David offered his hand and Eric engulfed it in a handshake.

"Hi, I'm David Thompson."

"Nice to meet you," he said.

"What team does your son play on?"

"Babson Concrete."

David realized it was Poser's team. "How is his season going?"

"I'm not one to complain," Eric said, "and I appreciate what you do and all, but he's not getting hardly any playing time."

David became incensed. The league rules stipulated that all players were to be given equal playing time. "That's not right. I'll talk to your coach."

"I appreciate it, but I don't want to cause any trouble," Eric said.

"Don't worry, I won't say you complained. I'll handle it."

"Thank you so much. What brings you here this morning?" he asked.

"Funny you should mention baseball. I have a meeting with the principal in a few minutes about that very subject. Could you tell me where his office is located?" David didn't have any idea where the principal's office had been relocated after all the remodeling projects. Since Christy wasn't yet in high school, David had no reason to revisit it before his meeting with Duffel. It had been thirty years since he had graduated and he might have been in the school only a few times since then.

"You just go through the entrance doors there and go straight ahead halfway down the hallway—that is 'A' hall. Main office is on the right, and the principal's office sits to the rear of the main office."

Just then, from around the corner of the building, a faint *beep-beep* of a backup car alarm could be heard. Eric dropped to his knees and started working again.

"Walk back to your car and come back after he passes," he said to David.

"What are you talking about?" David said.

"No time to talk. Just do as I ask, please."

"All right." David turned and started walking back toward his car. An electric golf cart swung around the side of the school from where the beeping sound was heard. In the seat driving was a chubby middle-aged balding guy in a too-tight suit jacket that clashed with his slacks. The man was puffing on a cigarette and looking around as he drove by the two men down the access road to the athletic fields on the other side. Once he passed, David walked back to where Eric was working.

"What was that all about?" David asked.

"Security."

"I don't get it. You aren't a student here. Why are you so concerned about him?"

"I don't want to be accused of loafin'. Word gets around here, ya know? I got a few years left here and don't want to give them no excuse to geezer-size me."

"Geezersize?"

"Yeah, that's what I said. When they tell ya they are downsizin' or right-sizin' what they really mean is they are geezersizin' the department—making life so miserable for the old employees that they leave." He stroked his gray sideburns. "And my hair color don't lie. They're probably going to outsource all of us custodians soon enough anyway. Been lots of layoffs 'round here. Lots of good teachers got their pink slips."

"Gotcha."

"You best be careful 'round here. You had better get to that meeting of yours with Principal Conway. He's a big muckety-muck. That man still gets his raise, you know, like clockwork. You don't want to keep him waitin'. Oh, yeah, don't scratch *his* barge there when you leave."

David stared into his dark brown eyes and looked perplexed. "You said *his* barge?"

"I said what I meant—"

"I know, I know, and you mean what you say."

"You're a quick learner," Eric said, smiling.

"Took me a few go-arounds. So how come the principal gets to park in a visitor space?"

"He's the boss."

"You said he parks there every day?"

"Every day. Saves him fifty yards of walking from the general parking lot where everyone else parks."

"If he's the boss, why not just make one of the visitor spaces the princi-pal's spot by changing the sign?"

"I dunno. Maybe he wants to show everyone that the rules don't apply to him, but you didn't hear that from me."

David didn't know what else to say at that point and had to get to his meeting. "Thanks for your help. Nice meeting you, Eric."

"Nice meeting you too," Eric said.

David turned and started walking toward the school.

"Be careful in there," Eric said for the second time.

What does he mean by that? David thought.

He trekked down the hallway and found the main office on the right just where Eric had said. He walked in and faced the service counter. Behind the counter, there were two frenetic older women hustling to deal with the two dozen students gathered in front. In the midst of all this confusion, and set back from the counter, sat a pretty young woman who was spot cleaning her immaculate desk, oblivious to the chaos in front of her. David moved down the counter to get as close to the woman as possible. She was seated with her back to an office that had its door closed. There was a nameplate on the door that read "Principal Conway." David leaned on the counter. She cleaned the same spots she had cleaned a few seconds ago once again.

"Excuse me," David said.

No response. The cleaning continued. She didn't hear him over the commotion in the office.

"Excuse me," David said again.

"Oh, I'm sorry. I didn't see you," she said with a smile.

"You keep a very neat desk," David commented.

"Thank you," she said. "But it's like my desk is a magnet for dust and dirt. It's never-ending. Can I help you?"

"I have an appointment to see Mr. Conway."

She flipped a page in her appointment book. "Are you Mr. Thompson?"

"Yes."

"I have here that you want to talk with him about baseball. Where does your son play?"

David paused. "Um, he plays here in town."

"Oh, I thought he was a college player somewhere."

"Ah, no, he's currently a student here."

"Oh, my mistake. I thought . . . never mind. You can have a seat here by my desk. I will tell Mr. Conway that you're here."

David walked through the swinging gate to the area behind the counter.

He sat in a chair next to her desk. He saw the secretary open the door to the principal's office and stand in the threshold. She said David's name and stood there for a second before going inside and closing the door behind her. It was a few minutes before she reappeared. She walked out of the office and her smile was gone.

She didn't look at David. She looked at her desk instead. "You can go in now," she said as she sat down.

"Thank you." As David stood up, she picked up a bottle of spray cleaner and started spraying the desk where she had cleaned before.

The door was ajar. David looked in as he opened it further to enter and saw Jerry Conway sitting behind his desk talking on a cell phone. He motioned David into the office and pointed toward a chair off to the side of his desk, and so David sat down.

The office had a large picture window to one side of Conway that looked out onto a courtyard. Conway was sitting behind a large modern desk with bookcases behind him and file cabinets on either side. The office walls were decorated with some lightly dusted educational plaques and an assortment of sports memorabilia. David noticed there was an open sports magazine on Conway's desk.

David was looking at some of the sports memorabilia in the office. There was a glossy autographed photograph of Josh Cribbs, the Cleveland Browns kick and punt returner, hanging nearby on the wall.

He felt a bit uncomfortable staring off into space and waiting for Conway to finish, so he stood up to read a framed magazine article. Conway spun his desk chair around to face the wall behind him as he talked to someone about issues relating to a website.

The article had been published in the local *Business Review*, a weekly magazine of the area's business news. The article was titled "Forty Under Forty: Jerry Conway."

There was a long table below the hanging article with various piles of handouts concerning the school. There was also a pile of the *Business Review* article. David picked one up.

He could hear Conway wrapping up, so he sat back down with a copy of the article and folded it in half while waiting.

Conway finished talking and stood up. As he did so, he put the cell phone back into its holster, which hung next to a second cell phone on his belt. He was wearing pinstriped gray slacks, a pressed shirt, and a salmon silk tie. He extended his right hand down. David offered his hand and Conway gripped it, pressing his large fashion ring into David's palm.

"Jerry Conway," he said as he shook David's hand.

"Hi, David Thompson."

"It's been a hectic morning."

"Thanks for seeing me," David responded.

As Conway was sitting down, one cell phone went off. Conway looked at the caller ID and then at David. "I'm sorry, but this guy has been trying to reach me. Do you mind stepping out? There's a seat outside the door."

"Sure, no problem."

"Hello, this is Jerry Conway," David heard while walking out the door to sit down. Not knowing if he should close the door, he half pulled it shut on the way out. Class must have been in session because there were no students at the service counter and the place was quiet. Conway's secretary clicked on her keyboard about twenty feet away.

David sat down in the chair right by the door opening. He could hear Conway on the phone. "First of all," Conway said, "this news caught both Correll and me by surprise this morning. When I found out, I talked to Correll, who said to me there is *absolutely* no validity to the allegation that was made. He did not purchase drugs from this individual or speak to this individual on the phone."

David figured that this Correll kid had found himself in some kind of trouble at school. David turned his attention to the *Business Review* article. It was about forty people under the age of forty who were up-and-comers in the region, and Jerry Conway was one of them. David read on, expecting to learn about Conway's educational achievements, while half listening to Conway's conversation.

"My concern," Conway said, "with a situation like this is we're not there to ask questions or dive into the allegations. We can't bring out things that might call into question the credibility of the information. This thing gets a life of its own because an individual says this on the stand."

David continued reading the article. There was nothing at all mentioned about Conway and his job as principal at Indigo Valley High School. It talked about a different Conway and went on to say, "Conway's firm has secured more than $130 million in contracts and marketing endorsements, a figure that Conway wants to grow to $1 billion. Today, Conway represents seventy professionals." David was confused.

He listened to Conway speak passionately about the Correll boy to whomever was on the line. "I've got to go by everything I know about Correll Buckhalter as a person; all I can tell you is he's *always* conducted himself and carried himself as a professional."

Professional? David thought. He didn't think Conway was talking about a student.

He tuned in to Conway's conversation again. "Correll is well aware of the NFL's personal-conduct policy. He has respect for the league and the rules. And he's going to continue to carry on that way."

Just as he heard Conway complete that sentence, David saw a small picture of Conway in the bottom corner of the article. He brought it closer and saw Principal Conway staring back at him. He read another sentence in the article quoting Conway: "The part that I enjoy most is providing guidance and assistance to the lives of athletes and helping them accomplish lifelong dreams and goals."

David furiously read the article and put it all together. *I must be dreaming,* he thought. *The principal sounds like he's a sports agent.*

At the end of the article, it mentioned that Conway stayed true to his Italian heritage in that *The Godfather* was his favorite movie and that he loved to dine at Italian restaurants. Suddenly, David's stomach turned inside out and he felt a heat rush throughout his body. *Wonderful,* David thought, *another godfather in the making. I could field an entire team of godfathers now.*

When Conway mentioned the last name "Buckhalter," David, a football fan, realized then he was talking about Correll Buckhalter, a running back with the Philadelphia Eagles who had recently signed on with the Denver Broncos. David listened to Conway ramble on about Buckhalter. From what he could gather from the conversation, Buckhalter was alleged to have bought marijuana from a dealer.

David sat outside trying to soak in the absurdity of it all while swimming in a state of disbelief. Here sat the principal of Indigo Valley High School at his desk on a school day, during school hours, defending a professional football player on drug allegations. *I suppose,* David thought, *the drug problems in our high school are not as weighty as the ones in the NFL.*

David wondered how Conway was able to get away with it. He had to assume the superintendent and the board of education knew about his sports agency business. *Perhaps,* he thought, *this is viewed as a quaint, maybe even a cool undertaking by those in charge.*

The phone conversation turned to Josh Cribbs. David listened while he tried to process all of his thoughts. But something wasn't sitting right with him. From what David could figure, Cribbs was holding out and seeking to reopen his contract for more money. "It's obvious that Josh has outperformed his contract," Conway said. "All he's looking for is meaningful dialogue from the team and an acknowledgment that the contract he's under is inappropriate. If we get that, he'll show at minicamp." *Well,* David thought, *we certainly can't have Josh miss camp. It would be a black mark on his permanent record. What would his parents say?*

David's mind drifted as he felt a surreal undertow pulling him out to a sea of turmoil. *Conway has seventy professional athlete clients,* he thought. David understood that Conway's clients were high-maintenance types who were suddenly awash with money and in need of lots of services and attention. They were a full-time job in and of themselves.

He looked back at the article and wondered if Conway would be so kind as to share some of that $1 billion in targeted revenues with a school district that was strapped for cash and laying off good teachers and staff left and right.

Conway continued talking about his contract discussions with the Browns over Cribbs. "We exchanged e-mails last night but there were no proposals or numbers discussed. It's time for the organization to step up and do the right thing for this *kid,*" Conway said.

Kid? Kid! David thought about that word and could not get it out of his mind. *KID?* The word hit him hard and it stung, like a fastball to the abdomen. An inner rage began to brew. At the same time, it cleared his mind and sharpened his senses. Here he was volunteering to care for kids in the town, to save their baseball program, and here was this guy, probably getting paid six figures to care for its kids, and they didn't seem to be anywhere near the top of his priority list.

Conway went on. "Look, a base salary of $1.4 million per year would be indefensible if offered by Holmgren. It would be crazy. It would be like they were trying to take advantage of him."

David squirmed in his chair. He could feel his face turning red. Now Cribbs, the kid, was being taken advantage of by being paid a mere base of $1.4 million per year. All David could think about were all of the Indigo Valley kids that were being taken advantage of by Conway. David couldn't believe he was sitting there outside the principal's office listening to

Conway pass on the fourteen hundred kids in the school. He recalled his
principal at Indigo Valley High School and how much he cared for and
involved himself in the lives of his students. The principal that followed him
was the same way. *These guys were role models*, David thought. But this guy
Conway seemed to be a role model for greed, selfishness, and arrogance.
David wanted to lash out. *I'm going to give this guy a piece of my mind when he
gets off the phone. I'm going to put this guy in his place and go over his head to
bring an end to this lunacy.*

But as he waited those last few minutes for Conway to wrap up his pitch
and get off the phone, and as he considered bringing an end to the lunacy,
he realized that he couldn't bring himself to do anything. The thought of
The *Godfather* rang in his head like an alarm gone haywire. The movie had
become the common thread that joined Moss in Mohawk City with Barkus
and Conway in Indigo Valley. This common thread that tied these two
worlds caused David to reconsider reacting at all.

David understood then and there that Conway was like Barkus on
steroids. If Barkus was fighting to keep his little gravy train on track,
Conway would fight tenfold to keep his lucrative sports enterprise going.
For all David knew, Conway, like Moss, had taken the lead role in *The
Godfather* to heart and was Indigo Valley's nutcase on the loose. After all,
some people in the town and school district had to know about Conway.
David's mind raced. *Who is backing Conway?* he asked himself. He guessed it
had to be the superintendent—as was the case with Moss—or maybe the
board of education. He wondered if there were gifts or tickets being kicked
back by Conway in exchange for looking the other way. He didn't have any
answers.

Conway was still blabbering about the Cribbs situation into the phone.
"I'm not sure what is happening with management," he said. "They said they
might be willing to open discussions yesterday, but no substantial talks took
place. I'm not sure they want to renegotiate. Josh is going to walk if that
happens."

David thought Josh Cribbs was on to something. *Maybe*, David thought, *I
should walk too.* He realized that Barkus probably was an outgrowth of the
sports-crazed environment created by Conway and his backers. Conway
seemed intent on grabbing his cut from his clients and to hell with everything and everyone else. He seemed like an empty suit as a principal; he
helped to create a culture in which Barkus and the Elite parents took root

in and thrived. It incensed David that this environment was responsible for killing off the town's community baseball program; it incensed him that in upsetting this entrenched culture, his family was at risk; and it incensed him most of all that he had come to believe that he could do nothing about it, nothing at all. He felt like a coward now; he felt like he was looking the other way, just like everyone else. And if Conway didn't make him feel sick, the thought that he was a coward did.

He felt as if he had no choice but to retreat. Johnny had already said that Barkus and Morgan were upset at losing teams and were going to do something to get back at the two of them. That was more than he could handle on one front.

He thought of the husband and wife who were Moss's victims. They slept with a shotgun under their bed. David understood then that he and his Sharps carbine were no different from them. He had assumed the victim posture of defending the homestead and this realization caused some resentment, as David fancied himself as a soldier on the move, a man of action who shaped events before they shaped him.

David reasoned that he had already put his family in danger by taking on the school baseball program and the Barkus machine. The retribution against Christy through the school coaches was a sign that the school was willing and able to reach David's family. *I don't need to push another button in the school hierarchy*, he thought.

Conway was finishing up. "When I learn anything more, you will be the first to know. Yes, absolutely, you can count on it. Yes, I have to go now. You bet, absolutely, I'll be in touch. Bye-bye now."

Conway called David back into his office and David sat down. At that moment, David saw a ring on his left hand, a white-gold ring with diamonds and rubies on his pinky. The rubies on the ring sparkled and David recalled the ring at the ball field, the one the man had worn that first morning. Then he remembered the black SUV the man drove that day, the same color as the one outside. He saw Conway's black wing-tipped shoe kick the air as he sat legs crossed, flicking his foot as he talked. David looked around and saw a beige trench coat hanging on a coat stand with Conway's suit jacket on a second hook. On the third hook, there was a pale blue lanyard hanging down with a card attached, an identification card with Conway's picture on it. His name was printed on the lanyard itself several times. David had seen enough. *Just like Cribbs*, David thought, *I need to walk out.*

"Sorry about that," Conway said. "I needed to take that call."

"Yes, I understand," said David. "You must be busy here to need two cell phones."

Conway tried to crack a smile but it quickly became a grimace. "My secretary says you wanted to talk about baseball or something?" Conway said, looking at his watch.

David had to think quickly—the last thing he wanted to talk about now was the high school baseball program. "Ah, yes . . . well, something related to baseball anyway."

"Oh, okay then. Why don't you tell me why you're here then?"

"My son, Christy, has an interest in baseball—"

"Yes, okay, good to hear . . . what of it?"

"You have an internship program available through the high school, right?"

"Absolutely."

David had figured a way out of the jam. "Okay then. Well, Christy is interested in interning with the Tri-City ValleyCats semipro team over in Troy maybe next year. I was wondering how we are supposed to go about doing that."

"Yeah, that's possible. You need to see Mr. O'Toole. He is an assistant principal here at the school. He oversees the internship program."

"Oh, I didn't know he handled the internships. I thought you did. My mistake. I'll go make an appointment with him."

"Absolutely, his office is down the hallway."

David stood up, while Conway remained seated. "Thanks for your time then," David said. Conway nodded and put up another smile. David turned toward the door and walked out before another "absolutely" was heard from Conway. He walked by the secretary, who was cleaning her phone receiver now with Lysol.

"I see what you mean," David said to the secretary.

She looked up. "Excuse me?"

"You're right, there's a lot of dirt around," David said as he walked to the counter gate.

"Yes, it seems so."

David closed the gate behind him and faced the vexed woman. "Thanks for your help," he said as he walked toward the main office exit. He turned left and strode down the hallway without hesitation. He wanted out of the school in the worst way. He sped past Mr. O'Toole's office, full speed ahead, and threw the entrance doors open.

He walked over and stood between Conway's shiny Navigator and his Mustang. He wanted to take a bat from his car and take it to the Navigator's side mirror. *Stupid security cameras,* he thought. He then spotted Eric on the grass digging up the "Visitor" sign overlooking Conway's vehicle.

"Hey, what are you doing?" David asked.

"Digging up the sign."

"Why?"

"Orders. Rumor is they wouldn't let him put a 'Reserved for Principal' sign up so he's takin' down the 'Visitor' sign over this space. He can grab it when he gets here as the school opens. No visitors show up that early, so he'll get his spot for the day, and nobody can criticize him then for taking a visitor spot as the day goes on. It's as good as having a principal sign over it. He's got it all figured out."

"Unbelievable," David said, shaking his head. *Grab a piece of the action, grab a parking spot, it's all about the grab.* He opened his door and looked at Eric. "I'll see you on the ball field."

"Yes, sir, it will be my pleasure."

"Take care now," David said. Then he ducked into the driver's seat and drove off.

23

FIELD ATTACK

D avid drove one block to the Indigo Valley library to do some research on the Internet. He didn't want to do it at home because Annie would be suspicious. He couldn't deal with her questioning. He was having trouble processing what he had learned about Conway.

An hour later, he walked out the library doors with a bundle of printouts. The petals of the pansies planted on either side of the walkway to the library fluttered in the wind. David looked up while walking to his car and saw white cirrus clouds streak like streamers thrown through the blue sky.

He wasn't going to talk to Annie about what had just happened in the principal's office or what he had found out in the library. Not now anyway. She would freak. There was only one person he could talk to about what he had discovered and that was Johnny.

He dialed him as he walked to the car and Johnny picked up on the second ring.

"What's up? How did the meeting go with the principal?"

For a second, David didn't say anything. He didn't know where to begin. The wind blew across the cell's microphone as David searched for words.

"What's with the heavy breathing?" Johnny asked. "You making an obscene phone call to me?"

"Sorry, it's the wind. I'm outside."

"What's on your mind?"

"I can't tell you over the phone."

"You think your phone is bugged or something?"

"Funny. It's just that I don't know where to begin. It's complicated."

"Nothing is ever simple with you."

"Look, I need to talk with you in person," David pleaded. "I've got some things to show you that you need to see."

They decided to meet at the Yellow Ribbon Diner that afternoon and David hung up. A second later his cell phone rang and Jack Masters's number was flashing on the screen. He thought about ignoring the call, but then decided he wanted to give Masters a piece of his mind.

"Hi, Jack. What do you want now?"

"Hey, David. I'm at work and was wondering if you could do me a favor."

"Let me guess. You want my resignation, right?"

"No, forget that."

"Easy for you to say, Jack."

"It wasn't my doing. Poser and Scully called that meeting. I couldn't do anything about it."

Way to shift the blame, David thought. True to form, Jack was trying to avoid being the bad guy. "Whatever, Jack. What do you want?"

"I got a call from a league parent who lives next to the fields. He said one of the fields has been vandalized."

"The Babe Ruth field?"

"No, one of the other fields. Could you check up on it for me? I called other guys on the board but nobody else can go."

"Sure, you want me to file a police report?"

"Yeah, that's a good idea."

"Okay, then. Later."

David dialed up Chief McNeal and told him what happened. He asked if he could go to the field complex and meet with him there to take a report. McNeal, a friend of David's since high school, said he would be at the field in a few minutes.

David drove into the empty field complex. There was a bunch of paper blowing on one field, a field for younger Cal Ripken kids. As David drove closer, he could tell it was toilet paper. It was wrapped around the backstop and fences along the baseline. Some toilet paper was breaking off from the fencing and was blowing wildly, like kite tails snaking their way around the ballpark until they were pressed against the fence by the wind. He got out of the car and approached the field. A blast of air whipped his unzipped wind-breaker behind him. The bases had been removed from their anchors and were strewn about the outfield, except for third base, which was placed about ten feet off the ground on one of the fence posts. He walked onto the field. He saw home plate had been broken in half by someone's failed attempt to pry it from its anchor. He walked out to the pitcher's mound. It was still in the ground but there was a pile of something on it about a foot high. He walked closer and saw it was a pile of dog shit of different colors, dimensions, and age.

David looked over his shoulder and saw a police cruiser drive up and park next to his car. Pete McNeal, a giant of a man, got out. He had played high school football with David thirty years ago. Pete gently closed the door as he looked in amazement at the field. He approached with his clipboard in hand and broke out a pen.

David looked back at the field. The wind started to swirl and the loose toilet paper started dancing in a circle around the dog shit on the mound as the sun hid behind a cotton-ball cloud and draped the field in gray. When the winds calmed for a moment, he could smell the dog crap. David turned around when he heard Pete's voice.

"What happened here?" Pete said as he shook David's hand.

"Looks like we had some visitors last night."

"What a mess. Any idea who would do this?"

"Yeah," David said indifferently.

"Who?"

David surveyed the damage. He knew Barkus and his clan were probably behind it. They thought they could take the Babe Ruth field on Indigo Valley Day but David had shut the door on them. They were pissed and showing their displeasure by vandalizing this field, the most remote one on the complex. "Let me ask you this, Pete. If I did have any idea, what difference would it make?"

"Well, I might go over and talk with them."

"Yeah, well that's the problem."

"What are you talking about?"

"You're not going to take any fingerprints here, right?"

"No, there's no point. There're prints of the entire town here."

"Right. And you are not going to do a DNA analysis on the dog shit to try and trace it, right?"

"No, of course not. Are you kidding?"

"I'm trying to make a point, Pete."

"Look, I'm just trying to help, David. I know you're doing a lot for the baseball program. My boys enjoy playing Babe Ruth. And I know the program is so much better because of you. I'm not sure what's going on. I hear things, you know. Some people are saying some nasty things about you. But I've known you for thirty years now and I know you must be doing what is right for our town."

"I'm glad your boys are having a good time. Pete, I appreciate your support more than you will ever know. You're a good friend, but your stirring the pot will only come back to bite me in the ass."

"I don't understand."

"You're not going to make any arrests, Pete. You will go out and question them, they will deny involvement, and that will be the end of it as far as you're concerned."

"David, I could shake them up a bit."

"No, it would just mobilize them against me. I can take them on one at a time, Pete. But I can't always take them on when they come at me all at once. If you go over there and try to rattle them, can't you just hear them? They would say, 'Thompson had the nerve to accuse us of vandalizing the field. How dare he accuse us! He's nuts; he has to go.' In an instant, I would become their common enemy and I would reenergize them. Then they would try and remove me from the board again. Long story there. Been there, done that, Pete."

"Are you sure of who did this David?"

"I'm a baseball guy. I think in terms of probabilities. I think I know the group behind it, but I don't know who actually did it."

"Maybe it was just kids."

"Whoever did this planned it. It was not just a bunch of kids walking around and then deciding on a whim to vandalize the field."

"Why do you say that?"

"Our bathrooms are locked. They had to bring their own toilet paper and lots of it. There is none available for miles at the taking. And the dog crap is old and from different dogs."

"How do you know . . . the age, and if it came from different dogs?" Pete asked with some regret.

David seized the opportunity to demonstrate why he considered himself the world's foremost expert in the area of dog excrement. "The fact that some is dried out shows the age; the different coloration and the different forms shows it was from different dogs. Trust me, I know my shit."

"Okay," Pete said, half impressed and half bewildered.

"They imported the stuff too." David pointed at some plastic grocery bags pressed into the backstop by the wind. "You can see the stains in those bags. They collected the stuff and brought it to the field."

Pete played along with David and walked over and picked up one of the bags. "Excellent observation," he said, sounding like Watson confirming a brilliant Sherlock Holmes deduction. Pete then looked around the field at the mess.

"Whoever did this put some thought and effort into it," David said. "It wasn't a bunch of roaming teens causing havoc." David paused for dramatic effect. "It was planned," he said, as if he were suggesting that some heinous crime, like murder, had been committed.

"What do you want to do about it then?" Pete asked, half amused by his friend. At this point, Pete wanted either a plan of action or to get back to the warmth of his patrol car.

"Nothing," David said. "Just file a generic report for any insurance claim and be done with it."

"Okay, David, but I want you to know that I'm here if you need me."

"I appreciate that, Pete. I'll remember that for sure. Just keep it in the back of your mind that Barkus doesn't have permission to play on our fields."

"Okay, David."

David thought about mentioning Conway to see if Pete knew anything about him. But David hadn't fully processed what he had learned that morning. He wasn't going to risk losing his friendship with Pete by talking about Conway before he had a grasp on the situation himself.

After the report was taken, both men went to their cars. David stopped to check the bottom of one shoe. He dragged his right foot across the pavement three times like a bull readying himself to charge. Pete looked back when he heard the shuffle of David's foot.

"You okay there, David?"

"I stepped in it. I hate stepping in it."

At that point, a blowing piece of toilet paper wrapped around David's waist. He danced a jig to try and free himself from the excrement on his shoe. Then another piece of paper wrapped around his forehead. Pete laughed at the sight of David dressed in toilet paper streamers doing the dog shit shuffle in the empty parking lot with his windbreaker flapping like a flag.

"You got some talent there, David. You should think about auditioning for the Indigo Valley Day parade. I hear they need dancers."

David laughed at himself. "Did I ever tell you how much I hate dog shit, Pete?"

24

REGROUP

When David walked through the door to the Yellow Ribbon Diner, he found Johnny at his regular table warming his hands with a cup of coffee. David cased the patrons and looked for any familiar baseball faces around Johnny. He saw none. He saw Susan, the waitress, as she attended to a table filled with kids and a stressed-out mother. He walked by the screams and giggles on the way to Johnny's table.

David threw his windbreaker on the far side of his booth and sat down. He looked at Johnny and was at a loss for words. He didn't know where to begin.

"Jesus, David, you look like you've seen a ghost. You want anything?" he asked as he slid the menu over.

"No . . . no thanks." He was dazed by the morning's events.

"How did your meeting with the principal go?"

David looked out the window and then back at Johnny. "You're not going to believe this. I'm not sure I believe it myself. It seems our principal is a sports agent."

"What are you talking about?" Johnny said.

"Jerry Conway, our high school principal, is a professional sports agent."

"Huh?"

"You know, he is like Scott Boras is to baseball, only football is his main sport. But he's looking to grow in other areas. He's growing a client list in baseball, basketball, and boxing. He's got like one hundred clients listed on his website in a bunch of sports, with some big names. He claims to be one of the biggest agents in the business."

With that, David read out loud some of the thirty-five NFL names from a printout that were listed on Conway's website as clients : Lorenzo Alexander, Corell Buckhalter, Kevin Burnett, Josh Cribbs, Dorin Dickerson, David Diehl, Letroy Guion, T. J. Houshmandzadeh, Adam "Pacman" Jones, Hakeem Nicks, Chris Ogbonnaya, Russell Okung, Mike Patterson, Josh Portis, Mike Scifres, Donald Strickland, Phil Taylor, Joe Thomas, J. T. Thomas, and Kraig Urbik.

Johnny sat there motionless with his mouth wide open. "This is unbelievable. Are you sure it is the same guy? Maybe it's two different guys with the same name?"

"Actually, he goes by a slightly different name when he acts as an agent. I ran *Jerry Conway*—that's his name—and the word *agent* through a Google search and did not find anything. But then I ran *J. O. Conway* through Google along with agent and found a number of articles on him."

"Are you sure J. O. Conway and Jerry Conway are one and the same person and it is the principal?"

"He's got his picture on the website. He's riding in the back of some limo with his cell phone looking like some big shot. It's him; it's the same guy."

"What do you make of it? What does it mean?"

"I know one thing it means. We are not going to get any help from him on the baseball front. Like you once told me, you're either part of the problem or part of the solution. J. O. Conway is not just part of the problem —he *is* the problem."

"How's that?"

"There is no way he can service one hundred or so high-maintenance clients and his growing businesses and not let it interfere with his work as principal."

"So, do you have to be one of his millionaire clients to get to see him during the school day?"

"I don't know. All I know is if there is a drug issue with both the kids and his clients at the same time, our kids won't be first in line."

"Sounds like another conflict of interest thing. Same deal as your baseball board."

"Yep, there's a huge conflict between his hundred big-shot clients and the fourteen hundred kids he is supposed to serve and protect as a full-time principal."

"Unfuckingbelievable. How does he get away with it?"

"I'm not sure. I don't know how many people know he's an agent. If people do know, they're probably too frightened to ask questions, don't know exactly what to do about it, or they just want to look the other way. Put me in that last category."

"I don't get you. You're taking on Barkus, your board, and the high school coaching staff. What's one more?"

"One too many. You know, there was this newspaper article in his office that said *The Godfather* was his favorite movie."

Johnny fidgeted in his seat. "So what? It's a good movie."

"It was Stanley Moss's movie too. Didn't you read that in the papers?" David wasn't about to tell Johnny about his meeting with Moss because of the attorney-client privilege.

"Yeah, yeah. Your point is . . . ?"

"Stanley Moss's life *was* that movie."

"Oh, and you think the principal is some kind of whackjob as well?"

"I have no idea."

"Why do you say that then?"

"Just speculating."

"Maybe it's nothing then."

"I can't take the chance on it being nothing. Something is going on here. I mean, this is nuts. We have a principal who is a full-time sports agent? Pinch me. He has got a website and he tweets on Twitter during the school day about his sport business that he wants to grow into a billion-dollar empire? On top of it, he's involved with other sports businesses. He does a sports radio show too on Friday evenings on a local ESPN radio station, according to his website."

"Oh, come on now. You've got to be kidding."

"I'm not. I'm dead serious."

"How can all this be going on without anybody saying anything?"

"I have no idea. Maybe somebody is covering for him."

"Maybe it's the superintendent?"

"Yes, like the superintendent in Mohawk City when he looked the other way with Moss."

"At least your principal is not trying to intimidate anyone with threats or bombs, or anything."

David sighed and started shaking his head, looking at the table.

"Oh, come on now. Here you go again. Do you think this guy, Conway, is Moss or something?"

"I don't know what to think. But look at this."

David handed Johnny a printout from the library. "You see this here? This is an article from the Cleveland Frowns website." David handed it to him.

"Cleveland Frowns website?"

"Yeah, some guy out in Ohio set up this site devoted to the Cleveland Browns football team. Anyway, you see this article here about Josh Cribbs and Conway, his agent?"

"Who is Josh Cribbs?"

"He's a kick returner and wideout for the Browns."

"Okay, just tell me what the article says."

"Evidently, the writer, who is an attorney, was critical of Conway's efforts to renegotiate Cribbs's contract and Conway wrote him an e-mail that he published. Read it."

And there stood Conway's late-night error in judgment for the whole world to see. Johnny read the e-mail out loud.

Peter,

Who the hell are you? You know me???

If you did, you would know that my marketing days are in the rearview mirror.

You should focus on your thriving law practice and scribing of current briefs before you comment about me.

Regards,

J. O. Conway President, J. O. Enterprises

Johnny's head slowly rose from the article. He sat there with a puzzled look on his face.

David leaned forward and met Johnny's eyes and said, "Does the Conway in this e-mail sound like he's a speaker at anti-bullying conferences —which he was, by the way—or does he sound like some wannabe mafioso like Moss is made out to be in the newspaper?"

"I see what you mean," Johnny said. He thought about it for a second. "I think this guy, Conway, is trouble but I can't believe it. Do you know what I mean?"

David stared out the window. "I understand. I don't believe this either. This guy may well be trouble and I don't need to find out the hard way. For God's sake, I am just trying to run a kids' baseball program. This guy isn't going to help us. He is just like the Elite league except on a grander scale: they are both using the school and kids to line their pockets. For all I know, Barkus and Conway know one another."

"You're kidding. Why do you think that?"

"Let's just say I think I saw them down at the Babe Ruth field one morning."

"You think Barkus is involved with Conway's operation?"

"I don't know what to think, Johnny."

Johnny shook his head. "Why not take it to the media?"

David sighed. "Conway represents a number of local media personalities too as their agent. How am I going to approach them if Conway might have them in his back pocket?"

"How about the school board? Why not go to them?"

"There's a board of education member whose son plays for one of the Elite teams."

Johnny got bug-eyed. "You're right. Stay away from this, David. Run don't walk to the exit on this one."

David looked down at the table and began spinning his knife. "I guess I need to look the other way."

"Yeah, that's how things are done in your town."

"I guess I'm going to have to become a part of that mindset."

"Cut yourself some slack there. You took on the Elite Travel Baseball program. You got them and the school off your field."

"For now. They're regrouping; they'll be back soon enough."

"Focus on that battle then. You can't be expected to take on the principal as a national sports agent and as a potential Moss twin."

"I'm glad you agree. Christy and Annie have already suffered enough. I know I can't open another battle front, but it still upsets me to see him get away with it."

"Doesn't Conway have some people helping with his business?"

"Supposedly—there's a guy in the school administration that seems to be running his website."

Johnny shook his head. "Okay, here's my take. You've got too many people sucking on the teats of this cash cow. They aren't going to give up their place willingly. Conway and every last one of them will go down kicking and screaming if you try and pry them from their teats. You don't need that now. You've got enough on your plate."

"Tell me about it."

"I told you this wasn't going to be easy."

"Yeah, well, you didn't tell me that this mess involved our principal as a nationally known sports agent."

"That's fucked up."

"Yes, but do you know what the sad part is about all this?"

"What?"

"People in town who know don't seem to care enough to do anything about it. I mean, what does it say about us if we don't think our kids are worth a full-time, dedicated principal?" He added, "I am disgusted and worn out with the system that seems to prevail." It was exactly what John Buford had said about the unwillingness of the Union ranks to pursue Lee in his retreat from Gettysburg.

"Maybe they don't know about it, or don't know how to do anything about it, or maybe they are just plain afraid," Johnny responded.

"Maybe." David grimaced and put his hand to his stomach. "God, my stomach is in knots. I'm getting sick from thinking about Conway."

"Steer away from this guy, David. Stay the fuck away."

"You're preaching to the choir, my friend." David knew full well that Buford would die from illness four months later after writing that dispatch. It was not a path he wanted to travel if he could help it.

25

IN A PICKLE

I t was Tuesday morning and David sat at his office desk shuffling thorough baseball paperwork when the phone rang. The name came up as Jim Fletcher on caller ID. David hadn't spoken to him since interviewing Stanley Moss the previous week.

"Hey, Jim."

"How goes it there, David. How does our team look these days?"

"We're a work in progress, that's for sure. Flash is looking good."

"Great, he's having a good time. Hey, speaking of baseball, I wanted to give you a heads-up on something."

"What's going on?"

"I was at a court appearance with Moss yesterday and there was this guy in the gallery who sat behind us. Anyway, the hearing is over and Moss starts talking to this guy about baseball or something. We moved out into the hallway and before they took him back to his cell, I asked him who this guy was he was talking with. He wouldn't tell me. So this guy hangs around and I get a court security buddy I know to go over and ask him some questions. My friend later tells me his name was Barkus, Rob Barkus. I got home last night and remembered you mentioned a name like that to me when we spoke last week. I wondered if it was the same guy. . . ."

David's stomach dropped to the floor and then shot to the ceiling like he was on some wild elevator ride. His mind was a mess of thoughts about

Barkus, his followers, and Moss. He was thinking about Poser and Scully at the board meeting and how Poser said that David would regret walking out.

He was thinking about what Barkus had said at the field, how he had told David to sleep well and then repeated the line while laughing. He was thinking about the meeting he had with Moss, how he'd made it a point to talk about the fear of living in a home under siege. He recalled Moss's technique was to issue a vague threat, before an attack, so he would get credit for it, though he would not say enough to get arrested by the police. David knew that Moss vandalized and bombed homes for friends as favors. He remembered Moss spouting off about respect, the need for respect, and recalled that Barkus had expressed the same need. He thought about the vandalized baseball field. He was piecing things together as best he could and it looked ugly, real ugly.

"David, are you there?" Jim asked.

David couldn't hear him for the moment. His mind shifted to Johnny and what he said about Barkus and Morgan, about them planning to do something bat-shit crazy against David and Johnny for all their efforts.

"David, are you okay?"

"Ah, sorry, Jim. I was just thinking."

"Do you think it was the same guy?" Jim asked.

"What did he look like?"

"I'll do you one better. Go to the Channel 6's website. You'll see a story on the hearing. You can see him in the gallery for a second or two."

"Okay, let me check it out. Hold on, I'm at my computer now."

David found the website and searched for news reports about Moss. He located one dated the day before and played it back in mute mode. He saw what he thought was him. He froze the picture and put it in full-screen mode. There was Barkus in the gallery a few rows back.

David's mind exploded with thoughts. He had refused to explore the connection between Conway and Barkus. There was no point because Conway's actions all alone amounted to a reason for staying away. But now there was a possible connection between Moss and Barkus.

He reminisced about his conversations with Moss and Barkus in search of a link between the two. He recalled that Moss said he had a lot of friends in Indigo Valley whose kids went to the high school. Moss also had discovered his interest in baseball during that meeting and had indicated that he had been in the area of the Babe Ruth field during the early-morning hours sometime prior to his arrest. On top of it all, it seemed Moss knew he had a single son who played baseball.

David thought about the vandalism to the other ball field and wondered if the Babe Ruth field was next. But then it hit him. Maybe it wasn't the Babe Ruth field at all. Moss had made it a point to tell David how attacking someone's home in the middle of the night was so terrifying. Maybe, David thought, the next target was his house, his family.

Then there were the vague threats coming from Barkus and his cronies over the course of the past weeks that served to support the notion that David's home could be a target.

"David, do you see him?" Jim asked.

"I'm looking for him now," David said, stalling for time to think it through. "Hold on a second."

David wasn't sure if Barkus and Moss were somehow working together, but he knew he couldn't take the chance—not with his family at potential risk. After all, Moss claimed that he terrified people as favors to friends. Perhaps Barkus was one of those friends.

Whatever the relationship between Barkus and Moss, David realized then he had made a huge strategic blunder by shutting down Barkus's access to the field on Indigo Valley Day. In doing so, it seemed possible that he had frustrated Barkus and his cronies so much that they might lash out against his home and family. He needed to think quickly to try and rectify the situation.

"Yes, it's him," David said.

"What do you make of it?"

"I don't know." David didn't want to discuss his predicament with Jim. It would take too long, it was too bizarre, and David saw no benefit in it. Jim had Moss to worry about—the biggest case of his professional life.

"Did you get the e-mail I sent you about my interview with him?" David asked.

"Yeah, thanks for that."

"Do you still need me on this case? Moss didn't seem too interested in me being part of it."

"I talked to him about it and I didn't get a clear answer. He said he'd think about it. That was last Wednesday."

"Do *you* need me, though?"

"I could use you, David, but I've freed up some time on other cases, so it's not essential."

David was relieved to hear this. He was going to have to back out of assisting to defend Moss anyway. He couldn't defend Moss, knowing he had a relationship with Barkus, and he wasn't particularly interested in working to set Moss free to create a threat to himself.

David thought it was quite possible that Moss was just trying to play David through Jim as a favor to Barkus. If that was the case, David saw an opportunity to turn the tables, to use Moss as a means to play Barkus before stepping away from the case entirely.

"Okay, do me a favor Jim."

"Sure."

"Is there anything scheduled for Moss this afternoon?"

"No, there is nothing on the calendar for him. He'll just be sitting in his cell with time on his hands."

"Okay, tell Moss I want to meet with him at 2:00 p.m. I want to go over some things we talked about last week."

"Sure, I can arrange that—"

"Good, I'll be in touch. I've got to run now. I'll talk to you later."

"Okay. Talk to you then."

David hung up and found his redwell file on the Moss case and began looking over some documents the district attorney had released.

He climbed the stairs, two steps at a time, and reached the kitchen, where Annie was working at the table.

"Good morning, babe," she said.

"Hi, you're looking great this morning," he said as he reached down to give her a hug.

"How's baseball treating you," she asked.

"Great. Ever since you marched into the board meeting and set them straight, things have been relatively calm on that front."

"I can't believe I actually changed their minds."

"I don't think they quite know how to deal with a woman who threatens to shoot them."

"I'm sorry I lost my cool last week. I don't know what got into me."

"Don't be sorry. You helped the cause. Last thing these guys want to be seen doing is getting into a fight with a woman. They don't want to risk losing their wives' support."

"Stop it, David," Annie said, trying to suppress a smile.

"Annie, did you happen to get the mail today?"

"No, can you get it? There's been a guy parked down the street the past week or so when I've walked out to the mailbox. He's giving me the creeps."

David looked out the front window. "I don't see anyone. Where have you seen him?"

"Down the street," she said, pointing left.

"Okay, well I don't see anyone."

Annie shrugged while writing out a check for a bill. "He's not there every day."

"I'll get the mail," David said. He opened the door and walked down the driveway, wondering if Barkus or Moss was connected to the mystery man. Was he scoping the place for an attack? He needed to remedy this situation with dispatch. He thought about confronting Barkus. But he knew if he did, Barkus would deny it all and tell everyone he had lost touch, was imagining things, was a risk to the league and needed to be replaced. No, the best way to get at Barkus was to go through Moss.

After he came back in the house with the mail, David went down to his office. He accessed the league website and announced on the home page that Babe Ruth would not be having games or practices on Indigo Valley Day. He notified the coaches through an e-mail so they could tell their teams. David was opening the field to give Barkus wide berth to execute his plan in taking the field for that day. David figured he would rather have them try and take the field than try and vandalize and bomb his home. He was planning to open one door and bait it while shutting the other door by visiting Moss in jail.

Later that afternoon, David walked through the security doors to meet Moss at the Mohawk City Jail. He was escorted to Room 3, an attorney meeting room no larger than a batter's box with a stainless-steel table and two stainless stools on either side all bolted to the ground. Moss was seated in his orange jumpsuit on one side of the table. His arms remained bound at the wrists and shackled at the legs at David's request. The guard closed the door behind David as the two looked each other over.

"I'd get up to shake your hand, but I can't," Moss said, looking up at David and raising his cuffed hands.

"No problem," David said as he laid his satchel on the table.

"What's with the restraints?" Moss asked.

David shrugged as he opened his satchel and took out his redwell and shimmied the elastic band up the folder to release the flap.

"You're my lawyer, get me out of these," Moss said, lifting his hands before resting them back on his lap.

"So, I'm on your team now?" David asked. He removed some papers from the folder.

"You're here, aren't you?" Moss stared past David and tried to look through the smudged and scratched small bulletproof glass window on the entrance door.

"Yes, it seems that way," David said, unwilling to sit down.

"What do you want? Fletcher said you wanted to see me. You got news on my bail?" The last thing David wanted to see was Moss out on bail and on his doorstep.

"Fletcher is handling that, but things don't look good for you."

"Jesus Christ, it's not like I'm accused of killing anyone. What gives?"

"Your mouth isn't doing you any favors on top of your reputation."

"What are you talking about?"

"Well, you've spent a considerable amount of time over the past decade building your reputation as the godfather—someone to be feared—and, well, by God, congratulations are in order because there are a number of people that are absolutely terrified of you."

"I've got no criminal record, though. That must count for something."

"Yeah, well, not if you are going around telling people you're going to get them, that you'll never be taken alive, that you'll blow your head off before you do a day in jail, that you will not die in jail like your father did. The district attorney has affidavits. The judge does not want the possibility of a murder-suicide rampage on his hands while you're out on bail."

"Whose side are you on, anyway?"

"I'm not on the side of denial, that's for sure. Have you made the necessary preparations?"

"Preparations for what?"

"I see by the letter you left your wife in case you predeceased her that you must care for her quite a bit," said David, putting a copy of the letter on the table.

"How did you get ahold of that?"

"When the police searched your home, they found it."

Moss twisted his hips to face the table so he could place his bound hands on it. He struggled to pick up the letter. David picked it up and put it in his hands.

"Does she live alone there?" David asked.

Moss was reading the letter, reading how he had promised to look over his "honey," his "sweetheart," after he was gone because there was nothing he couldn't do, even from the heavens above. In all caps he had written that she was the best thing that ever happened to him.

Moss was embarrassed that his private thoughts were now in everyone's hands; he feared people were making fun of his letter and of him.

"Stan, does she live alone there?" David asked again.

"Yes, what of it?"

"She's vulnerable there. How are you going to protect her if bail is denied or if you're convicted?"

"Who's threatening her? I'll take care of them. I know people."

"All your friends have abandoned you, Stan."

"Bullshit, I got friends."

"Yeah, what they say to you and what they actually do can be two different things, Stan. We're lucky to get anyone to testify on your behalf. They don't want to be associated with you anymore. It's bad for their personal and professional lives to be associated with you, to say anything favorable about you."

Moss looked up at David standing over him. "My *friends* will look out for her!"

"Well, I certainly hope so because there seems to be a number of people out there who resent the terror you caused them, and they might take it upon themselves to get even with you by returning the favor of doing *your* house and scaring the shit out of *your* wife."

Moss fidgeted in his stool, as one shackle was cutting off circulation to his foot. "They're all a bunch of pussies. They'd never do anything."

David put one foot up on his stool and rested his elbow on his knee. "You'd better hope so, because I know if I was in their shoes and someone came at my house, my family, I would retaliate for sure."

David waited for a reaction from Moss. His eyes darted around the room for a second but he didn't say anything. David felt that Moss was looking around the room for something to say while wondering at the same time if he should keep quiet. David had caught Moss off guard and by doing so he had revealed that Moss was up to something with Barkus.

David leaned over and locked eyes with Moss. He whispered, "Stan, you can screw around with the ball fields, but nobody messes with *my* house and *my* family."

Moss's eyebrows raised as his eyes widened. His lips parted as if to say something but the only thing that passed between them was his stale breath.

"Do you understand me, Stan?"

Moss looked away.

The point having been made, David recoiled from Moss's personal space. "I have a lot of respect for you Stan, I really do," David said, biting his tongue while pulling another piece of paper out of his folder, holding it in the hand that rested on his knee. "You and I see eye to eye on a lot of things. I mean, you say here that 'there comes a time in everyone's personal or professional life to stand up for what they believe in.'"

"What are you reading from there?"

"An unpublished letter to the editor that you wrote to the *Daily Gazette*. The paper handed it over to the police. Your life is an open book."

Moss shook his head.

"You say here, Stan, that sometimes 'in the face of too much adversity people choose the easy route of being silent.' I agree with you there, Stan. I see that happening in our town. I see that happening with respect to baseball and more, Stan, much more. And I'm taking a stand . . . Stan."

David put the papers back in his redwell and closed it.

"Good for you, counselor. Now what does this have to do with me and my case?"

"It has everything to do with you, Stan, and what you hold dear outside of your jail cell. I remember last time we met here, you said sometimes street justice is the only justice—"

"I know what I said."

"Is all this hitting too close to *home* for you, Stan?" David asked, putting the redwell in his satchel.

"Knock it off already. You've made your point."

"Good. Then this interview is over," David said, opening the door. "Guard . . . guard!" David called. He looked at Moss one last time. His face looked like a puppy that was being locked in the basement for the night. When the guard showed, David told him he was done and walked out.

26

CHOPPERS REVISITED

D avid's struggles off the field were mirrored by the play of the Choppers on the field. Losses had strung together like beads on a rosary and the Chopper dugout became a place to mourn past games lost too soon and a foretelling of losses yet to come.

It was Saturday, May 2, and the Choppers had worked themselves into last place in the league standings. They were playing the first place Babson Concrete Block team, which had beat them 14–3 a few weeks earlier.

David knew that Poser, the head coach, was probably seething in the Babson dugout after the boardroom failure. He knew Meeson was probably over there trying to calm Poser in a half-assed manner that would prove ineffective but would enable Meeson to claim that he tried.

Barry "Stretch" Anderson was on the mound for the visiting Choppers in the bottom of the seventh, the final inning of the in-house game, with the Choppers ahead by one run, 4–3.

Stretch was six foot four. His head was disproportionately small for his frame, which highlighted the fact that his head was not fully wired to his body yet. As a result, his pitching mechanics were stiff and he threw the baseball like he was throwing darts. His glasses gave him a studious look.

Despite his awkward appearance, David felt there was a man underneath, a man whose heart was surely not too small for his frame as he played with passion to match his stature on the mound.

"Bullwhip" Billy Wilson, the Choppers' only school player, was not allowed to pitch with the school season still in session and so it was up to Stretch to close.

David was growing concerned. The sun had been behind the clouds for most of the game, but at the beginning of the inning it had come out in all its glory. It was not only hotter now, but it was humid as well. David had been in this position before. He knew that a long inning under these conditions could grow only longer as the heat sopped the energy of the players whose bodies had not adjusted to the heat and humidity that was due to arrive in summer, not in early May.

There was a Babson player on third with two outs and Skit, the rowdiest of the bunch, was catching behind the plate. It was a full count and then Stretch pitched ball four. Men were now on first and third. The runner on first was Oscar Poser's son, Tony, a very good base runner.

And then it started, again. "You suck," said a player's voice from Babson's dugout. And then the laughter followed. The abuse from the other dugout had been going on all game. Poser was the third-base coach and he ignored the chatter and ran through his signals.

"Let's go, team!" Annie chanted from the front row of the visitor bleachers. She had now made a point of attending every game since the board meeting.

Stretch stepped off the mound and slapped his throwing hand and glove together as he walked a few steps toward home to get the return throw from Skit. But once Skit heard the comment and laughter from the Babson dugout, he asked for time and walked out to the mound to try and talk to Stretch.

David could see that the next batter, Alex Meeson, was right-handed as he took his swings outside the dugout. Normally the second baseman covers the steal at second with a right-handed batter, but Roots, the slowest player, was positioned at second base.

David called to Christy: "Christy, you got the bag. Roots has your back." It wasn't that David wanted to try and gun the runner down at second. He just wanted to give Oscar Poser some reason to think twice in having Tony steal second so as to give the Choppers an extra force option for at least a few pitches. Roots covering the bag would only induce Poser to steal; Christy covering would give him pause.

When Skit got to the mound and took off his catcher's mask, David recognized a mischievous grin unfolding beneath the sweaty dirt on Skit's face. He had seen that grin one too many times before.

David stepped out of the dugout. "Blue, I want to visit the mound," he said. The umpire called, "Time." David jogged over from the third baseline of the visiting dugout to the mound. "Infield in," he called.

Bullwhip came in from third; Sammy Jackson came in from first; Christy and Roots came in from their middle infield positions.

David started grooming the mound with his feet as he talked.

"Skit, what's the situation here?"

"What do you mean, coach?"

"Outs, inning, runner position, and score. Come on, we have been over this before."

"Two outs, bottom of the seventh, men on first and third, and the score is 4–3."

A voice from the Babson dugout said, "Look at that tub of lard." Then there was laughter. Everyone on the mound knew that the barb was directed at Skit.

Meeson was outside the dugout sitting on a bucket of balls while keeping score when the insult was fired. He turned to the dugout and thought about saying something before Poser called over to him from third base to confirm there were two outs. Poser asked the umpire to bring in a pinch runner for his injured player at third. The umpire allowed it under league rules and out trotted Eric Washington's son. David had learned that the boy's name was Drew.

David had the boys in a circle on the mound. "Ignore those guys," David said calmly. He looked over to third and saw the runner substitution and figured Eric Washington's son was the pinch runner because the father was black and the boy was the only black player in the league. It was the first time that Drew Washington had played in the game.

"Coach, I'm tired of this crap," Skit said to David.

"Me too," David said firmly, "so let's finish this game, finish this thing with a win."

"Look, coach, I know I can gun him down," Skit said.

David knew before coming out to the mound that Skit's plan was to try and throw the runner out at second when he tried to steal.

"That's exactly what they want you to do and we're not doing it. We need to play the percentages for one last out and get a win. We don't need to be heroes to do it. You know that the runner at third is going to try and score if you throw to second. That's the tying run." David knew that Skit was throwing rainbows to second on the steals earlier in the game and these airborne throws served to give any runner at third the opportunity to make it home. The worst-case scenario was that the throw wasn't fielded at second but rather found itself in center field where Mark "Steady" Prior was positioned, flanked by Flash in left and Gold Glove in right.

"But coach, we could have Christy cut the throw and go home—"

"No buts, Skit. That's too risky." David knew that Skit wanted to make the last out at home plate, to be the hero, to stick it in Babson's face. David looked to Stretch. "Stretch, you throw a few nice ones to Smiles at first to keep the runner honest for a few pitches, but we don't need to be heroes at second."

They called Sammy Jackson "Smiles" because that was his nature. Smiles was a wide body and a little below average in height. Smiles was a player, a boy who loved baseball and was determined to play to the best of his ability. He did not say much but was always smiling and was easygoing to the point of causing one to wonder if it was some kind of medication at work. He had a nice, relaxed swing that matched his disposition. He had a pretty good scoop too, but his reaction time made him look like he lived life in slow-mo. If the pitcher's throw got by him, it was like watching time stand still to see him move to retrieve the ball.

"Stretch, aim for accuracy when you throw to Smiles at first," David said. "Smiles, remind Gold Glove to back you up from right field. Remember, your real battle is at the plate. First pitch strike. And you have to throw it down at the knees. That's your best location. Get him to hit a grounder and let's count on our defense to get the final out."

The umpire approached the mound and David knew his time was up.

"Let's stay focused and play smart baseball," David said before jogging off to the dugout.

Alex Meeson came to the plate and banged his cleats clean with his bat out of habit, as they were spot clean except for a few grains of sand.

Stretch engaged the rubber and leaned forward to his lead knee to get the signal from Skit. He brought his lead foot back to stand erect. He saw Tony had a big lead. Suddenly, he stepped off the rubber and threw to first to keep

Tony honest. Tony dove at the bag. Smiles caught the ball, then threw it back to Stretch.

Stretch got the ball and readied himself again to pitch. Tony's lead was a bit shorter this time, so Stretch pitched one to Alex.

Alex watched the ball slide over his knees into Skit's mitt for a called first strike.

"Nice pitch," chanted Christy.

Alex had struck out when he first batted against Stretch a few innings back. David knew what was happening. He knew Alex was trying to gauge the speed of the ball. Stretch's pitch was slower than what he had seen playing for the school team. He had tried to hit it out of the park with his first at-bat.

Stretch received the ball from Skit and looked over to first as he positioned himself on the mound. Tony's lead was the same as the last pitch as he put one arm toward first and actually leaned toward first a little as he waited.

Babson's dugout threw out another barb. "You got this, Alex. This chump is throwing meatballs."

Stretch grimaced and got red in the face. He disengaged from the rubber to gather himself while removing his cap to wipe the sweat off his brow with his forearm.

David clapped his hands together. "Here ya go, kid. Let's go, kid."

Stretch got back in position on the mound. His eyes fixed like a laser to Skit's mitt. He looked over to Smiles at first. Tony now had a large lead, but Stretch didn't care. He was going to home and for that one pitch his gangly frame came together. He didn't look like he was throwing a dart on this pitch. His arm came all the way back and he then thrust his chest forward and the ball followed as if released from a catapult. The raised seams of the baseball hissed in the air and blew past the plate, with Alex swinging behind it as it popped into Skit's dusty mitt. Alex was expecting Stretch's slow stuff.

Christy looked at Bullwhip at third. "My God," Bullwhip said.

"He's got a gun!" Christy said, smiling.

No sooner had Skit thrown the ball back than Stretch was ready to go again. Sweat gathered behind his lenses but it did not bother him. Tony took a big lead, but Stretch was in a zone and was going home again. Even though he was out in front in the count, he wasn't about to throw a breaking pitch.

Tony ran on the pitch and for the second time in a row Stretch fired one to home right out of a cannon. Alex was ready—he knew he had to protect the plate. He had seen this speed in school games and he was ready for it now. He drove a line drive in the direction of the shortstop as the aluminum bat pinged in celebration on contact.

Christy jumped with his arm and glove extended. The ball sailed a few inches over his glove. The ball seemed to be gaining altitude as it soared over his head and into the gap between Flash in left field and Steady in center.

Drew Washington scored and Tony was halfway to third as Steady fielded the ball on the hop in left-center field. He gunned the ball to Christy, who had run to the outfield to get the cutoff throw as Tony rounded third. Christy launched a bullet to Skit and Tony went into a slide right before it reached Skit's mitt.

"Safe!" the umpire called while motioning with his hands.

Tony popped up with a fist raised in the air and ran over to Alex as the Babson dugout cleared and started chanting, "Walk-off, walk-off!" The announcer read the final score over the public address system: Babson 5, Choppers 4. The Choppers' losing streak now numbered six.

The Chopper players wandered to the dugout with the look of gloom on their faces. "Line up," David said, trying not to sound disappointed. The team knew the drill. The players on the bench lined up in front of the dugout and the players in the field jogged or walked in to join them. It was time for the good-sportsmanship handshake, where the players from both teams walked toward each other in the home plate area and shook each other's hand for a game well played.

David looked at the pained faces of his players as they lined up in front of him. After a few moments, David looked to the front of the line when he realized it was not moving toward the players from the other team.

The reason for the delay was near the pitcher's mound: Babson's team was not done celebrating. A dog-pile of players was still rolling around on the ground. The coaching staff looked on and shook hands with one another. It was as if they had won the league championship.

As it continued, Skit looked back at David. His head drooped but his eyes looked up to David as they squinted. His mouth then opened up, revealing his clenched teeth. Then one by one, the players looked back and checked in with David with looks of disgust, including Christy and even

Steady, as the celebration continued. When Smiles smiled no more, David knew he had to do something.

"Coach!" David's voice bellowed as he sought the attention of Poser, who was shaking hands with his players. No response. "Coach!" David said louder. Nothing.

David walked to the front of the line. "Hey, coach!" he said, raising his voice to a level that at least caught the attention of some Babson parents in the stands.

Arnold Meeson heard David at that point and tapped Poser on the shoulder, then pointed to David. "Oscar, we need to line up and get off the field," he said. "There's another game right behind us."

"Just a minute," Poser said. After a few more handshakes, he directed his players to line up.

Babson's line strutted toward the Choppers line, which moved like a chain gang. As the players passed one another, they exchanged handshakes. The Babson players excitedly said "Good game" as they passed; the Chopper players mumbled the same.

David had completed his pass and was returning to the dugout with many of the Chopper players as the lines wound up. Skit and Tony Poser were shaking hands at the end of their lines and exchanging "Good game" with one another when Poser put his other hand up to his throat and made a gagging noise and whispered, "Choke."

"How's your sister?" Skit said in return.

"Fuck you," said Tony, charging Skit.

Skit stepped aside and used Tony's momentum to push him to the ground. Before Skit could jump on him, Christy and Steady were holding him back.

"He's not worth it," said Christy.

Skit's face was red as he tried to struggle free.

"Let me go. I've had enough of this crap," said Skit.

Tony was starting to get up. He looked at Christy. "You stay away from my sister," he said.

Christy ignored him and turned to Skit. "We need you. You're going to get suspended if you keep this up."

Poser was now upright. David had run over to stand between Poser and Skit. "Enough," he said as the teams were converging. "Everyone, go back to your dugout."

Oscar Poser shouted from the third baseline, "Thompson, what's your problem? Can't you control your players?"

David had seen the entire episode between Tony and Skit. "We'll talk later, coach," he said.

Tony was shaking his hand and flexed his fingers as he walked back to his dad and the dugout. He had used his hand to brace himself from falling.

"Tony, are you okay?" asked his dad.

"I think so," he responded.

"You know, Thompson," Poser yelled, "that's why school players don't want to play in this league! They could get hurt!"

"Give me a break," David said. "They could get hurt walking in the school hallway or crossing the street too! Why don't you just lock him in the house until he gets his scholarship." David thought, *First they don't have the time and now they're afraid of getting hurt.* "By the way, coach," David said loud enough so the Babson parents and players could hear, "under league rules all players are to have equal playing time. You're not following that rule. The next time it happens, you'll forfeit the game. Got it?"

Poser waved him off saying, "Ahhhhh, just go away already!"

"It's not happening, coach," David replied. "By the way, all these young men want to play ball and it's your job to have them play equally. Do your job or I'll find someone else to run the team."

"You can't hold this field hostage every day," Poser said. Meeson quickly came over and put one arm over Poser's shoulder. Meeson knew if he didn't intervene, Poser would end up saying something stupid and Mrs. Poser would have to clean up after Oscar once more. Meeson had Poser turn away from David like a door closing on its hinges as they both headed back to their dugout. They walked slowly with Meeson talking to Poser in hushed tones while his other hand made brushstrokes in the air as if he were painting a picture.

Poser wasn't one to calm himself so readily and David knew that Meeson was probably explaining to him that he needed to play his players equally, something that Meeson had probably already suggested to him but that Poser had ignored. David knew that by publicly humiliating Poser, he would have to change his ways. Meeson knew it too.

David jogged toward the dugout to gather his things while talking to the team. "Everyone clear out of the dugout so the team for the next game can get in here. Meet me outside the fence, by the parking lot." The players slung their bags on their backs and slogged their way to a grassy area between the left-field line fence and the parking area.

When David arrived to the scene, the boys were talking about the game. He walked over to the scowls and frowns. Most of the boys were sitting on their rumps. Some were picking grass, others were fiddling with their hats.

"Eyes and ears on me," he said as he positioned himself facing the field. This way the boys would have to turn their backs to the field and focus on him without the distraction of the other game about to get underway. "Eyes and ears on me!" he repeated.

"Put your hats on, get off your bottoms, and take a knee," David said as he surveyed the dejected faces. He found each player's eyes in a moment of silence. The announcer introduced the first batter to the next game.

"You guys played a good game," he started. "Yes, you played well. You're matching up better physically now. I attribute that to all of our practices. But listen to what I'm about to say. You'll always have a tough time matching up to Babson physically. They have the better athletes overall—the school players."

Now the boys exchanged confused glances. "Coach, are you saying we can never win?" asked Roots.

"No, I'm not saying that at all. You guys are old enough now to understand that there is a mental aspect to this game too. And you guys are head and shoulders above teams like Babson right here," David said, pointing to his head. "You just need to learn to use that asset properly."

"I get it," said Steady, cracking a smile. "You've got to have faith. Like faith in God."

Skit rolled his eyes.

"God works. You need to get faith any way you can," said David. "It's one facet of the mental aspect. Faith is confidence; you, as a team, have to believe you can win before you *can* win. You guys understand what I'm saying?"

Silence.

David continued. "Your challenge now is to persevere and not to get discouraged. I don't care what the other teams say to you. They say you are too fat or too clumsy to win. Get used to it, boys, 'cause it's the real world slapping you in the face. There'll always be people telling you that you can't do this or that in life. It's your job both on the field and off to prove them wrong and to prove something to yourself in the process."

David began pacing as he let it sink in with the team and as he gathered his thoughts. He noticed a man standing about twenty feet away from the team with a white business-sized envelope in his hands. Annie came up from behind and tapped David on the shoulder. He turned to her, wondering why she wanted his attention.

"I'm sorry to interrupt, David. But that's him over there. That's the man who was hanging around our house. He says he needs to talk to you."

David looked at the lanky mustached man as he pushed up the glasses on his nose. He didn't recognize him.

"Tell him I'll be over in a minute," David said as he turned his attention back to the team. "Oh, sure you guys have come a long way the past few weeks. You used to just plain get trampled on the scoreboard. Now the scores are respectable, even quite close at times. But in the past three games we've found ways to lose our lead in the final innings. We need to learn how to close the deal, to finish the game."

Annie went over to the man and David could see her talking to him.

Flash was texting something on his cell phone faster than he could run, and David snatched the phone from his hand and slid it in his pocket without skipping a beat.

"Let's review this game. I think some of you got too giddy about your lead and, toward the end, you didn't have the focus, the absolute concentration required, to finish the game with a win. You were too pleased with yourselves for playing close to the other team. That was enough for some of you. Gentlemen, I've got news for you. We're here to win."

David looked at the team as he paced and their eyes, more or less, were looking off to the side. Christy did a little finger-roll wave in that direction, which caused David to look at what the boys were eyeing. It was a group of three chatting teenage girls, real cleat-chasers, who were looking at the boys from the parking lot. One started to tie her blouse at the waist, revealing her midriff; another loosened a button at the top of her blouse; the third girl was waving to the team, perhaps to Christy. David could see Annie in back of the girls heading toward the concession stand.

David raised his voice. "Concentration must trump distraction if you boys hope to win! Follow me with your eyes, boys," he said as he walked to the other side so the back of the players' heads would face the girls. "I think some of you other guys are looking for a way to lose. You expect to lose because you have lost so many; you're just wondering how you are going to blow the game this time around. If you think like that, you will have a tough time winning a game, ever. Losing feels like you've stepped in dog crap. But you've got to scrape that feeling off and then walk away to get ready for the next game."

For a brief second, David had their attention. The eye black some of them had put on before the game was running down from sweat now like black tears on their faces. David could sense that he had struck a nerve, if only briefly.

"Look, you *do* have the ability to compete with these other teams. One thing you have going for you is your passion to play the game. You're also head and shoulders above Babson when it comes to heart. That's another aspect of the game. But I have to tell you that your passion is unfocused some of the time. You've got to play the game with smarts and with your hearts." David paused for a second to gather his thoughts and looked at the ground as he paced.

Some boys started to laugh and pointed to something behind David. Other boys joined in and David wheeled around. He saw the man was behind him now, only ten feet away. Beyond him, back in the woods adjacent to the left-field corner fencing, were a group teenage boys, mostly camouflaged by the brush, who were smoking joints and puffing up a plume of smoke so engulfing that it looked like the trees were mired in a fog.

Skit cupped his hands around his mouth and called to the boys, "Dudes, you can't hotbox a forest!" The players all laughed, except for one.

David thought he recognized Gold Glove's older brother, Jacob Golder, as one of the smokers. He was sure of it when he saw that Gold Glove wasn't laughing. David stood in disbelief as the smoke billowed above the trees and sweetened the air.

Roots commented, "It must be National Weed Day." The boys laughed again except for Andrew. He looked away from the scene.

David yelled to the woods, "Hey, you guys knock it off and get out of here." With that the boys hurriedly disappeared into the forest.

Bullwhip weighed in: "No, National Weed Day is April 20. It was the other week."

"Are you sure?" asked Flash.

"Yeah, it's April 20. Same day as Hitler's birthday," Bullwhip said.

Roots thought for a second. "Come to think of it—"

"Knock it off already," David said. "Eyes and ears on me," he added as he moved so that the back of his players' heads faced the woods. It was the one direction David had left, as he was surrounded by the distractions of cleat-chasers, potheads, and a ball game.

As David turned the team again, he got a glimpse of the strange man. As the man glanced at his watch, one side of his windbreaker lifted just enough for David to see what appeared to be a handgun tucked into his belt. The man brought his hand down and whatever was tucked into his belt disappeared from sight. The man kept to David's rear.

David gathered himself and began to pace in front of the team. He tried to focus on delivering his team message as he thought about how to deal with the man. "Look, I like your spirit. You aren't a bunch of automatons playing ball in search of a scholarship. You play the game because you *love* it. That's why I love coaching you."

David looked at them all, surveying the faces one by one. He raised his voice. "I'm going to challenge you all right now. I'm going to challenge you to believe in yourselves. I have seen us losing close games the last three outings. And I believe there are enough of you here who don't think that you should win, that don't believe that you are worthy enough to share the same field with these school players. Yes, there are enough of you here that don't think you deserve to win so losing has become a self-fulfilling prophecy, an outcome you're satisfied with so long as the score is close."

David stopped pacing and stared at the team. The boys were all paying attention for now. He could sense the man inch closer but he wanted to finish what he had to say to the team.

David pressed on with his speech. "Don't fall into the trap of designing a fate for yourselves. I'm here to tell you right here that I *believe* in you as a team. But it doesn't matter what I think because I can't play on the field with you. You must believe too. You must look inside yourselves and figure out if your mental makeup is helping your team to win or to lose. And if you think your thought process is a losing one, it is up to you to try and change it and it is up to you to help your fellow teammates change the way they think for the betterment of the team. I'm telling you right now, if you don't change your focus as a team, you'll have a tough time winning another game this season."

David stopped surveying the team to try and gauge the impact of his speech. Christy's eyes met his. He knew Christy got the message. Other players' eyes hit his as well and, for that brief instant, there was a connection between a coach and his players, a moment that passed as quickly as it came.

The man was two steps behind him now. "Are you David Thompson?" he asked. David looked at the man. If it was any other man, he would have told him politely to wait until he was done. But this man might be packing a gun. David wanted to get him away from the boys.

David looked at the team. "Think about what I said, guys. I'll be back with you in a minute."

David turned around to face the man. "Yes, I'm him. You and I need to step over here to talk," he said to the man. They both walked off toward the woods.

"What's so important that this couldn't wait until I was finished with my team?" David asked as they walked side by side.

"Don't you know why I'm here?"

"Why would I know that? I don't know you, do I?" David looked for the gun but didn't see it, as the man had zipped up his windbreaker.

"No, you don't know me. I've been hired to give you this," he said, unzipping his windbreaker to reveal the gun. His back was to the team. David grabbed the gun from the man's pants and backed away, putting the gun in his front pants pocket. The boys were busy talking and didn't see what was happening.

"Who sent you?" David demanded.

The man's mouth opened wide as he stepped back, but then a smile came to his face. He started to reach into an inside pocket of his windbreaker.

"What are you doing?" David asked, pulling the gun out.

"Relax, I'm reaching for an envelope inside my coat."

"I'll get it," David said, and reached for it. He took it from the man and held it.

"The gun," the man said, "it's not real."

"What?"

"It's a starter's pistol; it fires blanks."

David pulled the gun out and could see the man was telling the truth by looking down the barrel. There was an obstruction in it. He looked in the chambers and found them empty.

"Why did you come to ballpark, filled with kids, with that gun in your pocket?"

"I go to some dangerous places in my line of work and I need to dress the part."

"What in God's name are you talking about?"

"I'm a process server. I came here to serve you the papers you're holding." David opened the envelope and unfolded the papers. He read the caption and could see that he was being sued personally along with Babe Ruth League, Inc., Brad Summers, and Johnny McFadden by the Elite Travel Baseball League. He glanced at the allegations and saw he was being accused of antitrust violations along with some other crap. He looked at the man.

"You realize, of course, that this is bullshit," David said. "You've got some nerve showing up here with the likes of a gun with all these kids here and then serving me papers."

"I was told to find you here and to serve them."

"My wife says you were hanging around the house this week. Is that true?"

"I tried to serve you there, but your car was never in the driveway. I asked the attorneys if I could serve your wife. They said to serve you at the field today."

"Here's your gun," David said, handing it back to the man. Some of the boys saw David give the gun back. They stopped talking among themselves and whispered to the other boys about the gun. "Now I've got a message I want you to serve to the attorneys and their clients who hired you."

"Okay, what is it?" the man said.

"You tell those bastards that they won't take baseball away from these boys . . . by threats . . . by force . . .. by lawsuits . . .by *any* means. I will simply not let it happen. Listen closely, real close, to what I am about to say." At that point, the words of Colonel Strong Vincent emerged from David's subconscious. He imagined hearing Vincent's orders to Colonel Joshua Chamberlain of the Twentieth Maine to hold Little Round Top at all hazards on the second day of the Battle of Gettysburg. The words began to reverberate in his head, carving out a notch in his vocal chords, searching for his chapped lips. "I will *defend* this field at all costs; I will *defend* the rights of these boys to play baseball in their own town. This *is* pure ground, it *is* sacred ground. This field is all that these boys have left in this town; it's the only thing they can call their own, especially during the summer. This is *their* game and *their* field. I would rather die right here on this ball field than see it occupied by all the greed, selfishness, and delusions of entitlement that have become entrenched in the feeble minds of adults gone wild. Did you get all that?"

The man stumbled backward, his gum-soled suede shoes squeaking on the pavement tar while he sought to maintain his balance. "I'll give them the message," he said. The man turned and left for his car. The boys looked at David, then at one another, and for the first time they realized their coach was fighting for them both on the field and off. Just then an oncoming truck blared its familiar "Turkey in the Straw" jingle as it entered the parking lot.

"It's the ice cream truck!" blurted Flash.

The tune registered with David as one that might have been played in a Civil War campfire on the eve of battle, perhaps in Joshua Chamberlain's campsite on the eve of his defense of Little Round Top.

David realized that his postgame talk had finished when the ice cream truck arrived. He had made a brief connection with the boys and that's all he could ever hope for on any given day. "Okay, you guys can go get some ice cream if you want. I don't have anything else to say."

"Bring it in here," David said, extending his arm. The boys gathered round in a circle and extended their hands on top of one another. "Choppers on three," David urged. "One, two, three," he said and the boys replied, "Choppers!" as their hands drooped down and parted.

With that, the team made a dash to the ice cream truck and David was left standing alone with Christy and Flash among the strewn equipment and bags.

"Okay, Flash, here's your cell," David said, flipping it to him.

"Dad, can I go?" asked Christy.

"Sure, Christy, but tell me something before you go. Why did Tony Poser tell you to stay away from his sister?"

"Oh, Becky and I are friends and Tony can't stand it."

"Why is that?"

"I'm not a school ballplayer, so I'm not good enough for her."

"Unbelievable," David said. He noted that this was the first time Christy had mentioned any girls in his life.

"Yeah, all Skit has to do is say *sister* and Tony drops an F-bomb and goes nuts."

"Wow, that's crazy."

"It's funny."

"Just be careful, Christy. . . ."

"Okay. Dad, what did that man want, by the way?"

"We'll talk about it later. Just don't say anything to your mother, okay?"

"Got it."

"Where is she anyway?"

"I think she's cleaning up in the concession stand."

"Oh, okay, see you back at the car in a few then," David said, thinking and hoping that Annie probably did not see the commotion he made with the process server.

David threw the equipment bags over his shoulder and picked up his bucket of balls and began walking to his car parked at the end of the lot near the left-field corner of the ballpark. When he got there, his cell phone was ringing. He dropped his load by the car. The caller ID flashed Johnny's number.

"Did you get served yet?" David asked, answering the phone.

"Those fucking dickheads," Johnny said. "They don't know who they're messing with. When they fuck with the bull, they will find the horns!"

"So is this the bat-shit crazy thing they planned to do to us?" David asked.

"Who knows? What do we do with these papers?"

"My league has got directors and officers liability coverage," David said. "So I'll turn the lawsuit over to the insurers so they can defend it. You need to check with your league and do the same."

"Okay then. How are you holding up?"

"Calm before the storm, my friend."

"What do you mean?"

"We've been playing defense. Now it's time to play offense. Are you game?"

"I thought you'd never ask. What's the plan?"

"Stay tuned. I gotta run. Christy and Annie are walking back to the car now. If Annie finds out I've been sued, she'll flip. Talk to you soon." David hung up and started loading the equipment in the backseat of his Mustang.

"Hi, David," Annie said, giving him a hug. "It was a good, close game."

"Yes, the boys played well. We just need to learn how to finish. Are you coming home with us?" he asked, throwing the catcher's equipment bag in the trunk.

"No," Annie said, "I'm getting a ride with Karen, Barry's mom. We're going shopping."

"Stretch's mom," Christy said, reminding David of Stretch's first name.

"Oh, gotcha," said David.

David finished loading the equipment into the car and closed the door and turned. Annie found his hands and held them.

"Who was that man that came to talk with you?" Annie asked.

"I didn't catch his name," David said, looking away.

"What did he want?"

"He had some information about our baseball league he wanted to share."

"Oh, so why was he hanging around our house?"

"You know us guys. We always want to share things with one another face-to-face. It was just a misunderstanding, a long story. Isn't that Karen over there waving to you?"

Annie looked back. She didn't see anyone.

"There, by the concession stand, next to the dumpster," David said, not knowing if it was Karen or not, but close enough for his purpose.

"Are you sure?" Annie asked.

"I think she ducked behind the concession stand," David said. "Have a good time shopping, Annie." David pulled her toward him and gave her a hug and then a kiss on the lips. Annie turned to Christy to give him a hug and to say how proud she was of him.

David watched Annie walk away and wondered how he was going to tell her, or if he was going to tell her at all. He got into the car and Christy was in the front seat already taking off his cleats and putting on his sandals. Neither of them wanted to talk about yet another lost game. Christy reached for the radio and turned it on to find a station. He looked at his dad.

"You okay?" he asked.

David nodded. "I'm good."

Over the years, there had developed long periods of silence between the two on the ride home from a loss, a silence broken only by the rush of air into the car as they drove with the windows open to rid themselves of the smell: the fermenting equipment bags holding the sweat of every team member in the foam helmet liners, the rain-soaked baseballs that had become moldy at the bottom of the baseball bucket because David did not get to drying them in the sun or in the oven.

"You okay?" David asked Christy this time.

"I'm fine," he said.

David knew that in Christy's mind the game was fading with each song on the radio. He knew Christy had already taken what he could from the game and that he might revisit it at times during the week. But he understood that for right now, the game had been filed away in Christy's mind, a memory that only he could access on his own terms. They reached the driveway.

"You okay?" Christy asked again.

"Yeah, I'm good."

"You look worried."

David exhaled. He was an easy read for Christy. "Baseball," he said.

Christy nodded.

David parked the car, switched the ignition to power mode, and turned up the radio. Christy put his soggy baseball socks on the dashboard to dry in the sun and then reclined in his seat. David pushed his seat back too and joined him. They both shut their eyes and rested, letting their minds drift to the music.

27

PREPPING FOR SUCCESS

A few days later, David sat in his office late at night inspecting his Sharps carbine to make sure his cleanings of the gun had removed all the black powder residue from the bore.

He felt surrounded by greed and corruption on several fronts. In his mind, the option of standing pat and doing nothing had run its course. He viewed his meeting with Moss as the prelude to a full-out offensive campaign. David just needed to iron out a plan.

David picked up a cleaning rod and dipped it in a soapy solution before swabbing the bore.

He thought about Annie. With the exception of Johnny, she was the only adult on his side willing to fight, but if their home was attacked her support would evaporate.

David pulled the hammer back to the safety position and depressed the plunger pin, allowing the lever hinge pin to move freely.

He considered moving openly under the cover of darkness to make his move on the Barkus forces.

David moved the lever hinge pin back and forth until it came out, releasing the breech block for cleaning.

No matter what, he decided right there that he needed to pick the time and place of battle to strike back.

David cleaned and oiled the entire mechanism and all the parts before placing them back in the gun.

In his mind, he needed to hit them hard. David looked in his cartridge box to make sure it was full with twenty rounds.

He saw an opportunity to strike first before being struck, to hit them hard so the sting was lasting and crushed their will to fight.

David replaced the lever hinge pin and locked the breech block in place. His gun was ready for action.

He decided to use rubber baseballs—those used in T-ball—because they were the same circumference as regular baseballs, but bounced more. The unraised seams allowed for easier handling and more effective targeting in the delivery mechanism he had designed.

He had bought hundreds of balls and they sat in the unfinished side of his basement in his workshop. They were hidden in a large bucket under a sheet in the corner where Annie would not find them.

With Annie asleep in bed, it was time to get to work on the balls. He had set a jig on his drill press to hold the balls as he used an electric drill bit to bore five-eighth-inch holes into each ball. He opened the storm cellar doors to allow the fresh air to diffuse the thick smell of burning rubber that the drilling produced. He worked for about a half hour drilling baseballs to the proper depth before setting them on his workbench.

Then it was time to insert the explosives. He thought about securing quarter sticks as Moss had done, but decided that M-60 firecrackers would be effective if used in bulk. The M-60s measured a little over an inch in length and a quarter inch in diameter and David stored them in the back of a drawer hidden by cat supplies.

The problem he faced was the length of the fuse. He calculated that he needed more time than the four-second fuse allowed, and so he had meticulously removed the plastic end cap at the top and replaced the fuse with a much longer one that he cut from a coil of fuse he purchased. He then replaced the end cap and made a pile of the devices in a shoe box on the floor.

The long-tailed fuses on the M-60s almost led to a disaster of epic proportions. The longer fuses reminded the Thompsons's two cats of their long-tailed mouse toys, and the fact that the M-60s were stored near catnip in the drawer caused them to bum-rush David's shoe box. The cats removed the devices one by one from it while David was repairing his jig assembly and they were off merrily playing with M-60s around the house.

Fortunately, David had made a mental note of the number of explosives he had made and put in the box. When he discovered them missing, he was able to recover all of them, or so he hoped. He found one in the cats' water bowl, another in the litter box, another in the little carpeted shelter that served as the base of a scratching post. He wrestled the final one from a cat playing with it on the bed between Annie's legs while she slept on her stomach. *No harm, no foul*, David thought after he returned to the work at hand with a newfound appreciation for Moss's operation.

In half of the baseballs, he inserted smoke bombs of the same size. The end caps were flush with the surface of the balls so only the fuse would stick out. He separated the explosive baseballs from the smoke-bomb baseballs by placing them in separate buckets.

David then heard someone coming down the basement stairs. He quickly covered his operation with the sheet. He thought maybe Annie had discovered a stray explosive in bed.

"Dad?"

"Yeah, Christy, I'm in the workshop."

Christy opened the door and looked around at the sheet covering the drill press and baseballs.

"Dad, what are you doing?"

"I'm getting ready."

"For what?"

"To fight back."

Christy had never seen his father so focused as he had been the past few days. He didn't smile and joke with him and always seemed at work in the basement.

"What's going on with you, Dad?" Christy asked. "You've been acting kind of strange."

"I didn't tell your mother but I'm going to tell you, and this is between you and me. Barkus and his gang of lunatics are suing me, and our family for that matter."

"I don't understand. For what?"

"Antitrust violations. Basically they're suing us so they can get the Babe Ruth field."

Christy sat down on the workbench stool. "Wow . . . that's crazy. What can we do?"

"Nobody sues us; nobody attacks our family. When that happens, it's time to do something; it's time to go on offense."

In his mind, David had warned Moss not to mess with him and his family and, despite his warnings, one week later Barkus and company had a process server lurking around his house and his family with what looked like a loaded gun. He then had the audacity to serve him in front of the kids and families at the baseball field. David was concerned that their next move would be late at night, at his house, targeting his family, just like Moss had done with families in Mohawk City.

"Dad, I should probably tell you some things," he said, his voice cracking. "I didn't want to say anything because I know you have your own problems to deal with. . . ."

"What's on your mind?"

"The Barkus players at high school. They're saying some awful things about you and they were trying to bait me into a fight with them when I was at the high school for the modified tryouts."

"Oh, geez, I'm sorry about that Christy—"

"I dealt with it."

"How?"

"I ignored them pretty much."

"Good for you."

"I'll be honest, Dad, sometimes I think, doing nothing makes me angrier. I'm tired of being pushed around or tripped—"

"Oh, Christy, I wish you had told me."

"Dad, you got other things on your mind. It's over 'cause I didn't make the modified team. I won't see these guys after school ends in a few weeks. But I want to pop some of those kids and someday I just might."

"You can't, not on the school grounds at least. Trust me, they'll find a way to suspend you. Mom wouldn't be happy."

"It's not just me. The older guys on our team are picked on too at the high school. The Barkus players want to fight them after school. Some guys on the team are thinking about taking them up on it and fighting them in the foxhole." The foxhole was a depression in the ground located halfway between the one-hundred-yard stretch of densely wooded area that separated town hall (which housed the police station) and the high school.

Located near the old business center of town, it was a busy playground for pot, alcohol, and the occasional fight.

"No, no, no! Tell them not to do anything in or near the high school. God, especially not at the high school." David was thinking about Conway. Something appeared to be going on between Conway and Barkus. David thought his boys would be the ones disciplined in any fracas while the Barkus boys, the school players, would be miraculously exonerated of all blame.

David decided then to enlist Christy and the boys in his plan. At least they would be under his supervision and off school grounds. "Look, Christy, I'm with you. It's time to take a stand but we need to do it on our own terms. We need to take the battle to them. Tell the boys not to do anything. I think I have a plan. Tell them to be ready on twelve hours' notice to take action."

"What's the plan, Dad?"

"I'm still working on it. But you tell the boys that they will need to wear costumes and masks for what I have in mind."

"You mean like Halloween costumes?"

"Exactly. The crazier, the better. It's important that people can't recognize your face. You guys will also need guns."

"Guns? But Dad—"

"No, no, no. I'm talking about squirt guns, long-range water rifles with those big reservoirs you guys use during the summer."

"Okay."

"You guys will also need a lot of urine."

Christy's eyebrows raised; his mouth dropped. "You want us to collect our own piss?"

"I suppose, but artificial urine will work just as well."

Christy looked at his Dad and wondered if he had lost his senses. "How do you make fake urine?"

"Some water, salt, yellow food coloring, and some ammonia should do it. Look it up on the Internet."

"What are we using this for, Dad?"

"To put in the guns, of course."

"To shoot at what?"

"You'll find out when the time comes. Just be ready."

"Okay, Dad, I'll talk with the guys. They're ready to do something after all the crap they've been taking."

"Okay, tell them to talk with no one about this."

"All right. What are you doing down here anyway?"

"I'm getting ready, just like you guys need to do." David didn't want Christy to carry the burden of knowing what he had in mind. Besides, he hadn't quite figured out his plan anyway and it was subject to change. "Christy, please go to bed now. It's past your bedtime."

David extended his fist to Christy and he bumped it with his own before going back upstairs. David grabbed a pad of paper off his workbench and started adding items: wire, flexible PVC pipe, reducers, couplings of various sizes, butane lighters, two gasoline generators.

28

ANNIE'S DISCOVERY

Annie had been doing the grocery shopping in Colonie to avoid the cackling of the Barkus women in Indigo Valley, but that was before her appearance at the baseball board meeting. Now she shopped back in Indigo Valley, in her hometown, in her store where she had worked behind the deli counter as a teenager.

Indigo Valley Co-op was a small, independent grocery store where the locals shopped. It was next door to Canfield's Pharmacy and in the center of town, a few hundred yards from the high school on one side and a few hundred yards from Stanley Moss's house on the other.

As Annie pulled out from one aisle and prepared to round the corner in the front of the store, Angela Meeson was reading the *National Enquirer* while waiting in a check-out line closest to Annie. She was placing the magazine back on the rack when she spotted Annie.

Angela looked away and touched some other tabloids on the rack, purposely ignoring Annie like she'd been doing since Barkus had e-mailed the world that David was the enemy. If anything, Angela was a socially adept woman, the perfect conformist. She ignored Annie around the field and in the bleachers. She did not want to be seen with the wife of David Thompson—it would do nothing for her sons' baseball careers. But Angela had not seen any other school players' wives in the store, so she felt she could say something to Annie then without jeopardizing her status in the brood.

Annie saw Angela's glance and maintained her resolve to reciprocate the cold-shoulder treatment. She began to enter the next aisle when Angela looked up again.

"I'm sorry to hear about the lawsuit," Angela said.

Annie heard her speak but wondered if Angela was talking to her or someone else. She looked over her shoulder. She saw Angela looking at her and asked, "Are you talking to me?"

"Yes," Angela replied.

Annie moved back a few steps toward Angela. "I'm sorry, I don't know what you're talking about."

"You know, Rob Barkus and the Elite Travel league?"

"What about them?"

"They're the ones suing your husband."

"Is that right?" Annie said, wondering what, if anything, David had failed to tell her. Annie was determined not to give Angela the satisfaction of any reaction. She might have been upset with David for not telling her about the lawsuit, but she was more upset with Angela for reveling in the news.

"You do know about the lawsuit, don't you?" Angela asked, hoping, praying to be the bearer of bad news.

"No."

"Really?"

Angela's smugness irked her. She could imagine Angela recounting this very moment with all the Barkus women. "If David thought it was important, he would have told me," Annie said.

"Yes, it's too bad he just didn't give them the field," Angela added, hoping to land a dig.

"Who are *'them'*?" Annie asked.

"Rob Barkus and the Elite Travel Baseball League."

"How come 'them' doesn't include you? Don't you play in that league?"

"Yes, but I'm not suing you."

This comment did not escape Annie, as she and David lived and talked about the law off and on through four years of night law school. "Where do you think all that money is going that you are paying Barkus? Don't you think some of it is going to fund this lawsuit?"

Angela just wanted to break the news; she didn't want to discuss it. "I'm really sorry this happened, but *your* husband should have given them the field."

"Angela, you're not sorry at all and stop trying to pretend you're not involved, like you're some kind of innocent bystander. You're enabling it; you've got blood on your hands."

"What do you want me to do about it?" she whispered loudly. "My sons want to play on the school teams so they need to play on the Barkus teams, just like the varsity coach's kids do," she said, banging her head like a hammer every few words for emphasis.

"Is there a parent in your home?"

"Excuse me?"

"You know, like an adult to give some moral guidance to your sons."

"Stop it," Angela whispered. "I shouldn't even be talking to you. Your husband is to blame, you know."

"What's with the whispering and what's with the field? Don't you already have two fields to play on?"

Angela pushed her cart toward the cash register as the line began moving.

"Don't you?" demanded Annie.

Angela reached the conveyor belt and bent down to pick up a case of red Gatorade from her cart. She came up with her neck extended like a periscope as she turned about, looking for any familiar faces. She plunked the plastic bottles down on the conveyor belt, the same kind of bottles David found strewn about the Babe Ruth field and its dugouts when he cleaned up. She then turned to Annie. "I'm warning you," she said like a cat growling. "Your husband *needs* to listen to Arnold about the field—"

"Is that some kind of threat or something?"

Angela eyed someone walking through the entrance doors. She recognized Jerry Conway walking down the first aisle toward the rear to the delicatessen. Angela quickly turned to Annie and mumbled, "Look, that's all I can say," before she went back to unloading her groceries.

Annie was not going to let Angela Meeson get the last word. "You people think you are something special: you bad-mouth us, you shun us, you sue us, and now you threaten us. I can't wait for your kids to graduate so you can move the hell away from us."

When Angela heard Annie's words, her forehead furrowed as her eyeballs bulged, but she continued about her business as if Annie were talking to someone else.

Annie shook her head in disgust. She resumed pushing her cart down the next aisle and hurried through the rest of the store. She wanted to get home and talk with David to find out what was going on. A few minutes later, she returned to the cash registers. Angela was nowhere in sight.

Conway was ahead of Annie but she didn't recognize him as anyone other than a businessman talking on a cell phone while he was dealing with the teenage boy cashier.

It was Jacob Golder's third day as cashier at the co-op and he was still a bit unsure of himself. He had taken a job there to earn some money, to try something different, and to pass the time away while he waited to graduate. He asked Conway if he had his co-op membership card. Conway was engaged in a phone conversation with someone about the future growth of his business. He waved Jacob off, indicating that he was either a nonmember or didn't have his card. Annie proceeded to unload her groceries from the cart to the conveyor belt.

Jacob thought the man was the same one that had tripped over his foot about a week ago in the school. He would have asked him but the man was on the phone and a line had formed behind Annie.

Conway forked over a crisp twenty and received his change. He clutched his lunch from the checkout counter with his free hand as he continued to talk on his cell with the other, pressing the phone hard against his ear as he walked out the entrance in search of his black Navigator.

Jacob greeted Annie with "Hello" and a smile, just like he'd been trained a few days earlier. He asked her if she had a co-op membership card and Annie had already gotten it out of her wallet and was waiting for Jacob's prompt before handing it over to him. As he took it from her, Annie noticed Jacob's large gold ring with a ruby-colored stone with surrounding engraving that read, "Indigo Valley High School, Class of 2009."

"Oh, that's a beautiful ring. You're graduating from the high school this year then?" she asked.

"Yes," Jacob said, scanning the card with a smile that was all his own.

"That's great," Annie said as Jacob handed the card back. "I have a son that's entering the high school next year."

"Oh, wow—"

"Yes, he's excited."

"That's great," Jacob said, beginning to scan the items.

"So what are your plans for next year?" Annie asked, while careful not to assume Jacob planned on going to college.

"College, the usual," Jacob said. Most of his friends were going on to four-year colleges.

"Well, congratulations." Annie removed her charge card from her wallet.

"Thank you," he said as he continued to scan Annie's items.

"Did your four years at high school go fast?"

Jacob laughed. "Sometimes not fast enough; sometimes too fast."

"How's that?"

"Well, there's not a whole lot to do here in town when you're my age." He made it a point to make eye contact with Annie in between scanning items. "Time goes slow then. But when you study hard and all you do is study, time goes real fast."

Annie smiled and nodded. "Same thing was true when I went to school here."

"Really? How long ago was that?"

"Oh, about thirty years ago."

"Wow, that's a long time ago," Jacob said as he finished scanning the items.

Annie laughed. "Yes, it seems like it."

"Your total is $20.09."

"Hey, that's your lucky number," Annie said while moving to the credit card machine.

Jacob chuckled. "So it is."

"Do you have any advice for an incoming freshman?" Annie asked, swiping her credit card.

Jacob had a ready answer. He had written a retrospective article about his experience at Indigo Valley High the previous week for the *Cornhusker*.

"I guess I just don't take it too seriously," he said, waiting for an approval of the credit charge.

"That's good advice—sounds like something my husband would say to his baseball team."

"He coaches baseball?" he said, waiting for the transaction to process.

"Yes, he runs the Babe Ruth program in Indigo Valley."

"Oh, that's neat. My younger brother, Andrew, plays Babe Ruth."

"Really? What team is he on?"

"I think it's Cycle Chopper."

Annie told Jacob that David was the coach of the team and they quickly started talking about the season. Jacob said he had only seen a few games because he had been too busy. He told her that Andrew was having a great time playing on the team and about how highly he spoke of David. At that moment, Annie felt a rush of pride in what David was doing for the kids and the town.

The charge approval went through and the printer spat out a receipt as Jacob searched for a pen.

"Do you play baseball?" Annie asked.

"No, I quit a few years ago. All my friends quit."

"Oh, that's too bad. What happened?" She took the pen from Jacob and signed for the purchase.

"I don't know. They really didn't pay any attention to us. All they seemed to care about was the school players. They played all the time. I got tired of sitting on the bench."

"I'm sorry," Annie said, handing the pen back. "My husband is trying to change things."

"Yeah, I know. Andrew tells me he plays all the time."

Jacob started packing Annie's groceries in bags while thinking about playing baseball as a kid and how he missed it. He was happy for Andrew but believed that graduation had put an end to his personal baseball career. He had spent his high school years studying hard, taking all the AP and honors courses that he was told to take in order to get into the best private colleges in the country. When he wasn't smoking joints in the foxhole or in the woods by the Babe Ruth field, the little free time he had was spent writing for the *Cornhusker*. Those were his outlets when he wasn't studying.

Annie said goodbye to Jacob and on the way home she thought about how baseball had the potential to enrich the lives of teens like him. When she pulled into the driveway and walked past David's mud-caked sneakers piled high under the water spigot, for the first time in memory they didn't remind her about the dirt David tracked into her home and how it sounded like sandpaper when she walked across the maple flooring. And while she also thought about the lawsuit that Angela had mentioned on the way home, she wasn't angry with David about it, though she knew she had to discuss it with him. Instead, she kept thinking about Jacob, Andrew, Christy, and baseball.

She had seen David's Mustang in the driveway and figured he was probably in his office. The hinges to the basement office door squeaked like a
bird chirping and she opened it to call down to David to ask for help
unloading the groceries from the car. He came up, two steps at a time, and
promptly kissed Annie on the cheek.

"Guess who I saw at the market today?" she asked.

"I don't know. Who?"

"Angela Meeson."

David's smile disappeared. "Lucky you."

"She spoke to me today."

"How gracious of her."

"She mentioned that Barkus and the Elite Travel Baseball League are
suing us. Is that true?"

David closed his eyes briefly, wondering if another baseball argument
was about to ensue. "Yes," he sighed.

"When were you going to tell me?"

"When I had some answers," David said softly, looking down. "I didn't
want to upset you unnecessarily. I don't want to hurt you." He was scouring
the high-gloss wood floors for any sign of dirt out of habit and fear that its
presence might push Annie over the edge and place him firmly in the
doghouse.

"Oh, okay, I understand," Annie said finally.

"You understand?" asked David, feeling as if he'd misunderstood her, like
he had been fooled by a pitch.

"Yes, that's what I said."

"Okay, I figured you'd be upset with me—again—over baseball."

"I'm not happy about it, but you taught me that anyone can sue anyone."

"Yeah, I guess I did."

"So do you have some answers now?"

"Yes, I've been working on getting them this morning."

"Okay, spill the beans then."

"Johnny, Brad, and Babe Ruth are also defendants. The Barkus people
are suing us for antitrust violations."

"What? You mean like you have a monopoly on baseball?"

"Something like that."

"That sounds ridiculous."

"Yes, I agree."

"How can they sue you as a volunteer?"

David shook his head. "I know. It's crazy."

"What do they want?"

"Damages and an injunction on paper, but they really want to intimidate us. That's what this is all about."

"Intimidate you over what? Baseball?"

"Yes, they want the Babe Ruth field so they can ring the cash register. We are in their way."

"So this is all about money then?"

"Yes, money and field access."

"Who's defending us?"

"The Indigo Valley league directors and officers liability insurance carrier. Our lawyer says Babe Ruth headquarters wants to fight the lawsuit."

"So the insurer is picking up the cost of defense?"

"Yes."

"How about if we lose or they decide to settle out of court?"

"It's a multimillion-dollar policy. So the policy should cover it all, defense costs plus any judgment or settlement. But they don't want to settle. They want to fight it."

"Okay then, I can live with the lawsuit."

David knew a "but" was coming.

"But I don't want you doing anything more. You've done enough already to save baseball. It's time to let it go and let whatever happens happen."

"I can't."

"What do you mean? You can't or you won't?"

"I won't because I can't."

"What's that supposed to mean?"

"This baseball situation is at my core, it's become a part of me. I don't want to live in this town without baseball for everyone and I don't want to move anyplace else because this is *my* town. I want to show Christy that some things are worth fighting for in life. I don't want to be sitting around the dinner table twenty years from now wondering if we could have saved baseball. I don't want to live a life of regrets."

Annie heard David, heard him loud and clear. "What exactly do you plan to do, David?"

"I'm working on a plan."

"Are you going to share your thoughts at this point?"

"No, I'm trying to protect you. The less you know the better."

"David, we always discuss everything. . . ."

"Not this time. You're going to have to trust me on this one."

"I don't understand."

"That's where the trust part comes in."

Annie's eyes closed and her head drooped. She did not know if she wanted to cry or lay into David. She felt tired of it all. She was worn out, totally exhausted. David put both hands on her shoulders and then touched her chin. She looked up and her eyes met his. He took her hands and warmed them.

"Annie, I'd like to think I've been a good husband. I don't smoke, drink, and I've never cheated on you. I listen to what you have to say, just as you listen to me. I can't make promises because when things change, I have to change my plan. It's like being at bat. You have to change your approach as the pitches are thrown, as the count builds. I can't talk to you in between pitches."

"What happens if I don't like what you do? Did you think about that?"

"Yes, but we'll talk about it after I've done something."

"You know, most wives wouldn't have put up with this nonsense."

"I'm hoping you're different from most wives. That's why I married you."

"You had better watch it because I just might leave you."

Annie's hair was almost covering one of her eyes. David raised his hand and pushed it back. "I realize that's a chance I'm taking."

"You know, I'm not a dummy. I understand you're going to do something I might not approve of and that's why you won't discuss it with me."

David didn't respond. He knew she was right.

"Whatever happened to doing things in a nonconfrontational way, like shifting the blame, or doing nothing sometimes?" asked Annie.

"Annie, deflection through blame-shifting was a handy thing for a time when we were fighting on too many fronts. But in the end, making somebody else the bad guy is really just failing to take a stand and hiding behind him. Doing nothing and being nonconfrontational might be the right approach at a certain time, but could be totally wrong at another. Isn't that why you walked into our board meeting?"

"I'm not sure. It seemed like the right thing to do at the time."

"Exactly. If you have tons of supporters, being nonconfrontational could work. If you don't and you're alone, or if there are only a few, then you are like the voice of reason clinging on to a life raft on a sea of insanity. That's me. Now, how do you survive that voyage to effect change? You can't, so you perish—unless you adapt your tactics to the circumstances, much like a baseball coach or general adapts to circumstances of any particular game or battle."

David continued. "At this point, doing nothing means baseball will die for these Babe Ruth boys as sure as I'm standing here. Oh sure, it might limp around crippled for a year or two before it's put out of its misery completely. But mark my words, it *will* die. And with it, a piece of you, me, Christy, his friends, and the other boys in this town will die too."

Annie stood still and didn't respond. She thought about Jacob and she knew David was right.

"All right, David. I won't press you on the topic any longer."

"Thank you," David said as he drew Annie closer and she embraced him. "Thank you," he said again. He felt good to have Annie's support, but he knew he had it under false pretenses and that did not sit well with him. David hadn't told her everything. He had withheld information about Moss, the Barkus threats, the vandalism of the baseball field, Conway, and more.

He realized he was risking his marriage with the very person he was hugging. David felt a bit dirty and ashamed for not telling her everything, but there was no turning back now. The pitches had been thrown, the count was full. He had to protect the plate; he had to protect his home. He was going to foul off anything close and wait for his opportunity.

Annie rested her head on his shoulder and he rested his head on top of hers. Annie whispered, "I just don't want to see you hurt."

David whispered back, "I know . . . I know." But David wasn't worried about himself, though. No, David was worried about Christy and Annie—worried about who would take care of them should death catch up to him the way it finally caught up to Buford.

29

THE EVE OF BATTLE

I t was the night before Indigo Valley Day and David was locking up the house before going to bed. Every night of the previous week, David had slept with his loaded gun stowed under his bed, out of sight of Annie. He slept lightly, if he even slept at all, as he investigated every noise in the depth of night with the light feet of a sharpshooter so as not to wake Annie. But the only enemy he encountered were the cats who playfully chased the shoulder strap hanging from the saddle ring of his carbine as David snuck around the house checking for any signs of Barkus and his minions.

His first concern was for Annie and Christy. He had thought about taking the battle to Barkus, to his home, to the homes of his followers, but he could never live with himself if he was not at home when they attacked. Besides, he thought, it was best not to fire the first shot and invite a retaliatory action from Barkus and his large army directed at his home. David saw himself, again, like General John Buford, seemingly locked in a defensive battle.

But as the day and nights passed and no bombs were found on his windshield or on his front door knob, the fear of a home attack subsided and David became increasingly confident that the battle would not be in his yard. The passage of time made it increasingly likely that his plan to steer Barkus and his army toward the Babe Ruth field had been effective. So

David, like any good commander, directed his focus more and more on the most likely battlefield: the Babe Ruth field.

David understood the advantage he had in knowing the location, time, and place of the enemy's troop movements so that he could orchestrate the battle on terms most favorable to him. He believed that such an opportunity would present itself the next day—Indigo Valley Day, the Saturday Barkus had mentioned at Canfield's Pharmacy for one of the Elite teams to defiantly play a game on the Babe Ruth field. David figured that Barkus, on this day, was determined to show his strength in numbers and his resolve in securing ground that he felt was his divine right to possess.

Indigo Valley Day was the one day each year when all Indigo Valley turned out as a community. On this occasion, the town celebrated its founding with a colorful parade loaded with homemade floats and children —more children than one would ever see at one place in town year round— laughing while either walking in the parade or watching it from the lawns along the route right to where it ended at the high school. The organizers did all they could to make the parade longer by creating large gaps in between performing groups—sometimes running fifty yards—and by adding an endless procession of every emergency vehicle from Indigo Valley and the surrounding counties, all sounding their horns and sirens. During the lean years, they even brought out the snowplows or the sewer truck to add some heft to the parade. Marching bands from all over the region came to play. They were all introduced over the PA system in front of the co-op, where the grandstand was located and the entire procession was filmed to be shown on public-access television. Indigo Valley Day culminated with a barbecued chicken dinner for purchase and alcoholic beverages of choice, provided you brought your own. The day was capped off by fireworks.

With all of Indigo Valley at the noisy parade three miles away from the Babe Ruth field and with every police officer in town either working crowd control or driving their newly washed cruiser in the procession, David knew he could not ask for a better day to do battle with Barkus.

Before David locked the front door, he stood outside and scanned the perimeter of his yard while a chorus of crickets chirped. He smelled the dead worms run over in the street after the heavy rains earlier that evening. But no sign of the enemy. David climbed the stairs and looked into his bedroom and saw Annie asleep. He turned to Christy's room and David could see a light shining underneath the door. He lightly tapped on the door and he heard Christy's desk chair slide on the wood floor.

"Christy, you awake in there?" David whispered.

The door opened. "Hey, Dad, what's up?" Christy said, stretching his hands up to the ceiling.

"Tomorrow is the day."

"Yeah, it's Indigo Valley Day. Looking forward to it."

"No, I mean tomorrow is the day we attack."

"Really?"

"Yes. You need to be armed and at Lock Seven Park at 8:30 a.m. sharp." Lock Seven Park was an access point from the main road to the bike path. The bike path ran along the river before climbing the rear of David's hill. "Get the boys there and await further orders. Can you get ahold of them now?"

"Yeah, I was just talking with them on Facebook," Christy said, sitting back down at his computer. "Are you sure about this, Dad?"

"This is as good as it gets. This is our opportunity knocking."

"Okay, can you tell me what we're going to do?"

"Yeah, sure." David proceeded to give him a rundown of the plan while Christy started typing to the boys.

After Christy sent messages to the boys, David leaned over his desk. "I need another favor from you, Christy."

"Okay."

"I need you to give this letter to your mother tomorrow morning before you go," David said, handing the envelope to Christy. "These are instructions for her to follow. I won't see her tomorrow because I need to leave before she wakes up. Can you give this envelope to her for me before you head to the park?"

"Yeah, sure, what's this all about? Is everything all right?"

"Everything is fine, but I need you to give it to her. You can read it if you want. If I don't see you in the morning, I'll see you on the field. Wait for my call."

Christy stood up and faced his father. David put his hands on his shoulders. "Son," he said, "tomorrow we're going to try and save baseball for this town."

David withdrew, thinking how broad Christy's shoulders had become. He noticed for the first time that maybe Christy was taller than he was. It struck him then that Christy would be leaving the house in a few years, perhaps to go off to college. He couldn't bear to think of it; he turned away to leave the room. He knew he screwed up Christy's high school baseball career; he didn't want to screw up tomorrow for him too.

He went downstairs and picked up his Sharps and went to his gun safe to get twenty rounds for morning. As he was loading his cartridge box, he heard it: the loud-pitched roar of an engine floored like it was starting a drag race. David peered out the narrow front-door side window to see the red taillights of a pickup in the middle of his front lawn kicking up turf like a rototiller stuck on full throttle. He tried to unlock the front door but it was jammed. After a number of tugs, he swung it open and moved to the front yard with his gun. The gas fumes still lingered. David could see and hear the truck speeding down the street. He looked down the street for any parked vehicles or anyone that might indicate that the pickup truck was part of a larger attack. He looked around the front yard. Nothing. The crickets returned as the engine's roar faded off in the distance. David heard a noise from behind him; he quickly turned and started to bring his Sharps up to his chin with both hands.

"Dad, it's me," Christy said, poking his head out the front door. He had run down the stairs when he heard the commotion outside. "What's going on?"

David didn't answer. He scoured the front bushes and then the side bushes for any signs of an ambush. He looked to the rear of the house and saw nothing moving under the spotlight that doused his backyard. He recalled what Moss had said at his first meeting with him: "Thinking or knowing some guy was at your house or even in your yard, that's an icky, awful feeling, don't you think?"

Christy came out and stood by his father's side and looked at the lawn. "What happened?" he asked.

"Lawn job," David said.

Christy looked at the two dirt tire tracks engraved in the lawn under the lamppost light. "Bastards," he said.

David briefly wondered if he should chastise Christy for his word choice, but that thought quickly disappeared when he recalled using the word a few times himself in Christy's presence.

"I think I recognized the truck," Christy said.

"You saw it?"

"Yes, from my bedroom window."

"Who was it?

"It looked like Poser's truck. I saw it at tryouts."

"Really?" David said, wondering if they were coming for his house tonight or whether this was a distraction of some type for the game tomorrow. "Did Mom hear anything?"

"No, she was still asleep when I came downstairs. She's got her sound machine on. What are you going to do, Dad?"

"First thing to do is take a picture of the damage. I'm going to call Chief McNeal and report it tomorrow. Fortunately, the driver didn't swerve, so the damage is just the width of his tires and pretty cleanly cut. Go get a wheelbarrow and get some topsoil from the back and let's fill these tracks in and then sprinkle some of that green-colored grass seed and throw on some grass clippings. With any luck, Mom won't see it tomorrow. I'll get the camera."

"You think they're coming back?"

"I don't think they're coming back tonight. But just in case, I'll sleep downstairs with my Sharps."

"Jesus, Dad, this is crazy," Christy said. "I just want to play baseball with my friends."

"It is nuts, Christy. Sometimes you're forced to fight crazy with crazy to get your point across. That's what tomorrow is all about."

After they repaired the lawn, they went in the house. David locked the door behind them while Christy went to bed. David got his pillow from his bed and gently kissed Annie on the forehead. He found a quilt in the linen closet and a travel alarm clock. He set the clock for early morning and slept downstairs on the living room couch. He set his loaded Sharps down on the rug beside him. He lay there half asleep with the windows partly open as the bushes and trees rustled in the spring breeze. He was looking for a sign that Barkus was sending a second wave of minions. But David felt comfort in being in a room surrounded by the Mead Schaeffer wartime illustrations. There was one in particular that soothed him, a 1943 Christmas *Saturday Evening Post* cover illustration entitled *Lone Soldier*—David's favorite.

It depicted a World War II soldier standing on guard, rifle in hand in the moonlight against the backdrop of a clear, star-filled sky. He got glimpses of it as car headlights shined through a window as they passed the home. The illustration calmed him and cleared his mind. As he lay there and as the time passed, he found himself unafraid. He felt Barkus and his toadies had fired shots first with the e-mail assault, the lawsuit, and now with the attack on his home. He was ready to do battle that night, from his living room, or tomorrow at the Babe Ruth field. The time had come.

30

THE BATTLE

A fter he had spent a few hours getting his equipment in place on the hill, David stood atop it precisely at 8:00 a.m. with his Sharps carbine in hand. Against the blue sky, the sun was shining and white, puffy clouds cast shadows that rolled across the ball field, then up and over the hill, and then down the Mohawk River. Though the clouds were moving above, there was only a very slight breeze at ground level, a breeze that David could easily account for in making his artillery adjustments.

David relished the possibility of an offensive launch from his hill—his high ground—onto the field below. On the second day of battle at Gettysburg, Colonel Chamberlain was positioned on the Union far left flank with orders to hold the ground at all costs. He had nearly depleted his ammunition after refusing a number of Confederate attacks on his line. A large number of his men were either killed or wounded. Chamberlain could see the Confederates were forming below to attack his line again. He heard musket fire to his rear and thought his position had been surrounded by Confederates. In his mind, he was faced with the decision to do nothing and lose the fight for sure or to do something to try and win it. In the end, history was made when Chamberlain ordered his men to fix bayonets and the soldiers under his command then charged. The Confederates, exhausted themselves, were caught by surprise in the face of this maneuver and were pushed back. It was the turning point of Gettysburg, perhaps the war.

David saw this day as his opportunity to change the tide in his war. Dressed in a Federal blue uniform and cap adorned with brass buttons and golden trim, David was disguised as Joshua Chamberlain of the Twentieth Maine. He sported Chamberlain's famous walrus mustache as a mask of sorts and, with the exception of his gray loose-fit baseball pants and his white sneakers, he looked the part of the famous colonel.

Whether David's great-great-grandfather had any role at Little Round Top and Big Round Top at Gettysburg while serving under the command of Colonel Joseph Fisher was always a matter of debate in David's mind. Colonel Joshua Chamberlain and Fisher vehemently disagreed over whether Fisher should receive any credit for taking Big Round Top at the end of the second day. Now David saw a clear path to redeeming his family's name. Today was his chance to be in command. It was his chance to be Colonel Joshua Chamberlain and to defend his Round Top at all hazards. Then he would take the battle to all those who would destroy baseball, his town, and his family.

He looked down over his neglected baseball field. The infield dirt and baselines were pockmarked with the cleat movements of a thousand plays. David had told the last teams to play there not to rake the infield after they were done. He had also instructed the lawn-care contractor to skip the mowing for the week to ensure long, dewy grass for the game.

David heard the swishing sound of someone walking in the high grass behind him. He stood up and turned, expecting to see Johnny. Instead, David saw a man dressed in a kilt and holding bagpipes. David's stomach dropped for a second. He looked closely at the man. Finally, under the Balmoral cap and behind the muttonchops, David recognized Johnny.

"What the hell are you supposed to be?" David asked.

Johnny smiled. "I'm a piper from the Royal Highland Regiment of Canada."

"You look insane."

"You said the crazier, the better."

"So I did. Thanks for bringing the bagpipes. Nice touch."

"Sure."

"I'm appointing you to the position of company musician."

"Yeah, okay, whatever that means."

"Where did you park the truck?"

"Down the hill from you a bit."

David looked at the dark black, blue, and green tartan colors of Johnny's kilt. "You know, they didn't wear kilts in the Civil War and there was no record of pipers in battle either."

"So what," Johnny said, pointing at David's feet. "Do you think we're doing some kind of Civil War reenactment here?"

David looked down at his sneakers. "I suppose not."

At the house, Christy was ready to bolt out the door to bike over to Lock Seven to meet up with the rest of the boys at 8:30 a.m. But first he knew he had to give his mom the letter as he'd promised. He found her at the dining room table reading the morning paper.

"Hi, Mom. Dad wanted me to give you this note."

"Oh, I was wondering where he was this morning. Have you seen him?"

"Not since last night."

Annie opened the letter and read it to herself, with Christy reading over her shoulder. Christy was reading it for the first time too.

Dear Annie,

Ever since I've known you, we've watched the Indigo Valley Day parade together. But today I'm afraid we're going to break that tradition.

I know baseball has come between us. I'm sorry it happened. But I need to finish what was started because that's who I am. It's the right thing to do.

I've asked Christy to help. If that is what he wants to do, please don't stop him. We need your help. Please go up to the Indigo Valley Police Office and keep Pete McNeal's wife, Elle, company starting at 9:15 this morning until I text you. She's going to be working dispatch today while the rest of the police force will be overseeing the parade. I know you two haven't seen each other since last baseball season, so consider this an opportunity to catch up.

Don't ask Christy what we are doing because it's better that you don't know now. All you need to know is that there are no games scheduled for the Babe Ruth field today. Don't forget that, and everything will be okay.

I love you more than anything. We will be back with you around noon.

David

"What's this all about, Christy?"

"It's something we have to do, Mom."

"What are you two up to?"

"I can't say," Christy said, looking at his cell phone to check the time.

"Why not?"

"I promised Dad and I think he's right. I have to go now, Mom." Christy began to move toward the door.

"Where do you think you're going?"

"I'm going to bike to meet the other Babe Ruth players," Christy said, packing his disguise in a bag under his arm.

"Are they a part of this too?"

"Yes."

"You boys and your baseball." She looked at Christy and saw the same determination in his eyes that she saw when he was playing ball. "There is probably nothing I can say to change your mind."

"No, my mind is made up."

"I guess you and Dad outnumber me then."

"I suppose. This is important to us, Mom. It's important to all of us." Christy began to open the door but then came back in and gave Annie a hug and a kiss.

Annie sighed. "Please be careful, Christy. Look after your father."

"I will," Christy said on the way out the door. He found his bike in the garage and began to pedal.

At the Babe Ruth field, David was on the phone with Chief McNeal with Johnny by his side looking for any signs of Barkus.

"Pete, our house was vandalized last night."

"What happened?"

"Somebody backed into our front yard, spun out, and dug up the lawn."

"Oh my God. Really? Any idea who did it?"

"Christy saw the truck. We think we know who did it."

"I'll come out and take a report then. But with the parade and all, it won't be until later."

"Don't worry about that now. You might not need to do that at all. I'll talk to you about it some other day. I just wanted to give you a heads-up in case you hear anything."

"Sure, no problem, David."

"Good luck with the parade today."

"Thanks. You know how wild things get in town today. I'm glad it only comes once per year."

"Talk to you soon, Pete," David said before hanging up.

Johnny turned to David. "I don't get you. We should go over and take out the headlights on that pickup truck. What are we waiting for?"

"Let them come to us."

Johnny looked at his cell phone to check the time. "I thought you said they'd be here by eight fifteen. It's almost eight thirty."

"They should be here. Their pattern is to be at their field one hour and forty-five minutes before a game."

"Maybe they didn't get your memo."

"Be patient."

Johnny scanned David from head to toe. "Who are you supposed to be anyway?"

"Colonel Joshua Chamberlain, Twentieth Maine."

"You look ridiculous," Johnny said, grinning.

"You should talk. At least I got the right country. Canada? Really?"

"You know, they play baseball in Canada."

"Thanks, knobby knees, like I didn't know. Do me a favor today, Johnny."

"What's that?"

David put his binoculars to his eyes. "Don't bend over today. I don't want to see the Loch Ness Monster."

Johnny exhaled a puff of air and shook his head. "I'm feeling stupid waiting here dressed like—"

"Wait," David said, pointing, "I think I see Barkus's SUV."

Sure enough, Burkus's red and chrome beast barreled into the parking lot, kicking up stone dust as it headed back to the Babe Ruth field. Two other cars followed along with a pickup truck in the rear. Johnny and David crouched down below the grass line.

Barkus pulled up to the chain-link backstop between the concession stand and the home team dugout set back from the first baseline. He got out and already had a cigar lit. Fog got out of the passenger side. Barkus put his hands on his hips and surveyed the field. Fog imitated the pose. Meeson emerged from one car and Melotti from another. Poser got out of the driver's side of the pickup truck and Scully got out of the passenger side.

"Let the fun begin!" Johnny said.

"It's a good day to save baseball," David said, handing over a spare pair of binoculars to Johnny. Hidden by the grass, they both lay on their stomachs to watch the show unfold. David took out his cell and dialed up Christy.

Christy and the Babe Ruth boys were all at Lock Seven Park hidden in the wooded trails along the riverbank. There were thirty of them, including all the players from the Choppers, and they were all busily putting on their disguises behind trees and in the thicket. After a few minutes, what emerged were a number of comic-book superheroes and characters of every dimension carrying piss-filled water guns.

Christy's cell phone rang and he pulled it from his pocket.

"Yeah, Dad."

"Christy, are you guys set to go?"

"Yep, just about."

"Okay, pedal up here and lay your bikes against the hill and climb to the top to meet us."

"Okay, Dad. See you in a few."

Christy hung up and said, "Time to mount up, guys." The Babe Ruth players put their street clothes behind the trees and got on their bikes for the ride along on the paved bike trail along the bank of the river. Usually, the trail might have a few walkers and bikers on it at that hour, but not on Indigo Valley Day. Everyone was getting ready to view the parade starting at 10:00 a.m. The Babe Ruth players sped like a swarm of bees down the paved bike path along the Mohawk to the ball field.

On the hill and out of sight of the men below, David and Johnny spied on Barkus and company as they talked about what to do with the field.

"What the fuck is going on with this field?" Barkus asked, assuming he would be spared from doing field prep work that day.

"No problem," interrupted Meeson. "I'll get the groomer." Meeson sauntered over to the garage about thirty feet from the concession stand and field entrance. He opened the door with his league keys. He climbed on the groomer and reached for the key in the ignition to turn the riding machine over. He looked over his shoulder to Barkus. "There's no key, Rob."

"Where is it?" Barkus asked the men.

"Should be in the ignition," said Meeson. "That's where we leave it."

"Is there a spare?" asked Melotti, walking to the garage.

"Not that I know about," said Meeson.

Back on the hill, David reached into his pocket and held the key up to Johnny's face. "Houston, they have a problem."

"Nice," Johnny said, chuckling while looking through the binoculars.

Down on the field, Fog suggested raking the infield dirt and so he and

Melotti searched the garage for rakes. They both came out with a ground rake and walked to the home plate area. Melotti started raking the third baseline and Fog started raking the first baseline. Scully and Poser emerged from the garage with ground rakes of their own and started raking the home plate area.

Meeson found the dry line marker, also known as the "chalker," and pulled it out of the garage to outline the batter's box. He flipped open the lid to the holding bucket to make sure there was enough powdered limestone in the machine to do the batter's box and the baselines. The machine had a hundred-pound capacity and Meeson could see it was filled to the top. He closed the lid and grabbed the batter's box template—a series of metal strips welded together in the shape of the batter's box—to mark the location of the lines for the box. Meeson headed out to the home plate area while Barkus sat in the bleachers talking on his cell phone.

Melotti was halfway down the third baseline when the hard steel rake head separated from its long wooden handle, leaving him holding a pole.

"Fuck!" Melotti said so loud that David and Johnny could hear him easily on the hill.

"Sounds like his *tool* broke," Johnny said, looking through his binoculars.

"What a shame," David said.

The other men kept raking for a minute while Melotti fiddled with his rake. "What's with the rakes!" Fog screamed. Fog was now standing with a rake pole detached from its head too.

"Hey," David said to Johnny, "I think I know what the problem is with those rakes."

"What's that?" asked Johnny.

"Ah, shit!" Scully said as his rake head separated from the pole.

David smiled while peering through his spyglasses. "Seems if you loosen the set screw, the pole handle tends to fall out and the rake head won't stay on. Imagine that."

Johnny put his binoculars down and looked at David. "You did this?" David pulled his field glasses from his head and winked at Johnny before resuming his watch.

"Nice. Is that guy's rake going to break too?" Johnny asked, pointing at Poser.

"Nah. They say hope can be a great motivator; one functional rake is like having hope in a bottle when prepping a ball field."

Poser finished raking the home plate area while the rest of the men returned to the garage with their broken rakes.

Barkus walked over to talk to the men and said, "Okay, I gave the all-clear signal and the boys are on their way over to warm up."

"Good," Fog said. "The bases are riding high and are wobbling. We need to find the clean-out tool to clear out the base anchors."

A base anchor was a hollow rectangular prism set in the ground designed to accept a rectangular insert attached to the underside of a base. Sometimes dirt would get inside the anchor bottom and the insert could not go all the way down, causing the base to protrude above ground level and wobble.

Fog went to the garage and located the two clean-out tools—two long, chisel-like devices designed to clean the anchor holes. "Here they are, Benny," Fog said. He walked over to give Benny one. "You take third base and I'll take first. We'll meet up at second."

"Okay."

"Where can we find some more rakes?" Barkus asked the men.

"I'll check the other garage to see if there are any more," Scully said.

Poser had finished raking the home plate area.

Meanwhile, Meeson had laid down the template on both sides and walked on it to form an imprint in the dirt to guide the chalker. He put the chalker over the imprint so that the axle and the two wheels in the front straddled it and would lay white dust on top of it. He moved the engage lever forward to open the crevice on the bottom to allow the powdered limestone to flow.

But when Meeson walked, only a few drops of powder spurted through the crevice. He moved the machine back and forth to try and loosen the chalk but still only a few drops came out. He closed the engage lever and shook the machine side to side, trying to loosen the chalk dust, but that didn't work either. Again, he closed the engage lever. He pushed down on the two handlebars, lifting the front wheels in the air and then let the machine drop to try and loosen the powder. Over and over again he shook, rattled, and rolled the machine, trying to coax powder from it like he was trying to get the last drops out from a ketchup bottle. The machine coughed up just enough splotches of powder every so often to encourage Meeson to continue his ritual dance. He wiped the sweat on his forehead with his white hand and chalk-marked his face. When he realized he was wiping chalk on his face, he wiped his hands on his pressed black slacks and stained them white. His lemon chiffon polo shirt began to reveal sweat stains just below his chest and down his back.

On the hill, David asked, "Johnny, did you ever try to sift wet flour through a flour sifter?"

"Can't say I have."

They both watched Meeson open the lid to the bucket to stir the powder with a screwdriver, but it couldn't reach the bottom. Meeson got even more powder on his slacks in the process.

"Well, that's what Meeson is trying to do down there," said David.

"What do you mean?"

"I filled the chalker up about a third full with powder and then added water and mixed up some glop. Then I topped it off with nice, dry powder all the way to the top. He doesn't know about the muck at the bottom that has clogged the works."

"Are you kidding me?" Johnny said, removing his binoculars.

David smiled. "Yeah, the only way for that thing to work is for Meeson to dump out one hundred pounds of powder and clean out the bottom before filling it up again."

"You're an asshole and I love it!"

Meeson tipped the machine over at a forty-five-degree angle against the backstop before trying to poke the crevice clear from underneath the chalker. He walked back to the batter's box imprints to try again. As he worked, his pale yellow polo turned a darker shade—the color of a lemon— as the sweat poured.

"That's not going to work either," David said to Johnny.

After probing the bottom a few times, Meeson went back to the batter's box to dance with the machine again. The home plate circle was now filled with footprints despite Scully and Poser's work to rake it clean.

"When do you think he'll figure it out?" Johnny asked.

"I don't know. Meeson will have to admit his approach is wrong and then start over. That might be too much to ask of him."

In the meantime, Melotti and Fog were hard at work cleaning out the dirt from the base anchors while Poser was raking the back of the infield between second and third.

"Fuck!" David and Johnny could hear Melotti say from third base. Both he and Fog were trying to work magic with their clean-out tools to break up the dirt in the anchors. Sometimes they looked like they were churning butter in the ground; other times they looked like they were tenderizing a steak with a fork by stabbing holes in it.

Johnny asked David, "How come those guys are taking so long to clean out those base anchors?"

"Well, the dirt can get compacted in there sometimes," David said, "especially when someone adds some mortar to the dirt trapped on the inside of the anchors." David pulled his binoculars away and winked at Johnny.

"Nicely played," Johnny said.

Barkus walked over to give a hammer to Fog and then to Melotti to help them work the cement-like mix out of the anchors. They whacked the top of their clean-out tools with the hammers like they were using rock chisels.

Fog finished clearing the first base anchor and set so that it now sat at ground level. He wiped the sweat from his brow and he began slowly walking over to second to fix that base.

Johnny saw him begin his walk and his face lit up. "You see that guy walking over from first to second," he said, his voice bubbling with glee. "Watch him."

"I got him in my sights," David said, eyeing his head and shoulders through his field glasses.

"Keep your eye on him."

"Okay," David said before blinking. But when he opened his eyes, Fog was gone and Johnny was trying to contain his laughter while rolling on his back.

"What happened to him?" David asked, scanning from left to right. "I don't see him."

Johnny tried to explain but he couldn't speak through his laughter.

"Keep it down, Johnny. They're going to hear you." David looked to where Poser had been raking between second and third—his was rake was lying on the infield but he was gone too. "Oh my God, where did Poser go?"

Johnny tried to get ahold of himself. "Was . . . was . . . he the guy between second and third?"

"Yeah, I see his rake but I don't see him."

Johnny started to pound the ground, laughing while on his back.

"What the hell is wrong with you?" David asked Johnny.

David wondered for a second if Barkus and his men had heard them below and were now flanking them on either side of the hill.

"Relax," Johnny finally managed to say. "Look at the ground between first and second."

David scanned the ground from second to first. He saw something lying on the ground. It was the color of human flesh. He zoomed in on it. It was a hand, but it wasn't attached to anything.

"Johnny, what the hell did you do? I think I see a hand on the infield—it looks like a severed hand!"

"Really?" Johnny said, rolling to his stomach and pressing the binoculars into his eye sockets.

Then, with both of them watching, the hand moved.

"Did you see that?" David asked.

Johnny began laughing again. "Oh my God, I don't think I've laughed so hard in my life."

"You've absolutely lost your mind."

While zooming in on the hand, David saw Scully from above grasp the hand and pull it upward. As he pulled, an arm seemed to emerge from the ground, then a head, then the other arm, then the torso, and finally the legs. It was Fog. Scully had pulled Fog from a hole in the infield that David couldn't see.

"What did you do?" David asked Johnny.

"Don't you remember our talk?"

"Talk? What talk?"

"We talked about the craters at the Elite Travel fields. You know, 'I dropped Jimmy off at the ball game and he dropped off the face of the earth'? Well, there's the proof right there."

Johnny explained to David how he and his cousin had dug some holes last night and made two pit traps on the infield.

"There's more than one?" David asked.

"Yeah, there's one between second and third too."

They both zoomed in on that area of the field and saw Melotti pulling Poser out of that hole.

"I wish you told me what you were doing," David said, shaking his head. "Subtlety is not your middle name, for sure."

"What's the big deal?"

"The groomer, the chalker, the rakes, and the bases left them guessing as to what was going on. Pit traps in the infield kind of give us away. That wasn't part of my plan."

"Thompson!" Barkus shouted from below on the pitcher's mound. He slowly turned in a circle with his hands cupped over his mouth yelling "Thompson" again and again.

"That's what I mean," David said to Johnny.

"Aren't you going to answer him?" Johnny asked.

"No, I'm not identifying myself."

"Thompson!" Barkus screamed. "If you're out there, know that we're going to play a game on this field today. Nothing is going to stop us!"

David was relieved to hear words of defiance and determination coming from Barkus. He was afraid that Johnny's aggressiveness might cause Barkus to turn tail and leave. Fortunately, Barkus was acting just like Lee at Gettysburg: intent on pursuing battle because the fight had started and withdrawal might appear cowardly to his men and those who would hear of it later. The last thing David needed was someone like Arnold Meeson to talk Barkus out of the fight, to try to convince him to fight another day on conditions more favorable, to try to dissuade him much like James Longstreet had tried to do with General Lee at Gettysburg. No, David wanted to fight Barkus on a day where he had the advantage.

Meeson had abandoned his chalker and had walked toward the pitcher's mound to talk to Barkus. By this point, he was covered in chalk dust and his shirt had soaked through. The pair of three-foot-deep, body-length holes that swallowed Poser and Fog shocked his sensibilities and he was afraid of more holes, afraid of what else was waiting for them. "Rob, maybe we should let the field go," he said.

"Thanks, Arnold. If I wanted your opinion, I would've asked for it. Now get back to the chalker there and get it working."

"Okay, Rob, I didn't mean to upset you," Arnold said, now fearing for his sons' baseball futures. He wheeled the chalker back to the garage to consider his options.

David and Johnny observed Poser, Scully, Melotti, and Fog probing the infield for more pit traps with their rake poles, like blind men tapping their canes searching for the curb. After they came up empty, they gathered shovels and wheelbarrows from the garage and began loading soil from the adjacent woods to fill the holes, tamping the dirt as they went along.

"They sure want to play ball," Johnny commented.

"Sure do. But they're not playing on this field."

Suddenly the grass rustled behind David and Johnny. They kneeled and looked down the river side of the hill. Johnny saw a uniformed police officer in the high grass below.

"It's the cops," Johnny whispered excitedly.

David's stomach dropped as he saw the uniformed officer. But then someone else came into view.

"There's a guy next to the cop," Johnny added. "He's dressed up like a . . . like a dog? Is that Clifford the Big Red Dog or something?"

Stretch's height gave him away and David recognized him as the dog. "No, I think that's Underdog."

"What's going on?" Johnny asked.

A bunch of other boys came into view in their costumes, including Christy dressed as Spider-Man.

"Those are the boys from our league. That's our infantry," David said.

David moved down the hill and then stood up and waved at the boys. Christy took the lead up the hill and the rest of the Babe Ruth players followed wearing costumes that ranged from the homemade to the profes- sional mascot variety. They were all carrying water blaster guns with large reservoirs, and some had squirt handguns too. They made it to the backside of the crest of the hill and kneeled next to David.

"Great costumes, guys," David said. "Well done. Does everyone have a mask?" Some boys nodded and the rest held up their masks. David recog- nized Chief McNeal's two boys as well as Drew Washington in the crowd.

"Okay then," David continued, "I know Christy has gone over the general plan with you. Here are some details. By the way, this is Johnny here with the pipes."

Johnny tipped his cap to the boys.

"Boys, years from now you're going to look back on this day as a special one, a day when you made a difference, a day when you saved baseball. I don't expect you to understand everything we're doing today, but some day you will. Down below, the Indigo Valley team you see does not have permission to play on your field. Only a few of the kids on that team play in our league; even they think they're too good to be playing with you. The parents of these players think that they can take your field any day they want while saying that you guys suck. It's time to send these guys a message that we will not be pushed around anymore on our field, on our sacred ground. It's time to take back your field and your right to play baseball with everyone in this town. Are you with me?"

Some boys said yes, some nodded, and a few gave the thumbs-up. The excitement and determination in their faces was palpable.

"I love the smell of piss in the morning, coach," Skit said in his Hulk costume. "It's time these green guns did some damage," he added, flexing his green foam biceps.

"Some days you're the hydrant," Christy said, holding up his gun, "and some days, like today, you're the dog!"

Stretch, who was Underdog, replied, "Woof, woof."

David laughed as he petted the back of his neck.

"Coach," said Roots, disguised as Evel Knievel, "I got my own brew." He struggled to hold his huge water bazooka in the air. The rest of the players laughed.

"Gentlemen," David said, "it's a great day to take back our ball field."

David looked at the other boys from his team. Steady was Moses and carried a staff instead of a gun. Flash was dressed as his namesake and was bouncing on the balls of his feet with anticipation. Bullwhip wore a Lone Ranger outfit and was rolling two six-shooter water pistols around his index fingers. Smiles, dressed as Shrek, had a huge grin. Gold Glove, with his long hair, was dressed as a hippie from the 1960s.

"Now come up here where you can see the ball field," David said. The players stayed low and huddled around David and Johnny while looking down on the field.

Car doors were closing below as the players from one of Barkus's Indigo Valley Elite Travel teams were being dropped off to warm up. The team was dressed in tackle twill red jerseys with their names on their backs, gray pants with red piping on the side, and fitted hats to match with raised embroidered insignias. They all wore titanium necklaces and eye black.

The players from a rival Elite Travel team arrived in a few cars along with their coaches. They were wearing navy-blue silkscreened jerseys with just their numbers on their backs. They all sported pants in various shades of gray, and one had black pants. They wore adjustable snap-back blue hats with silkscreen insignias.

"Do you know where that other team is from, Johnny?" David asked.

"Mohawk City. I can tell by the uniforms. That is the Elite Travel team that's driving the Mohawk City Babe Ruth program into the ground."

The Mohawk City team walked together to the third base dugout that was enclosed by a chain-link fence and gate. The Barkus team had pretty much settled into their first base dugout and was already pairing off and warming up in right field. Poser, Scully, Melotti, and Fog were finishing up filling the infield holes.

"Did you get them?" David asked Johnny. "I forgot to look this morning."

"Yep. Watch this, boys," Johnny said.

The Mohawk City team started to file into the dugout when one of the players said, "What the hell?" Another chimed in, "Very funny!" A few players stepped out of the dugout while a few remained inside. All of a sudden, several Rhode Island Red hens were chased out of the dugout, flapping their wings and clucking.

Poser and Melotti were at the hole between second and third base and didn't know what to think when they saw the chickens.

The Indigo Valley team in right field saw the chickens running from the dugout onto the field and started laughing and pointing, wondering who among them had pulled the prank on the other team.

Seeing this, Poser and Melotti smiled and shook their heads, thinking their team had a part in it somehow.

The Mohawk City head coach looked in the dugout and then looked at Poser and Melotti. "There's chicken shit all over the dugout floor!" he said, at which point the Indigo Valley team started laughing louder and carrying on. "We'll see who's laughing at the end of the game!" the coach yelled to the Indigo Valley players.

Players and coaches from both sides chased the chickens around the field to the delight of the Babe Ruth players looking on. They finally chased all the chickens outside the gate and into a grassy area by the woods. But the damage had been done, the hook had been set. Barkus, his players, and his men all denied involvement, but their outward display of pleasure while watching the prank play out said otherwise to the Mohawk City team.

"Coach," Barkus pleaded on the pitcher's mound, "we had nothing to do with this, really."

The Mohawk City head coach got in Barkus's face. "I'm tired of the bullshit, Barkus! Ever since they busted Moss, we've been the butt of jokes, like we're a bunch of patsies too afraid to speak up and do something. Well, we're dealing with our problems, thank you very much. More than I can say for you!"

Everyone on the field and on the hill heard this exchange.

Barkus glared at the coach, angered that he had been shown such disrespect in front of his men, his team. "What is that supposed to mean?"

"Look in the mirror, Barkus. You guys have your own problems and you don't do anything about them because *you're* chicken. We address our problems—we arrest Moss—while you snoots from Indigo Valley look the other way at your school problems. You're the joke, not us."

"Well, I never," Barkus said. "You should worry about your own school," he added.

"Ha," the coach responded, "your school's reputation is getting flushed. Either you don't know it, won't admit it, or don't care."

"Mind your own business!" Barkus said.

"Fuck you and your chickens!" the coach said. "What goes around comes around, as you'll find out!"

The two separated and headed back to their dugouts.

David and Johnny looked at one another and smiled at their good fortune in having heard the Mohawk City coach say these words.

"You thinking what I'm thinking?" Johnny asked.

"Yep. On it," David said.

David looked to the boys. "Boys, come closer and listen up. Stay low and spread out on top the hill on either side of the pitching machine. Spring up and show yourself when I give the word. When my fist goes up in the air, roar like savages. When it comes down, go to silent mode. We're going to soften them up a bit before going after them to give you some cover. Wait for my word and then attack. Pay attention to this point: we're only going after the Indigo Valley team. Keep your masks on and cheer for Mohawk City."

David went on to explain to the players how to attack in two lines before they all scurried below the grass line to find a position.

David turned to Johnny. "Can you start the generators?"

"Yes sir, colonel." Johnny went down the hill a little and started the gas-powered generators.

When the Babe Ruth players were in position, David grabbed the wireless microphone he and Johnny had rigged to the loudspeakers mounted on the stadium lighting posts around the ballpark. He stood atop the hill in full military dress with his Sharps carbine hanging by his side and in plain view to those below.

"Gentlemen," his voice echoed over the PA system, "your attention please. I regret to inform you that there'll be no game on this field today."

Barkus was startled as he looked up in the announcer's booth atop the concession stand to see who was announcing, but there was no one there. All of Barkus's men converged around him, looking around the Babe Ruth complex for the source of the voice.

David set his microphone down on the ground. He pulled his Sharps up and loaded it with a cartridge from his box. He looked through the gunsight, found his target, and squeezed the trigger. The shot crackled and a plume of smoke shot forth.

The men spotted the plume of smoke but, before any could say anything, David's bullet struck a baseball lying in shallow center field, causing it to roll toward the infield and Barkus's dugout.

"Jesus Christ," Melotti said, "that crazy fuck on the hill is shooting at us."

"Rob, I'm not sure playing here is a good idea," Meeson said.

"Shut up," Barkus replied.

"He's just trying to scare us," Poser said.

"He's doing a good job," Melotti said.

"Meeson might have a point," Fog said. "You know how I don't like confrontations."

"Shut up," Barkus said, growing irritated.

"Tell him to come down here and I'll beat him with my bat," Scully said.

"No offense, but my money is on the guy with the gun," Melotti said.

"Will all of you just shut up and let me think this through," Barkus said.

The Mohawk City team saw what had happened and fled. They knew to take cover when there was gunfire. A side wall of their third baseline dugout faced David's army and served as protection against it.

The Indigo Valley coaches told their players to go inside the dugout while they remained just outside. The front of their first baseline dugout faced David and the Babe Ruth players. They were exposed to the full wrath of David's frontal assault.

Barkus cupped his hands around his mouth. "Thompson, is that you up there?"

"What goes around, comes around," David said, parroting the Mohawk City coach over the loudspeaker. "You've got one minute to leave the Babe Ruth complex or else."

"He's bluffing," Poser said.

"What's he going to do? Shoot us all?" Scully asked.

"No, he's not going to shoot us over a baseball field," Barkus said. "He'll back down." He cupped his hands again and yelled, "It's all over. Go home already. We're playing on this field today."

"Now you have less than one minute!" David said.

"You're all alone," Barkus shouted. "Run along. Nobody on your side cares."

Scully decided to take it up a notch by calling up to David. "You suck, Thompson . . . and Babe Ruth sucks too!"

"All right, let's show them who cares," David said to the Babe Ruth players. "Move into position."

With that the Babe Ruth players slowly rose from the grass from one end of the hill to the other, like they had been created from the refuse and gases below and the hill was giving birth to them. They sported a variety of costumes that were unremarkable, maybe even comical, when viewed individually. But collectively the sight was frightening to those on the ball field below, especially when they all held their guns across their chests. Ranging from conventional costumes to the absurd, thirty vastly different costumed boys stood there perfectly still. There were traditional costumes: a skeleton, a hobo, a ghost, a pirate, an Indian, a vampire, and the policeman. There were superheroes: a Power Ranger, Batman, Robin, Ironman, and Superman. And there were some odd costumes too like a banana, Barney, Elvis, Snoopy, Tom and Jerry, and a caped cow with udders.

There the Babe Ruth players all stood at the top of the hill in all of their glory and to the astonishment of those below on the field. When David pumped his fist in the air, the players all roared at the top of their lungs, some pumping their guns in the air, their faces red with the anger of having been told one time too many that they sucked. Their cries blared through the microphone and the PA system speakers. The sound was deafening, blasting down onto the field and echoing. Barkus tried to talk to his men. His lips moved but the men heard nothing over the voices of thirty enraged teenage voices amplified. David then brought his fist down and the players went silent.

Below, Melotti said, "Who are those guys? Are those guns?" The men couldn't tell if these figures were men or teens or if the guns were real like David's Sharps carbine.

Barkus stood there silent for a second, wondering if this was all a bad dream, his mouth hanging half open. "What the hell? What the hell?" is all he could say before David raised his fist again and the boys went crazy in anticipation of the attack.

David moved his loaded baseballs within reach and then brought his fist down to quiet the boys again.

"Johnny, it's time we had some music," David said, pointing to the microphone.

"It would be my pleasure, colonel."

Johnny warmed up his bagpipes and began playing "Scotland the Brave" into the microphone.

Like any good military commander, David realized the importance of the artillery to soften the enemy lines before sending in the infantry. David,

Christy, and a few of the players uprighted the pitching machine and its tripod base like they were raising the flag on Iwo Jima. The machine glistened like a showroom car: metallic green, trimmed with chrome with two large, shiny black rubber wheels—one top of the other. The wheels could launch baseballs a distance of four hundred feet in any direction using the swivel top and with any trajectory using the height adjustment. Ty Cobb once said that baseball is not unlike war and that batters are the heavy artillery, but Ty Cobb never met David's pitcher, a machine that could pitch balls at over one hundred miles per hour as rapidly as David could load them.

David turned the machine on and the rubber wheel whirled. He aimed it at center field and taped a long-neck lighter to one of the tripod legs so he could easily light the devices. He lit the fuse of one of his explosive balls and pushed the ball through the two revolving wheels. The machine went *thunk* when the ball launched and arced above center field with its fuse whisping through the air before dropping to the ground, bouncing, and then exploding in a flash of light, blowing the rubber baseball into little bits.

With the short shot into center field, David had effectively warned those below that these were not your ordinary baseballs and shouldn't be fielded. He sent some more in the same general area to drive home the point. They bounced in center field and rolled toward second base before exploding and leaving a cloud of smoke.

Barkus and his men backed toward their dugout but remained outside. They were stunned by the sheer lunacy of what was happening and couldn't talk to one another over the sounds of exploding baseballs and the blaring bagpipes.

David began to alternate between exploding balls and smoke balls, adjusting the speed and angle of his artillery piece so as to spread the shells across the entire outfield. *Thunk, thunk, thunk,* the machine went with each passing ball. The smoke began to envelop the infield below, creating a grayish-white curtain that obstructed the view of both the outfield and the hill from the dugouts. David's vision of the field was impaired as well but it didn't matter as the machine delivered consistent throws. David increased the speed a notch when he wanted to hit right field and brought it down a notch when he was targeting left field. He played that machine like he was a musician at Carnegie Hall.

David ran his hand across his throat, giving Johnny the cut sign to stop playing. David raised his fist in the air and the boys, inspired by the artillery attack, let out a thunderous holler that Johnny added to by offering a war whoop. Some of the boys moved closer to the microphone to make sure their yells were heard below.

With his fist still raised, David pointed to the rest of the smoke balls and motioned to Johnny to feed them to him. David sent one last rapid-fire volley of smoke bombs down onto the field before yelling "Chaaaaaarge!" to the boys on both sides and into the microphone. With their guns held high, his costumed infantry ran down the hill hooting, hollering, and doing their best imitation of the rebel yell. Johnny started playing "Scotland the Brave" again into the microphone and David shot some exploding balls onto the field to keep Barkus off balance.

With his eyes on the boys, David quickly moved to his gas shutoff valve and turned the handle on full force. The candy-cane-shaped pipes on the dump had all been rigged together by a series of hoses that met at a junction and connected to a main hose that ran around the right-field fence and through the irrigation box to one circuit of sprinkler heads located around the outside perimeter of the dirt infield. David had removed the sprinkler popup devices on this circuit and replaced them with holed metal collars. This allowed the highly flammable landfill gas to vent directly upward through the windproof lit butane lighters he had placed over each opening.

The main hose jerked to attention as the gas whooshed through on its way to the field. Within moments, the butane lighters lit the methane gas as it surged through the six modified sprinkler heads around the infield. Large billowing plumes of flame shot up over forty feet into the air. David returned to his artillery and continued to launch smoke balls.

The players and coaches on the field were terrified but at the same time mesmerized by the flames rising out of the ground amid the smoke, explosions, and bagpipes. The ball field had been transformed into an apocalypse within a few minutes' time. From either dugout, they could barely see the infield. The outfield was a mass of flames and smoke speckled with the flashes of exploding baseballs. The Mohawk City coaches peered out from behind the chain-link fence protecting the front of the dugout. The Indigo Valley men stood frozen in front of their dugout looking up at the flames as if they were tracking a ball hit high into the outfield.

Barkus decided then that his best course of action was to bring in some support. He turned to Melotti and yelled, "Call the police!" Melotti nodded and left the field to try and find a quieter place to make the call.

When the call came into the police station, Annie was sitting with Elle McNeal in the police dispatcher's room. They were catching up with one another, exchanging baseball season stories about their boys.

"Hold that thought, Annie, let me take this call."

"Sure."

Elle picked up the receiver. "Indigo Valley Police. How can I assist you?" Elle started writing some notes and a puzzled look came over her face. "You'll have to speak up, sir. I can hardly hear you." At that point, Elle turned to Annie and covered the receiver. "You've got to hear this," she said as she flipped on the speaker switch. "Sir, please start over."

"We're being attacked by a bunch of guys in costumes," Melotti said. Annie and Elle could hear the bagpipes blaring in the background and then an explosion. "Did you hear that?" Melotti pleaded.

Elle shook her head and smiled. "What was your name again, sir?"

"Melotti, Benny Melotti."

"Mr. Melotti," Elle said, writing his name down, "did you know today is Indigo Valley Day and there's a parade going on now in town?"

"Yes, but there's no parade around here."

"I believe you're mistaken, Mr. Melotti. I hear bagpipes. Are you in your house?"

"I'm not in my home!" Melotti shouted. "I'm at the Babe Ruth field trying to play a baseball game."

Elle flipped the mute button on as she looked to Annie. "Do you know what he's talking about? Is there a game going on over there today?"

At that instant, Annie understood that David wanted her to give Elle the information in his instructions. She wished she understood why, but she told herself that she needed to trust David. "David told me that there were no games scheduled at the Babe Ruth field today. He wanted players to have Indigo Valley Day off."

Elle pressed the mute switch off and said, "Mr. Melotti, there are no games scheduled at the Babe Ruth field today."

"Are you fucking listening to me? I tell you there's flames the size of buildings, people in crazy costumes running around, and bombs shaped like baseballs being thrown at us."

Elle started to snicker but got ahold of herself. "Mr. Melotti," Elle said, "are you sure you might not have started a little early this morning?"

"What are you talking about?"

"What have you been drinking this morning, Mr. Melotti?"

"What, you think I'm drunk or something?"

"*Have* you been drinking this morning, Mr. Melotti?"

"I don't fucking believe this shit."

"Mr. Melotti, there's no need to get nasty."

"Are you going to send someone over here?"

"Let me have your home address, Mr. Melotti."

"Never mind," Melotti said before hanging up.

Elle shook her head. "I get at least one call like that every year on Indigo Valley Day," she said to Annie.

Back at the Babe Ruth field, the players had climbed the left-field fence with their water rifles and bazookas strapped over their shoulders and had landed on the other side. They formed two lines and moved on the double quick toward the Indigo Valley dugout over on the first base side. David held off on the explosive balls as his infantry took the field. When they reached center field, the two lines separated with the first line moving around right field and the other line positioning itself in short left field between second and third base.

The first line took a position in right-field foul territory, near the fence, under the haze of smoke cover. They knew where they were in relation to the Indigo Valley dugout and spotted the outlines of a few coaches. They knelt on the peripheral side of an enemy captivated by the show that was underway in front of them.

The second line took a position between second and third base in shallow left field and waited under the cover of smoke and flames, invisible to anyone in the dugouts.

Christy pulled out his cell phone and hit his Dad's number. David felt the phone vibrate in his pocket. He saw it was Christy's number and motioned to Johnny to stop playing. The bagpipes ceased and all that could be heard on the field was the whoosh of gas-burning flames that looked like wind-dancing inflatable figures outside a car dealership.

"Christy, are you in position?"

"Yes."

"Hit and run and cheer for Mohawk City! Got it?"

"Yep."

Christy hung up and motioned the first line to attack. They moved forward to within twenty feet of the players and coaches. On Christy's signal, they fired their water rifles and bazookas both at the Indigo Valley men and entrenched boys, dousing them with their loads.

Some Elite Travel men and players wiped their faces and shook their hands off and looked down at their uniforms before looking at each other.

The Babe Ruth players cheered "Mohawks! Mohawks!" as they ran away toward the gap between second and third. The Mohawk City team started coming out of the dugout talking among themselves, trying to figure if they knew any of the attackers.

After a few seconds, a bat-wielding Tony Poser along with Alex Meeson and a few of the Elite Travel boys gave chase to Christy and his line as they retreated to left field. The second line, led by Skit, moved into visible position between second and third to thwart that chase. Steady, dressed as Moses, stood of to the side of the line and raised his hands and staff like he was parting the Red Sea, when the second line blasted the pursuing Elite boys. "Mohawks! Mohawks!" the Babe Ruth players cheered while launching their loads.

The Elite boys were plastered and retreated. Stretch, dressed as Underdog, jogged a few steps closer to them and lifted his leg as if he were relieving himself on a hydrant and then ran away with the rest of the Babe Ruth boys into the smoke-screened outfield.

By the dugout, Barkus brought his wet hand up to his nose. "This . . . this smells like piss!" he yelled.

"It *is* piss!" Poser screamed in disgust.

Melotti returned to the field. "The police aren't coming," he said to Barkus.

At that point, the entire Mohawk City team and a few of the coaches were laughing at the prank, thinking, perhaps, that the attackers were from their city. They enjoyed the retaliation for the chickens they thought were placed in their dugout by Barkus's team.

On top of the hill, David and Johnny saw the Babe Ruth players climbing back over the fence to join them. David turned the gas flames off. David's troops were laughing so hard they could hardly get over the fence. As they managed to get over and climb the hill they were backslapping one another and giving each other high fives.

The smoke was beginning to clear. Johnny and David heard a lot of screams from both men and boys on the field. Slowly but surely, a large dog-pile of bodies came into view, red versus blue. The two teams, the two armies—one dressed as Confederate colors and the other dressed in Yankee colors—were engaged in a bench-clearing, pile-on brawl on the infield. At first, the coaches tried to separate the teams but they started to fight among themselves and joined in the battle. The Babe Ruth boys stood by David and looked at the mass of boys and men change shape and move around the infield like a swarm of birds darting about the sky.

David spoke to his boys, his troops. "Boys, today we stand united, while the other boys from Indigo Valley have fallen. I hope that someday you'll all be united to play on this field as one so that baseball will be available to all. Baseball was meant to bring us all together, not drive us apart. Please don't talk about what we did here with anyone. Please understand that on rare occasions, you have to respond with crazy when faced with crazy, but I'm not advocating delinquency as part of your everyday life. Do you understand?"

The boys removed their masks as they nodded. David surveyed their faces. It was at that point he saw her long blond hair in the crowd of boys. Melissa Meade, the only girl in the Babe Ruth league, had taken her Power Ranger mask off and was grinning ear to ear.

"Glad you could join us this morning, Melissa," David said.

"I wouldn't have missed it for the world, Mr. Thompson."

Johnny was so inspired by the scene below that he then picked up his bagpipes to play a verse of "Amazing Grace" while they all looked on as the brawl moved about the field.

When Johnny finished his verse, David had the boys and Melissa quickly help load Johnny's truck and his Mustang with all the equipment and the leftover artillery balls. Afterward, David called everyone over by his car.

"We've accomplished our goal. There'll be no game on the Babe Ruth field today. We need to get out of here in case some of them decide to come looking for us. Get on your bikes and go home and tell nobody about this." The boys and Melissa disbanded and headed down the hill.

"How can you be sure there'll be no game?" Johnny asked David.

David looked at his watch. "In about ten minutes, the in-ground sprinklers that are still attached to the water line will turn on. They're set to water the infield for about eight hours."

Johnny laughed. "Brilliant! They can't turn them off?"

"No," David said with a grin. "I locked the irrigation box in the ground and locked and disabled the irrigation control panel in the garage. I doubt they know where the shutoff valve is, but I removed the valve handle anyway."

"It's over then."

"Yes," David said while texting Annie to meet him at the parade grounds. "Chalk one up for the good guys, chalk one up for baseball."

31

THE AFTERMATH

L ater that afternoon, David and Christy caught up to Annie at the Indigo Valley Day festivities at the high school. She asked what had happened at the Babe Ruth field. David brushed her off by saying that everything was fine and that they should enjoy the rest of the day as a family.

Annie's mom was there and provided David with needed interference in the pursuit of the topic. And when her mom wasn't around, Annie was preoccupied with all the distractions of the exhibits, craft sales, entertainment, and old friends.

Christy split his time between family and his baseball teammates and friends. The boys talked among themselves about the day's events but it was their secret to hold and share with one another.

By the time of the fireworks show that night, the topic of the Babe Ruth field had all but been forgotten by Annie. As they were pulling out of the parking lot after the fireworks had ended, David saw Chief McNeal directing traffic and rolled down his window to wave and say hello. David prayed that he wouldn't say anything about what happened on the Babe Ruth field that afternoon. Pete nodded and smiled but couldn't say much of anything with all the traffic and the whistle stuck between his lips.

David was relieved. He glimpsed Christy through the rearview mirror.

He was smiling and looking out the window at the crowd of revelers trying to cross the street.

Annie yawned several times while catching up with Christy on the way home. She was too tired to say anything when David pulled up into the driveway and said that he had to go back to the Babe Ruth field to check on a few things.

Under the cover of darkness, David and Johnny cleaned up the field while reviewing the day's events. They disconnected the landfill and reconnected the sprinkler system and cleaned up what was left of the baseball devices. Johnny had a large cage on the back of his truck and was able to round up the chickens by throwing a piece of batting-cage netting over them. The holes Johnny dug were mostly filled already; they topped them off with some infield mix and then firmed up the dirt with a hand tamper. They congratulated each other for a job well done and exchanged a man hug upon parting for the night.

The next day, a Sunday, David got up early to cook for Annie and Christy. He called up to them and they stumbled down the stairs in their bathrobes. They were surprised that David was not at the ball fields and had made them breakfast.

They all sat around the dining room table. David had a view of the driveway out the front window that wasn't shared by Christy and Annie. As David sat at the table helping himself to bacon and eggs, he saw a town police cruiser pull up into the driveway. Pete McNeal was in the driver's seat.

As he opened the door to get out, David interrupted the conversation between Christy and Annie to give them a heads-up. "Chief McNeal just pulled into the driveway and he's walking to the door."

Annie's eyes woke up in an instant. "David, this is about the Babe Ruth field yesterday, isn't it?"

"That's a good guess."

"Oh my God. What did you do?"

"Not now, Annie. Let me handle this. You guys follow my lead."

The doorbell rang. David could see Pete through the door's half window and motioned Pete to come in as he got up. Pete opened the door and David was there to greet him.

"Good morning, Pete," Annie said.

"Hi, guys," Pete said, stepping into the room.

"Hey, Pete. What's going on?" David said, shaking his hand.

"The usual," he said. "Can we talk?"

"Sure, you want to join us? Can I at least get you some coffee?" David asked.

"No, thanks. I can't stay for long."

"What's on your mind?"

Pete looked at Annie. "Hey, thanks for keeping Elle company yesterday. It gets lonely there on Indigo Valley Day."

"My pleasure, Pete. I had a good time."

Pete looked back at David. "I called into the station this morning and found out the night dispatcher left a message for me to call Rob Barkus. Something about filing a complaint. So I called him a little bit ago and found out that he wants to file a complaint against you."

Annie's eyes bulged as she wiped her face with a napkin. Christy reached over and put his left hand on her forearm and rubbed it.

"Anyway, Barkus told me about some crazy attack you orchestrated yesterday: exploding baseballs and smoke bombs. He said he has proof of it and e-mailed me some photographs. Here, take a look." Pete handed the photos to David, and Annie glanced over to see them. She was about to stand up and look over David's shoulder, but Christy pressed on her arm to keep her sitting down while discreetly waving her off with his other hand.

"So I pulled these pictures up on my desktop," Pete continued, "and all I saw were some crazy-looking people dressed in costumes running around with water guns. I couldn't even tell where they were with all the smoke and flames in the background. I told him I don't think that a bunch of loonies running around in costumes with water guns is a crime. Besides, who am I going to arrest? Moses? The Hulk?"

Annie looked at Christy. He just smiled at her before digging back into his cereal bowl.

Pete went on. "I asked Rob where all this took place. He said on the Babe Ruth field. I said there's nothing in the pictures to indicate that this took place over on the field. All I saw was smoke and flames and some crazies running around. I remembered our talk at the baseball field—the one that was vandalized—when you said they didn't have permission to be on the field. I asked him, you know, if he had permission to be over there from you or the league. He didn't really answer me. I told him that if he didn't have permission to be there, you had cause to file a complaint for trespassing against him and maybe the players. I said to him that this wouldn't look good for the school players going into the state sectional tournament. Then I asked him if he knew anything about your lawn damage. All of a sudden, I hear his wife in the background raising her voice and telling him to drop it, telling him that she's sick of baseball. So he told me to forget it all, then hung up. Anyway, thought I would stop by and let you know."

"Thanks, Pete. I appreciate your support."

"No problem, David, you know I appreciate what you do for the kids in this town."

"Thanks. Sure you can't stay for some breakfast, Pete?"

"No, thank you, I'm on duty now so I have to run." Pete extended his hand and David's met his with a hearty shake. David felt something in Pete's hand and David looked him in the eye. Pete winked.

Annie and Christy said goodbye to Pete as David released his handshake. He gripped tightly the thing Pete had given him. Pete turned and opened the door and walked out to his cruiser, whistling a tune. David closed the door behind him and with his back to Annie and Christy looked in his hand. It was a charred piece of an exploded baseball marked by its seams. David slid it into his trouser pocket and rejoined his family for breakfast.

Annie looked across the table at David. "What was that all about?" she asked. "You know something, never mind—I don't need to know."

32

SWEET DREAMS AND NIGHTMARES

Over the next several weeks, word of what happened on Indigo Valley Day quickly spread across town. Nobody said anything more to David about Barkus accessing the Babe Ruth field. The school baseball season ended with the varsity team continuing its record-breaking fifty-year streak of failing to win a sectional title. Barkus and his teams started their travel season sentenced to the school fields for the duration. Moss was still fighting to get out of jail on bail.

Jacob Golder was working hard on his next opinion piece for the *Cornhusker*. He bemoaned his fate as a student having to work harder in college than in high school in order to achieve his goal of becoming a doctor. This bothered him to no end because he wanted to have a good time in college but also do well at the same time. He didn't think this was possible and it troubled him.

Jerry Conway was preoccupied with more important things, to him anyway. He was constantly trying to use the media to position himself in negotiations with the Browns over Josh Cribbs. There was the big drama of whether Josh Cribbs would join the voluntary minicamp starting May 19. Conway was all over the media saying that Cribbs would not show up to minicamp if there was no progress on talks for a new contract. During the afternoon of Monday, May 18, and the evening as well, Conway was reportedly working the phones for a new deal. When that did not pan out,

Conway said to Cleveland.com that "Josh is starting to get a sense that there's no appreciation for him." Cribbs, according to Conway, wanted to be traded if a new contract was not signed, as the remaining four-year contract pegged at $6.7 million was inadequate. Cribbs expressed his dissatisfaction with the progress of the talks by failing to show at the first voluntary minicamp.

Jacob Golder, on the other hand, was not in a position to skip school for the rest of the year. He had to finish out his senior year in order to graduate in June. But if he had one thing in common with Josh Cribbs, it was that he felt unappreciated too.

Another voluntary minicamp was set to begin in late May and Conway again worked the media for Cribbs. He wanted to see "meaningful dialogue" toward a new contract in order for Cribbs to attend. Cribbs did show for this minicamp.

A few days later, the *Cornhusker* ran Jacob's article. In it, Jacob argued against doing too much work in high school and college. The words *stress, depression,* and *suicide* repeated themselves in his article; he discussed in detail—citing statistics—how stress at college resulted in a large amount of depression and suicidal thoughts among students.

When May turned into June, the question for Conway was whether Josh Cribbs would attend the mandatory minicamp starting on June 11. Conway said he was in contact with the Browns, but the talks hadn't reached the "meaningful stage." Nevertheless, Cribbs reported to the practice session.

Jacob was an emotional train wreck going into June. Classes were about to end. He was leaving high school behind and beginning a new journey into an unknown world. The last edition of the *Cornhusker* had circulated for the school year. So Jacob turned to his only other writing outlet: his secret blog, which he made available only to his closest friends.

He wrote a story about a nerd named Zack. Jacob told about how Zack's life sucked, how he'd been picked on his entire miserable life, how the world would be better off without him. He then went on to talk about Zack's desire to relieve his emotional pain by replacing it with physical pain.

Jacob told how Zack cut his wrists with a razor blade. He wrote that it felt good, real good to Zack. The more cuts that Zack made, the better he felt.

At the end of the story, Zack plunged the razor straight into his neck and took his own life.

Jacob wrote that no one came to Zack's funeral even though they didn't have anything else to do. Nobody cared. "Why did I write this?" Jacob wrote at the end. "So it doesn't really happen. If you see Zack, go talk to him. Have a conversation. It will mean a lot more to him than you think it will."

33

THE CHAMPIONSHIP GAME

I t was late June and the events of Indigo Valley Day faded with the arrival of the humidity as spring marched toward summer. Starting in the morning hours, the hum of the dog-day cicadas came and went, sounding like the seams of a fastball cutting the heavy air pitch after pitch. The tar on the Babe Ruth parking lot began to bubble in the heat of the day, promptly popping by midafternoon. Thunderstorm clouds like black anvils formed more frequently near the center of town before rolling toward the baseball field, dumping their loads or casting shadows sprinkled with sunlight. On either side of the baseball field, the woods and underbrush grew as thick as a tropical rain forest. Foul balls hit there were given up for lost without a search. And with each passing night, the voices of the crickets and mosquitoes multiplied, drowning out the whispers of the Barkus parents.

The events of Indigo Valley Day were stuck in the minds of the Chopper team. After that day, the Choppers went on a winning streak right into the playoffs. Although they were seeded last in the playoffs, they took everyone by surprise by making it to the finals to face Babson Concrete for the championship and town bragging rights.

It was Tuesday night, June 23, 2009, and by virtue of their top seed, Babson Concrete sat in the home dugout along the first baseline. The rear of their dugout faced the sun so the inside was shaded. The angle of the sun had also created some shade in front of it.

The Choppers sat in the visitors' dugout along the third baseline. It was ten minutes before game time and the sun was beating on the Choppers' dugout, making the cinder-block walls hot to the touch, like a brick oven. The sun beamed directly inside and there was no place to hide. It was so hot out that David had brought a cooler filled with ice and water for the boys to dip their hats in to cool themselves down.

The Chopper players sat with their elbows on their knees and their hats dripping ice water and sweat onto the dirt on their cleats, creating a fine mud that ran like butter off pancakes. Some of the boys chewed on sunflower seeds, biting the shell on its side and spitting it out before chewing on the seed. But there was no talking. There was nothing left to say. Everyone knew what the other was thinking. They looked over every once in a while to the Babson dugout. Many of the players had said earlier that the home dugout rightfully belonged to them.

The dugout had become their safe house, their place of refuge from home or school, a place where they could discuss anything that came to mind before or after a game, so long as the focus was baseball once the umpire shouted "Play ball!" Everyone had their issues to deal with, but they all fell by the wayside when the game began. For two and a half hours, the boys dropped their baggage at the dugout door and found bliss in uniting to accomplish something, and that evening anything seemed possible. They all wanted to beat Babson if it was the last thing they did on earth.

Bullwhip got the start on the mound and had already warmed up with Skit. He sat there flipping and catching a ball with one hand and looking across the field into the Babson dugout. Bullwhip hadn't played an inning all season long on the school team. Yet the school coaches still refused to let him pitch for the Choppers. They wanted to conserve their pitching for the school team just in case. With each passing school game, "just in case" became "just bullshit" to Bullwhip as he sat on the bench. Bullwhip had something to prove that evening to all the school players in Babson's dugout.

David approached home plate. After Indigo Valley Day and with the ending of the school season, the Elite Travel Baseball season had kicked into full gear. Barkus and his followers were busy trying to play a baseball season and, after Indigo Valley Day, the Barkus crowd didn't want to have anything more to do with David.

Poser and David shook hands with the umpire and with each other. Poser kidded, "Do you want to play for the field today?"

"No," David said, "we're playing for the town championship today."

After the ground rules were discussed, the meeting broke and David walked back to the dugout and waved to Annie sitting in the bleachers. She was the first parent there and the last one to leave, always sitting in the front row of the bleachers if she wasn't working in the concession stand.

David looked into his sweltering dugout and saw the boys' drenched heads and determined faces.

"Men, gather around me out here," he said. The boys' pants peeled off the bench as they lifted themselves up and then shuffled through the swinging dugout door to surround David. "Men, you've worked hard to get here," he said, looking at each player's face. "Your focus has been excellent during our win streak. Now it's time to finish what you've started. Play your hearts out for the full seven and leave nothing in your tank when you walk off that field today. Remember Indigo Valley Day." The players nodded in agreement. David knew they were ready. "Bring it in here," David said. He raised his hand and the boys raised their hands and touched his arm or the arms of each other. "Hits on three," David said.

"One, two, three, hits!" the boys chanted, before bringing their hands down and breaking the huddle.

Though Tony Poser had issues hitting, he was an excellent pitcher. By league pitching rules, he could go the full seven innings since he did not pitch in Babson's last playoff game. Oscar Poser had taken a chance by not pitching Tony in the semifinals, knowing he would want to pitch against the Choppers to avenge his dousing by the piss brigade. You could tell by the quick pacing and velocity of his warm-ups that Tony wanted this game badly.

David acted as third base coach and Bullwhip acted as first base coach until he batted last in the order. In the first inning, Flash batted leadoff and was walked by an overthrowing Poser. He went to second on a passed ball before advancing to third when Steady, batting second, grounded out to the right side. Christy hit a sacrifice fly deep to left field that scored Flash from third. Skit then hit a hard grounder to third that almost went foul. He ran like never before but couldn't beat it out. The score was 1–0 after the top of the first.

After his team took the field, David sat down alone with his scorebook in the dugout. He was lost in thought as his team warmed up on the field before the bottom of the inning began. *Baseball on a summer night is like heaven on earth,* he thought. A full moon was rising over his hill, behind one of the eight light poles that surrounded the field. The poles had a beam that supported the lights on either side that made the poles look like a lowercase *t,* or eight crosses. One cross split the moon in half, resembling the crosshairs of a gun against the backdrop of the moonlight. The scene prompted David to recall aiming and firing his Sharps at a baseball just a few weeks ago on the field on Indigo Valley Day.

Since then, his boys, his team, played the game with the resolve of soldiers fighting for their lives. They had some inkling about the larger meaning of this game, but it didn't seem to weigh on them or even concern them in the least now. It was personal for them.

Over the last few games, David coached less and less. The players knew what to do and he could watch almost as a spectator as he admired their determination. These young men were not pretenders using the game to chase a scholarship. They were real ballplayers who played for the love of the game.

A part of David wanted to explain to them that they were fighting for much more than the league championship. For years, the parents of the Elite Travel players had complained about the lack of competition in Babe Ruth baseball. But here was his team with only one school player—and a benched one—against a team stacked with five school players in the lineup. David wanted a victory to put the competition argument to rest. He wanted to do everything in his power to bring more school players to the Babe Ruth league. If winning was the only thing they understood, then that was one more reason that David longed for a victory.

David wanted to tell his boys that they were also fighting for the future of baseball in their town, in the region, maybe even the state. He didn't know if Babe Ruth League, Inc., would try to settle the lawsuit. David knew the case was weighing heavily on Brad Summers, New York State's Babe Ruth commissioner. After letting the Elite Travel Baseball League take root in his Babe Ruth leagues, Brad decided to draw a line in the sand at Indigo

Valley. If he lost here, his concern was that the other leagues would fall like dominoes to the Elite Travel Baseball League.

David had asked Babe Ruth corporate to fight the case and not to settle for one nickel out of court. Up until that point, Babe Ruth League, Inc., had been steadfast in their resolve to defend the lawsuit. But David knew this lawsuit could go on forever and that people could change their minds. Already there were rumors being floated by the Barkus parents that Babe Ruth would fold and settle. The Elite Travel Baseball League's website was advertising their lawsuit in an effort to paint David and the defendants as wrongdoers. They were using it as a marketing ploy. David understood that any settlement at all would only serve to embolden Barkus and his followers by suggesting that Babe Ruth and David were guilty of something.

But David decided that it would be unfair to have his team shoulder the burden of baseball's future going into the game and by possibly losing to Babson. He was satisfied that he had at least managed to buy these and other boys in the league this one season. Win or lose, he wanted to let them enjoy the game on their own terms and create their own memories in the process.

Except for buying the league an additional year, David was unsure if anything lasting would come out of his efforts despite some positive signs. Jack Masters had finally seen the light. He sent an e-mail out to the board backing David; he began the process of replacing any resigning Barkus backed board members with Babe Ruth parents, including women. But David didn't know if things were changing for good or if he had merely applied a Band-Aid to a situation too far out of control to remedy. He realized that looking away and doing nothing would have meant the end of the league, the end of baseball as the town knew it. At least by doing something, his boys, and boys like them, had a chance to continue playing baseball in their hometown. At least he had reached out and touched the lives of as many teens as he could.

David looked on fondly at all the boys playing each other for the town championship. In an ideal setting, in a Rockwell setting, David knew that it should have been all about them. Baseball, in David's mind, was simply about teens making friends and playing together. It was about teamwork and cultivating relationships. It was about boys—and sometimes girls—having the time of their lives playing in their community, in their hometown, playing outside and not on some game console. Playing baseball wasn't about travel ball, college scholarships, or the pros. Baseball, at its heart, was about casting some footings in the crazy lives of teenagers. It was about instilling a way to carry oneself in times of adversity and in times of success; it was about building a foundation that would last a lifetime. *Anyone who dares take aim at the innocence and defenselessness of community baseball,* David thought, *is a sniper without a conscience, a murderer of the human spirit, the lowest form of life.*

Babson Concrete matched the Choppers' one run with a run of its own in the bottom of the first inning thanks to Drew Washington's base hit. David was pleased that Eric's son was seeing equal playing time since he had called Poser out.

The game was a see-saw battle up until the bottom of the sixth, when Babson Concrete came up to bat with the score tied 3–3.

Roots was playing right field when he started waving frantically to David. "What's going on?" David called out. Roots crossed his legs and twisted side to side and bobbed up and down. He had to go to the bathroom. "Are you kidding me?" David shouted. Roots shook his head. David flashed one and then two fingers to Roots. Roots flashed one finger in return. "Jesus," David said under his breath, "I'm back coaching T-ball again." He called out to Roots, "Tim, they're two outs. Try and hold it in for the team!" The team laughed and started yelling out to Roots, "Do it for the team, Roots!" Roots danced for a few pitches to the delight of the Babson bench. Three pitches later, Stretch fielded a ground ball at first and touched the bag for the third out. Roots then ran as fast as David had ever seen him run; he rolled over the waist-high fence and headed toward the men's room.

It was the top of the seventh and Christy came up to bat against Tony Poser. The first pitch was a fastball and Christy found the handle and drove a frozen rope so taut and long you could hang the entire town's laundry on it. It pierced the right center gap for a double.

Skit came up to bat next and he was slow to take the box. He stepped in and a tired Poser shook Alex Meeson, the catcher, off several times before Skit asked for time. The umpire called time and Skit stepped out. He looked through the galvanized fence backstop to his rear and saw Becky Poser standing there with her two friends watching the boys. Skit waved to the girls and they all smiled at him. Poser saw it all happen and pounded the ball in his glove as Skit stepped back into the box. Tony quickly came set and delivered a chin-strap fastball that made Skit spin backward into the dirt.

Skit got up and brushed himself off and waved at the girls again. Tony was all ready to pitch when Skit stepped back in the box. The next pitch was a fastball that hit Skit in the shoulder.

"Dead ball," the umpire said. "Batter, take your base."

Skit tossed his bat toward the dugout.

"Don't rub it," Gold Glove said.

"We got ice," said Steady.

David stood up from sitting on a bucket of balls in front of the dugout and was about to walk toward the field of play to check on Skit and talk to the umpire when all at once his players yelled, "Sister!"

Tony received the ball from Alex and slammed one foot down on the mound as he heard them. He spun toward Skit on his way to first and saw him whisper "sister" as his hips swayed side to side ever so slightly as he jogged. Poser couldn't take it anymore. "Fuck off!" Tony thundered in the direction of Skit. Along the first baseline, Tony's dugout, Babson's parents, and their kids in the bleachers all heard the F-bomb go off.

The home plate umpire couldn't believe what he had heard. He removed his mask and walked toward the mound. "Son," he called out. Tony turned toward him and the umpire said, "You're done!" For emphasis, the umpire lifted one foot off the ground and punched the air above. Tony Poser had been thrown out of the game.

While a little swearing under the breath might be given some leeway by the umpires, even whispering the *F* word was cause for ejection. Tony's F-bomb had silenced the crowd. Little children playing around beneath the bleachers stopped cold and sought their parents out. They understood by the tone of Tony's voice and the umpire's reaction that Tony had done something terribly wrong. "What did he say, Mommy?" one little boy asked. "What did he do?" one girl asked her father. Parents cupped their hands over their ears and whispered explanations while every emotion played out on the children's faces.

David walked back to the dugout and put his hands on the chain-link fencing that guarded the players inside of the dugout. All his players were standing and enjoying Poser's ejection.

"So you guys planned this all along?" David asked.

"We talked about it before the game," Steady said.

"Controlling your temper is a mental aspect of the game, coach," said Stretch. "You taught us that."

"I remember you telling us to use the mental aspect to our advantage because it's our strength," Flash said.

"Unbelievable," David said, turning around to face the field.

Oscar Poser was walking his son off the field while Alex Meeson was taking off his catcher's gear to get ready to pitch. Alex was a good pitcher, but he'd only played catcher on his teams.

Stretch was first to bat against Alex. He hit a nice shot to shallow right field that was caught. Christy went to third after tagging up while Skit remained at first when the ball was thrown in to second.

Roots was at bat next. David waited a few pitches before sending Skit to steal second. He ran hard and went down like a two-hundred-pound sack of flour and flopped into the base. "Safe," the umpire called.

On the next pitch, Roots hit a hot grounder deep to the right side that was fielded by the second baseman. Christy scored and Skit went to third. Roots didn't beat the throw to first but he had done his job by getting Christy across the plate. The score was 4–3 in favor of the Choppers with two outs.

Smiles got up to bat and a nice easy swing made contact with the Alex's fastball, sending it into right center field for a single, scoring Skit. The bottom half of the order was taking it to Babson.

Gold Glove was next in the lineup and after working a full count he went down swinging.

It was 5–3 in favor of the Choppers and all they had to do was hold the lead for three more outs. The Chopper players were giddy as they gathered up their gloves to take the field.

"Gather around, men," David said. "Let's huddle up." The boys surrounded him. "Don't fall into the trap of thinking this game is over. You still need to get three more outs. Stay focused and let's *finish* the game." They broke the huddle with a chant of "defense." David gave them their fielding assignments for the inning and off they ran to take the field.

David sat on the bench and hoped for the best. Roots was scheduled to play second base on David's position grid. With his disability, Roots had the lateral movement of a rusty stepladder. He couldn't bend over so his throws to first were weighty and labored, like he was throwing a medicine ball. His reactions were accurate but his timing was after the fact. But David had decided earlier that morning that he was going to reach out and give Roots an opportunity and his grid served as a steadfast reminder.

Bullwhip went back to the mound. He had pitched a great game, but this was his first time going seven innings during the season. He was tired but determined.

He struck out the first batter and then the second batter fouled out to Gold Glove in right field. Two down, one to go.

David now heard a new voice from the Babson bleachers, a voice he recognized and loathed. Rob Barkus had arrived at the field and was cheering. David recalled how General Buford discovered a spy in his camp a few days after Gettysburg and hanged him.

But David was surprised to see a group of school players who played only on Barkus's teams cheering too. He hadn't seen them at the field all season. Sure, they were cheering for Babson, but they were certainly not rooting against the Chopper team. They were smiling and enjoying themselves. They were leaning against the backstop and gripping the chain link so tight that it made their knuckles turn white. It was like they were in jail and wanted to break out; only this time "out" was "in" and on the playing field with the rest of the boys.

Babson Concrete was now back at the top of their order, a place where all the school players were stacked. The first batter promptly lined a single to right, only to be followed by a double to left. Runners were now on second and third and Alex Meeson was up to bat. He took two balls before fouling one off. But on the very next pitch, Alex hit a belt-high laser up the middle over to the right side like it was shot out of David's pitching machine.

David's stomach dropped to the ground as he believed the ball would find a hole in his defense and allow two runs to score, tying up the game. But Roots took one side step to his right, then another, before bending over to catch the line-drive knee-high effortlessly, like he was born to make that one play. He held his glove high in the air and the umpire signaled the third out. The place went crazy on the Chopper side. Roots ran to the mound and pulled the ball from his glove before tossing it in the air. He kept running and the ball hit the ground and lay there still behind the mound. The players all rushed together and did a dog-pile on Roots and Bullwhip. David jogged out to join them but then suddenly veered to find the ball. He picked it up and found Roots in all the chaos and placed the ball in his glove.

"Roots, this ball is yours. Don't ever forget today."

"I won't," he replied. "Thank you, coach."

The Choppers, the team least likely to win the town championship, had prevailed. Only David knew that the absolute last player chosen in the league draft in 2009 had made the defensive play that won the game.

The Chopper parents stood and applauded and Annie cheered the loudest. David looked over to the Babson bleachers. The Barkus parents politely clapped before packing up to go and play a travel game in some other town. The school players outside the backstop were gently ribbing the school players on the Babson team. Rob Barkus was nowhere to be found.

One hour later, David was in the dugout gathering his equipment. The trophies had been presented to both teams and the pictures had been taken under the stadium lighting. Afterward, David had hugged Annie and given her a trophy too.

It was just Annie, David, and Christy left at the field. Annie was in the concession stand making sure everything was in order before locking up. Christy walked over to the dugout to check up on his dad. He saw him moving in the shadows of the dugout. When David saw Christy, he sat on the bench and leaned back against the dugout wall. Christy sat down beside him.

"You okay, Dad?"

"Yeah, I'm good. How about you?"

"I'm good."

"What are you thinking, Dad?"

David sighed and clasped his hands together. "Right this second, I'm thinking about . . . how good this field looks under the lights . . . how beautiful the moon looks rising over our hill. I'm thinking about our season and about how proud I am of you and all the boys. I'm thinking about how much I love watching you play . . . about how much I'm going to miss that in a few years. I wish tonight could last forever." Christy couldn't see David's eyes misting in the darkness. "How about you?" David managed to ask. "What are you thinking about?"

Christy leaned back against the wall next to his Dad and looked onto the field. He wore a smile that didn't waver, like Rockwell had painted it on. "All I can say, Dad, is what a season."

They sat there a bit longer looking at the field and taking in the stillness of the night under the peacefulness of a spotlighted empty field surrounded by an ocean of darkness speckled with stars.

"How'd we win that game, Dad?" Christy asked.

"Roots made a great play."

"He did," Christy said, "but he's missed that play all season long and in practice too."

"I guess it was his time to shine," David said.

"You know what Steady said?"

"No, what did he say?"

"He said you can look for God in a lot of places, but on summer nights you can likely find him at a baseball field."

David turned his head toward Christy and smiled. "I like Steady," he said.

David got up. He grasped Christy's hand and pulled him up out of his seat. "Let's go get your mom," he said. "It's time for this family to go home." They gathered up the equipment bags and the bucket of balls and walked over to the lighting control box like they had done all season after a night game. There were two breaker switches in the box that controlled the field lights. David turned around and looked at the field, the base of the hill, under the lights. *God, how I do love this field,* he thought.

"One more time to close the season," David said to Christy as he reached into the box. "Long live the spirit of baseball," he proclaimed as he flipped one switch off. Half of the field nearest to the hill immediately went dark. "Your turn, Christy."

Christy reached into the box for the other switch and flipped it. The entire field went to black as Christy said, "Long live the boys of summer."

THE END

ALSO BY TOM SWYERS

~

Thank you for reading *Saving Babe Ruth*. If you enjoyed this book, you can make a huge difference in the writing career of a struggling author (me) by taking a few seconds to review *Saving Babe Ruth*. You only have to write a few words if you'd like and I'd really appreciate your support. I am an independent author who faces off against the powerful publishing houses with unlimited budgets every day. Please help me so that I can write more for you. Google "Amazon Saving Babe Ruth" to find the book on Amazon to leave a review. (In order to leave a review on Amazon, you need to have bought something from them at some point in your life). You can also enter this link in any browser to locate the book so you can leave a review on Amazon: http://hyperurl.co/ReviewSavingBabeRuth If you are a member of Goodreads, you can also leave a review there if you choose. Thank you!

~

Saving Babe Ruth is the prequel to the Lawyer David Thompson Series and was the 2015 recipient of two Benjamin Franklin Book Awards for "Best First Book, Fiction" (first place) and "Best Popular Fiction" (second place).

The Killdeer Connection, a legal thriller, is the first book in the Lawyer David Thompson Series and was selected as a 2017 winner in Amazon's international Kindle Scout competition.

Read the book description that follows to find out what *The Killdeer Connection* is all about:

Hang out with the wrong friend, end up a wanted terrorist . . .

Worn-out lawyer David Thompson is on a mission to prove his innocence. Falsely accused of murdering his friend, he must desert his family and seek out a secret society of bird-watchers in a desperate search for the truth. When the feds talk of adding a terrorism charge, the death penalty looms and Thompson is on the run from both the law and the real killer. With Thompson out of the way, his family becomes a target. Thrust on a riveting thrill ride through the oil fields of North Dakota, Thompson's quest to save his own skin explodes into a race to save both his family and the nation from a deadly tidal wave of terror. But he may be too late ...

Don't miss this action-packed, realistic, and thought-provoking legal thriller filled with mystery, family secrets, conspiracy, financial intrigue, captivating characters, deception, prejudice, greed, courtroom drama, and a bird!

∼

Join my Readers Group to get special offers available only to members. You'll also get exclusive news on upcoming books. There is already another book in the works that follows *The Killdeer Connection* in the Lawyer David Thompson Series. Learn about it plus more and join the Readers Group by typing out this link in your browser: http://hyperurl.co/JoinReadersGroup

∼

You can purchase a paperback copy of *The Killdeer Connection* by ordering it through your bookstore or by purchasing it on Amazon by typing out this link in your browser: http://hyperurl.co/AmazonKilldeerPage

EPILOGUE

Little did David know, the day the Choppers won the championship would be the last time Rob Barkus would set foot near the Indigo Valley Babe Ruth field. That fall, men and women dedicated to Babe Ruth baseball were elected and replaced all the Barkus-backed members on the board.

As a result of the efforts of Brad Summers, a large number of teams left the Elite Travel Baseball League and joined the Empire State Baseball League. Brad Summers retired from serving as New York State commissioner of Babe Ruth. In 2013, he was elected to the Babe Ruth Middle Atlantic Region Hall of Fame.

David Thompson's improvements to the Indigo Valley Babe Ruth program convinced the school players to rejoin the league next season. Mayor Reed and many others returned. Babe Ruth enrollment increased by forty-five percent over a two-year span. School ballplayers played in-house baseball side by side with community ballplayers. The league fielded travel teams in the Empire State Baseball League and also fielded all-star teams in all the age groups for the first time in memory. The Elite Travel Baseball League teams became extinct in Indigo Valley.

In both 2012 and 2013, the Indigo Valley Baseball League won back-to-back berths to the Babe Ruth World Series in two separate age groups, the first berths ever earned by the league during its entire fifty-five-year history. Both teams played well and made it to the semifinals.

David Thompson was formally recognized by Babe Ruth League as a *Volunteer of the Year* for "his outstanding service and unselfish generosity for the time and never-ending commitment." Christy finished his baseball career with Indigo Valley Babe Ruth and now attends college, where he is heavily involved with cancer research. David Thompson remains happily married to Annie. She is a baseball fan again and David still volunteers his time to youth baseball leagues in the region.

The lawsuit against David, Johnny, Brad, and Babe Ruth League backfired and generated sympathy for David Thompson's cause. It proved to be an embarrassment to the school district and to the Barkus followers. In 2012, after three years of litigation, the Elite Travel Baseball League's lawsuit was thrown out by the judge for its failure to appear at depositions to answer questions about its operations, including its financial records.

Johnny McFadden continues to sell frozen foods from his truck and is president of Empire State Baseball League, Inc.: a nonprofit organization serving nearly forty communities and four thousand youth annually by providing travel baseball opportunities to youth that support their community baseball programs, like Babe Ruth. Joan McFadden, Johnny's better half, schedules nearly three thousand games per year for the league.

Stanley Moss never made bail and was convicted of eighteen out of twenty-two counts against him. He was sentenced to twenty-three years to life and is serving his term in New York State's largest maximum-security prison.

Correll Buckhalter was never charged. With the assistance of Jerry Conway, Josh Cribbs secured a new contract with the Cleveland Browns in 2010. He played for the Browns until he was released in early 2013. After a brief stint with the Oakland Raiders, he played for the New York Jets during the 2013 season.

Jacob Golder faced many challenges in his life after high school, but tragically ended up taking his own life. He is dearly missed by family and friends.

Jerry Conway is still the principal of Indigo Valley High School and continues to increase the size and scope of his business interests. As of 2014, his website says that he is "one of the most successful agents in the country today."

ACKNOWLEDGMENTS

I first met Jeal Sutherland in the fall of 2008. It was a meeting that changed my life. Jeal has always been willing to share his vast knowledge of baseball and the inner workings of youth baseball programs with me. He has been a great resource, but he has been much, much more. Without Jeal, there would simply be no story to tell, period.

I also would like to acknowledge Jeal's better half, Rose. For years, she has given her all to help children play baseball in their community program and has supported Jeal in doing the same.

For nearly thirty years, Jerry Francis volunteered his time to Babe Ruth League up until his recent retirement. Jerry risked and sacrificed so much for the love of Babe Ruth baseball and all that it represents. Without Jerry, there would be no story to tell either.

I also want to express my sincere thanks to my son, Randy, who encouraged me to write this story and served as an early editor for the manuscript over the course of an entire summer and also when he was on break from college. Randy, I'll never forget the intense give-and-take sessions we had that spanned days. But then I'll never forget laughing with you for days on end too. You were always there to motivate me when I needed it. Thank you for being my editor, friend, and son.

Jane Rosenman did a tremendous job as my developmental editor. She was always there to field my many questions and to brainstorm with me about ways to provide the reader with a richer, more meaningful experience. Thank you, Jane, for being in my corner.

Michael Trudeau did the copyediting and offered his skilled suggestions on how to clarify and simplify. Thank you, Michael, for a job well done.

Margot Livesey, Joanna Scott, and Amy Wallen are terrific authors and inspirational teachers. I met all three during the 2012 New York State Summer Writers Institute held at Skidmore College. Margot and Joanna were both generous in their direction and guidance. Amy read an early draft of my manuscript and provided wonderful suggestions and encouragement.

I want to thank Bob Winchester, who has been my high school teacher, class advisor, and friend over the span of the past thirty-five years. Bob means so much to me and our community. He is an author, school board member, volunteer, and mentor who goes out of his way to try and touch the lives of as many people as is humanly possible, even in retirement. He represents a guiding light connecting our community's past with its future and we are so fortunate to have him in our lives. Thank you, Bob, for always lending your ear and your support.

I'm indebted to my sister, Karen Swyers, an artist and graphic designer who spent countless hours helping me with my website and book design. Thank you, Karen. I hope someday that the entire world knows the talent and beauty you bring to the world in your paintings and volunteer work.

I want to acknowledge Derek Murphy who led the cover design effort and also Joel Friedlander who helped guide me through the publishing process.

I want to express my gratitude to the many young coaches that I worked with over the years and the Babe Ruth teens who played on my teams and in our league. I sincerely wonder if I learned more from them than they learned from me. I truly miss them all and I'm grateful for all the time we spent together.

Special recognition goes out to all of the players on the 2009 Babe Ruth baseball team. My screensaver for the past several years has been a picture of all of you. Every morning you greet me and give me inspiration. Never forget what you accomplished.

I also want to acknowledge all the wonderful people who oversee the Empire State Baseball League. Thank you all for everything you do to keep the flame of youth baseball lit.

More than anything, I want to express my undying gratitude to my wonderful wife and partner, Cher, who is simply the kindest and most giving person I know. Her generosity knows no bounds and she is inspirational to me every hour of every day. Thank you, Cher, for everything. You have always been there for me ever since we climbed that mountain on senior skip day back in high school.

Finally, there are others whom I would like to acknowledge and thank. But, unfortunately, they will have to remain anonymous.

ABOUT THE AUTHOR

Award-winning author Tom Swyers first had an audience on the edge of their seats (and the girls giggling) when his play, "The Great Train Robbery," made its debut in the seventh grade.

After high school, he worked his way through several of the best colleges in the country. Employed in a variety of positions ranging from a late-night convenience store clerk to a fine jewelry salesperson, Tom eventually graduated from college and worked his way through law school in the caverns on Wall Street.

Since then, he's been a lawyer for much of his career. He is also a former judge. Tom studied at the New York Summer Writer's Institute at Skidmore College.

Along the way, he married his high school sweetheart and raised a family. Tom is usually running (literally) away from trouble on the back roads of Upstate, New York where he lives with his family and two cats (really two dogs working undercover).

Contact

www.tomswyers.com
swyerstom@gmail.com

Made in the USA
Lexington, KY
26 January 2018